MW00413425

Avalina

(Ahh-va-lee-na)

Timeless Fear, Inextinguishable Lust for Vengeance…And She's Dying to Know You!

A Mystical Thriller Novel By

Manuel Rose

$15.99 USD
$17.99 Canada

DEDICATION

To my family,
thank you for all your support
in all of my ventures.

Published by MMRproductions.com &
Ingram Spark a Lightning Source Company

Cover designed by Robynne Alexander of Damonza.com © 2022

Melissa Rose and Heather Rivera, Editors

Printed in the United States of America

PUBLISHER'S NOTE
This is a work of fiction. Names, characters, places, and incidents either
are the product of the author's imagination or are used fictitiously,
and any resemblance to actual persons, living or dead, business
establishments, events, or locales is entirely coincidental.
This novel is not intended to insult, discriminate, embarrass, or degrade
any group of people in any way.

Books and audio books can be ordered.
For more information, please write to:
MMRproductions.com
815 Route 82 # 51
Hopewell Junction, New York 12533

Author's Note

This novel was not intended to insult, discriminate, embarrass, or degrade any group of people in any way. This novel was written purely from my own imagination, and from experiences around me from some closed-minded people I have known in my lifetime. If I offended anyone, it was totally unintentional.

CONTENTS

ACKNOWLEDGMENTS

To my beautiful daughter, Melissa Rose, thank you for all your help editing and formatting this book; and to Robynne Alexander and Damon Freeman of Damonza.com for the fabulous cover design. Also, to Heather Rivera for final editing; and to Ingram Spark a Lightning Source company.

1

1969

It was a moderately cold Monday afternoon, February 3rd, 1969. The sun was trying to shine through some dreary clouds, making it look overcast. Some folks were even saying that it looked like a snow sky, and they were right. A winter storm was coming into a small suburban town called, "Merryville," just outside of New York City. The storm was expected to dump up to twenty-five inches of snow with blizzard-like conditions. Everyone was doing their food-shopping and getting supplies ready for snow removal. The local patrons were looking at the newspaper headlines in the supermarket, many of them were saddened to learn that legendary English actor, Boris Karloff, had just passed away at age eighty-one. The famed film actor that was most notably known for his role in the movie, *Frankenstein*, died of pneumonia.

Not too far away from the shopping district, two teenage girls, Melissa Conley and Avalina Bishop, were just getting out of Merryville High School. The girls had decided to walk home and get some fresh air instead of taking the school bus home today. Melissa and Avalina were both fifteen-years-old and were best friends; even though, the two girls had only shared one class together in the tenth grade: History. Melissa had a baby face with short, black curly hair, she looked five years younger than her actual age. Avalina, on the other hand, was a little taller than Melissa and looked much more mature for her age. Some people thought that she was about twenty-one-years-old. Avalina had long, straight, and shiny raven-colored hair framing her beautiful face. Her bright blue eyes were the envy of every girl in school. Melissa was Avalina's only friend; most of the other students had thought that Avalina was a weirdo. The other students didn't even want to associate themselves with her; some of them even feared her, so she pretty much kept to herself.

The two girls had become friends since the beginning of the school year, but Melissa was always a little jealous of Avalina. *How come you have such pretty straight hair and I don't?* Melissa would ask her. She was also jealous of Avalina's, shapely body. There was one other thing, though. Melissa always thought that there was something weird about Avalina; she couldn't quite put her finger on it, but Melissa knew it was something very strange.

As pretty as Avalina was, she was not popular with the boys at all; they seemed to fear her, especially after what happened to David Scholl. David had tried to take advantage of her, but Avalina proved beyond a shadow of a doubt that she could defend herself. Avalina claimed that the boys in school just weren't mature enough for her.

Then, one day Avalina told her friend, Melissa, that her grandmother was a real live witch. *Does that make you a witch, too?* Melissa had asked her, but Avalina didn't answer her; instead, she just gave Melissa a devilish grin and laughed. The two girls talked as they walked home from school in the cold, thinking that maybe they should have taken the school bus home instead.

"Hey, Melissa, you wanna come over to my house to watch TV?" Avalina asked her.

"Nah, that's alright. I've got a book report I got to finish," Melissa replied.

"Are you sure? My folks are visiting my grandmother in Salem, Massachusetts so I have got the whole house all to myself 'til tomorrow."

"Nah, thanks, anyway."

"Oh, well. I guess I'll have to watch my favorite television show all by myself, then."

"What are you watching, anyway?"

4

"Dark Shadows."

"You still watch that show?"

"Doesn't everybody?"

"I don't, not anymore, anyway. I stopped watching it over two years ago. It got more boring instead of it being scary."

"Oh, no. Not now. Not since they got a vampire on the show."

"They've got a vampire on it now?" Melissa asked with extreme curiosity in her voice.

"Yup, his name is Barnabas Collins and he is so dreamy. He can bite me anytime, any day, and anywhere he wants to," Avalina said with a sexy grin on her face.

"I guess he's good-looking then, right?" Melissa asked her.

"Hell yeah! He is so damn handsome and I get to see him in living color."

"Color? You've got a color television set at your house?"

"Doesn't everyone?" Avalina asked with a smirk on her face.

"Well, excuse me, Miss Rich Bitch, not everyone can afford a color TV set, you know."

"Oh, come on now, I was just playing."

"Sure you were," Melissa said with a sneer.

"Hey, you think we'll have school tomorrow; I mean, because of the snowstorm?" Avalina asked with a worried look on her face, hoping the schools would be closed.

"I hope not. How much snow are we supposed to get?"

"They said about two feet."

"Really? That's so cool!"

"Well, this is where I live. See you tomorrow…maybe," Avalina said as she walked over to her house.

Melissa kept on walking down the road while Avalina walked towards her home. The outside of the two-story colonial home, with its white aluminum siding, had seen better days, but inside it was in decent repair. The home was nestled at the end of a secluded dead-end road, with no neighbors around.

Avalina unlocked the front door and went on inside. She took off her grey winter coat and black shoes. She put everything into the hall closet. The girl went into the family room and lit a fire in the fireplace. Avalina noticed the burn mark on the wood floor in front of it; that was caused by the last time she lit a fire. She caught hell for that mistake and vowed to be more careful in the future.

Avalina looked at the grandfather clock in the foyer as it chimed. It was now three o'clock. She had an hour just before her favorite show came on. The teenage girl put a frozen TV dinner into the oven and decided to take a short bath, before she would watch television.

Light snow flurries started coming down as Avalina started to fill up her bathtub. She took off all of her clothes and looked at herself in the bathroom mirror.

"Man, I'm fine," she said to her reflection as she fondled her fairly large and shapely breasts.

Avalina clutched the golden pentagram locket around her neck. It was a gift that was given to her by her grandmother when she was only six-years-old. *Never ever take it off, Avalina, it has got great powers,* her grandmother had told her. The golden pentagram locket had an inscription engraved on the inside that read, *"Avalina: Goddess Of Eternal Life."*

Angela Bombay, her sixty-six-year-old grandmother on her mother's side, was a real witch living in Salem, Massachusetts. Angela had been practicing witchcraft ever since she was very young. Unbeknownst to everyone, except for Avalina's mother, Angela had been teaching the art of witchcraft to Avalina, for almost a decade.

Avalina got into the light green bathtub that was full of warm, soapy water. She was careful not to splash any water onto the old white tiled floor, since some of the tiles were already coming loose. Avalina didn't want to get blamed for that again either. She grabbed the sponge and started to wash her body with it. Avalina rubbed her breasts until her nipples got rock-hard. Then, she slipped some of her fingers down towards her thighs. Avalina started to masturbate; knowing that there was no one at home to hear her, Avalina freely let out a big scream of ecstasy as she quivered with her first orgasm, then another. After her third climax, the teenager walked out of the tub feeling satisfied and cleansed. She drained the tub and then dried herself off. Avalina decided to put on her mom's red robe instead of her pajamas.

It was now five minutes to four o'clock. Avalina grabbed her Salisbury steak TV dinner from the oven. She went into the family room and turned on the console television set. After the TV set had warmed up, Avalina looked at the screen. She was not happy with the picture quality; there were ghosts in the image on the screen. Avalina looked at the chart her father had made up for the outdoor TV antenna rotator. The chart said that for channel seven, the antenna should be at the "SW" position. Avalina turned the dial on the rotator control that was on top of the set to the "SW" position. The remote motor on the outdoor roof pole turned the antenna towards the southwest position and stopped. The picture was now very clear. *Daddy's gadgets really work,* Avalina thought to herself. The fireplace was keeping her warm, as she sat down on the old red sofa and watched her favorite TV show.

Avalina felt a certain kind of warmth that was emanating from her gold locket. *Never ever take it off, Avalina, it has got great powers,* she remembered her grandmother saying to her. *Gee, maybe it really does,* she thought. One thing was for sure though; it felt really good in between her breasts.

Outside, snow flurries were beginning to pile up. There was already a coating of snow on the grassy surfaces. Avalina took a quick look outside the window during a commercial break and smiled.

"Who knows? Maybe I won't have any school tomorrow. Well, fine by me," she said to herself.

Avalina finished her Salisbury steak TV dinner and she was going to throw the tray away, but then her show returned from its commercial break. The telephone rang, but the teenage girl wasn't talking to anyone until *Dark Shadows* was over. *It could be mom and dad,* she thought, but Avalina *still* didn't get up to answer the phone. After seven rings, the person hung up.

Later on that evening, Avalina had fallen asleep in front of the television set. The fire died out in her fireplace, but something wicked was brewing outdoors. Melissa and four boys: Michael Resnick, David Scholl, Gilbert Johnson, and Benny Smith were outside looking in through Avalina's family room window. They had been watching her for quite some time now. Melissa told them that Avalina would be home all by herself. The five teenagers had placed crumpled up newspapers, wooden kitchen matches and sticks all around the house. Then, they poured two large cans of lighter fluid on everything to make sure it would still burn, even with the snow falling.

"Do you really think we should be doing this?" Melissa asked the four boys.

"Yeah, man, if she's a real witch and I think she is, she's fricking evil. I'll never forget the day I tried to kiss her. She gave me this evil eye, grabbed my balls, and squeezed them real tight. That shit really hurt, man! Then, the bitch told me to piss off," David said.

"I'm with you on that shit. There's no room for the devil in our school, and witches were all part of the devil," Michael added.

The other two boys, Gilbert and Benny also agreed. With that, the four boys lit the fire with their cigarette lighters. Since Avalina Bishop's house was situated at the end of a dead-end road, she had no nearby neighbors to see what was going on. There wasn't anyone around for at least a quarter of a mile.

The fire spread real fast in the old wooden structure. As it burned, the five teenagers chanted, *burn, witch burn*, over and over again. Avalina woke up to the sound of a ground floor window exploding from the heat of the flames. She looked out of the family room window and saw the five teens chanting and laughing at her.

"Why?! Why are you doing this to me?!" Avalina screamed out in fear for her life.

"What did I ever do to you?!"

She tried to go through the front door, but it was too late. The fire was already making its way inside the house, consuming everything in its path. Draperies, curtains, carpeting and the wood floors were all burning. Avalina was horrified; she didn't know what to do. The young teen decided to run upstairs. More windows exploded as the flames licked the sides of the old wooden structure, melting what little snow accumulated around it. Avalina went into her room and thought about jumping out of her own bedroom window, but she was too high up and the red and yellow flames were everywhere, turning white hot in certain areas. *Think fast, girl, think fast,* she nervously thought. The poor girl was beginning to cough and choke on the smoke from the raging fire as it relentlessly devoured her home. Avalina decided to grab a piece of white chalk. She drew a large circle on the wood floor around her. Then, the girl drew a five-pointed star inside of the circle to resemble a pentagram, similar to the one that was hanging around her neck. Avalina clutched her golden locket and prayed.

"Oh, Prince of Darkness, ruler of all evil, save me from being destroyed. Guard and protect my spirit. Save my soul from my mortal enemies that wish to extinguish me. Let me be able to walk again amongst the living and seek revenge," Avalina chanted.

The five teenagers split up and ran away as the house burned. Melissa was the only one who felt guilty. She ran into her house and placed an anonymous phone call to the local fire department. Within minutes, fire engines came racing down the road to reach the scene. The firemen desperately tried to put out the fire, but it was just too late. The fire had been burning long enough to spread all over the old structure. The entire Bishop home was completely engulfed by the raging fire. Firemen desperately searched the ruins of the structure for any signs of life. One of the men came out carrying Avalina's body in his arms.

"Is she alive?" the captain asked him.

"No, captain; she's dead, apparently from smoke inhalation. You know, it's the darndest thing, everything around her was burned to a crisp, except her and the floor she was on," the fireman replied.

Two days later, Mr. and Mrs. Bishop had returned from Salem, Massachusetts. They were supposed to come home earlier, but the roads were rendered impassable due to the big snowstorm.

When the Bishop's finally arrived on their road, the couple were shocked to find that their home was completely burned down to the ground.

"Oh, my God! What the hell happened to our house?!" Sabrina Bishop asked her husband.

"I don't know, dear, but I sure hope our daughter wasn't in it when it burned," Zachary Bishop replied.

The couple decided to get back into their blue station wagon and head on down to the local police station. They had no idea what was in store for them. The two of them were extremely worried about their daughter.

Mr. and Mrs. Bishop walked right into the police station and explained who they were, the chief brought them into his office to describe what had happened two days earlier.

"Please, have a seat," Chief Smith solemnly told the couple.

Chief Smith loved his job, but this was something that the forty-eight-year-old man hated to do. Smith found it extremely difficult to give people bad news, especially about their own children; that really stressed him out. That was the main reason he had stomach ulcers and grey hair, or so he thought.

The couple sat down in the two wooden chairs that were next to each other in front of the police chief's desk. They each had a worried look upon their faces. Zachary and Sabrina both knew that it wasn't going to be good news. Sabrina had a nervous habit of twirling her long brown hair around her fingers. The forty-year-old woman still looked good for her age, but she knew that her baby-making days were pretty much over. Avalina was her only child; if something happened to her, she wouldn't know how to go on. Zachary, who was five years older than his wife, was out of shape and balding. The man couldn't handle stress very well and being overweight with high blood pressure didn't help him at all. Zachary began nervously rocking back and forth in his chair, waiting for the chief to start explaining what had happened to their home.

"We suspect that your house was the target of arsonists. There were traces of accelerants around the foundation of the building," Chief Smith told them.

"Who would do such a thing to us?" Zachary asked.

"We were hoping you could tell us. Do you have any enemies?" the chief asked them.

"None that we know of…I mean…none that would do such a horrible thing like that to us," Sabrina replied.

"Where's our daughter?" Zachary asked.

"Your daughter didn't make it. I'm so sorry," Chief Smith somberly told them.

"Oh, my god! No! No! Please, say it isn't so…please," Sabrina clutched her husband's hand and sobbed.

"Wh-where is she? Where's our daughter?" Zachary nervously asked the chief.

"Her body is at the county morgue. Would you like me to have one of my men take you down there?" the chief asked them.

"That's quite alright, chief, I know where it is," Zachary Bishop said as he stood up from his chair.

"Again, I'm so sorry. I want you to know that we're doing everything we can to find the perpetrators," the chief sorrowfully said to them both.

"Nothing can ever bring her back now. Nothing can bring back my ba-by," Sabrina said as she sobbed in her seat.

*
**

The couple left the police station, got into their car, and drove down to the county morgue. After driving for fifteen minutes, they arrived at the morgue. Charles Malloy, the medical examiner, brought them over to the room where the bodies had been kept. Charles was almost ready to retire. His prominent belly, long grey hair, beard, and glasses, made him look like Santa Clause. Charles pulled out one of the stainless-steel drawers in the wall where Avalina's body was kept.

"Is this your daughter?" Charles asked the both of them.

"Oh, my god! My baby, my beautiful baby girl. Why, lord, oh why?" Sabrina cried on her husband's shoulder.

Zachary Bishop tried to calm her down, but he, too, started to cry. Avalina looked peaceful lying there. She was still wearing her mother's red robe.

"Yes, that's our daughter," Zachary quietly replied.

"She was found clutching this in her hand when they discovered her in the house," the medical examiner said as he handed Mr. Bishop a small bag.

Zachary Bishop opened up the bag in front of his wife. They both knew what it was. It was the only piece of jewelry that Avalina ever owned.

"It's the locket my mother had given her when she was only six-years-old. She never took it off," Sabrina said while she cried.

"Come, baby, we have to go plan her funeral," Zachary Bishop told his wife.

The two of them thanked the medical examiner for his time. The Bishops' went down the road to check into a nearby hotel. Zachary and Sabrina had lost everything. The couple knew they had to deal with their homeowners' insurance company, plus the funeral arrangements that had to be made for their daughter, Avalina.

A few days later, at Merryville High School, the principal was making an announcement over the school's public address system.

"Attention, all students and faculty members! In case you haven't heard the news, one of our students, Avalina Bishop, has just passed away in a horrible fire at her home. The police department suspect it was arson. If anyone has any information about this terrible tragedy, please notify the Merryville Police Department. Our hearts go out to the Bishop family during this time of deep sorrow. This is Principal Mary Croce signing out," the principal stated.

Later on during lunch period, the five teenagers: Melissa, David, Michael, Gilbert, and Benny all convened at a corner table in the old school lunchroom.

"Did you hear that announcement this morning?" Melissa asked the four boys.

"Yeah, we all heard it," Michael replied.

"Who didn't?" David added.

"Yeah, well, we all went too far. We *killed* her. This was supposed to be a practical joke! She never made it out alive," Melissa said.

"Nah, man, we knew what we were doing alright. Some witch, shit, she couldn't even escape a damn fire," Gilbert said.

"Listen, guys, let's all just keep our voices down. Nobody saw us. As long as we keep quiet about it, no one will ever know,"

Benny logically stated.

"Keep quiet? You're forgetting something, boys. Avalina saw us," Melissa pointed out.

"Avalina? Shit, she's dead! Didn't you just hear that shit this morning? The bitch is dead," Michael said.

"She could have called somebody on the phone before she died. You never know. Besides, she was a witch, remember?" Melissa said.

"Yeah, right, some witch she turned out to be. Anyway, I don't believe in any of that hocus pocus shit," Benny replied.

"Yeah, well you better because that's for *real*. Avalina told me that her grandmother was a real live witch living out in Salem, Massachusetts," Melissa stated.

"A *real* witch; you mean like that show *Bewitched* on TV?" David asked with a curious look on his face.

"Yeah, that's right, only she's for real!" Melissa replied.

"Man, later for her ass. If she really was a witch, she got what the hell she deserved," David added.

"That's not nice! She didn't deserve to die," Melissa said.

"Listen, like I said before, let's just keep our asses quiet about this shit, alright?" Benny asked.

They all agreed, but the five teenagers were still very worried. They knew deep down inside that what they did was wrong, very wrong. The teens finished their lunches and headed on back to their classes with guilt on their faces. High above them in the cafeteria, close to the ceiling, a spirit had been watching and listening to every single word that they said; a spirit that would seek out revenge against each and every one of them all, someday...

2

THE LOCKET

Almost fifty-one years later in the town of Midland, New York: the townsfolk were enjoying a relatively light winter for late January. The news media was talking about a new virus called the Coronavirus (COVID-19) that had infected many people in Wuhan, China. The United States president said it was contained in China and that there was no need to worry.

Anna Nuñez was in the kitchen of her small ranch home. She had been on her laptop trying to get a birthday gift for her fifteen-year-old daughter. The forty-year-old single mother decided to go to the auction site called: *Win It Easy*. Anna had been bidding on a beautiful gold pentagram necklace, and so far, she had been the highest bidder.

"I've got to win this necklace for my little Susan," Anna said to her laptop as she twirled her long black hair.

Anna hoped that her ex-husband would send her some money for his daughter's birthday, but nothing came from him yet. *He's probably too damn busy with his new blond floozy*, she thought to herself. Her daughter, Susan, was going to be sixteen-years-old in just six days. The girl had grown up looking like her so much. Some people actually thought that they were sisters instead of mother and daughter, especially since Anna looked young for her age; plus, she stayed in shape. Both Anna and Susan had pretty faces with similar facial features. They each had long straight black hair. Susan even took after her mother in having a petite and shapely figure.

Finally, after fifteen grueling minutes of watching the countdown timer on the computer, Anna had won the necklace for a hundred and fifty-three dollars and fifty cents. She had come real close to her highest bid of one hundred and fifty-five dollars. Anna was so happy, but she didn't realize that there was a fifteen-dollar shipping and handling charge on top of that. *Oh well, I have to put it on my card anyway,* Anna thought to herself.

"She's gonna love it," Anna said while entering her credit card information on the website server.

Susan Nuñez had just walked through the door while her mother was on the computer.

"Hi, mom!" Susan said while her mother closed up her laptop.

"Hi, honey, how was school?" Anna replied as she hugged her daughter.

"It was alright; school is school. What's for supper?"

"Rice, beans, and steak."

"Didn't we just have that over the weekend, mom?"

"Yes, we did, dear, it's called 'leftovers' and you *will* eat it," Anna said sharply.

"Ok, mom, I'm going to my room to do my homework. Call me when it's ready, alright?"

"I will, honey, go on."

Anna was hoping that the necklace came in time for her daughter's birthday. It wasn't easy being a single parent. Anna was holding down a job at the college as an administrative assistant, but she was only getting fourteen bucks an hour. It wasn't enough to pay for the small three-bedroom house that she rented, plus the food and utilities. Whenever there was overtime available, Anna had jumped on it, but she often had to share it with her other coworkers. Anna kept her eyes open for any possible promotions on the job.

***

About thirty miles away in Merryville, New York, ninety-year-old Sabrina Bishop was printing out a sales receipt from her computer and an address label for the necklace she had just sold online. It had been about fifty-one years since Sabrina had lost her beloved fifteen-year-old daughter, Avalina, to that terrible house fire in Merryville. Sabrina knew it was time to let go. If her daughter was ever going to come back, she would have done so by now. *So much for being a witch like my mother was,* she thought. Sabrina had lost everything. Zachary Bishop, her husband, had passed away over twenty-five years ago, leaving the woman all alone. Sabrina's mother and father had been gone long before Zachary.

Sabrina took one last look at her daughter's necklace, she kissed it goodbye, and packed it up into a small carton. The old lady was living in a small two-room apartment that she rented. It was all her social security checks could afford. Her health was beginning to fail, but she kept on chugging right along.

"I'll just bring it down to the post office later," Sabrina said to herself.

She taped the box up and affixed the label on it. All of a sudden, an eerie apparition of her daughter appeared right in front of her, as she had last looked, wearing her mother's own red robe.

"I love you, mommy, I always will," Avalina's phantom said in a ghostly voice.

Sabrina freaked out; she nearly dropped the package on the floor.

"My baby, is it really you?" Sabrina asked.

"I will come back to you, mommy, soon, in another form; you'll see."

"You had better hurry up, baby. I haven't got that much

time you know; after all, I'm ninety-years-old and my heart is starting to fail me."

"I would have come back sooner, but you wouldn't let me, mommy, you wouldn't let me go."

"What do you mean by that?" Sabrina asked the ghost.

"You held on to my locket. You should have given it to another girl," the apparition told her.

"I'm sorry; I didn't know. It was all I had left of you. I just couldn't let it go."

"You must, mommy, you must mail it. Do it today. Do it now. I must have my revenge, please!"

"Revenge? Revenge against who and why?"

"Revenge against all of those that killed me, especially the woman who wrote that book of yours over there."

Sabrina looked at the book the spirit was pointing to on the old coffee table: *Hope to Stay Alive* by Melissa Waters. The author's picture was on the cover.

"What have you got against Melissa Waters?" Sabrina asked her daughter's spirit.

"Her name was Melissa Conley. She and her friends started the fire that killed me years ago in our home," Avalina's spirit said in a hauntingly evil tone.

"Why, why didn't you tell me that years ago? Why didn't you tell your father?"

"I couldn't, mommy. I just didn't have enough power to materialize, not until now. I need a young host to help me carry out my revenge. Please, mommy, please mail the locket out now."

"I will. I'll go ahead and mail it out right away, anything to see my baby again," Sabrina eagerly replied.

With that last remark, Avalina's spirit disappeared from Sabrina's presence. Sabrina got dressed and took her daughter's locket out to the post office. Even though her customer had only paid for first class mail, Sabrina was going to splurge by sending it overnight. *You must, mommy, you must mail it. Do it today, do it now, please,* she remembered her daughter's ghost telling her. Sabrina couldn't believe what her daughter's spirit was telling her. After all these years, the truth had finally come out. Sabrina realized that her house was not just a target of a random arsonist, but the *real* victim was her daughter.

"They all murdered my little girl, those bastards! Too bad Zachary wasn't around to hear what really happened to our little daughter," Sabrina said to herself.

The next morning, sixty-five-year-old Melissa Waters woke up from a nightmare in her Bright Falls, New Jersey home. She was in a cold sweat with visions of Avalina. *I'm coming to get you, bitch. It's time to get even; time for you to pay for what you did to me.* Avalina had said in her dream.

"It can't be you! You're dead!" Melissa screamed out loud.

"Honey, are you alright?" her husband, John, asked.

"I'm sorry. I'm sorry I woke you up, dear. I had a bad dream, that's all," Melissa replied.

"Dream? The way you just screamed out, it sounded more like a damn nightmare."

"Yeah, I guess it was."

"Well, what was it about?"

"Nothing, dear, it wasn't anything important, really."

"It must have been something that really upset you. It helps to talk about it you know."

"There you go again, playing psychologist on me. I'm not one of your damn patients! Forget it already, will you?"

"Fine. I'm just trying to help, that's all," John solemnly replied.

Melissa didn't want to talk about it to anyone, especially her psychologist husband. Melissa knew what she and her friends did to Avalina over fifty-one years ago was wrong. Back then, she was known as Melissa Conley, and that was a part of her past that she had kept locked up and didn't want to discuss it with anyone. Melissa never even told her parents about what had happened that night in 1969. The only ones that ever knew what truly happened to Avalina were Melissa and the four boys: Michael Resnick, David Scholl, Gilbert Johnson, and Benny Smith, but Melissa was the one who orchestrated the whole event. *That was almost fifty-one years ago, why am I thinking about her now?* Melissa mentally asked herself.

Melissa Waters made a successful lifestyle for herself. She had become a New York Times best-selling author, married a successful psychologist, and had a very nice two-story home in the suburbs. Unfortunately, it wasn't all a bed of roses for her. Melissa never got the one thing in life that she really craved: to be a mother. Melissa was barren. Her body had let her down. The doctors told her that she could never get pregnant because she had polycystic ovarian syndrome.

Melissa tried to stay in shape. She had joined a local gym and watched what she ate, but the pounds just kept accumulating on her anyway. The middle-aged woman got so overweight that her own husband got turned off from her body.

Melissa dyed her curly grey hair black again, hoping that it would help her land the gym instructor that she liked. *If I can't get any sex from my own damn husband, I'll just have to get it from someone else,* she thought. Unfortunately, her instructor only showed professional interest in her, even though the man had asked her to autograph a copy of her book for him. She went to the bathroom and looked at herself in the mirror.

"My belly is bigger than my boobs," Melissa said to her reflection.

All of a sudden, a ghostly image appeared in her mirror. It was the spirit of someone she helped kill years ago. Avalina Bishop was looking straight at her in a ball of flames.

"I'm coming to get you, bitch. You thought I forgot all about you, but I didn't. You're gonna pay for what the hell you did to me. You're all gonna pay!" Avalina's apparition said in a haunting voice.

"No! You're dead! We killed you years ago! Go away! Go awayyy!" Melissa screamed at the image that taunted her in the bathroom mirror.

"Melissa, are you alright?!" her husband shouted as he walked into the bathroom.

Melissa just wept on his shoulder. She knew Avalina was a witch, and after almost fifty-one years later, Melissa had something to really worry about…her own life.

Later on that evening, Anna Nuñez was coming back home from her job at the college. She noticed something small sitting there in front of her white front door; it was a small package.

"Oh, it's the locket I won for Susan! That was quick!" she said while bending down and picking up the package.

Anna brought the small box inside and closed the front door behind her.

"I think I'll give it to her tonight, even though it's not quite her birthday yet," she said to herself.

A few minutes later, Susan walked through the front door.

"Hi, mom!" Susan said while kissing her mother on the cheek.

"I have something for you, baby. Happy birthday!" Anna shouted as she gave her daughter the small brown package.

"But, mom, it's not my birthday yet!"

"So, what? It's only a few days away. Open it up, honey, come on!"

Susan grabbed a butter knife from the kitchen cabinet drawer. She proceeded to cut open the little brown box. Susan became breathless when she pulled out the small, golden pentagram locket and chain out of the package.

"Oh, mom, it's beautiful! Where did you get it from? It must have cost you a small fortune, right?"

"Whoa, one question at a time please," her mother replied.

"I love it! Help me put it on, please?"

"Sure," Anna replied as she put the necklace around her daughter's neck.

"It's so beautiful, mom. I'm never ever gonna take it off."

"I'm so glad you like it, dear."

"Oh, look! There's an inscription inside the locket!" Susan said as she opened it up.

"There is? What does it say, Susan?"

"It says, *'Avalina: Goddess Of Eternal Life.'* Who's Avalina, mom?"

"I have no idea, no idea at all," Anna nervously replied.

Anna didn't know it was a personalized locket; she thought it was brand new. The seller never really clarified that on the listing and there were no pictures of it open either. *Who the hell is Avalina?* she wondered.

Anna thought she may have heard that name years before, but she just wasn't sure.

That night, while Susan slept, she had a frightening dream that caused her to wake up screaming in a panic. Anna came into her room and turned on the light.

"Susan! Susan! Are you alright?" Anna shouted.

"Mom, it was terrible and it seemed so real!" Susan tearfully replied.

"Did you have a bad dream, precious?"

"It was more than a dream, it was a nightmare, mom."

"Well, sometimes it helps to talk about it. What was it all about, sweetie?"

"Oh, mom, I was in this old house that was burning, and when I looked around, I was standing in a circle, but it wasn't really a circle, it was like a pentagram. It was similar to the one I'm wearing around my neck. It was awful mom, absolutely awful," Susan said as she cried on her mother's shoulder.

Anna began to worry. Her daughter never had nightmares

before. Anna wondered about the locket she had gotten for her daughter and the strange inscription inside that read, "Avalina: Goddess Of Eternal Life." *What did it all mean? Who the hell was Avalina, anyway?* The questions kept playing in her mind, begging to be answered.

Susan wasn't the only one having a nightmare. Across the river, in New Jersey, Melissa Conley was also waking up from a similar nightmare in a cold sweat. The spirit of Avalina was taunting her in a burning house, only there was no pentagram there to save her. Melissa kept hearing Avalina's ghost saying, *it should have been you burning, I'm coming for you, bitch, I'm coming to get all of you.*

"Noooo, leave me be! Leave me the hell alone!" Melissa screamed as she woke up from her nightmare.

"Honey, are you having another bad dream?" her husband asked as he woke up next to her.

"I-I'm fine, John," Melissa said while hyperventilating.

"No, you're not, you're shaking," John said while hugging his wife.

"She's coming to get me…after all these years…she's coming back for me."

"Who's coming for you, honey?"

"Avalina."

"Avalina? Who the hell is Avalina?"

"It's a long story, John, but I can't tell you. I just can't tell you anything about it."

"Why not? We're married. We're supposed to be honest

with each other."

"I'm sorry, but some things are better off left unsaid."

"I-I'm afraid I don't understand."

"Precisely, that's why I'm not telling you. Forget about it, dear, just forget all about it. Let's just try to go back to sleep," Melissa told him.

John couldn't go back to sleep at all...neither could Melissa. John kept thinking about what his wife said, *"It's a long story John, but I can't tell you. I just can't tell you anything about it. I'm sorry, but some things are better off left unsaid."* John thought about asking the computer search engines online tomorrow. *Avalina is a pretty unique name. How many people here could be named that?* he mentally asked himself.

The next morning, Susan woke up feeling very strange. She went to the bathroom and looked at herself in the mirror. Susan was horrified to see that the reflection in the mirror was not hers.

"Who are you?!" Susan shrieked.

The ghostly reflection just laughed at her. Susan began to feel weak. She grabbed her head, then the young woman held on to the bathroom sink, holding on for dear life. Susan finally collapsed onto the white tiled bathroom floor. Anna heard the noise and ran towards the bathroom to see what happened.

"Susan! Susan! Are you alright?" Anna yelled out.

Susan was now unconscious. Anna ran to the phone in the kitchen and called 911, as she feared the worst for her daughter. A few minutes later, the ambulance was taking Susan away to the local hospital.

Later on that day, Susan finally regained consciousness in the emergency room.

"Are you alright?" the young ER doctor asked Susan.

"Yes, yes, I'm fine; at least I think I am. Where am I?" Susan asked in a groggy voice.

"You're in Midland General Hospital. I'm Dr. Foster. You passed out at home and slipped into a coma," the young doctor informed her.

Susan was checking out the handsome young doctor in his white lab coat. She thought he was cute. Dr. Stephen Foster was only twenty-seven-years-old with an athletic build. His bright blue eyes and short brown hair had all of the nurses after him. Stephen was single and he had no intentions of getting married any time soon. He enjoyed his freedom and he loved his job at the hospital as a resident doctor. Midland General Hospital was a large facility, but it was slightly run-down and in dire need of a major upgrade, but the hospital funds were low. Dr. Foster liked working there since his commute to work was less than fifteen minutes each way.

"Can I please have something to drink? I'm very thirsty," Susan asked him.

"Sure, but first, let me tell your mother you're alright," Dr. Foster replied.

"My mother? Is she here?"

"Yes, your mother's back in the waiting area. She's worried sick about you. I'll go get her," he said with a smile on his face.

The doctor walked out of the emergency room and went to find Susan's mother. He looked in the waiting room full of people and called out her name.

"Ms. Nuñez? Ms. Anna Nuñez?" Dr. Foster called out.

"That's me, doctor, is she alright?" Anna asked him.

"She's fine, Ms. Nuñez. Would you like to go see her?"

"Yes!"

"Follow me, please."

The young doctor took Anna towards the emergency room to visit her daughter. When Anna saw her child lying down on the bed, hooked up to all of the hospital equipment, her eyes filled up with tears.

"My, baby, are you alright?" Anna asked her.

Her daughter just looked right up at her with a confused expression on her face.

"Who are you?" Susan asked.

"You don't remember me? You don't remember your own mother?"

"You're not my mother."

"How can you say such a terrible thing to me, Susan?"

"Susan? Who the hell is Susan?"

"Ok, now, that's enough games, honey. Are you ready to come home or what?"

"Not with you. I don't even know who the hell you are!"

The doctor watched in sorrow, not knowing what to say or do. Clearly, this wasn't going to be easy for any one of them.

"Oh, please, doctor! Something's happened to her memory. Maybe she hit her head on the bathroom floor when she fell. I mean,

I don't know. Maybe she has a concussion or something. Please, you've got to help her. She's all I've got!" Anna cried out to the doctor.

"We can run some more tests on her, Ms. Nuñez, maybe a CAT scan of her brain," Dr. Foster replied.

"No! There's nothing wrong with me! I want to go home! Who is this strange lady that keeps calling me, Susan, doctor?" Susan asked.

"I'm your mother, Susan, I'm your mother!" Anna shouted in disbelief.

"No, you're not; and my name's not Susan, it's Avalina!" Susan screamed out.

"Avalina?"

"That's right, Avalina Bishop and I live in Merryville, New York. I demand to know what the hell am I doing here in this damn hospital?! Why is this strange woman calling me Susan?!" Avalina's spirit shouted out through Susan's body.

"But you are Susan. Your name is Susan Nuñez and you're my daughter," Anna tearfully told her.

"Miss, nothing for nothing, but I'm not your daughter, and I've never ever seen you before in my damn life!"

Anna was completely stunned. Something was clearly wrong with her teenage daughter, but she didn't know what it was. *Avalina,* she thought, *wasn't that the name that was on the locket I gave her?*

"What's wrong with her? What am I going to do now? My own daughter doesn't even know who the hell I am. What am I going to do?" Susan kept asking herself over and over again while the tears flowed from her eyes.

3

THE ENCOUNTER

Late in the evening, Susan Nuñez, driven by the spirit of Avalina Bishop, was planning her escape from Midland General Hospital. She had packed up all of her clothes and was waiting for the nurse to finish making her rounds. Susan had fifty dollars on her, and she didn't know how far that would take her, but Susan knew where she was heading. As soon as the coast was clear, the girl snuck out of her semi-private hospital room and went down the emergency stairs.

Susan Nuñez had hailed a taxicab to go down to the Port Authority Bus Terminal in New York City. She took a bus that was heading into Bright Falls, New Jersey. Susan didn't really know why she had to go to Bright Falls, New Jersey, but something very strong inside of her told her to get there and to get there fast.

The next morning, Anna Nuñez got an urgent call from the hospital where her daughter was recovering.

"Hello, is this Ms. Anna Nuñez?" the male nurse asked her.

"Yes, yes, it is," Anna replied.

"This is Midland General Hospital. Your daughter, Susan Nuñez, has left the hospital."

"She what?!"

"I'm sorry, ma'am, but we're trying our best to locate her. Do you know where she could have gone?"

"No, no, I don't. She's lost her memory and she doesn't even know who I am."

"I'm sorry to hear that, Ms. Nuñez. We'll notify the proper authorities. If she does come home to you, please let us know."

"I will. Please find her; she's my only child," Anna pleaded.

"We're doing our best, ma'am," the nurse had said before hanging up the phone.

Anna didn't know what to do. *Where could she have gone to in her present state of mind?* Anna thought to herself. One thing was for sure, Anna knew it had something to do with that gold pentagram locket she gave her. Anna was sorry that she gave her daughter that locket.

Anna decided to get dressed. She wasn't going to leave this situation up to the hospital staff or to the police either. *The nerve of them! What the hell kind of hospital is that place anyway? Don't they have any kind of security? I've got a good mind to sue their asses.* Anna thought. She grabbed a cup of coffee and a doughnut from her kitchen and left.

Later on that morning, Susan Nuñez had been waiting outside of someone's home in New Jersey…waiting for the right time. It was seven o'clock and the sun was beginning to shine. Susan spotted a middle-aged, heavy-set woman with curly black hair, stepping out of her two-story colonial home. The woman had come out to pick up the morning newspaper that was thrown on her front porch.

"That's her," Susan muttered to herself.

Susan Nuñez cautiously approached the woman, looking as innocent as she could be.

"Excuse me, Miss, I seem to be lost. Is this Lodi, New

Jersey?" Susan asked the woman.

"Lodi? Oh, heavens, no. You're in Bright Falls; you're off by about twenty-five miles, Miss," the woman replied.

"Really? Oh, man, I don't know what I'm going to do!"

"I can show you how to get there. You see, you just have to go down this road and...well... where's your car?"

"I don't have one," Susan replied.

"You don't? Well, how did you get here?"

"I got off the bus and walked. I guess I got off at the wrong stop. The driver never announced the stops, you know."

"I wouldn't know that; I travel by car. I'm sorry. You seem awfully young. Do your parents know where you are?"

"I'm over eighteen and my mother knows I'm going to visit my uncle. I'm just lost, that's all."

"I'm sorry. I didn't mean to offend you; it's just that I'm a little bit leery about strangers showing up on my front doorstep, especially because of the profession I'm in."

"Well, what profession are you in, if you don't mind me asking?"

"Well, I'm a writer."

"You are? What kind of books do you write, Miss?" Susan excitedly asked her.

"Mostly thrillers and mysteries. I'm sure you must have heard of me. My name is Melissa Waters."

"I'm sorry, but I've never heard of you."

"Really? But I've been on the New York Times best sellers list several times!"

"Like I said before, Miss, I've never heard of you, but I really don't read many books."

Melissa was appalled by the fact that this young upstart never even heard of her. *How rude*, she thought to herself. *To think I was going to give her my autograph.* Suddenly, Melissa noticed something strange on the girl; it was the golden pentagram locket that was around her neck. *I've seen that locket once before, but where?* Melissa wondered.

"I don't know how I'm going to get to my uncle's house. He's probably at work by now," Susan stated.

Melissa started to feel sorry for the girl, maybe because she saw the girl was shivering; after all, it was only about fifty degrees out. The girl had a short, thin dark blue jacket on with blue jeans.

"Would you like to come inside and warm up for a bit? We could try and call your uncle," Melissa asked her.

"Yes, I'd like that very much," Susan replied.

Melissa brought the young girl inside her home. She showed her where the downstairs bathroom was and put on a pot of coffee. Melissa was all alone with this strange young girl; her husband had already left for work about an hour ago. Melissa went over towards the refrigerator to get some milk. Before she could open the fridge door, Melissa was struck in the back of her head with a wine bottle and slowly, collapsed on the floor with a thud.

A while later, Melissa finally regained consciousness. She wondered what happened to her and why she couldn't move. Melissa had been tied up to one of her kitchen chairs. Her arms and legs were securely tied to the arms and legs of the wooden chair. By now,

Avalina had complete control over Susan's body. The possessed girl was standing right in front of Melissa, waiting for her to awaken.

"Ow...my...head. What the hell is going on here? I brought you into my own home and *this* is how you repay me?" Melissa asked, barely conscious.

"Well, it's about time you woke up, Melissa Conley," Susan sarcastically stated.

"Melissa Conley? You *must* be mistaken; my name is Melissa Waters," Melissa nervously replied.

"Yeah, right, that may be your married name, but we *both know* who the hell you *really are*, don't we? Do you remember what you and your hoodlum friends did to Avalina Bishop?"

"I'm sorry...I've never heard of an Avalina...whatever her name is. You...you obviously got me confused with someone else."

"Do I really? How would you like to burn like she did, *bitch*?"

"This has *got* to be a mistake, Miss...besides, that happened a very long time ago, before you were even born."

"Oh, so you do know about it, bitch! I thought I was your best friend! I even invited you to come over and watch *Dark Shadows* with me, remember?"

"How could you know that? You weren't even there! I've never seen you before in my life!"

"Oh, yes I was and you know who I am. I've come back now, Melissa, I've come back to get even with you for that horrible thing you and your friends did to me in 1969. You are my first encounter," the possessed girl stated with an evil glare in her eyes.

"Look, I really don't know how that's even possible, but I'm really very sorry. It was a mistake. It never should have gotten that far. I am so sorry. Can't we just let bygones be bygones?"

"No way, bitch, you've got to pay for your sins! I want revenge!"

Susan tore down the white kitchen curtains from the window and poured cooking oil all over them. Then, she poured the rest of the oil around Melissa's chair and all over the wooden floor. Susan reached for the wooden kitchen matches she found in one of the cabinet drawers.

"Any last words, bitch?" Susan asked.

"No, please! I have a lot of money. I can help you out!" Melissa cried out.

"Are you that stupid or what? I'm not interested in your damn money. I want my revenge!"

Susan lit the match. She then lit up the white curtains and threw the fiery hangings onto the floor. Then, Susan casually walked out the front door and closed it behind her. Melissa screamed and begged for her life, but it was of no use. Her screams fell on deaf ears. Susan showed no mercy on her.

"You'll never get away with this, you crazy-ass bitch! Help! Help me, somebody! Please!" Melissa screamed out at the top of her lungs.

The flames climbed up the legs of the old wooden chair that Melissa sat in.

"Oh, God! Help me, please!" Melissa kept screaming while she burned in her surroundings.

Susan watched from behind a nearby tree on the front lawn. She waited for the house to burn down, just like Melissa and her friends did to her years before. Avalina's spirit was using Susan's body like a puppeteer and she was out for vengeance. Suddenly, one of Melissa's few neighbors came out to walk her dog as the house started to burn. Melissa finally stopped screaming as her soul painfully left the remains of her charred body. Unlike Avalina, her victim years before, Melissa died in complete agony. Avalina's spirit got more retribution than she had bargained for. Mrs. Jones, who was walking her dog, called 911 from her cellphone to report the fire and the screams that were coming from within the house. By now, the house had become completely engulfed in flames. Susan, knowing she had succeeded in her mission, started to run away as fast as she could from the flaming house, that once belonged to Melissa Waters.

The fire department finally arrived with two fire engines, but it was too late. The house was completely destroyed. Melissa had initially tried to break herself free, but Susan had done a great job of securing her to the heavy wooden chair. A police patrol car came down the block and Mrs. Jones flagged them down.

"There she is, officer! That woman was running away from the scene! She did it! I know she did it!" Mrs. Jones yelled out as her German Shepard barked.

The officers turned the police cruiser around and went after the running girl. One of the two officers yelled out over the car's public address system.

"Freeze, Miss! stop right there and put your hands up where we could see them!" Officer Robinson ordered.

Susan Nuñez stopped in her tracks and put her hands up. Officer Robinson and Officer Bolden handcuffed her. They read Susan her rights and brought her down to the police station. Susan had refused to answer any questions during the car ride. The officers firmly believed she was guilty of arson, and possibly, premeditated murder.

*
**

Anna Nuñez was franticly looking for her daughter. She had just come back from the police station to report her daughter missing, but the hospital had already informed them of the situation. Before Anna had gotten a chance to sit down in her home, the kitchen telephone rang. She went over to pick it up, hoping it was some good news about her daughter.

"Hello?" Anna asked the caller.

"Hello there. This is the Bright Falls, New Jersey Police Department. We're looking for a Mr. or Ms. Nuñez. Is this Ms. Nuñez?" Officer Robinson asked.

"Yes, yes, it is! Did you say, New Jersey Police?"

"Yes, ma'am, we have your daughter right here. I'm afraid she's been arrested, Ms. Nuñez."

"Arrested? On what charge?"

"Arson and possibly premeditated murder."

"*Murder?* No, not my child, it can't be. You must be mistaken, sir. What's your name, officer?"

"My name is Officer Robinson, ma'am, and I assure you I'm not mistaken."

"But, officer, we live in New York. How the hell did she get to New Jersey?"

"I don't know, ma'am, but her ID says that her name is Susan Nuñez and that she resides at 15 Park Lane, Midland, New York. This phone number was listed as 'Home' in her cellphone."

"Officer, can I please speak to her?" Anna asked with a cry in her voice.

"Sure, ma'am, hold on while I get a cordless in her cell," Officer Robinson replied.

*
**

Officer Paul Robinson was a husky, middle-aged Caucasian man of English heritage. He worked for the police department for over thirty-five years. Robinson had been passed up for promotion to chief twice, but his chance was coming up again. *This time, I'm going to get that bloody promotion,* he thought to himself as he sat at the chief's desk. Robinson did have a heart of gold, but he had zero tolerance for public offenders.

"What are you doing here with your feet up on my desk, Robinson?!" the chief bellowed as he entered his office.

The chief was a tall, thin man with snow-white hair. He kept in shape, but at sixty-five-years-of-age, Chief Landing was ready to call it quits. Landing had thought about finally giving his position to Robinson, but not yet.

"I'm sorry, chief," Officer Robinson nervously said while removing his feet from the chief's desk.

"I hear we have an arsonist in one of our cells. Is it that young lady in cell two?"

"Yes, it is, chief, her mother is on the phone. I was just getting the cordless phone to bring to her cell, sir."

"It breaks my heart to see someone so young go down the drain like that. How old is she?"

"She's fifteen, chief."

"What a fricking' waste, pretty young thing, too."

"Yeah, I know. Let me bring the phone out to her cell so that she can talk to her mother," Officer Robinson said as he got up from the chief's desk.

The police station was an eighty-six-year-old building with

two floors and four holding cells. It had recently been scheduled for demolition in three months. A newer, modern, larger facility had already been constructed a block away and it was almost ready for occupancy. Officer Robinson took the phone out to Susan's jail cell and offered it to her through the bars.

"Miss Nuñez, your mother wants to talk to you," Officer Robinson said as he held out the phone to her.

"My mother? She knows I'm here?"

"Yeah, that's right, we called her."

"What's her name, officer?"

"What is this, guessing games, Miss Nuñez? Here, take the phone, will you?"

"My name's not Miss Nuñez."

Susan reached out, pretending to grab the phone, but instead, she quickly snatched the service revolver from the officer's holster and pointed it at him. Officer Robinson was stunned. *Clearly, this lass is quick,* he thought.

"Get your damn hands up!" Susan yelled out.

"Now look, Miss, we don't want any trouble here," Robinson said as he raised his hands and dropped the phone.

"I said, get 'em up, and don't try any funny business! I don't wanna hurt anyone, but I will if I have to!"

"What's going on here?!" the chief asked out loud as he entered the area.

Susan was so stunned by his presence that she shot the chief. The bullet entered his heart and he collapsed right in front of them onto the grey tiled floor.

"I'm so sorry, chief. I was going to warn you that she was armed!" Officer Robinson tearfully told him.

"Shit, you just blew your pro-mo-tion, Rob-in-son," Chief Landing said just before he closed his eyes and died.

Susan Nuñez turned the gun back onto Officer Robinson.

"What's going on? Susan, are you alright?!" Anna yelled out over the cordless phone that was now on the floor.

Susan smashed the phone with her boot while staring at the police officer.

"I'm sorry about your chief. I told you I didn't want any trouble," Susan said. "Now, unlock this cell, give me the keys and *you* get in the jail."

Officer Robinson obeyed her command. Susan locked him inside the cell, but before she got a chance to turn around, she was shot in the back by Officer Bolden. The young African-American officer showed no remorse in shooting her. *Pure white trash*, Bolden thought. Susan collapsed on the floor, but she wasn't dead yet.

"I failed this time, but I'll be back. You can count on that," Avalina stated through Susan's dying body.

Seconds later, Susan passed away in front of the two police officers. Officer Bolden took the gun out of her hands and let Officer Robinson out of the jail cell.

"Is she...dead?" Officer Robinson asked.

"Yes, she is," Officer Bolden replied.

"We have to notify her folks," Robinson stated.

"Yeah, I know," Bolden replied.

Officer Robinson got back on the desk phone and called the

deceased girl's mother. When Anna Nuñez heard the news, the woman became so distraught, that she dropped the phone and broke down crying.

"My baby, my beautiful baby! My only child!" Anna cried hysterically.

Officer Robinson felt bad for the woman. *I hate having to inform parents that their child passed away. That really stinks,* he thought, but Robinson knew it was all part of the job. The officer hung up the phone. Officer Robinson then made another call to have the bodies of Susan Nuñez and Chief Landing removed from the police station. There was a lot of paperwork that had to be done, and he wasn't looking forward to that at all.

On the New York side, Anna Nuñez was trying to pull herself together. She had to make that trip out to New Jersey to claim her daughter's body. *A parent shouldn't have to bury their child,* the woman thought. Anna wondered if her daughter ever regained her memory. *I guess I'll never really know.*

"She called herself, Avalina Bishop. Who the hell is Avalina Bishop? Shit!" Anna kept asking herself the same question over and over again with no answer.

Anna believed one thing, though. This all started when her daughter put on that damn pentagram locket she had given her, the one that Anna won at the online auction site. *That name, Avalina, was inscribed in the pentagram locket. I never should have gotten that damn thing for her,* she thought. *Maybe this could have all been avoided. Maybe I would still have my daughter with me.* Anna broke down and cried some more, knowing that she was going to have to plan a funeral for her beloved daughter.

4

A NEW VEHICLE

Tuesday morning, February 4th, the sun was shining really bright and there was a warm breeze blowing, which made it perfectly delightful outside. This was very unusual weather for the middle of winter. Anna Nuñez had just woken up to the sound of songbirds singing outside of her window. Anna had lost most of her will to live after her fifteen-year-old daughter, Susan; her only child, her only baby, had been taken away from her. It had been almost two weeks since Susan was shot and killed by that police officer in New Jersey, after she had killed the chief of police, but to Anna, it all felt as though it just happened yesterday. The officer claimed that he shot her in self-defense at the police station, but Anna thought that was bullshit. Anna's boyfriend, Hector Rodriguez, came over and tried to cheer her up, but the woman was too distraught. She just wanted to be alone.

Anna remembered the funeral as though it just happened. She had her daughter dressed up in a beautiful white dress. She looked just like an angel, dressed up for the last time to go in her white coffin and be buried. Anna made sure that all of Susan's favorite jewelry went with her, all but one piece: the golden pentagram locket and chain that was her last birthday gift. Anna firmly believed that it was cursed with evil and she didn't want it anywhere near, her little Susan's body. Anna thought about throwing it in the garbage, but she decided to resell it back on the internet auction site. *As much as I hate the damn thing, I could sure as hell use the money,* Anna thought.

After being listed for three days online, people were finally bidding on the pentagram locket Anna Nuñez was selling. Anna got out of bed, grabbed her laptop, and turned it on. She logged in to the auction site and realized that her seven-day listing had just ended. The locket was sold to the highest bidder for one hundred and sixty-five dollars. Anna had made a twelve-dollar profit on the deal. *I'd rather have my daughter back,* she thought to herself. Anna turned on her printer, printed up the sales receipt, and proceeded to pack up the locket.

"Goodbye and good riddance," Anna said to herself.

Back in Bright Falls, New Jersey, sixty-six-year-old John Waters was rummaging through an old fire-proof safe. John had salvaged the safe from the basement of his old home. It was one of the few items that survived the fire that utterly destroyed his house and killed his wife, Melissa. John wondered why a total stranger, a young girl like that, would want to do such a terrible thing to his wife. John's younger brother, Richard, had allowed him to stay at his house in Parkville, New York until John's house was rebuilt. The big delay, of course, was waiting for the insurance company to issue him his payment check. John found his wife's high school yearbook in the safe and started going through it. There was a picture of Melissa Conley and Avalina Bishop in the school yard. The picture was labeled: "me and my friend, Avalina Bishop."

"Avalina? Oh, shit! That's the name she screamed out from her dream!" he exclaimed.

John had remembered how really scared his wife was after mentioning her name. *"She's coming to get me...after all these years...she's coming back for me."* That's what his wife, Melissa, had told him, but John also remembered that she wouldn't explain why. *What could have come between the two of them? They looked so happy together in this picture,* John had thought to himself. There were other pictures of her friends, mostly boys: Michael Resnick, David Scholl, Gilbert Johnson, and Benny Smith. John decided to borrow his brother's computer and do a little research.

"Now, I got a complete name, 'Avalina Bishop.' Let's see what I can find out about her online," John said to himself.

John Waters went upstairs to his brother's home office and turned on the computer that was on his desk. After searching online for a few minutes, John discovered an old, town newspaper article:

TEENAGER DIES IN MYSTERIOUS FIRE

A female teenager, described as fifteen-year-old Avalina Bishop, died of smoke inhalation in her own home yesterday. Local police officials suspect arson. The teenager was all alone upstairs in the house at the time of the fire.

John had taken note of the date the article was printed: February 4th, 1969.

"Why, she's dead! Her friend, Avalina, died long ago when they were teenagers," he said to himself.

John still wondered what it all meant. He wondered why a total stranger, a teenager, would want to kill his wife. The only similarity John could see was that the girl was the same age as Melissa and Avalina were fifty-one years ago. *This is preposterous,* he thought. Nothing made any sense to him at all.

**

Three days later, in the town of Brighten, New York, twenty-one-year-old, Joan Sanders, drove up to her mailbox and looked inside it.

"It came!" she excitedly said to herself.

Joan grabbed the small package from her mailbox and held it close to her breasts. She looked at the flawless blue sky that was above her. It had been a perfect spring-like day for the month of February. The sun had been shining all morning and afternoon, even though the meteorologists had forecasted snow for the rest of the evening.

Joan was a modern-day hippie who wished she had lived during the 1960s. Her long, straight, bright, shiny red hair, great shape, and deep piercing blue eyes had all the young men turning their heads. However, some felt intimidated by her height since she was nearly six feet tall, without heels. Joan always wore a pink headband, love beads, and one of her ten different tie-dye blouses, except when she was at work. Joan got back into her old, black Ford four-door sedan, and drove up the rest of the driveway of her rented split-level ranch house.

Joan was looking for another roommate to help pay the bills. *This time, it's just got to be a woman*, she thought. Joan didn't plan on having a relationship with anyone, but Harry Nash, the young man who had shared the house with her for three long months, had a different idea. Harry was young and attractive, he had a nice muscular build, shoulder-length black hair, and a cute face, but Harry was *way* too possessive. *Ain't nobody gonna tell me who I can see and when I should be home. Christ, I may as well be married! Screw that shit*, Joan thought to herself. So, after three long months, she had asked him to leave. Harry didn't want to leave at first, but when Joan threatened to call the cops on his ass, he agreed to leave.

Joan was working as a secretary for The Johnson Law Firm. Her job was only five miles away from her home. Since it was Friday, she got to get out of work by four-thirty. The office always closed early on Fridays.

Joan drove up into her garage. The young woman pressed the remote-control unit that was clipped on to her sun visor to close the door. She walked up the basement steps and headed straight towards the grey living room sofa. Joan sat down and opened up her package with excitement.

"Oh, my! It's beautiful. It's much nicer than the pictures show of it online," she said to herself.

Joan tried on the necklace and went straight towards the full-length mirror that was hanging in the hall. She suddenly felt strange as she touched her forehead with her right hand. A ghostly image appeared in the mirror in front of her reflection.

"Different. Sometimes, it's alright to be different. You're mine now," the spirit of Avalina said as she looked at her new vehicle through the mirror...

"Who...who are you?" Joan asked the girl with the long black hair in the mirror.

"Never mind, bitch," the spirit said as she tightened up the gold chain around her new victim's neck.

Joan grabbed the golden pentagram locket that was now tightly attached with its gold chain around her neck. She caressed it until its grip got even tighter. Joan began struggling to breathe. Then, the young woman went back to the sofa and laid down, feeling very weak. As she slept, Avalina started taking over her body.

***

The next morning, Joan Sanders woke up as a new, younger woman. She was now fifteen-year-old, Avalina Bishop. Joan became a woman with a purpose: a purpose to kill for revenge again.

"I won't fail this time," Avalina said through Joan's body.

Avalina's next target was Michael Resnick. She had to find Michael and terminate him. She went upstairs to one of the three bedrooms. She walked into the room that was used as a home office, to use her host's machine, the thing they called a *computer*. Avalina didn't know anything about computers. They weren't around back in the sixties, at least, not for the average Joe. However, her host, Joan, knew everything about computers and how to use them to get information. Finding Melissa was easy; she had always talked about becoming an author, plus Avalina's mom had one of her books on her bookshelf. Finding Michael was going to be a bit trickier. Avalina guided her host, Joan, over towards the desk where the computer was kept.

"Now, find us 'Michael Resnick' on this machine," Avalina said to her host.

Together, they searched for Michael Resnick. After a couple of hours, the possessed young woman had finally located him. Michael had a social media presence, but it showed a lot of instability. His looks hadn't changed all that much, with the exception of him putting on some weight. His hair was also thinning out and turning grey, but Michael's face pretty much looked the same, except for a few wrinkles of course. Avalina noticed that things went down the tubes for him when his wife had left him...for another woman. Michael had a hard time dealing with that, knowing that there wasn't any way for him to compete with a woman. He had lost his job at the newspaper as an editor. The distraught man had become suicidal. Michael was also in and out of rehab for alcoholism, and because of that, he lost custody of his only child. She also noticed that he always hung out in a particular bar.

"Oh, man, this guy's a real fricking loser. I almost feel sorry for his ass," Avalina said.

But she couldn't forgive or forget what he and the rest of them had done to her; how they set her house on fire and watched it burn...with her inside of it. Fifty-one years may have come and gone, but how could she ever forgive them for taking away her whole life? How could Avalina forget the fact that she had missed out on everything and that her parents were devastated, too? Avalina would have her revenge on all of them. One by one. No hesitations. No mercy.

It was Monday night and Michael Resnick was sitting in a New York City bar. Michael had been nursing a scotch and soda. He had been there for over three hours after his third job interview had gone sour. Michael was feeling sorry for himself. Today was his birthday; he had just turned sixty-four, but Michael had nothing to celebrate about. The small bar was pretty full, mostly with middle-aged men and a few women. Someone went over to the jukebox and played some oldies from the sixties. There were three wall mounted television sets, each one showing news stories of the Coronavirus instead of TV shows. The virus was now reported in the United States. Somebody had lit up a cigarette and was promptly yelled at by the bartender.

"Hey, buddy! This is a smoke free bar! Put it out or get out!" George, the burly bartender, shouted.

The man took one look at the angry bartender, not wishing

to create a scene, and walked out of the bar. Michael looked at his watch. It was 9:00 pm. A beautiful young woman, wearing a light brown leather jacket and blue jeans sat down on the stool next to him at the bar. *Wow, this girl's a real looker! What's she doing here all by herself?* Michael thought as he checked her out. The woman started making small talk with him, then she asked him what he was drinking.

"Scotch and soda," replied Michael.

The young woman called the bartender over and bought him a drink. Michael was stunned. *Wow! No woman ever bought me a drink before,* he thought.

"I know you may have probably heard this before, but what's a nice girl like you doing in a place like this, all by yourself I might add?" Michael asked her.

"The same as you, just hanging out," the woman replied.

"Are you new in town?"

"Not really, but I do live in New York, just not in the city. Do you come here often?"

"Yes, I do, especially since my wife left me for someone else."

"Oh, I'm sorry to hear that. Was he someone you knew?"

"No, and it wasn't a man. She left me for a woman."

"Wow, I'm sorry. I guess you can't compete with that."

"Nope. She said that she had been fighting the feelings for women ever since we got married...until...well...you know..."

"Look, I'll be honest with you. I know you're a little bit older than me, but I know what I like and it's mature men, like you, and *I'm* not gay," the woman said as she placed her left hand on Michael's right thigh.

"Wow, you come on pretty strong and quick, don't you?" Michael replied.

Michael was beginning to get aroused. The woman noticed it and gently, but playfully, gave him a little squeeze in between his thighs. Michael got so excited that he almost dropped the drink he was holding.

"Like I said before, I know what I like. What do you say we go somewhere more private?" she said with a sexy smile.

"Sure thing, we could go over to my place; it's not far. I live alone uptown just a subway ride away...unless...you'd rather go to your place?"

"No, your place is fine," she replied.

Michael finally had something to cheer him up on his birthday, which was also the anniversary of the day his wife had left him two years ago. Michael just couldn't believe he was about to score with this beautiful young woman, a woman he had only known for about a half an hour. She put on her hat, they both got up from their bar stools, and walked out holding hands. The couple walked down the streets of midtown Manhattan under the bright city lights, enjoying each other's company. The streets weren't that crowded, but there were a lot of hustlers around trying to sell their goods. It had gotten cool out. Michael offered the woman his black suit jacket, but she refused it. He noticed that he spilled his drink on his shirt, but he didn't remember when.

Michael Resnick and his new girlfriend, finally got to the subway entrance and went down the stairs. Michael had purchased a round trip metro card for the woman since he had his own card. They swiped through the turnstiles and headed down for the subway platform to wait for the uptown train. Michael extended himself over the platform and towards the tracks below when he thought he heard the train coming.

"I think the train is coming. Hey, you know, I just realized that I don't even know your name?" Michael said as the train started barreling into the station.

"You don't need to!" she bellowed.

Avalina, through Joan's body, pushed him down onto the subway tracks below the platform, just in time for the speeding train to run him over. The few passengers that were around, watched in horror as the train put three cars over the torn-up body of Michael Resnick, before it came to a screeching stop towards the end of the station.

"That lady pushed him! I saw it!" a woman screamed out.

The train operator got off his train and went down on the tracks to investigate. Michael Resnick had become the latest victim to feel the wrath of Avalina Bishop's revenge. The possessed woman ran down the platform and up the stairs as fast as she could while people screamed. Within minutes, she was at the self-serve parking lot a couple of blocks away and back in her car. Avalina made her way down the streets and onto the highway as fast as she could.

"I'm not getting caught and killed this time; that's for sure," she said to herself as she drove back upstate to her new home.

Avalina hoped that no one got a good look at her. Her large brown floppy hat did cover a good portion of her face, plus it wasn't that bright at that station. The maintenance crew hadn't yet gotten around to replacing the few fluorescent lights that had burned out.

"Two down…three more to go," Avalina said through her host.

The next morning, Carrie Sanders was watching a breaking news story that interrupted her favorite daybreak show. The newscaster was being shown split screen, with a dark grainy image of what appeared to be a woman.

"Police are on the lookout for a woman, that witnesses say,

pushed a middle-aged man in front of a speeding train to his death last night at the forty-second street subway station. The woman is described as being in her twenties, tall, with long bright red hair, and a thin build. The suspect was wearing a light brown leather jacket, blue jeans, and a large brown hat. The victim has not yet been identified. Police are asking if anyone knows who this woman is to please call the number on your screen," the reporter said while the police hotline number was shown on the lower portion of the screen.

Carrie Sanders looked at the image up on the screen. The picture was obviously taken from someone's cellphone and it was of very poor quality. Carrie thought the woman in the photograph looked familiar, but she couldn't quite tell. The photo was just too dark and grainy to make out the details. The forty-eight-year-old woman was thinking about her daughter, Joan. Her friends had told Carrie that Joan looked like a younger version of herself. Carrie enjoyed the compliment; she worked out to keep in shape, but now, the attractive, red-headed woman was worried. Carrie turned off the TV set and thought about what the reporter had said. *The woman is described as being in her twenties, tall, with long red hair, and a thin build,* Carrie remembered hearing. *The suspect was wearing a light brown leather jacket, blue jeans, and a large brown hat,* the television reporter also said.

"Oh, my god…it can't be!" Carrie said in astonishment.

Carrie knew that her daughter had an outfit similar to that one. Feeling nervous and upset, Carrie decided to call her daughter up on the phone. She went into the kitchen, grabbed the phone off the wall, and dialed the number. The phone rang four times until the answering machine picked up.

"Hello, thanks for calling, but I'm not available to take your call right now. If this is a telemarketer, *buzz off!* Anyone else can just leave me a message and I'll get back to you soon. Wait for the beep," Joan's recorded voice said.

"Hello, honey, it's your mom calling. I'm just checking to see if you're alright. Can you please give me a call later? I love you," Carrie said as she hung up the phone.

On the other end, Joan Sanders heard every word as she screened the call over the machine. Joan wanted to talk to her mother, but Avalina wouldn't let her. She decided to go back to her host's information machine, the computer.

"I must find David Scholl. He's next on my agenda," she said to herself.

The possessed woman went back upstairs to the spare bedroom, turned on the computer, and waited for it to warm up again.

Later on, that day in Bright Falls, New Jersey, John Waters was watching the evening news. The reporter said the police had now identified the man that was pushed in front of the subway train last night as Michael Resnick; the man was sixty-four years old. The police were now calling it a homicide and they were looking for any witnesses to the crime.

"Michael Resnick? That name sounds very familiar," John said to himself as he started to think.

Michael Resnick...now I remember! He was one of my wife's friends in that high school yearbook. I wonder if there's a connection, he thought. *The reporter said he was sixty-four years old. That's got to be the same guy.* John took a good look at the man's image on the TV screen, then he got up to look at his wife's yearbook to make a comparison.

"Yup, that's him," he said to himself.

John took note of his wife's other high school friends. His inner detective was beginning to emerge. He made a list of Melissa's three remaining friends: David Scholl, Gilbert Johnson, and Benny Smith. John thought it was just a little too coincidental that his wife, and one of her classmates, were both slain by young women.

5

MY FIRST TIME

Joan Sanders woke up early in the morning to a severe thunderstorm. The mid-winter storm took down trees and flooded several roads. Folks in the town had never seen anything like it. This type of storm was much more common in late summer during the hurricane season. The storm jostled Joan right out of her pleasant dream; she tried to break free from Avalina's power, but it was no use. The entity had an extremely strong hold over her host and she wasn't about to slack off. Joan was lucky that she didn't have to go in to work today. Her boss at The Johnson Law Firm told her they would be closed for the storm. The telephone began to ring and she leaned over the nightstand to pick up the phone.

"Hello?" Avalina asked through Joan's body.

"Hi, baby, it's me, Harry," the caller said.

Avalina didn't know who the hell this guy was. She searched her host's memory and found out that he was Joan's old roommate and boyfriend, Harry Nash. Avalina thought about getting rid of him. *I should just hang up on him,* she thought, but Avalina decided to have some fun with the boy.

"Why, hello, handsome. What cha doing?" she asked him in a very sexy voice.

"I'm home all alone, watching the sky open up. I miss you, baby. I'm really very sorry about how things turned out," Harry replied.

"Wow, isn't that funny? I miss you, too. Let's just forget it even happened, alright?"

"Sure, sounds great to me, baby!"

"Hey, I've got a great idea. Why don't you just bring your ass over here so we could watch the sky together?"

"Sounds like a plan to me! Let me check to see what roads are open and I'll be right over."

"Ok, love, I'll be waiting right here for you," Avalina said smiling while she hung up the phone.

"Nooo!" Joan screamed out to her captor.

"Sucks for you, dearie. He's mine now and we're going to have some fun together, so just shut the hell up and enjoy it," the spirit commanded.

Avalina never had sex with a boy before; she never got a chance to fall in love with anyone in her short life. The possessive spirit knew that her host was not a virgin, but Avalina was. Things were very different back in the sixties. Avalina went to her host's bedroom closet to pick out the sexiest lingerie she could find. Avalina was looking at her new body, naked in the full-length mirror that was hanging inside of the closet door. *Wow, this chick's got a real nice body. She's even got bigger boobs than I ever had,* Avalina thought.

Avalina went downstairs into the kitchen to try and cook some breakfast, but she didn't know how to use any of the modern appliances that were at her disposal. The possessed young woman didn't know what a microwave oven was or how to use it. Low-cost microwave ovens weren't commercially available until the late seventies. She thought about getting that information out of her host, but not now. There wasn't enough time; Harry was coming over. Avalina compared the house to her old home when she lived with her parents. *This place is nice and roomy, maybe even a little bit larger than our old home, but not as cozy,* she thought to herself.

An hour had gone by. Suddenly, the doorbell rang. Harry

Nash was at the front door getting wet from the pouring rain. It was ten o'clock in the morning, but it sure looked like ten o'clock at night. The sky was filled with dark, ominous clouds.

"Wo is it?!" Avalina called out behind the door.

"It's me, Harry! I'm getting wet out here!" he yelled.

The front door opened with Joan wearing nothing but a see-through, low-cut, black French negligée.

"Come on in, darling, you look like a wet rat," the possessed woman said to him.

Harry walked into the house, staring at Joan's breasts. Her nipples were literally popping right through; just barely covered by the sheer cloth she was wearing and her long, auburn hair. Harry was starting to get aroused. *Wow! She never looked that damn hot before. It must be that gown. I've never seen her in that before,* he thought to himself. Joan locked the front door behind him and escorted the young man upstairs into the bedroom. Avalina stared at him through Joan's eyes for a moment. She noticed his large throbbing dick bulging right through his wet jeans. Avalina was quite pleased with him. *Damn, I finally found me a real man,* she thought.

"I really missed you, babe," Harry said as he put his arms around Joan and kissed her on the neck.

"Not as much as I missed you," she replied.

Harry held her so tight that Joan could feel his dick pulsing against her crotch. Avalina's spirit was getting horny. A roar of thunder came from outside as the storm grew worse. Lightning was flashing so much in the darkened room that it made them look like they were moving in slow motion. Harry grabbed her ass and squeezed it so tight that Avalina almost had an orgasm.

"I want you," Avalina moaned.

Harry peeled himself away from her and began to strip. He loosened his belt and dropped his wet blue jeans on the carpet next to his jacket and shirt. Avalina sat down on the edge of the bed. She gazed at Harry's pulsing wet penis protruding through his briefs. When Harry finally pulled off his remaining underwear, his member sprung up like a rocket. Avalina gasped. *Wow! Is he going to put that big thing inside of me?* she thought. Avalina was beginning to get nervous; she didn't know what to do. Back in the sixties, there was minimal sex education. It was presented in a class called, "Hygiene." Avalina never had any experience with boys. The only sexual pleasure she had ever known was masturbating. She had never even seen a naked boy before, except in pictures; still, Avalina wanted to please this handsome young man, and more importantly, she wanted to please herself. The possessed young woman gave Harry a worried look.

"What's wrong, Joan? You're acting like it's your first time," Harry said to her.

Avalina tried real hard to search her host's memory for any insight into sexual intercourse. Clearly, her host had relations with this man before, but Joan clammed up tight as a drum, as if to say, *you're not getting any help from me, bitch.* Joan didn't want anything to do with this boy; to her, it was all over between them. But Harry wouldn't take "no" for an answer. Harry just kept on calling her and begging her for forgiveness. Harry desperately wanted to get back together again with Joan.

Avalina kept staring at the boy's large member, throbbing with every heartbeat. She scrutinized it in awe through Joan's eyes. Avalina just couldn't believe how big his penis was. She wanted him, but she was still worried about having that big thing being inserted inside of her.

"I'm just a little bit nervous, that's all," she replied.

"Nervous? There's nothing to be nervous about, darling. We've done this before you know."

Harry approached her on the bed. He put his loving arms around her and started kissing her on the neck again.

"There, isn't that much better? You said you wanted me," Harry whispered in her ear.

"Yeah, but, can't we just kiss first?" she nervously asked him.

"Sure, we can kiss," he replied.

Harry kissed Joan again on her neck, while working the shoulder straps of Joan's black negligée off of her body. A flash of lightning came through the window again and casted an eerie glow on the couple. Harry rolled his wet tongue over to Joan's right breast while putting his left arm around her back. He made circles around her nipple before Harry completely engulfed it with his mouth and began sucking. Avalina was getting turned on again. Her nipple became hard as a rock. The young man withdrew his mouth and started massaging her breast and nipple with his left hand. Then, Harry began sucking on Joan's left breast while still rolling her right nipple in between his fingers.

"Oh, my god...this feels so damn good," Avalina said breathlessly.

"Lie down, sweetness," Harry softly said to her as he picked his head up from her breast.

Avalina laid down on her back in the bed with her legs dangling right over the edge. Harry gently pulled off her remaining negligée and propped her head up on a pillow. He then buried his face completely in Joan's fiery red and wet bush in between her legs. Harry fiercely began sucking and licking her while still grabbing her breasts. Avalina became so excited by this sensual act that she finally climaxed. Joan was trying to stop Avalina from enjoying her body, but Avalina pulled the reins in on her tight as if to say, *I'm going to enjoy every last moment of this shit, so sit back and enjoy the ride, bitch.* Harry became so excited watching his ex-girlfriend climax, that he dribbled pre-ejaculate all over the floor from his throbbing member.

Harry reached back from underneath Joan and grabbed her behind, while sticking his tongue entirely inside Joan's soaking wet vaginal area.

"Oh, God…Oh, shit…I'm cumming again!" Avalina screamed louder than the thunder outside.

This time, her climax was so strong that Avalina squirted all over Harry's face. He pulled back just to watch her.

"Wow! I've never seen you do *that* before. Come to think of it…I've never seen any girl do that!" Harry exclaimed.

"Do with me what you want, boy, I'm ready for some more," she said.

Harry eased himself up on top of Joan and slid his big hard member inside of her. Avalina screamed in ecstasy while being filled with him. She never felt anything like this before in her life. Joan was worried about getting pregnant since none of them had any protection, but Avalina didn't give a shit. She used all of her powers to suppress the host's control over her own body. Avalina wanted to enjoy it all with no restrictions whatsoever.

"Oh, shit! This feels so damn good! I'm cumming again!" Avalina said while using her host like a puppet for her own pleasure.

"So am I!" Harry said.

Harry quickly yanked his member out of Joan and shot his entire load off, onto Joan's belly until he was completely empty and satisfied.

"Shit…that felt so damn good," Harry said with great sexual relief as he tried to catch his breath.

The two of them kissed and hugged each other for a while until they both fell asleep in each other's arms. The storm started to ease up outside. Joan didn't get to experience any of the sexual pleasure that just happened between her and Harry; Avalina had stolen it all away from her, but Joan didn't care.

Later on that evening, Harry woke up next to Joan in her bedroom. He thought about getting back together with her. The sex between them was never, ever *that* good before. *What happened to her? It was like making love to a horny young virgin,* Harry thought to himself. Suddenly, he noticed something very weird about the woman lying next to him on the big queen-sized bed. Joan was glowing with the face of another girl, superimposed over her own. Harry freaked out. He jumped out of the bed, completely naked. Harry couldn't believe it. He closed his eyes and gave them a good rub, but the vision was still there when his eyes were reopened.

"I've got to get the hell out of here. I'm seeing things," he softly said to himself.

Harry began to put his clothes back on. He went downstairs to the main bathroom to relieve himself before leaving. After washing his hands, Harry opened the bathroom door to find Joan standing right there, completely naked. She looked extremely sexy with her fiery long auburn hair, but she also looked very deadly. Her facial expression showed Avalina's true feelings.

"Where are you going, honey?" Avalina sarcastically asked him.

"I'm…I'm going home, dear. I have to get to work," Harry nervously replied.

"Work? It's seven o'clock at night. When the hell did you start working evenings, Harry?"

"J-just recently...I'm doing overtime...yes, overtime...you know, got to make that money."

"Really? Well, I happen to know for a fact that the real estate office where you work closes up at five. You'll have to come up with something better than that, dear."

Avalina had squeezed that information out of her host. She had a strong feeling that Harry was somehow suspicious of her. Something had to be done about him.

"But, it's the truth! I swear it!" Harry nervously cried out.

"Bullshit! I'm so sorry, dear, but I just can't let you go. I think you know way too much."

Avalina's spirit began ghostly glowing over Joan's body. *It's time to get rid of him,* she thought.

"You can't let me go? Who the hell are you, or better yet, *what* the hell are you?"

"Someone much more powerful than you...hon."

Avalina stared into his eyes and willed him to go into the kitchen and open up the silverware drawer. Harry grabbed a large kitchen knife from the drawer and held it up against his throat.

"What are you doing to me, Joan?" Harry cried out.

"For the record, my name's not Joan; it's Avalina, and now you know *way* too much for me to just let you go. It's time for you to die!" Avalina said in an authoritative voice.

"Wait! I won't say anything to anyone. I promise!"

"That's right, you won't be able to...you'll be dead."

Avalina exerted all of her willpower on him, forcing Harry to commit suicide. He tried to resist, but it was no use. Avalina was much too powerful for him to resist. Harry proceeded to slit his own throat. The young man's own precious blood was squirting out all over. He finally collapsed onto the white tiled kitchen floor, bleeding profusely from his wound. Harry's heart was giving out on him from the lack of blood, struggling to pump. Harry Nash finally died, still holding the bloody knife in his own hands.

"I'm so sorry it had to end this way, dearie. I really liked you. The sex was great. It sure was really enjoyable, but you would have spoiled my plans for revenge. Oh, well…look at it this way, honey, you died satisfied, and oh, what a great way to go. Right, love? It's been fun," she laughed.

The possessed young woman went over to the phone hanging up on the kitchen wall. She picked up the receiver and called the police.

"Hello?! Please, please help me! My boyfriend just killed himself!" Avalina cried to the police officer over the phone.

A few minutes later, two police officers were at Joan's front door ringing her bell.

"Who is it?!" Joan called out.

"It's the police!" one of the officers yelled.

Joan slipped on a light blue night gown and pair of brown leather sandals. She came out of her bedroom and went over to answer the front door.

"Evening, ma'am. We got a report of a possible suicide. I'm Officer Ramos and this is my partner, Officer Lorenzo." Ramos stated.

Officer Pedro Ramos was a tall, light-skinned Latino that shaved his head clean. He was only twenty-nine-years-old with over five years on the force. Ramos had a good record and was bucking for a promotion. Officer Ramos wanted to be a detective; he was tired of walking the beat.

Officer André Lorenzo, on the other hand, was an ole timer. The short, grey-haired Italian man had just gotten demoted to the beat after being a detective for over twenty-five years. Lorenzo was lucky he still had a job, after failing to assist his partner during a stakeout last month.

"Come on in, officers…he's…he's on the kitchen floor," Avalina said with fake tears through Joan's body.

The two police officers followed Joan into the kitchen. They both took out their books and got ready to question her.

"Jesus H.!" Officer Lorenzo said while looking at the body on the floor that was surrounded by blood.

Officer Ramos bent down and tried to take the victim's pulse just to verify that he was dead.

"Yeah, Lorenzo, this man's dead alright," Ramos stated.

"Well, hell, I could have told you that; just look at him," Avalina said sarcastically.

"Lorenzo, call the chief and let him know that we have a body here, and to get forensics over on the double," Officer Ramos told his partner.

"You got it," Lorenzo replied as he grabbed the microphone from his two-way radio.

"Alright, ma'am, this is now being treated as a crime scene. Now, just tell me exactly what happened here tonight," Ramos asked her.

"Well, we had a little fight," Avalina stated.

"A fight? What kind of a fight? Was it a 'knock-down, drag-out fight,' or was it a, 'I'm-seeing-someone-else type of fight?'"

"No, no, it wasn't that extreme, at least not to me, anyway. I simply told him that I didn't want to see him anymore. He was smothering me. I mean, what's a girl supposed to do? I needed some space. You could see that, officer, can't you?"

"No, ma'am, I can't. All I see is a man lying there dead on your kitchen floor, in a pool of his own blood, holding a large kitchen knife to his throat."

"I-I didn't think he would do such a thing. Harry was talking about marriage and I really wasn't ready for all that, so I broke it off with him."

"You said the victim's name is Harry. Harry, what?"

"His name is…was…oh, I don't even know anymore."

Avalina cried hysterically in front of the officers. She was definitely putting on a great act for them.

"Look, I know this is hard for you, ma'am, but I really need to know the victim's name," Officer Ramos said.

"Nash…his name is Harry Nash," she said while crying some more.

"And your name, Miss? What's your full name?"

"Avalina…I mean, Joan! Joan Sanders, officer."

"Alright, Miss, for the record, did you see Mr. Nash do this to himself?"

"No, no, I didn't. I was in the bedroom; I thought he left when I told him to leave. I didn't hear him anymore…now, I know why," she said while trying to put on a good show for the two officers.

"Did he say anything, anything that would have clued you in on what he was about to do to himself?"

"No, he didn't. Harry did seem upset, but I didn't think he would ever go this far. I just can't believe he did that to himself because of me."

"Hey, Ramos, the chief said the forensics team is on their way," Officer Lorenzo stated.

"Alright, Lorenzo," Officer Ramos replied.

The officers were both a little bit suspicious, especially, Officer Ramos. The woman's story just didn't sit right with him. Within twenty minutes, the forensics team had arrived to investigate the scene. Avalina was getting scared; she wanted all of the men to leave and to take the body with them. Joan was highly distressed by this parasitic spirit that invaded her body. Not only did it kill her ex-boyfriend, but now it was getting her in trouble with the law.

Joan was so sorry she had ever bought that stupid necklace. She tried to rip it off of her neck, but Avalina was way too strong for her. The only time Avalina would be weak and tired was when she was asleep; by that time, Joan herself was tired. The specter seems to lose some of its grip on the host when it's weary; that's why Harry saw Avalina's spirit superimposed over Joan's body when he woke up.

The next day, Joan woke up in a strange bed. She leaned over to look at the digital clock on the nightstand. It read twelve-thirty. The sun was shining through the window of the unfamiliar room, so the possessed young woman realized it was daytime, not nighttime.

"Where the hell am I?" Joan said to herself.

"You stupid bitch, don't you remember?! We got kicked out

of our house by the forensics team. They told us to check into a hotel until they were done," Avalina's life-force loudly informed her host.

When the forensics team arrived, they had asked her to leave so that they could conduct the investigation. The team also told Joan that she would be notified when they were finished. Joan Sanders was also informed by the team, that she would be responsible to have a cleanup crew come over and clean up after them, and to have the body removed from her premises.

Avalina began working on her revenge hit list. There were three more names left. *They must all pay for what the hell they have done to me. My life was robbed from me by those assholes,* Avalina thought to herself.

"David Scholl would be next, that's for sure...David Scholl," Avalina said through her host.

Avalina was going to need a computer with internet service to locate David. There was a computer back in her host's home, but obviously, she couldn't access it now. Avalina was going to have to wait until the forensics team finished their investigation. Then, there was that little matter of contacting the cleaning crew and waiting for them to finish their job. The apparition used her host's eyes to scan the room she was in.

"Low-budget...*definitely* a low-budget hotel room. Shit! Delays, delays, nothing but delays. How's a girl supposed to get things done around here?" she asked out loud.

Avalina looked in the nightstand drawer and found a bible, a pad, and a pen. She began writing her plans on the pad. *It'll have to do for now until I get back,* she thought to herself.

6

THE VISITORS

Saturday, February 15th, turned out to feel almost like a wonderful spring day. The temperature was sixty-two degrees, sunny with a nice cool breeze. The robins came early and were having a field day out on everyone's lawn, scouting about for food.

Carrie Sanders was ringing her daughter's front door bell, wondering if she was even home; after all, it was the weekend and it was a nice afternoon. Carrie thought that Joan may have gone out, but Joan was home; at least, her shell was, while being invaded by Avalina's spirit. Joan went across the hall to answer the front door wondering who it was.

"Hello, may I help you?" she asked, not recognizing the woman at the door.

"Joan, it's me, your mother. Don't you recognize me?" Carrie asked her.

Avalina tried to search her host's memory, but it was of no use. Joan was unwilling to help; she was tired of this parasite and was determined to chase her the hell out of her body, but the malevolent spirit was just too powerful for her. Avalina was going to have to pretend to know the woman.

"Mom, how nice it is to see you!" Avalina replied.

"Are you feeling alright, dear? You acted as if you didn't even know your own mother," Carrie stated.

"I'm so sorry, mom, I'm just under a great deal of stress from school...I mean work, that's all."

"Well, aren't you going to ask me in?"

"Sure, sure, mom. Come on in," Avalina begrudgingly said to her.

Avalina and Joan had just finally returned from the hotel yesterday. The police had taken their sweet time investigating the death of Harry Nash, still suspecting Joan Sanders in the back of their minds. Avalina needed to rest; her host was fighting her, which was making Avalina's spirit grow weak. She hoped this visitor would be brief.

"So, what brings you here, mom?" Avalina asked her.

"Well, my dear, I was watching the news just the other day about that poor man, the one that got thrown to his death in the subway. Have you seen that story on the news?" Carrie asked her.

"Y-yes, I think I have. Is that what you came here for?"

"Well, yes, sort of. You see when they gave the description of the killer...well...it sounded like they were describing you. Funny, isn't it? I knew right away it had to be a mistake. I know my daughter is not a murderer. Um...by the way, you weren't in the city a few nights ago, were you?"

"Of course not, mom. How could you even think such a thing?" Avalina nervously replied.

"I'm sorry, dear. I just wanna be sure, that's all."

"Listen, mom, I don't mean to be so rude, but I'm very tired and I just want to go take a nap. You understand, don't you?"

"Sure I do, you're kicking me out, right?"

"Well, I didn't mean to put it that way, but I am really tired," Avalina said with a yawn.

"Ok, dear, I get the message. Mama's leaving."

"Thanks, mom, thanks for being so understanding."

"Alright, I'll come back some other time when you're not so tired."

"Ok, mom, I'll see you later," Avalina said.

Carrie gave her daughter a hug, not knowing that she was possessed, but she still had a strange feeling about her. Avalina closed the door behind her and sighed. She watched through the window to make sure the woman was leaving. *Man, that was a close one*, Avalina thought to herself.

*
**

Avalina went upstairs over to her host's computer in the spare bedroom to do a little searching, before retiring for the evening. The witch had learned enough from Joan regarding how to operate the machine. The possessed young woman sat down in front of the computer and turned the power switch on, waiting for it to warm up. A message came up on the screen that said, *Windows is updating.*

"Updating? What the hell does that mean?" Avalina asked herself.

After a few minutes, the machine was online and ready. She looked at the keyboard, thinking.

"Now, let's see, it's time to search for David Scholl," the young witch said to herself.

The controlled shell of a woman, that was once known as Joan Sanders, started searching the internet for David Scholl. After a while of searching, the doorbell rang again.

"Who the hell is it this time?" she said aloud.

Avalina got up from the computer and walked downstairs

towards the front door to see who it was. She opened up the door, but didn't recognize the attractive, middle-aged woman with long black hair.

"Hello, are you Joan Sanders?" the visitor asked.

"Yes, yes, I am," Avalina responded.

The woman's eyes were drawn to the gold pentagram locket around Avalina's neck; a sudden chill went straight through the woman's body. She knew she had the right person. Anna knew deep down in her heart that the pentagram locket could only bring death and destruction to anyone that wore it. *I'm so sorry I sold the damn thing. I should have just destroyed it like it had destroyed my daughter; I'm sure of that now*, Anna thought.

"Is there something I can help you with?" Avalina asked her.

"My name is Anna Nuñez. I'm the one that sold you that necklace that's around your neck," Anna replied while pointing to Joan's neck.

"This necklace?"

"Yes, 'Win It Easy,' the internet auction site. Don't you remember?"

"Yeah, I remember."

"May I come in for just a bit? I just want to see how you like it and ask you some questions about your experience on the site with me, that's all."

"Well, I don't know, I'm really quite busy."

"Oh, please, it won't take long at all."

"Alright, then, come on in," Avalina reluctantly said as she let the woman in.

"I brought along my notepad with a list of questions to ask, if that's alright."

"Sure, let's go into the kitchen, shall we?" Avalina asked as she lead the woman inside the small room with its white, painted cabinets and white tiled floor.

The two women sat down at the round, walnut-colored kitchen table. Unbeknownst to Anna, Avalina had been analyzing her from the beginning, trying to read her thoughts.

"I'm just trying to get some feedback from you on your purchase," Anna said to her.

"Feedback? What's that?" Avalina asked her.

"You don't know what that means?"

"Well, I'm afraid I don't understand you."

"When someone buys something from that website, it's customary to leave some sort of a review, you know, to let others know what kind of an experience you've had with that seller."

"Oh, I see, and I didn't leave you any on that site?" Avalina asked her.

"No, you didn't."

"Sorry, it must have been an oversight on my side. Surely, we could have communicated this on the internet and saved you this trip, right?"

"I guess I just wanted to see who was going to wear my old necklace, that's all."

"Really, or could it be something else, Miss Nuñez?"

"I'm afraid I'm not following you, Miss Sanders," Anna apprehensively replied.

"I think you do, Miss Nuñez. You've come here to see if you could retrieve the locket. You're sorry you sold it and you think it's evil. Isn't that the reason, Miss Nuñez?"

"No, not exactly, I, I-"

"You think this locket is responsible for your daughter's death, don't you?"

"Yes, yes, I do! How did you know?! Did you research me or something?!"

"Yes, I read your mind. You're absolutely right about this locket, but it's not evil. It merely wants what I want."

"What's that?"

"*Revenge.* You see, Miss Nuñez, years ago, I was wrongfully killed by a few stupid and selfish teenagers. Now, it's time for me to get even-Steven. I'm going to kill them all, one by one and no one's going to stop me...not even you."

"I didn't plan on that at all. I'm really sorry I've taken up your time...well...I must be going," Anna said as she quickly got up from the table, ready to leave.

Avalina grabbed her arm and flung her back into her seat.

"I'm so sorry, dearie, *but you know way too much.* I can't possibly let you leave this house, alive," Avalina said through Joan with an evil expression on her face.

Avalina looked deep into Anna's frightened eyes. She willed Anna's heart to pump faster and faster. Anna clutched her own chest.

"Please, please...don't kill me...I promise...I won't say anything...*please,*" Anna begged as her heart raced up to dangerously high levels.

"You know, I feel a heart attack is surely coming your way, Miss Nuñez. Yes, a heart attack."

The possessed woman exerted all of her witch willpower into Anna Nuñez while looking into her eyes. Anna's heart pumped rapidly, until, finally, it completely exploded in her chest, killing her instantly. Anna's limp body collapsed on to the cold, hard white tiled kitchen floor.

Avalina had dragged the woman's body out towards her host's car. She placed the body into the trunk of the old, black four-door sedan. Then, the malevolent spirit was able to force her host to drive her own car towards the nearby lake. The possessed young woman summoned all of her strength to drag the body out of the trunk and roll it into the lake. She waited there to make sure the body would go down under. After a short time, Anna's body began to sink deep down into Pond Lake. Avalina had taken a precaution to make sure the body would sink. She had previously loaded Anna's clothes up with some rocks and pebbles. Avalina got back into the car and commanded her host to drive them back home.

Sabrina Bishop had stopped by to visit Joan Sanders. She didn't know Joan, but Sabrina had a vision that her daughter's spirit was inhabiting this woman's body. Sabrina wanted to be sure and the only way to be sure, was to see if this woman was wearing Avalina's golden pentagram locket around her neck. Sabrina rang the doorbell three times, but there was no answer. Just when she was getting ready to call it quits, a black car was pulling into the driveway.

"Oh, great...more visitors...just what I need," Avalina said to herself while getting out of the car.

She didn't recognize the elderly woman with long grey hair standing in front of her door right away. As Avalina walked closer towards her, she knew exactly who the lady was.

"Mom, what are you doing here?" Avalina asked her.

Sabrina took a good look at the pretty young redhead. Sabrina stared at her, until she noticed the gold pentagram locket around her neck.

"Oh, my god! It is you…Avalina!" Sabrina exclaimed.

"Yes, momma, it is! I'm back!" Avalina said as she gave her mother a big hug.

"So, this is your new look? Your new body?"

"Yes, momma, how do you like it?" Avalina happily said as she twirled around for her mother to see.

"Very nice, can we talk?"

"Sure momma, let's go inside."

The two of them went inside the split-level ranch house, not knowing they were being watched. John Waters had followed Sabrina, hoping to find some answers about why his wife was horribly killed by a total stranger, a teenager no less. He researched and found out that Sabrina Bishop was Avalina's mother. This scenario still didn't make any sense to him at all. *Who is this attractive young woman with long red hair, and how does she come in to play with this?* John thought to himself. He stood outside and waited…

Sabrina had given the possessed young woman a stern look. She wasn't happy about her daughter's spirit inhabiting this woman to seek out revenge.

"So, how long do you plan to possess this young girl?" Sabrina asked her.

"As long as it takes to get my revenge, for what they did to me and to you and dad," Avalina responded.

"I want to know one thing, dearie. Did you have anything to do with the death of Michael Resnick?"

"He was my second victim."

"Your second victim? You mean...you've killed before?"

"Yes, Melissa Conley."

"Melissa Conley, why? She was your best friend!"

"No, momma, it was all an act. Don't you remember me telling you that? Melissa orchestrated the whole damn thing. Melissa was very instrumental in my death; she was the leader of the pack."

"This isn't right, Avalina and it is not fair to this young woman you're possessing either."

"It isn't fair? Boy, you're singing a different song now, aren't you? I'll tell you what the hell isn't fair; momma, those bastards robbed me of my youth and my whole life, that's what isn't fair."

"You are absolutely right, baby, but what's done is done. What are you going to get by killing them all now?"

"Sweet revenge and satisfaction, that's what. I've got three more to get, momma."

"No, I've got to stop you!"

"You?! Look, momma, please don't make me kill you, too. You are old and weak. What could you possibly do to me? Why don't you just run along now? Go home."

With that, Avalina exerted her powers to make Sabrina Bishop turn completely around and face the front door again. She willed her elderly mother to go out and return home.

"Now, let me see, where was I? Oh, yes, I've got to go find my next victim, David Scholl," Avalina said to herself while closing her front door.

*
**

Outside of Joan's home, John Waters was watching the zombie-like old creature leaving the house. He had heard some of their conversation, but it didn't make any sense to him at all. John decided to try and get the old lady's attention.

"Pssst…excuse me, Mrs. Bishop?" John loudly whispered, trying not to be too loud. "Mrs. Bishop, can you hear me?"

It was no use; the old woman was obviously in a trance. Sabrina Bishop just kept on walking…walking with a purpose. It was getting dark out. John looked at his watch; it was going on six o'clock. He decided to confront the young woman. John gathered up all of his courage and rang the front doorbell.

"Oh, shit, who the hell is it now?" Avalina said aloud.

She went over to the front door and opened it.

"Excuse me, you don't know me and I don't know you, but that woman that just left here, Sabrina Bishop, I know her," John declared.

"Well, that's just hunky-dory, Mister. Who the hell are you?" Avalina sarcastically asked him.

"My name is John Waters."

"Sorry, Charlie, but that name doesn't ring a bell to me."

"Yeah, well, maybe you know my wife, Melissa Waters."

"I never heard of her, Mister."

"Melissa Waters, the novelist!"

"Like I said before, the name doesn't ring a bell, sir, sorry."

Avalina started to close the door on him, but John stuck out his right foot to keep it open.

"Listen up, Miss, I don't know how you come into play here, but if you know Mrs. Bishop, then you knew my wife and I want some answers," John firmly said while keeping the door ajar.

Avalina was getting extremely annoyed with this man, but she knew he wasn't going away.

"Very well then, come on in, sir," she hissed.

John cautiously walked inside the woman's home. He was upset, to say the least, but something in the tone of her voice made him feel mighty unwelcome here. The woman looked evil to him; her pretty, innocent look was now just a fond memory. John decided to hold his ground and question her; after all, he came this far. It would have been ludicrous to just chicken out now; that was not an option at all. He had to follow through.

"Like I said before, Miss, I need some answers about my wife," John tried to say calmly.

"Why don't you just go on home and ask her?" Avalina sarcastically asked him.

"I can't, because she's dead and I have a feeling you and Mrs. Bishop know something about it."

"Now, you listen to me, Mister, don't you dare come into my house and make assumptions that I had something to do with your wife's death."

"Surely, you must have heard that she was burned alive in her own home. It was all in the news."

"As I said before, I don't know *shit* about your wife," Avalina said.

Though as far as I'm concerned, she got what the hell she deserved. Now, she knows what it's like to be burned alive, Avalina thought to herself.

"You know, the way you and Mrs. Bishop were carrying on before, it looked like you two were close relatives." John stated.

"So, you were spying on us, too?" Avalina asked him.

"I may have seen and heard something; for one thing, you kept calling her, 'momma.'"

"You're a regular nosey-hole, aren't you?"

"I just want to find out why a young teenager, a total stranger, killed my wife in such a horrible way."

"How the hell would you like to join her ass, mister?!"

"Excuse me, are you threatening me?"

"Call it whatever you like, asshole. It's time for your ass to die!"

Avalina grabbed the man's neck with her right hand and lifted him off the floor. John was gasping for air as her hand clenched tighter and tighter around his neck. She squeezed his neck until it shattered in her hands. It sounded like a chicken bone snapping in two. John finally stopped kicking and thrashing in her hold. Avalina dropped his limp body down onto the floor, not realizing she had the strength to do what she just did.

"Oh, well, here's another damn body I have to get rid of. Shit, shit, shit!" Avalina said in disgust.

A few miles away, Sabrina Bishop was parking her car, not knowing how she even got home. The last thing Sabrina had remembered was talking to that woman whose body was being inhabited by her daughter's spirit. *I was supposed to convince her to quit, to give up her quest for revenge; instead, I'm back home again. How the hell did that happen? She must have put a spell on me, a hex or something,* Sabrina thought to herself. In reality, Sabrina was very lucky to have made it home alive. She had driven all the way home in a trance-like state, not really seeing her surroundings and nearly colliding with three vehicles on the road with her.

"Avalina is going to keep on killing until she gets them all, one by one, or until I do something about it. I've got to stop her, but how? Clearly, she's much too powerful for even me," Sabrina said to herself.

Sabrina got out of her old, white four-door sedan and went inside her home. The old ranch house had seen better days, but she didn't have any money to fix it up. It was getting late and the old woman was really tired. It was way past her bedtime. Sabrina was going to have to come up with a plan by tomorrow, if she was going to stop her daughter from killing the next victim she had lined up. Sabrina understood the reason why her daughter was doing what she was doing, but to kill everyone that was involved fifty-one years ago was just beyond her capacity, especially since Avalina had already killed two of them.

"She threatened to kill *me*, too, didn't she?" Sabrina asked herself.

7

THE NEW BEAU

David Scholl was coming home from work; he had stopped by the pet shop on his way home. The sun was still out, but it was cold outside, feeling more like winter as it should. The temperature had gone down to thirty-five degrees at five-thirty in the evening. David was happy it was Friday. The young man had been working hard as a computer technician for the past five years at, Computer Servers Plus in New Jersey. He had just brought a new toy for his beloved pet cockatiel. David parked his old white Thunderbird in his assigned parking spot. He walked up his steps and opened up the front door of his ground floor, Campton, New Jersey garden apartment. David called out to his little bird as he took off his black winter coat.

"Michael, daddy's home and I've got a big surprise for you!"

David expected to hear his bird whistle out a reply to him from the bedroom, but the three-room apartment he rented was dead quiet. Michael was all he had. Sometimes, the bird would fly out to greet him and land on his head, since David left his cage door open; but this time, there was no response, just dead silence.

"Michael, I'm home!" David yelled out again as he whistled for his pet bird.

He walked on over towards the bedroom, looking for him.

"Little boy, where are you? Here, little boy!"

David looked at the small white bird cage sitting on his dresser, expecting to find his little grey feathered-friend with bright orange cheeks sitting on his perch, but there was nothing. The cage was completely empty; only the bird's toys, food, and water were present.

"Michael, where are you?!" he nervously yelled out as he cautiously walked around, being careful not to step on him.

David carefully scanned the room, until he spotted a horrible site. Michael was lying dead on his bed. He went over and gently picked up the little bird's lifeless body.

"No, no, no! Not my little boy! Not my little baby!" David wailed over and over again.

The bird had been his only companion for over fifteen years, a lot longer than any of his girlfriends had been.

"My little baby," David cried out as he sat in the white chair by the bed and cradled, the dead bird in his lap, petting his tiny feathers.

The man was totally devastated. David was all alone now.

After grieving over his beloved pet for over two hours, David finally got up out of his chair and decided to look for a small box to bury his bird. The front doorbell rang and David wondered who it was. He put the dead bird back in its cage and went over to answer the door, wondering who the hell it could be at this hour. David wasn't in the mood to talk to anyone right now, especially not to some high pressure salesperson trying to sell him some shit that he didn't need. *I'll just have to tell him or her to go piss off,* he thought to himself.

When David finally opened up the front door, he was pleasantly surprised to find a very attractive young lady standing there. The woman was wearing a light pink dress and a tan colored trench coat. She had a concerned look upon her pretty face.

"Excuse me, sir, is this the residence of David Scholl?" the young woman asked him.

"Yes, yes, it is," David nervously replied.

It was clearly love at first sight, at least on David's part, but the woman looked at him strangely, as though she had found the wrong man.

"I'm looking for David Scholl," the young woman said coyly.

"Well, you've found him, Miss," David responded while staring at her beautiful, piercing, bright blue eyes.

The gorgeous young redhead stared at him completely bewildered. *This can't be, it must be some kind of a mistake. This man is way too young to be the David Scholl that I knew back then; unless, it's his son,* the woman thought to herself.

"Are you David Scholl junior?" she asked him.

"Nope, my dad's name was William. He's been dead now for quite a while, so is my mother," David replied.

The woman just stared at him dumfounded, not knowing what to do or say next. *This just isn't possible,* she thought again. *It's got to be some kind of a mistake.*

"Miss, are you feeling alright? You look like you've seen a ghost," David asked her.

"Maybe I have…maybe I have. I'm ok, no need to worry about me," she nervously replied.

"Oh, no, where are my manners? Please, won't you come in? I really think you should sit down, Miss."

"Ok, maybe just for a little while."

David happily escorted the young woman into his living room. He tried to check out her behind, but her bright red hair and trench coat were both long enough to cover it. David was definitely concerned about this extraordinary young lady; he wondered if she was alright. The two of them sat down on the green sofa.

"Would you like something to drink, Miss? I'm afraid I didn't get your name," David asked her.

"Some water would be just fine, sir, and it's Joan."

"Joan?"

"My name, it's Joan, Joan Sanders," she replied.

"Ok, Miss Joan Sanders, one glass of cool water coming right up," David said with a big smile on his face.

Avalina's spirit sat up in Joan's body, wondering what the hell was going on here. *This just can't be him. I traveled all the way to New Jersey for nothing,* she thought. *This boy is about as young as my host, in his early twenties.* Avalina was expecting a much older man, a man in his sixties, not twenties. She thought that the crazy high-tech machine, the thing that they called a "computer," was dead wrong. Avalina wanted revenge on all of her killers, but this guy was obviously not one of them. *He's really handsome, though. I really dig his muscular body and shiny brown hair. He looks good from behind, too,* Avalina thought as she checked out his butt. Then, Avalina looked at her surroundings. The place looked like it had been furnished from the sixties. There was a banjo clock hanging on the wall. The floor of the living room was covered with a bright green shag rug. A purple lava lamp sat on and old-fashioned desk in the corner, and an old glass-top coffee table was in the center of the room. Over in the foyer, there was a large picture of The Beatles. The décor was definitely something she could relate to, but not for a young person from this day and age…not *this* guy. David Scholl finally came back to her holding a glass of water.

"Here you go, Joan," David said as he sat down next to the woman and gave her the glass.

"Thank you very much. You're very kind, sir," Joan replied

as she looked into his warm, brown eyes.

"You can call me, David."

"Ok, David," she said hesitantly.

"Are you feeling any better now?"

"Yes, yes, I am."

"So tell me, Joan, who were you *really* expecting to see here? Obviously, it wasn't little ole me."

"I was looking for someone I knew."

"With the same name as me?"

"Yes, that's right, but you can't be him."

"Oh, what a shame. I would really like to get to know you better. Forgive me for being forward, but, are you married?"

"No," Avalina replied as she blushed through her host's body.

"This other David, the one you were originally looking for, is he your boyfriend or something?"

"Oh, good heavens, hell no, just someone I knew, that's all."

"I'm so sorry. I really didn't mean to intrude or to sound presumptuous; it's just, well, I don't get too many visitors here, especially beautiful young women, like you."

"You think I'm beautiful?"

"Extremely."

"I-I really should be going. I've imposed enough upon your hospitality already," Joan said as she got up from the sofa.

"Oh, please, won't you stay a little bit longer? I don't feel like being alone tonight. I just lost my only company before you came."

"You had someone else here?"

"Not anymore. It was my pet, a cockatiel. He was over fifteen-years-old."

"What's a cockatiel?"

"It's a small grey parrot with bright orange cheeks and a yellow head. Anyway, I feel so all alone now."

"I'm sorry," Avalina said as she placed a loving hand on his lap.

The two of them stared into each other's eyes for a minute. David tenderly gave her a quick kiss on the cheek. After that, Avalina cautiously placed her arms around the young man and intensely kissed him back on his lips. David was getting an extremely aroused. They kissed and hugged until Avalina noticed the bulge protruding in between the young man's pants.

"Oh, my, did I do that to you?" she said in a surprised sexy voice.

"Apparently, you did. I'm sorry; it's been awhile since I've been with a woman, especially a groovy looking chick like you. I guess you just turned me on," he said while feeling embarrassed.

"Well, it's certainly nothing to be ashamed of. In fact, I find it exhilarating."

Avalina grabbed the young man's member and massaged it through his pants. David was getting really horny; his penis was extremely large and hard. She was having fun with him and her host. Avalina was also getting wet in between her thighs. The possessed young woman decided to take things into her own hands…literally.

She decided to unzip his trousers, pull out his penis, and placed her mouth completely over it.

"Oh, shit, that feels so damn good," David whispered.

Avalina sucked on him as though she were sucking on a lollipop.

"Stop! I want you...I want you now," he sensuously told her.

David escorted the young woman into his bedroom and began to strip in front of her. Avalina was so turned on by this that she also started dropping her clothes onto the bright, green carpeted floor. They stared at each other for a moment, admiring each other, until David made the next move. He grabbed her big firm nipples and drew her closer towards him. David began sucking on her breasts like a hungry baby looking for milk. The two of them laid down on the bed, right in front of the white bird cage that his dead pet was in. David slid down and placed his mouth in between her thighs. He inserted his whole tongue deep, down into the woman's wet vaginal area. Avalina climaxed instantly into his mouth with a big sigh of relief.

"Oh, God...I want you...but do you have any protection?" Avalina asked him.

"Protection? Protection from what?"

"Don't you have any condoms? I, I don't want to get pregnant," she nervously stated.

"You won't get pregnant from me, dear. You see, I'm sort of sterile, Joan. I have a very low sperm count. I hope you're not turned off by that."

"Turned off? No, I'm relieved. Stick it in me. Please," she

begged him.

The young man mounted Avalina and began pumping her. The girl's body quivered with ecstasy as she had another climax.

"Don't stop! Don't stop!" she begged him.

David Scholl tried his best to hold on, but he couldn't wait any longer.

"Oh, shit! I'm cumming! I'm cumming!" he screamed.

David had shot his entire load inside of her, making her have yet, another orgasm. The boy pulled himself out of her and began licking the girl's vaginal area. Avalina had another climax. David was really wearing her out. He took his tongue and started licking her up towards the girl's stomach and back up towards her breasts, swirling his hungry tongue around each erect nipple.

"Oh, God, I can't take any more. Kiss me, please," Avalina whispered to him.

The young couple kissed and caressed each other until they fell asleep in each other's arms. They laid down on the big queen-sized bed, right under the light blue blanket, as darkness fell outside. While she slept, Avalina was still thinking about revenge to those that had killed her years before.

The next morning, Sabrina Bishop was at Joan Sanders' doorstep again ringing her bell.

"Avalina, I know you're in there! open up, I want to talk to you!" Sabrina yelled out while ringing the doorbell again.

After five minutes of trying, the woman decided to go back home. *I guess she's really not home. I'll catch up with her sooner or later, and when I do, we'll have our little talk,* Sabrina thought to herself.

As much as Sabrina loved her daughter, she knew that what the girl was doing was wrong. It was bad enough that Avalina had taken over someone else's body, but doing it to fulfill her own revenge by murdering all of her attackers, was dead wrong. Killing them all would not bring her back.

Avalina's spirit may be alive and inhabiting a human body, but that's the best it could be. *She should feel lucky to have a second chance at life, stealing some poor young girl's body. Instead, all Avalina is seeking is revenge. She must be stopped,* Sabrina had thought. The woman knew that kids did stupid things in life, and this was about as stupid as one could get.

Sabrina couldn't forgive them for taking her daughter away from her, but killing them all, fifty-one years later, that was just ludicrous. What would it accomplish? Nothing could ever really bring Avalina back again, at least not completely. Avalina was dead and buried…it was time to move on.

David Scholl was waking up next to the beautiful young redhead that drove him wild with delight last night. As he looked at his sleeping beauty lying next to him, David began to get aroused again. *Man, she's so damn hot; what a body, what a face and what beautiful fiery red hair. A real fox, that's for sure, but who is she really and who was she really looking for?* David mentally asked himself.

The young woman started to awaken in front of him.

"Hey, stranger, how'd you sleep?" David asked her.

"Like a baby, and you?" Avalina groggily replied.

"Oh, completely satisfied. Hey, how about I fix us up some breakfast," David asked her.

"As much as I'd like to stay, I really must be going. How about a rain check on that?"

"Sounds good to me. When will I see you again?"

"Real soon, honey, real soon."

Avalina got dressed and was ready to leave. She kissed him goodbye, but before she could leave, David stroked her hair once more and asked her to stay a little longer.

"I can't…I really must go," Avalina replied.

"But, I don't even know where you're from. I'd love to come by and visit you, if that's ok with you," David asked her.

"I live in New York."

"New York, the city?"

"No, I'm in a town called Brighten; it's upstate. Give me a piece of paper and a pen. I'll write my address and phone number down for you."

Avalina wrote down her address and number for him, then she kissed him goodbye again. The possessed young woman walked out to her car and left. While she drove herself home, Avalina thought about David. *Wow, he's an even better lover than the last guy I had, although Harry wasn't bad at all. He just found out about me…and that cost him…that cost him dearly,* she thought to herself. Avalina thought about how sweet and old-fashioned David was, but now it was time to go home and get back to work. There still was some unfinished business she had to tend to.

After over an hour of driving, Avalina finally returned to her host's home. She couldn't wait to get back to that bullshit computer, the one that lied to her about David Scholl. Avalina didn't plan on getting romantically involved with anyone, but it happened. *I must stop thinking about him and get back to work. I must find the REAL David Scholl and kill that sonofabitch,* she thought.

Avalina sat down in front of the strange contraption again. *Too bad we didn't have these machines when I was going to school; it would have helped me with my homework,* she thought. Avalina searched David Scholl's name online through the search engine. The computer came up with a few more David Scholl's, but they were either too young, or dead.

"Some information machine…junk…just pure junk," she said to herself. "Maybe he's just too private to be listed on the internet."

Avalina decided to skip David Scholl for now and focus on her next victim, Gilbert Johnson. The computer came up with Gilbert's social media pages. Avalina decided to join one of the sites and message him. She passed herself off as one of his old high school girlfriends. Avalina found out he was local to her, only just two towns away in Daytonville. She asked Gilbert to meet her at the local park on the square, tomorrow at three in the afternoon. Gilbert had readily accepted her invitation.

"Finally, I'm getting somewhere," she said to the machine.

After being on the internet for over five and a half hours, Avalina was getting tired. She couldn't wait to meet up with Gilbert tomorrow. *At last, I'm finally going to get some work accomplished. Time to get even-Steven, but for now, I think I'll just turn in early…after I eat something of course. That machine is really hard on the eyes after a while,* she thought.

Avalina went downstairs to the kitchen and made herself a ham and cheese sandwich with a glass of water to go with it. After she finished eating, the possessed young woman went back upstairs, washed up, and went straight to bed. It was only six o'clock in the evening, but both the spirit and the body were extremely tired. As she slept, Avalina thought about David Scholl, how he had made love to her, and how she was falling in love with him. But Avalina also thought about the *real* David Scholl, Gilbert Johnson, and

Benny Smith. They would all have to be dealt with…accordingly.

Avalina had missed out on everything in life, including boys. The girl never had the opportunity to become someone, to fall in love, to have a home with children, or even have a career. They took everything away from her. How could she ever forgive them? Her own best friend, Melissa Conley, sold her ass down the river and orchestrated the whole damn vengeful act. *But why?* Avalina had wondered in her sleep. *What the hell did I ever do to her? What did I do to any of them? What did I do to deserve that?* Although, Avalina had burned Melissa alive, she still didn't feel satisfied. Avalina had gotten a second chance in life, but it wasn't the same. Possession was quite different. There was always a chance that she could be exorcised out of her host's body by a priest.

8

THE NEXT VICTIM

On Monday, mid-afternoon, February 24th, the weather was so spring-like that everyone was calling it, "the winter that never was." Gilbert Johnson was getting ready to meet his high school sweetheart, Natasha Elder. She had messaged him to meet her at Daytonville Park at three o'clock. Gilbert hadn't seen her in years; he wondered what ever happened to her. The two of them had been an item throughout their high school years. Once Gilbert and Natasha graduated Merryville High School in 1971, the two of them went their separate ways. Natasha went to an out-of-state college that was over two thousand miles away from Gilbert's hometown. Natasha wanted to become a registered nurse. Gilbert, on the other hand, wanted to stay close to home and work as an insurance broker.

It had been about forty-nine years since Gilbert Johnson had seen Natasha Elder. He wondered what she even looked like today, since there wasn't a recent picture of her online. Back in the days, Natasha was a hot Russian babe with long blond hair and blue eyes. She was a real head-turner with the boys in school, but Natasha was a good girl. She wouldn't hang out with any of them; her school work always came first. One day, Gilbert got up the nerve to ask her out on a date. Natasha was stunned. Gilbert had been the only boy she had ever really liked in school. Gilbert was tall with wavy light brown hair and a muscular build, but the most important thing that Natasha had liked about him, was that he was a book worm just like her.

Gilbert looked at himself in the bathroom mirror after reminiscing about the good old days. The middle-aged man was not impressed at all by his reflection. Time had caught up with him. Gilbert was now sixty-five-years-old. He had lost all of his hair and had gotten fat. *What would she want from me now?* Gilbert had thought. But still, he thought it would be really nice to see an old friend and reminisce about the old days. The man had never gotten married. He waited and wished that his only true love, Natasha, would return to him, but Natasha never did…until now.

Gilbert Johnson had gone over to Daytonville Park on the square. It was almost three o'clock in the afternoon. Storm clouds were now threatening and casted an eerie darkness outside. Gilbert thought that it looked almost like nightfall. The wind was blowing so hard that it made it feel cooler than it actually was. *I should have brought a warmer jacket and an umbrella,* thought Gilbert. A beautiful young woman was approaching him in the park. The young lady looked absolutely stunning in her tan trench coat. She had on a matching floppy hat, barely covering her long auburn hair.

"Excuse me, sir, but, you wouldn't happen to be Gilbert Johnson, would you?" she asked him.

"Why, yes, I am. Have we met somewhere, Miss?" Gilbert asked her.

"Yes, we have, over fifty years ago."

"Excuse me, did you say over fifty years ago?"

"That's precisely what I said, Mr. Johnson."

"Is this some kind of joke? Surely you jest."

"I can assure you, this is *not* a joke."

"Miss, I'm sorry to disappoint you, but I've never seen you before in my life. I mean, I would never have forgotten a woman as attractive as you. You *did* say over fifty years ago, right?"

"That's correct, Mr. Johnson, now, what part of that didn't

you understand?"

"Well, all of it. This is ludicrous! Over fifty years ago? You weren't even born then!"

"Oh, I was born then alright," the woman sternly said while holding her ground.

"Listen, Miss, whoever you are, I'm waiting for a friend, so if you don't mind…"

"Your friend, Natasha Elder, is *not coming!*"

"How the *hell* would you know that?!" Gilbert asked her while raising his voice.

"Because, she's dead."

"What do you mean she's dead?!"

"She had died in a plane crash going on a trip to London, England about thirty years ago."

"Miss, this is preposterous! I demand to know who the hell you are!" Gilbert yelled with a cry in his voice.

The young woman looked around to see if anyone was near them. Besides the two of them, the park was completely deserted. Everyone was indoors, waiting for the impending storm to come. She stared at him with a smirk on her face, watching him sizzle, savoring every moment of it, until he furiously yelled at her again.

"I said, Who the hell are you, bitch?!"

"Bitch, eh? Does the name, Avalina Bishop mean anything to you, asshole?"

"Avalina Bishop? I haven't heard that name in years."

"Really? You mean you forgot all about what had happened

to her?"

"No, I haven't. Avalina Bishop has been dead for a long time. She died in an accidental house fire in the late sixties," Gilbert said.

"You're partially right. She died in a fire, alright, but it was *no* accident! You helped set it! You and your damn hoodlum friends!"

"How dare you?" Gilbert hissed. "How dare you accuse me of murder?"

"But you *are* a murderer, a cold-hearted murderer."

"How the hell would *you* know what the hell happened back then? That was over fifty years ago! You act as if you were there, getting a bird's eye view."

"Oh, but I was there!"

"That is utter nonsense. You weren't even born yet, you young upstart!"

"I was there. I felt her pain. You creeps tortured and killed that poor girl. What the *hell* did she ever do to you? What did she do to deserve that shit? *Tell me*, you damn bastard?!"

"That bitch was a witch and it wasn't even my idea, anyway."

"So, that makes it alright? You could have stopped it, but instead, you chose to participate in it. Isn't that right, Mr. Johnson?"

"Why the hell are you so damn interested in something that happened so long ago?"

The woman gave Gilbert a cold blank stare. At that very moment, she wanted to destroy him. She wanted him dead right then and there.

"What are you, a long lost relative or something?" Gilbert

asked her.

"Yes, something, alright. It's *me*, you *asshole*, Avalina Bishop! I've come back from the grave to avenge my death!"

"You're a fricking psychopath," Gilbert said laughingly.

"You think this shit is funny?" Avalina furiously said. "You, you and your deranged friends burned me in my own home. You watched me die! Now, it's time for you to die you sonofabitch!"

Gilbert just kept right on laughing. This infuriated her even more. The man was *not* taking her seriously at all. Avalina raised her hand towards his neck, and without even touching him, she made a squeezing motion using her witchcraft, until Gilbert finally stopped laughing.

"W-what, what are you doing to me?" Gilbert croaked. "I-I can't breathe."

"That's the whole idea, asshole. I want you to join your dead friends," Avalina coldly said.

Gilbert was suffocating. Avalina was cutting off his oxygen supply, making his face turn beet-red, but the middle-aged man came prepared. Before he would face death, Gilbert reached into his pocket and pulled out a .22 caliber revolver. He had purchased the gun, hot, from a junkie last year. Gilbert shot Avalina in her chest, right between her breasts. Avalina and her host, Joan Sanders, collapsed onto the ground in front of the park bench that Gilbert was sitting on. A nearby police patrol car heard the gunshot. The police car started making its way towards the scene of the crime. Gilbert jumped off of the park bench and bolted.

"Freeze!" the officer shouted through the squad car's public address system.

Gilbert kept on running; he was scared. The patrol car was gaining on him as he ran into the street. Officer Malloy kept shouting at him to stop running, but Gilbert just kept on going. Finally, the officer discharged two shots at the assailant. One of the bullets struck Gilbert straight into his heart. Gilbert Johnson collapsed right down onto the cold hard pavement. His heart had finally stopped pumping as he bled out all over the road.

*
**

Later on that evening, Joan Sanders was beginning to wake up in the hospital recovery room. She had been brought over to Daytonville Medical Center after being shot in the park. Her mother, Carrie Sanders, had been sitting by her bedside, waiting for her to awaken. The nurses had removed Joan's pentagram necklace, leaving Avalina's spirit temporarily dormant. Joan was gaining control over her own body, at least for now. She looked up at her mother, feeling dazed and confused.

"W-where am I?" Joan weakly asked her mother.

"You're here in the hospital recovery room, in Daytonville, honey," Carrie replied.

"Hospital? Daytonville? W-what am I doing here? I mean, what happened to me, mom?"

"You've been shot. You're lucky to be alive, dear. The doctor said that if the bullet was any closer, it would have hit your heart. You're gonna be just fine."

"Shot? Where, how, and why? Who would want to shoot me?"

"Well, that's what we're trying to find out, dear. Do you remember anything, anything at all?"

Joan tried to remember what had happened, but her mind drew a complete blank. Avalina had full control over Joan's mind and body for a very long time. The last thing she remembered was searching on the computer for someone. Avalina had used her as a puppet to get some information, but Joan couldn't recall what it was about.

"I'm sorry, mom, I just can't remember anything. My chest hurts," Joan replied.

"I'll have the nurse come in here and give you something for the pain, but first, the police detective has been waiting outside to talk with you," her mother said.

"The police? Why?! I don't know anything."

"Oh, dear, he just wants to ask you some questions about what happened, that's all."

"But, why, mom? I didn't do anything to anyone," Joan barely cried out.

"You see, honey, they think you may have known the man that shot you in the park. Just cooperate with them, it's for the best."

"But, mom, I don't know of any man in the park. I don't even know what the hell happened to me, can't you see that?"

"Well, then, you just tell him whatever you know, dear. I'll be waiting outside, all right?"

"Ok, mom, but I'm afraid I'm not going to be much help to him."

Carrie Sanders walked out of the recovery room, leaving her daughter there waiting for the detective to question her. Joan was worried; she didn't know anything about the incident. *What possible help can I be to the police,* she thought to herself. Joan started to remember something about losing control over her body. *I think I was possessed or something, maybe by some kind of evil spirit,* Joan thought. *But, why, and more importantly, by whom or what?*

Detective Wiretrak quietly walked into the hospital recovery room. The detective was a tall, slender Caucasian man of Irish heritage. Michael Wiretrak was fairly young to be a detective. The man was only twenty-eight-years-old. Due to his knowledge and quick-wit thinking, Wiretrak had moved up through the ranks rather quickly. The detective seemed to be very popular with his coworkers, especially the females; although, he showed no interest in them. The man just wanted to do his job. Wiretrak's fiery red hair and good looks seemed to peak interest in several of his female coworkers. Detective Wiretrak stared at the beautiful young woman lying there helplessly on the hospital bed.

"Miss Sanders, I'm Detective Wiretrak. I'd like to ask you some questions if you're up to it," the detective said.

"Sure, Mr. Detective, but I don't think I can be of much help to you," Joan replied.

"Well, now, let me be the judge of that, Miss Sanders. You see, in my opinion, any help is better than no help at all."

"Ok, sir, if you say so."

"Good, now tell me everything you can remember, from the beginning, please."

"Well, that's just it, sir, I don't remember anything at all. I don't even know how I got there, or even in this hospital."

"It sounds like to me you have a slight case of amnesia, Miss Sanders."

"Call it whatever you like, Mr. Detective, but it's true. I can't remember anything about it at all."

"Well, then, why don't you just tell me the last thing you *do* remember, ok?"

"Well, the last thing I *do* remember is searching on my home computer for someone."

"And, who were you searching for, Miss Sanders?"

Joan decided to think about what she was going to say to the detective. *If I tell him I was being possessed by an evil spirit, they'll lock my ass up in the loony bin for sure,* she thought to herself. Joan decided to lie about looking for an old friend online.

"I remember looking for one of my old friends on social media...that's all I remember," Joan finally replied.

"So, you don't have any recollection of meeting Mr. Gilbert Johnson?" Detective Wiretrak asked her.

"Who's he?"

"Gilbert Johnson is the man that just shot you in the park. You're lucky to be alive, Miss Sanders. The doctor said the bullet just barely missed your heart, only by a few millimeters."

"I still don't recognize the name. Was he trying to rob me or something?"

"We don't know for sure, Miss Sanders. We were hoping you could enlighten us."

"Didn't you question him at the police station?"

"No, ma'am."

"Well, I think you should."

"That won't be possible, Miss Sanders."

"Why not?"

"Because Mr. Gilbert Johnson is dead. He tried to get away and one of the officers on the scene shot him down."

"I-I'm sorry, but I still don't know him, or what the hell happened," she tearfully said to him. "Please, please leave me alone, detective. I cannot help you anymore; I'm in pain," Joan added.

"Ok, Miss Sanders, but if you *do* remember anything, anything at all, please give me a call."

Detective Wiretrak placed his card on the bedside table next to her and left the room, feeling disappointed. Joan broke down and cried. She wondered what this was all about and what it all meant. The nurse came back in the room and asked her if she wanted a sedative.

"Yes, please give me something for the pain...something to make me go back to sleep," Joan replied.

Detective Wiretrak went back to the police precinct to report to the chief of police. The chief was sitting at his desk smoking a big cigar. Chief Charles P. Valentine was a heavy-set, middle-aged Caucasian man. He was always stressed out about something. Valentine was ready to retire from the force, but he had to put in another three more years to fulfill his obligation with the department. Chief Valentine noticed Detective Wiretrak walking into his smoke-filled office, hoping he had some information on the recent shooting in the park.

"Hey, Wiretrak! You got any info for me on the park shooting?" Valentine asked him.

"I got nothing, boss," the detective replied.

"Are you fricking serious? You're putting me on, right?"

"I'm afraid not, chief. She doesn't remember a thing. I think Miss Sanders has amnesia."

"Shit, did you try and jog her memory?"

"Yes, I did, boss. I'm sorry; I know it's not what you wanted to hear."

"Well, we'll just have to try a little bit harder until we get some leads, right?"

"You got it, boss, I'm on it," the detective said as he eased himself out of the chief's office.

A week had gone by. Carrie Sanders was bringing her daughter, Joan, back home from the hospital. Joan wanted to go back to her own home, but Carrie wouldn't have it any other way. Her mother insisted that she'd stay with her until she completely recuperated. Carrie brought Joan into her living room and helped her sit down on the old brown sofa.

"Do you need anything, dear?" Carrie asked her daughter.

"I'm a little sore, mom," Joan replied.

"Well, do you want to lay down for a bit? The sofa opens up into a bed, you know."

"No, momma. I just want some Tylenol for the pain, please."

"Ok, honey, I'll go get you some."

"Mom, where did you put my things from the hospital?"

"They're in a shopping bag in the trunk of my car. Let me go get you some Tylenol and water first, then I'll go out to the car and get them for you, fair enough?"

"Ok, mom, thanks."

Carrie left the room and went to the kitchen. Joan was checking out her surroundings. It's been awhile since she's lived with her mom; the place still looked the same. Joan's mother was living all alone in that big ole house. Her father, Tom, had passed away over five years ago from a stroke. Joan had tried to convince her mother to sell the house and move into an apartment, but Carrie didn't want to leave. She enjoyed staying there along with her job as a teacher in Brighten High School. There were plenty of memories there in that old two-story colonial home, some good and some bad. Carrie wanted her daughter to move back with her, but Joan enjoyed her independence.

Carrie finally returned with the medicine for her daughter.

"Here you go, dear. Here's your Tylenol and water," Carrie said as she handed the pills and water to her daughter.

"Thanks, mom, I appreciate everything you've done for me," Joan replied.

"The pleasure's all mine; after all, what are mothers for?"

"You said you would get my things from the car, mom…"

"Oh good heavens, I forgot. I'll go out right now and get them for you."

Carrie Sanders went back out to the car to get her daughter's things. She unlocked the trunk of her old, white Ford sedan. Carrie noticed that the shopping bag fell on its side and spilled half of its contents all over. She started putting things back in the bag, until the woman noticed the gold pentagram necklace. *What a strange necklace,* she thought. I wonder where she got it from.

Carrie walked back into the house and approached Joan with her new findings.

"Honey, here are your things, but I do have a question for you," Carrie said.

"What is it, mom?" Joan replied.

"Where did you get this necklace from? I know I didn't give it to you."

"Oh, I was looking for that."

"Well, it fell right out of the bag in my trunk."

"I won it online at one of those auction sites, mom."

"How much did it cost you?"

"It was about a hundred and something."

"For that ugly old thing?"

"It's not ugly, mom."

"Yes, it is. It's gaudy."

Joan felt compelled to put the necklace back on, but at the same time, she was frightened by it. Joan suddenly remembered that her possession had something to do with the gold pentagram necklace. The young woman stared at the locket in her mother's hands. It had a hypnotic power over Joan, compelling her to put it on.

"Give it to me, momma, please?" Joan asked her.

"Here, dear, if it will make you happy..." Carrie replied as she handed the chain over to her daughter.

Joan greedily accepted the golden pentagram locket from

her mother. She really didn't want it, but Joan was forced into putting it back on. She placed it around her neck. Avalina began infiltrating her body all over again. Joan looked at her surroundings again, then she looked at her mother in disgust.

"Where am I?! What the hell are you doing here?!" Avalina sarcastically asked her.

Joan's mother was clearly shocked. She wondered what the heck happened to her daughter. *Oh, god, I hope she's not going crazy on me. I don't think I could handle that,* Carrie thought.

9

A TIME TO DIE, AGAIN

Sabrina Bishop was waking up to a warm Tuesday morning on March 3rd. It was already seventy-five degrees outside, but the humidity made it feel worse; this wasn't normal for late winter. Sabrina wished she could afford a window air conditioner for her small, hot ranch house, knowing that summer was near. Even if she could afford an air conditioner for the bedroom, Sabrina knew that she probably couldn't afford the electric bill to run it. Her social security checks were barely enough to make ends meet, let alone have any kind of luxuries. The small window fan wasn't doing much to help alleviate the heat inside her home. The poor old woman was mainly focused on her daughter. *I have got to find a way to stop my Avalina,* Sabrina thought as she wiped the sweat from her face. Sabrina knew that her daughter had something to do with the recent death of Gilbert Johnson, even though she couldn't prove it.

"Avalina has got be stopped before she kills again," the woman said to herself.

Sabrina got out of her bed to take a cool shower. The water felt refreshing on her back and cooled her off so that she could think more clearly. After bathing, she went to the kitchen to have a bowl of cereal and a cup of coffee. Sabrina finished her breakfast, got dressed, and left her house. She was on a mission to destroy her daughter's spirit, even if it meant killing her host, too. *I love my daughter dearly, but all of this senseless killing must come to an end,* she thought to herself.

Meanwhile, back in the town of Brighten, New York, Avalina Bishop was glad to be back inside her host, Joan Sanders' body and in the young woman's own home. Joan's mother, Carrie Sanders, had flipped out when her daughter told her that she wanted to go back home. What Carrie didn't realize was that her daughter had gotten repossessed by Avalina once she put that gold pentagram back around her neck. The scorned spirit tried real hard to control her temper, but she grew too impatient. Avalina had to diligently explain to her host's mother that she wanted her freedom and independence. After being insulted, Carrie finally had agreed and brought Joan back to the woman's own rented home.

Avalina, wearing a light pink house dress, turned on the room air conditioner and sat down in front of her host's computer. She started to think about David Scholl again and how he had made love to her. Avalina wanted him. She wanted him badly as the young woman slid her right hand in between her thighs, but the possessed young woman knew it was time to get back to business.

"It's time to find my next victim. It's time to find Benny Smith," Avalina said to herself.

The controlled woman waited for the computer to load up, then she started typing into the search engine. Suddenly, the front doorbell rang. *I wonder who the hell that could be. Interruptions, always interruptions, shit,* she thought to herself.

Avalina Bishop had gotten up from the computer desk chair and went downstairs to answer the front door. She was shocked to see the familiar old woman standing there again, this time in a light green dress with her grey hair up in a bun.

"Hello, dearie," Sabrina Bishop softly said.

"Hello, momma, what brings *you* here again?" Avalina asked her.

"I've come to put an end to your reign of terror."

"Oh, momma, don't be silly, come on in."

"No! This will be quick. Listen, I love you and I always will, but all of this senseless killing must come to an end. I don't know what the hell you've become, but you're *not* my daughter anymore. My daughter wasn't evil; my daughter was *not* a murderer. It's time for you to die, again…this time for good."

Sabrina pulled out an old snub-nosed pistol from her purse and pointed it directly at her daughter's host. Avalina was shocked. She didn't expect this, not from her own mother. Her heart began racing. Sweat began emerging from her face, knowing that her mortal life on Earth was about to end abruptly, again.

"Mother, you can't be serious! Put that thing away!" Avalina cried out.

"I really don't want to kill an innocent person, so please, leave your host, and go rest in peace," Sabrina firmly said.

"If you kill my host, I'll only find another one; you know that, don't you, momma?"

"No, not if I destroy your locket, or bury it where no one will ever find it again."

"You wouldn't do that to your only child, would you?"

"Like I said before, you're not my daughter anymore. What you have become is simply pure evil. You're a monster!"

The two of them stared at each other in the front doorway. Avalina kept looking at the gun that was pointing right at her. She had become attached to her fine young host. Avalina's spirit didn't feel like having to go and look for a new body all over again, but there really wasn't much she could do about it right now. Clearly, her own mother held all of the cards right now.

"I love you, honey, I'll always love you. I'm sorry," Sabrina said with a tremble in her voice as she cocked the loaded gun in her hand.

Suddenly, someone grabbed her from behind in a choke-hold. The gun went off into the air and missed Avalina. David Scholl managed to get the weapon away from Sabrina and pointed it at her.

"No, don't shoot her!" Avalina cried out to him.

"You know this woman?!" David asked.

"Yes, she's my...grandmother."

"What?! Why the hell would your own grandmother want to kill you, Joan?!"

"She...she's just not feeling well...it's her mind. My grandmother is very old and suffers from schizophrenia," Avalina responded through Joan's body.

"Are you alright?"

"Yes, yes, I am. Thank you for coming to my rescue."

"No problem, but what are we going to do about her?"

Before Avalina could answer, Sabrina grabbed her chest and collapsed in front of the two of them. Her heart couldn't take it anymore; the excitement was just too much for her to handle. Avalina was shocked. There was nothing she could do but cry out in agony.

"Mother! Nooo!"

David Scholl bent down to check Sabrina's pulse. He looked

up at Joan and shook his head, "no."

"I'm so sorry, Joan, but I can't seem to get a pulse. I think she's dead," David sadly reported.

Avalina collapsed over her mother's body and sobbed like a baby. David reached for his smartphone in the right front pocket of his blue jeans, then he called for medical assistance. Avalina became so distraught that she started punching him, until she finally collapsed on him and cried all over his light blue shirt.

The ambulance finally arrived after about twenty minutes. Two men stepped out of the medical vehicle: one emergency medical technician and one paramedic. The trained team tried really hard to resuscitate the old woman, but it was just too late. Sabrina Bishop was gone. After the medical team gave Joan and David some information, they took Sabrina Bishop away and left the couple there holding each other. David took the teary-eyed young woman back inside her home. The two of them sat down on the living room sofa. David placed a consoling arm around her.

"Are you alright, Joan?" he asked her.

"I'll survive," she replied.

"I took a chance and came by to visit you since you didn't answer your phone, but I didn't expect all this drama. I'm sorry."

"It's not your fault, David. I told you she was sick, but I'm sure glad you came by. She was going to kill me and you saved my life."

"What brought all that on?"

"I really don't know. She just came by to visit me, and the next thing I knew, she was pointing a loaded gun at me."

"I must say I'm a little confused though, you said that she was your grandmother and yet you called her, 'mother.'"

"She was like a mother to me, so I called her that after my real mother had passed away."

Avalina looked deep into David's brown eyes. She could see the warmth and gentleness in the man. Before Avalina could kiss him, the doorbell rang.

"I wonder who that could be…excuse me for a moment," Avalina said as she got up to answer the door.

Detective Michael Wiretrak had come by to ask Joan some questions. Wiretrak also wanted details on the incident that just happened at her house. The detective decided to ring the doorbell once more; this time, Avalina was there to open the door.

"Hello, Miss Sanders, do you remember me?" the detective asked her.

"Yes, you're that detective I met at the hospital," Avalina nervously stated.

"That's correct, Detective Wiretrak. May I come in and ask you some questions?"

"Sure, Mr. Detective, come on in."

The redheaded detective walked into the woman's home and stayed in the vestibule. Avalina closed the door behind him. The possessed young woman wondered what he wanted. Avalina tried to read his mind, but David came over and broke her concentration.

"What's this all about, honey, who's this?" David asked her as he pointed to the detective.

"Oh, I'm sorry, I didn't know you had company. I can come back later," Wiretrak said.

"Nonsense, it's alright. This is David; he's a good friend of mine. David, this is Detective Wiretrak."

"Detective? Are you in some kind of trouble, Joan?"

"No, it's nothing like that. The detective just wants to ask me some questions, that's all," Avalina replied.

"Do you need me to leave?" David asked her.

"That's up to the detective."

"Well, I would like to ask you some questions in private, Miss Sanders, if you don't mind," Detective Wiretrak responded.

"Sure. David, could you please come back a little later?" Avalina asked him.

"Ok, if you don't need me, I'll go," David said as he walked out the door.

"Listen, I'm going to extend my leave of absence from work, so call me, ok?"

"Sure," David replied.

David kissed her goodbye and walked out the door. The young witch escorted the detective into the kitchen and asked him to sit down at the table with her. Avalina tried to read his mind. She knew the detective was suspicious of her.

"So, do you have *any* recollection of what happened to you in the park that day?" Detective Wiretrak asked her.

"No, I still don't," Avalina replied.

"And you still don't remember why Gilbert Johnson wanted to hurt you?"

"Like I told you in the hospital, I didn't even know who the hell he was."

"Alright, then, tell me, Miss Sanders, did you know the elderly woman that just passed away in front of your doorway?"

"Yes, she was my grandmother."

"Really? Well, I didn't see any relation between you and Miss Sabrina Bishop. You see, I did my homework, Miss Sanders, since I've seen her here before," the detective doubtfully replied.

"What I really meant was that she was like a grandmother to me."

"Oh, I see. Then, tell me why would Miss Bishop want to pull a gun on you? It seems that lately, everyone is trying to kill you. Now, is there something that you want to tell me? If you're in some kind of trouble, I can help to get you some police protection, Miss Sanders, but you've got to level with me."

"It's nothing like that, detective. Sabrina was sick; she was a schizophrenic."

"Oh, I see, but you don't know what set her off like that, do you?"

"No, I don't. I'm sorry."

"Well, there must have been something you said or did that made her snap like that. I mean if this woman was like a grandmother to you…"

"I'm sorry, but I just can't think of anything that I did or said, for that matter, that made her snap. It had to be all in her own mind."

Avalina tried to read his mind some more. She gave him more appropriate answers to help satisfy the detective's suspicions. After a few more minutes of questioning, Detective Wiretrak left her premises feeling only a little satisfied. Avalina knew that he was on to her. She was going to have to play it cool, at least for now.

Carrie Sanders wondered what happened to her daughter. *She acted so strange, like she didn't even know who the hell I was, or where she was,* Carrie thought. *It's as if she was a different person, altogether. Maybe, I should go over to visit her and see how she's doing.* Carrie got dressed and headed for her car, wondering if her own daughter should see a psychiatrist. She drove almost halfway there, then Carrie just pulled over to cry.

"What's wrong with her? Oh, God, what's wrong with my daughter?" Carrie cried out in her car.

Later on that afternoon, Detective Wiretrak was back at his desk receiving a phone call from a worried medical director.

"You said he's been missing for how long, Mr. Roberts?" Detective Wiretrak asked the caller.

"The last time we saw him here at the Brighten Medical Clinic was on Friday, February the fourteenth," Paul Roberts replied over the phone.

"That's over two weeks ago. Did he have any vacation time that he may have wanted to use?" Wiretrak asked the man.

"That's a negative on that, sir. John had just come back from a two-week long vacation. Besides, John wouldn't just disappear like that; I mean, not without asking for permission."

"Well, maybe he's out sick or visiting a sick relative."

"Without calling in and letting someone here know that? I don't think so, that's not like him."

"Did you drop by his residence to see if he was at home?" Detective Wiretrak asked.

"Yes, I sent my Human Resources man over there to check on him, but there was no one home at the time. This isn't like him. John Waters takes great pride in his excellent attendance record here at the medical group. John always puts his patients ahead of any personal problems he may have."

"Well, then, my question is, why did you wait so long to call it into the police?"

"John just recently lost his wife; she was murdered. Some crazy young girl set fire to their home in New Jersey, while he was here at the clinic. The police found his wife tied to a chair in the kitchen while she was burned alive. It was horrible. John never really got over it, so we gave him some space. I told him to take some time off for a while."

"I remember that incident. She was a well-known author in New Jersey, right?"

"That's correct, detective. Melissa Waters was her name."

"Yes, yes, that's right, Melissa Waters. Ok, Mr. Roberts, next question: if he's in New Jersey, then why are you calling us in New York?"

"He's been living with his brother in Brighten, New York while his house gets rebuilt from the fire. The address is, 1534 Sycamore Road, Brighten, New York. He's a great psychologist, I hope everything's alright with him."

"Alright, let me get your phone number in case we need any more information from you."

"Will you please keep us informed of anything you find, detective?"

"Yes, I will, sir."

"Ok, then, the number here is (914) 393-7575."

"Alright, then, we'll keep in touch," Detective Wiretrak said as he hung up the phone.

Chief Valentine had just walked into the detective's office. Wiretrak looked up and noticed the concerned look on the chief's face. He knew right away something was wrong.

"What's up, chief?" Wiretrak asked him.

"We have a report of a missing person," Chief Valentine gravely stated.

"Another one, or is it the same one that I just got."

"I don't know. Who's the missing person you got?"

"It's a male. His name is John Waters, a psychologist. He was married to that famous author, Melissa Waters. Is it the same one?"

"No, the call I got was for a female; her name is Anna Nuñez. She's been missing since Friday, February 14th; at least, that's the last time her boyfriend, Mr. Hector Rodriguez, claims that he'd seen her."

"No, shit! That's the last time that *my* victim was seen!"

"Hey, something funny's going on around here and I don't like it."

"Well, do you think they're related incidents, or completely separate, chief?"

"I don't know, but we'd better go check it out."

"There's also that new victim, Sabrina Bishop."

"No, she was old with a bad heart. It probably was just her time to die. These other two cases; however, really need to be thoroughly checked out, ok?"

"I'm on it, chief," the detective replied.

Back in Brighten, New York, Carrie Sanders was ringing her daughter's front doorbell again. Avalina and her host, Joan, were both tired. The possessed young lady had gone off to bed for a late afternoon nap. Carrie kept ringing the doorbell. *I wonder where the hell she is,* Carrie thought to herself. *I sure hope she's alright. I know she hasn't gone back to work yet,* Carrie kept thinking while she rang the door some more.

After ringing Joan's doorbell for a good solid five minutes, she decided to give it up. Carrie got back in her car. She started the engine again of her old white Ford sedan. *It's got to be trauma from being shot,* she thought. *My daughter almost died; I've got to be a little more understanding.* Carrie buried her face into her hands in front of the steering wheel and cried again. After she regained her composure, the concerned mother put her car in gear and drove off. A few yards away, a figure stood in the upstairs bedroom window watching her drive off. Avalina was standing there, livid, wondering what the hell was she going to do with that meddling woman. *If she keeps this shit up, I'll have to kill her, too,* Avalina thought with an angry look on her face. Her host, Joan, knew what the witch's spirit wanted to do. She would try her best to help protect her own mother.

10

WHO'S THERE?

Avalina had gotten up in the middle of the night with a real strong urge to urinate. *That's what I get for drinking too much water before going off to bed,* she thought to herself. She pulled the light blue comforter off of her body and got out of bed, wearing only a white night gown. Avalina went to the bathroom down the long hall, of her host's rented home and sat down on the toilet. Suddenly, Avalina thought she saw a shadowy figure flash by her. The young woman was so startled, that she leaned over and slammed the bathroom door shut. *I've got to get a hold of myself,* Avalina thought. *There can't be anyone there. I'm tired and I probably just imagined it,* she tried to reassure herself. Avalina got up, flushed the toilet, and washed her hands. The nervous young lady cautiously opened up the bathroom door and looked around. Again, the shadowy figure flew by her.

"Who's there?!" Avalina screamed out.

Her heart was beating so fast that she felt it pounding in her chest; Avalina thought it was going to burst. She looked around some more, then the young witch went back towards her bedroom, hoping to find safety and comfort again in her bed. A bolt of lightning flashed through the windows, casting an eerie shadowy light. The lightning was followed by a crack of thunder that broke the sound of her labored breathing. Avalina flew into her bedroom and closed the door behind her. She started hearing thrashing sounds emanating from the hall outside. The frightened young woman locked the door and jumped into bed, eager to find security under her blanket. It was only three o'clock in the morning; there would be at least two more hours to go, before any daylight would be present to help alleviate her night fear. Joan, on the other hand, was relishing the fact that Avalina was so frightened. *Good…be scared…be very scared, and get the hell out of my body, you witch bitch;* Joan's soul was trying to convey to her captor.

Later on, that Thursday morning of March 5th at the Brighten Police station, Detective Wiretrak was going over his notes. It all seemed too coincidental and strange to him. Two people, living in different areas of the same town, not connected with each other at all, had disappeared at the same time. Wiretrak had always thought this was a quiet town; *I guess I was wrong about that,* he thought to himself. The detective took a break and he decided to go get a cup of coffee and a doughnut, at the local diner down the block. *Maybe some coffee and food will help me think clearer,* Wiretrak thought. The young detective walked out of his office to let the chief know where he was going. He didn't expect a breakfast list from the chief. *I guess I'm treating again,* Wiretrak thought. He stepped outside and marveled at how nice and warm it was. It sure didn't feel like winter weather in March, that was for sure. The only problem was that, since the Coronavirus was spreading fast, the governor stated that this was going to be the last weekend, that anyone could go eat out in a restaurant. It would have to be take-out food only. Also, no one was to have any kind of social gathering of over fifty people. This new order was to help stop the spread of the new virus.

David Scholl decided to pay another visit to his new love, Joan. He remembered her saying that she was going to extend her leave of absence from work, so he decided to take the day off to spend some time with his new sweetheart. After driving over an hour from New Jersey, the young man started thinking about the last time he had come over to visit Joan. *I sure hope that everything's alright with her,* David thought. He got out of his old, white Thunderbird and walked on over to ring the young woman's doorbell.

"Who is it?!" Avalina called out through Joan's body.

"It's me, David!" he replied.

Avalina was so excited. She ran over as fast as her host's legs could carry her. The young woman thought about changing out of her white nightgown, but decided to answer the front door instead.

"Oh, thank goodness, it's you!" Avalina excitedly said as she threw her loving arms tightly around his neck.

"Whoa, what brought all that on? Is everything alright?" David cautiously asked her.

"It is now, come on in, love."

David had followed her inside the house as she closed and locked the door behind him. He could see that the girl was frightened of something, but he didn't know what. David hugged Joan back and gently stroked her long hair.

"You're shaking…what's wrong, honey?" David tenderly asked her.

"I think there is someone in this house, someone that's trying to harm me," Avalina nervously replied.

"Are you sure?"

"Yes, I saw a shape pass by me last night; it was too dark to see who it was, but I saw someone."

"Really? Let's go check it out."

"I'm scared!"

"Ok, you sit here and I'll go check it out myself."

"NO, I don't want to be all alone! Please don't leave me!"

"Well, we haven't got much of a choice now, do we, Joan?"

"Ok, I'll go with you," she hesitantly replied.

Avalina led David around the split-level ranch house. She took him into the kitchen, the living room, the dining room and to the downstairs bathroom. Next, Avalina took David upstairs to the spare bedroom where her computer was. Finally, she took him to the upstairs bathroom.

"This is where I saw him last night while I was in the bathroom," she said.

"Oh, so it was a man?" David asked.

"Well, I assume it was. Like I said, I couldn't get a very good look; it was dark out."

"About what time was it, Joan?"

"It was around three o'clock in the morning."

"And you didn't put on any light?"

"No, because then I would have had a tough time going back to sleep."

"So, if it was pitch-black outside and inside, how the hell did you see him, or even know where you were going?"

"There's a little nightlight on in the hall over there," Avalina said as she pointed to the plug-in light on the wall.

"What did you do then?" David asked her.

"I ran down the hall to my bedroom here," the possessed young woman said as she led David into her master bedroom.

"Isn't it possible that you *thought* you saw someone? I mean, it was still dark outside and you didn't put on any lights, plus you were tired," David clearly stated.

"No, I wasn't seeing things. I also heard noises, like there was someone walking around or something," Avalina retorted.

"Well, this is the last room in the house and we've found no trace of anyone. I'm sorry, hon."

"Thanks, at least you humored me."

"I wish I could have done more," David sympathetically said as he put his comforting arms around her.

"Isn't it funny how we wound up in the bedroom again?" Avalina said.

"If you'd like, I could spend the night."

"Here, with me?"

"Precisely, my dear; I mean, it's only fair since you spent the night over in *my* apartment."

"Yeah, and who's idea was that?" she jokingly asked him.

"I'd like to think it was mutual," he said while gazing into her bright blue eyes."

"Boy, aren't *you* the smooth talker?"

"I just thought it would make you feel safe and comfortable, that's all, but if you want me to go, then I'll go."

"*No*, please stay with me tonight."

"Well, alright, then. You've twisted my arm, but we've got a long wait for tonight; after all, it's only ten o'clock in the morning."

They both laughed for a bit and then they started kissing one another. This time, Avalina took charge. She dropped her white night gown right in front of him, exposing her lovely naked body. David was beside himself; he didn't expect that. The possessed young woman gently, but firmly pushed David down onto the queen-sized bed. Avalina then proceeded to unbutton David's shirt and unzipped his blue jeans. She helped him remove all of his clothing. David was so turned on by this, that he instantly got aroused. Avalina started kissing him on his member, then she moved up towards his nipples and playfully kissed them, too. Avalina picked her head up and lovingly gazed into his eyes with a seductive smile.

"Now, sit back and enjoy the ride," she told him in a very seductive voice.

The young witch mounted David and inserted his big hard penis inside of her. It was easy for her since she was already wet from excitement. Avalina bounced up and down on him while rubbing her thigh with her right hand until she climaxed. David was doing his best to control himself; he wanted to hold on for as long as he could for her. While Avalina leaped up and down on him, David noticed something. In between her breasts, there was a round golden locket, a pentagram hanging down from a gold chain. *I've seen that thing before, but I don't remember where or when,* he thought. David didn't pay much attention to it before, partly because the last time he had made love to her, was at night, but now it was much easier for him to see it since she was on top of him, in broad daylight. Avalina climaxed again and this time, it was so strong that she was quivering and screaming. David got so turned on by her loud moans and her tightness around his member, that he just couldn't hold out any longer. David yelled out and expelled his entire load right inside of her. Avalina looked at the satisfied young man lying there under her. David touched her face with his right hand.

"That was so much fun, babe," he said while gazing into her blue eyes.

"Yes, it was baby," Avalina said to him.

"Come here, babe."

Avalina was so worn out that she just collapsed right on top of him. The couple fell asleep in each other's arms again. They were both exhausted from all of that hot sex.

***

Later on in the evening, at around eight-thirty, Avalina woke up to a strange sound. She tried to wake up her lover, but David was so out of it. The two of them had been sleeping all day.

"Honey, wake up," Avalina said.

"*Avalina*," a ghostly voice called out.

"W-what, who's calling me?" she asked.

"*Avalina*, you must stop all of this senseless killing," the apparition cried out.

"Who the hell are you?!" Avalina cried out.

"Honey, are you alright?" David groggily asked her while finally waking up.

"Did you hear that?" Avalina asked him.

"Hear what?"

"Someone was calling me."

"No, I only heard you."

"Oh, I see, you think I'm making all this shit up, right?"

"I didn't say that I just said, I only heard you. Remember, I just woke up. What exactly did you hear?"

"Never mind, it's not important."

"Yes, it is, it clearly upset you. You said someone was calling you just now. Who was it?"

"I don't know."

"Was it a man or a woman?"

"It sounded like a woman."

"Ok, at least now we're getting somewhere. What did she say?"

"She just called out my name, that's all."

"Did the voice sound familiar to you at all?"

"No, it did not, it was echo-like."

Avalina had a feeling that she knew who it was, but the possessed young woman wasn't revealing anything more to David, especially anything that might incriminate her. Avalina wondered if this was the same ghost or entity that had spooked her yesterday at night. David placed his loving arms around her and tried to comfort his young lover. He knew that she was clearly upset and worried about something.

"Come on, baby, maybe a good movie will help get your mind off of it. Let's go see what's on TV," David told her.

"*Well*, that's going to be a little difficult, sweetie," Avalina replied.

"Why is that?"

"Because, I don't have a television set here in this house."

"Really? I thought I saw one in your living room."

"Where? There's nothing in there except a sofa, loveseat, and two end tables with lamps."

"Come here, honey, I'll show you."

David escorted Joan into her living room. He scanned the area around and showed her where the set was.

"There it is, and I don't even live here!" David ecstatically replied while pointing at the flat screen TV, that was hanging on the wall above the fireplace.

"That's not a TV. It looks like an empty picture frame," the young witch replied.

David started laughing. He couldn't believe what she was saying. *She has got to be kidding*, David thought.

"Didn't you buy all this stuff here?" David jokingly asked her.

"No, I didn't. It came with the house," Avalina said with an annoyed tone in her voice.

"I'm sorry, babe. I didn't know you got a furnished house. I thought this was all your stuff," he said with a chuckle.

Avalina walked over to the TV set that was hanging on the wall. She looked all over it to see if there were any buttons or knobs. Then, Avalina turned around and faced her boyfriend.

"You see that? I told you it's not a TV!" she declared with a smirk on her face.

"Sure it is," David replied.

"Then, where the hell are the controls? There's nothing on this thing to turn it on."

"You have to find the remote."

"What remote?"

"Come on now, are you putting me on or what?"

David decided to look around the room. After a while, he found the TV remote control unit behind the lamp on one of the end tables. David picked it up, aimed it at the set up on the wall and pressed the power button. After a few seconds, the TV set sprung to life.

"Holy shit! I can't believe it! A TV on the wall. How did you turn it on with that thing?"

"I can't believe you, girl. This is the remote control for your TV. What are you, living in the stone ages or something? No, I know, you're getting back at me for not believing in you, right? This is a gag, right?" David asked with an inquisitive look on his face.

Avalina never had any interest in looking for the TV in this house with all its modern appliances. She was only seeking revenge. The only machine that was of interest to her was the computer, knowing it could be used to help locate her killers. That was all that Avalina needed. *However, a television set could also prove to be useful to me, if not entertaining. I better go along with him so he doesn't get suspicious of me,* she thought to herself.

"Yes, it is and you fell for it, ha, ha! Fooled ya, huh?" Avalina said with a big phony smirk on her face.

Detective Wiretrak was back in his office, receiving a phone call from a local fisherman. The man claimed to have seen a body floating around in Pond Lake while he was fishing.

"Isn't it kind of early to be fishing, mister?" Wiretrak had asked the man.

"Are you going to check out the body or nitpick? I didn't have to call this in, you know," the man said angrily.

Wiretrak hung up the phone and told Chief Valentine.

"This may be the big break we've been looking for," the chief said.

Chief Valentine assembled a team of men consisting of

forensics, two officers and Detective Wiretrak to investigate the scene. Wiretrak rode in the patrol car with the two officers. The detective felt confident that this would crack the case wide open, at least for one of the missing persons, anyway. Wiretrak didn't know if the body was a male or female.

On the next morning, Avalina was kissing David Scholl goodbye. She wanted him to stay another day, but David had other plans. The young witch didn't want to be alone.

"Are you sure you can't stay another day, darling?" Avalina begged him.

"I wish I could, babe, but I have to get back to work," David replied.

"You could go to work from here and then come back!"

"I wish I could do that, but it would be too much back and forth driving, hon. I live and work out of New Jersey, not New York; besides, all of my clothes and stuff are at home. You understand, don't you?"

"Will you come by over the weekend to visit me?"

"Of course, babe," David said as he tenderly kissed her again.

Avalina closed the door and went back to her bedroom. The young witch started to sob, wondering if she would hear that voice again now that she was home alone. One thing was for certain, the possessed young woman had fallen head over heels for David Scholl.

Later on that morning, the police crew had arrived at Pond Lake. Detective Wiretrak and the forensics men were examining a swollen body. A corpse had been pulled out of the lake by the two police officers.

"It's badly deteriorated, like it's been here a long time," Joe Chandler, one of the forensics men said.

"Like maybe about three weeks?" Detective Wiretrak asked.

"Yes, it's quite possible. It looks like whatever fish there are in this lake had a feast on it, but it's a female. I'm certain of that," Joe replied.

The forensics team took pictures and samples from the body and the area. Detective Wiretrak had a gut feeling that the victim was Anna Nuñez, one of the missing persons. Wiretrak phoned the chief and reported their findings back to him. Suddenly, one of the officers saw something else floating in the lake…another body.

"One thing's for sure, men, this is no damn accident. This is definitely foul play and we've got to get to the bottom of this," the detective stated.

*
**

Back in the rented home of Joan Sanders, in the town of Brighten, New York, Avalina had been sleeping like a baby in her host's body, until she was rudely awakened once more.

"*Avalina*," the ghostly voice called out to her again.

"W-what?" Avalina asked in a sleepy voice, just barely awake.

"Avalina, it's me."

"Who are you? What do you want?"

There was no answer this time. Avalina turned on the lamp

on her nightstand. She looked at her alarm clock. It was only three o'clock in the morning.

"This shit has got to stop; I need my sleep. Leave me the hell alone," she said out loud.

The possessed young woman turned the light off. She pulled the light blue comforter over her head and went back to sleep. A few minutes later, the voice called out her name once more.

"Avalina…please…stop the killings," the ghostly voice said to her.

"Who the hell are you and what do you want?" Avalina quietly asked.

"It's me," the strange voice said in a haunting tone.

"Who's 'me?'"

"I am your mother, Avalina."

"What? My mother's dead."

"Look at me, look at me, Avalina. I'm here!"

Avalina turned her head and looked towards the window where the voice was calling her. Slowly, an apparition of her deceased mother, wearing a light green gown, was appearing right before her eyes. Avalina started to tremble.

"Well, what's the matter, dearie; are you afraid of your own mother?" the ghost asked her in a haunting voice.

"It…it can't be you. I saw you die right in front of me," Avalina cried out.

"Yes, your boyfriend killed me…"

"He did not. My David never shot you, momma! You died

of a heart attack, that's what the doctors said in the hospital. David never hurt you."

"There are many ways to hurt, or even kill someone. Don't become a part of it, sweetie."

"I don't understand. If you're dead, how the hell are you here?" Avalina asked.

"You are not the only witch in town, you know," the apparition replied.

"So, you're a ghost, right?"

"For now, yes."

"Why are you tormenting me, mother?"

"I am here to warn you. Stop all of this senseless killing, or be prepared to accept the consequences."

"I don't know what the hell you're talking about. I am only seeking revenge for what was done to me."

"Let it go. No good can come from it, Avalina."

"I cannot. They killed me, momma! You weren't there. You don't know what I went through; it was horrible, momma."

"I know and I was devastated along with your father, but it was so long ago. Now, you've had a second chance in life. You should have just been enjoying the body that you've been in, instead of seeking revenge."

"It's not that easy, momma. I can't rest knowing that my killers are still alive and enjoying life, without any remorse. They all thought this was a game. They thought it was fun to watch me burn in my own home. None of them gave a shit about me."

"You have completely taken over this poor girl's life and

you're still not happy; that is being very greedy and very selfish. I did not raise you up to be like that. Your father is resting in peace, why can't you?"

"Because I can't! He wasn't murdered, momma, I was. I will NOT rest in peace until I get them all. They must ALL pay for taking my life away from me."

"If you do, would you leave this young girl's body and rest in peace?"

"I don't know, momma. I had originally planned to do just that, but someone may have changed my mind. I still might decide to harbor her body and live life to the fullest."

"I see. Avalina, you must be dealt with, properly. I'll see to that, dearie, I'll see to that."

"And just *what* do you mean by that remark, mother? Just what the hell are you trying to say?"

"You'll see."

"Is that a threat, momma?"

"You have been warned!"

Lightning and the roar of thunder shook the whole house as the spirit of Sabrina Bishop left. Avalina was startled. She was worried about the so-called consequences her mother's ghost had warned her about.

"I will get my revenge if it's the last thing I do. They're all gonna be sorry they did that shit to me," she muttered under her breath.

Avalina tried to go back to sleep, but she just kept on

thinking. She thought about finding her next killer. Avalina thought about the warning, but she mostly just thought about her lover, David Scholl. Avalina wished that David was here with her now to comfort her. She needed him. Finally, after two long hours of tossing, turning, and thinking, the possessed young woman finally fell back to sleep.

11

BENNY SMITH

*B*enny Smith was outside looking in through the family room window with the rest of the gang. They had been watching Avalina for quite a while. Melissa told them that she would be home all by herself. The five teenagers placed paper and sticks all around the house. Then, they poured lighter fluid on everything.

"Do you really think we should be doing this?" Melissa asked the four boys.

"Yeah, man, if she's a real witch and I think she is, then she's fricking evil. I'll never forget the day I tried to kiss her. She gave me this evil eye and grabbed my balls and squeezed them really tight. That shit really hurt! Then, she told me to go piss off," David Scholl said.

"I'm with you on that. There's just no room for the devil in our school and witches were all part of the devil," Michael Resnick added.

The other two boys, Gilbert Johnson, and Benny Smith, had also agreed. With that, the four boys lit the fire with their cigarette lighters. Since Avalina Bishop's house was situated at the end of a dead-end road, she had no nearby neighbors to see what was going on. There wasn't anyone around for at least a quarter of a mile.

The fire spread really fast in the old wooden structure. As it burned, the five teenagers chanted, "burn, witch, burn!" Avalina woke up to the sound of a ground floor window exploding from the heat. She looked out of the family room window and saw the five teens chanting and laughing at her.

"Why, why are you doing this to me?!" Avalina screamed.

She tried to go through the front door, but the fire was already inside of the house, consuming everything in its path. Avalina decided to run upstairs. More windows were exploding as the flames licked the sides of the whole building.

Avalina jumped out of the top floor window, her body burning in flames. She fell on top of Benny Smith, screaming.

"Die with me! die with me now, you sonofabitch!" Avalina screamed over and over again.

"Help, help! Help me, somebody, please!" Benny screamed in his sleep.

It was three o'clock in the morning when Benny Smith woke up in a cold sweat, gasping for air from that horrible dream. It was always the same old dream he'd been having for the past fifty-one years. It had become his worst nightmare. It was always the same vision, except *this time*, the ending had changed. This time, Avalina escaped and she was coming to get him.

"But, how can that be? She's dead," Benny quietly said to himself.

Benny Smith was now sixty-six-years-old and living alone. He was well overweight, bald, and he had several health problems, including a bad heart. Back in 1969, the man was a fifteen-year-old teenager without a care in the world. Benny didn't have a conscience for what he did back then...or so he thought. The boy didn't want to talk about it to anyone. He hoped that it would all just go away like an unpleasant memory, but it didn't go away. Benny had denied ever being with those other kids on that fateful night. Still to this day, Benny never discussed it with anyone at all. He knew the others would also keep quiet about it because, no one wanted to go to jail for some dumb shit like that. Benny had distanced himself from everyone that was involved with Avalina's fiery death, but the man wondered why the dream had finally changed all of a sudden...after all this time.

"Is Avalina Bishop still alive, somewhere? Was she really a witch?" Benny asked himself aloud.

"Nah, it couldn't be. I think I would have known by now," he reassured himself.

Benny never believed in any of that hocus pocus witchcraft shit, but maybe, just maybe, this time he did. He reached up over the nightstand and turned on the lamp.

"Shit, it's only ten after three in the morning," he softly said to himself.

The middle-aged man looked at his surroundings. It was a small bedroom that was part of a three-room apartment in New York City. The building was an old, rundown apartment house. What made the place even worse was that it didn't have an elevator. The building was a five-story walkup. Benny's apartment was on the top floor. The man often struggled to climb all of those stairs to the top, especially when he was carrying groceries. His bedroom was painted in a drab grey color. The old parquet wood floor had loose boards that creaked and squeaked when he walked on them.

"Shit, I'm back in the same crummy ole apartment," he muttered under his lips.

Benny wished that he could move to a nicer place, but this was all he could afford. The man didn't make much money as an editor working for a small publishing company. He would often ask for overtime, but there never was any available.

Benny would always play his lottery tickets, usually twice a week. He got tired of the machine spitting out the same old message, "sorry not a winner," but he'd still play. *Well, I guess I'm a glutton for punishment,* he would often say to himself. Benny would waste over two hundred dollars a month gambling with lottery tickets. *I've got to hit it sooner or later. You've got to be in it to win it,* Benny thought to himself. After thinking for a few more minutes, he finally fell back to sleep.

*
**

Avalina woke up at the crack of dawn on Saturday morning, March seventh. She had a dream about Benny Smith. The young witch was trying to send him a message in her sleep. Avalina hoped that David Scholl would stop by today, but she was still on a mission to find Benny Smith and exterminate him. Avalina got out of bed and headed straight towards the computer room down the hall. She flipped on the computer's power switch, but nothing happened.

"Shit! What the hell?" the possessed young woman said to herself.

All of a sudden, an eerie image of her late mother, Sabrina Bishop, had appeared upon the computer screen.

"Stop what you are doing, my child. Let it rest," the spirit said in a haunting voice.

"Never!" Avalina shouted.

The computer screen went black again. Avalina bent down to check the wires under the desk. The possessed young woman didn't really know what she was looking for, but she figured it had to be something out of the ordinary. After only a few minutes, Avalina spotted something.

"Ah-ha!" Avalina shouted as she found the problem.

The electrical cords from the computer system were all unplugged from the surge suppresser power strip. Avalina plugged everything back in and the computer sprung back to life. Then, it suddenly hit her. *How the hell was my mother on the screen when the machine wasn't even plugged in? How did everything get unplugged?* Avalina asked herself. She sat there in awe for a few minutes before looking for Benny Smith.

Avalina had searched and searched for over an hour on the computer. She finally found something very useful to her about

Benny Smith. The witch located where Benny worked.

"Oh, so he's an editor for Little House Publishing," she voiced.

Avalina looked at his recent bio picture and was shocked to see how different he looked, since that fateful day fifty-one years ago. Life hadn't been kind to him at all. The man clearly had aged, considerably.

"Man, he looks so damn old and fat. I almost feel sorry for his ass," she said to the computer.

But the young witch didn't really feel sorry for Benny. She got his address, from one of those people finder websites and wrote it down on a piece of paper, from a nearby notepad.

Avalina took off all of her clothes and looked into the full-length mirror in the hallway. Again, the entity admired the hot body that she had stolen from the innocent, young woman with long red hair. She guided her host into the bathtub to take a hot shower, thinking of how she was going to dispose of Benny. The hot water felt good. Joan Sanders had given up her fight to claim her own form...at least for now. Joan finally realized the evil spirit that inhabited her body, got its powers, and hold over her, through the golden pentagram locket that she wore around her neck. Joan only needed to figure out, how to get that damn necklace off of her neck and destroy it.

After Avalina finished bathing, she got dressed and went to the kitchen. The young witch decided to have a bowl of cereal with some orange juice. Avalina finished her breakfast as quickly as possible, then she went back to the computer room, to get the address she had copied from the computer screen earlier. She put the address into the right pocket of her tan colored raincoat. *Now I'm ready to get his ass,* Avalina thought to herself while walking out of the front door.

Benny Smith was not doing so well. After waking up again, this time at nine o'clock in the morning, he felt sick and run down. Benny was cold and shaking. The middle-aged man got out of his bed and went straight to the bathroom.

"Man, where's my damn thermometer?" Benny asked his medicine cabinet.

After searching all of the shelves and drawers for a good ten minutes, he finally found his digital thermometer. Benny took it out of the package and turned it on. He inserted it inside of his mouth, then he sat down on the toilet seat waiting for it to register. After a couple of minutes, the thermometer started beeping. Benny Smith pulled the unit out of his mouth and read the reading. His temperature was 102.1 degrees.

"I guess I'll have to call my doctor," Benny said to himself.

Avalina had finally arrived at Benny's apartment building in New York City. She parked her car on the street and walked over towards the tenement. The young witch read the names on the intercom's list and found his apartment number.

"That's it, apartment 5H!" Avalina exclaimed.

Avalina pressed the button for 5H, but nothing happened. *It's either broken, or he's not home,* she thought. Avalina waited to see if anyone was coming down the stairs to let her in. She waited for about fifteen minutes and decided that it was time to leave; until, a young Spanish woman with long black hair came down the stairs.

"Excuse me, do you live here?" the attractive young woman asked her.

"No, I came here to see my father," Avalina replied.

"Oh, who is he and what apartment are you looking for, miss?"

"His name is Benny Smith. He lives in apartment 5H."

"Yes, I know him, but I didn't know he had a daughter. I've never seen you here before. Why don't you just ring his bell?" the woman suspiciously asked her.

"I did, but he didn't answer. I just wanted to make sure he was alright, that's all."

"Ok, I'll let you in."

"Thank you. Thank you very much, Miss."

Avalina walked on past the woman and started climbing up the stairs of the old tenement.

Avalina finally got up to the top floor of the old apartment house. The possessed young woman started looking for Benny's apartment. She had noticed that the apartments were all situated in alphabetical order. After going down the hallway, the young witch found what she was looking for.

There it is, apartment 5H, Avalina thought to herself. She rang his doorbell and waited. After a few minutes of no response, Avalina rang the bell once more.

"Who is it?!" Benny asked through the door.

"Are you Benny Smith?!" Avalina asked him through the green painted front door.

"Yes, I am. Now, who are you?!"

Avalina decided to think fast for a good excuse. It had to be something that would flatter him enough to make him want to open his door. Then, she had a great idea. The possessed young woman was going to pose as someone of interest to him…a journalist.

"I'm a reporter for a major magazine. We're looking to do a feature article on you as a long-time editor for Little House Publishing!"

Benny was feeling intrigued by all of this attention. *An article on little ole me?* Benny thought, but he couldn't believe it. The man looked through the peephole of the door and was very impressed by her face. *Wow, she's fricking gorgeous. I feel like shit, but I'll let her in,* he thought to himself.

"Just give me a minute or two, miss. I've got to throw on some clothes and I'll let you in!" Benny replied through the door.

Benny was weak and he really didn't feel well at all, but the man wanted to see this beautiful female that was outside his door. He went as fast as he could towards the bedroom closet to get some clothes. After about eight minutes, the man was dressed and he opened up the front door.

"Come in, come in, Miss!" Benny exclaimed after getting an even better look at the attractive young woman.

Avalina walked into his apartment and scanned Benny from top to bottom. She looked at him in disgust. *Shit, will ya just look at him? He must be over three hundred pounds…sloppy, too. I'd be doing his ass a favor by putting him out of his misery,* Avalina thought. The editor had on a triple extra-large worn out pair of blue jeans with suspenders. He also sported a torn white t-shirt showing his man boobs and belly. Benny felt like he was being dissected by her. The overweight middle-aged man sensed the disgust that was emanating from her beautiful, bright blue eyes. The editor was no longer turned on by her. Benny figured he would never stand a chance with her anyway. In fact, he started feeling very uncomfortable around her in his own apartment.

"Just what magazine are you from, Miss?" Benny nervously asked her.

"Avalina," she replied.

"Avalina? Nope, I never heard of it. Is it a new magazine?" Benny asked her.

"No, stupid, Avalina Bishop! Doesn't that name ring a bell to you?" she said angrily.

Benny was getting very nervous. He knew very well who the hell Avalina Bishop was. The lonely editor was almost ready to collapse on his own floor as his face went flush.

"Judging by your own expression, Mister, I'd say you damn well know who the hell I am, *don't you?*" Avalina sarcastically asked him.

Benny remembered the dream he just had last night and how after all these years, the ending had changed. He remembered Avalina jumping out of the top floor window, her body was burning with flames and how she fell on top of him screaming, *die with me, die with me now, you sonofabitch!* Then, Benny thought that it wasn't just a dream, after all and that it must have been some kind of premonition of what was going to happen to him.

"No, no, this can't be! You're dead!" Benny fearfully said to her.

"Oh, so you admit to killing me!" Avalina said with such hatred.

"No, it wasn't my fault, it wasn't my fault at all!"

"Please, that's what they all say. I've come back to end your miserable stinking life, you fat slob."

"I don't understand. You don't look anything like her...you look...different. How can this be?"

"Different, eh? Well, sometimes it's alright to be different. Now, don't you worry about all the details. I can assure you it's me. I've taken care of all of your friends, especially that Melissa Conley bitch."

"You killed Melissa Conley?"

"I killed them all...well, almost all. You and David Scholl are the only two left. Prepare to die, asshole!"

"No, wait! Give me another chance...I..."

Before Benny could finish his sentence, he collapsed face down on the old parquet wood floor. His fever went up and had gotten the best of him. Avalina looked at him, wondering if it was a trick. All of a sudden, two emergency medical men came in right behind her through the open front door. Benny forgot to close the door behind Avalina when she walked into his apartment.

"Excuse me, Miss, we need to get to him," one of the men told her.

Avalina noticed something about the two men. They were both wearing respirator masks and safety goggles. She found that quite strange. The young enchantress knew that something was up, something serious.

"He's Benny Smith, right?" the other man asked her.

"Yes, yes he is. What's this all about?" Avalina asked them.

"You need to step back, Miss. His doctor called us and said that he had a fever; he may have the Coronavirus," the paramedic replied.

"I don't know what you're talking about."

"What? Haven't you been following the news, lady?" the EMT responded with a shocked look on his face.

"No, I haven't," Avalina retorted.

"His temperature is 103," the paramedic replied.

The two men placed Benny on the stretcher and started carrying him out of his apartment. Avalina knew that she wasn't going to get to him. The young witch tried to control them, but it was no use. Her powers weren't strong enough to control two people simultaneously.

"Wait! Can't I go with you? I mean, what hospital are you taking him to?" Avalina asked them.

"Are you his relative?" the EMT asked her.

"Yes, I'm his daughter!"

Benny was trying to get their attention by slowly shaking his head "no," but they didn't seem to notice. The paramedic did see the terror in his eyes, though.

"Sorry, ma'am, but in this case, you can't. This disease is highly contagious, assuming that he has it; but for the record, we're taking him to City Medical," the young paramedic replied.

Avalina followed the medical team down the stairs towards the street. She watched them carry Benny Smith and load him into the red and white F.D.N.Y. ambulance. The paramedic stayed with Benny, while the EMT closed the doors on them and stepped into the driver's seat. Within seconds, the vehicle took off with lights and sirens blaring, as it spewed muddy water from a puddle all over Avalina and her nice, clean tan coat. She had been standing a little bit too close to the ambulance when it had left. Avalina was pissed off to say the least. She felt so cheated. The possessed girl didn't want Benny to die from some dumb old virus. It wouldn't be right...it wouldn't be right at all. There wouldn't be any kind of retribution for her, no consolation. She wanted to kill Benny Smith herself. The young witch wanted him to suffer like she did back in 1969.

"I'll get you. I'll get your ass, you fat, sloppy, disgusting sonofabitch...if it's the last thing I do...you'll see," Avalina said to herself through clenched teeth.

Benny had escaped Avalina's wrath, at least for now, but she would be back to finish the job. She walked on over towards her car and headed back home, planning her next move.

12

THE VIRUS

On Monday morning, March 9th, everyone was trying to deal with a new pandemic: The Coronavirus, also called COVID-19. The new disease, that had originated from Wuhan, China and came from an animal infecting a human being, had now taken over the entire United States of America. The new, vicious, predatory virus wasn't discriminating either. Everyone was in danger and everyone was at risk of acquiring it. Restaurants were only serving food for take-out. Movie theaters, shopping malls, Broadway playhouse shows and most businesses were now closed. Some people were working from home. Streets were practically deserted and the stock market was diving every single day. Individuals everywhere were all worried about the economy heading into a recession and possibly even a depression. The only businesses that seemed to really be making any kind of money were gun shops, as everyone panicked for their safety and wanted protection. The governor of the state of New York, had mandated that there would be no social gatherings of groups at any time. This was to help stop the spread of the dreaded Coronavirus. Governors in the other states, such as New Jersey and Connecticut, were also adopting the same plan.

Avalina took a trip to City Medical Center in New York City to check on Benny Smith's condition. She walked into the hospital lobby and went straight to the information center. There was a young woman sitting there at the counter with short brown hair, staring at a computer screen while chewing on a chocolate bar.

"Excuse me, I'm Benny Smith's daughter; I heard he was brought here. I just wanted to see how he was doing," Avalina said with a concerned look on her face.

"I'm sorry, ma'am, but we're not allowed to give out any

information regarding our patients without their consent," the receptionist sternly replied.

"Really? But I'm his daughter! I just wanted to see how he was doing."

"I'm sorry, ma'am, but rules are rules. I don't want to lose my job here."

Avalina knew that this was going to take some work. She stared right at the young woman's eyes and exerted her persuasive hypnotic powers on her. Then, Avalina asked the woman again while she had the woman under her control.

"The patient was brought in with a high fever. Mr. Smith was intubated and placed on a ventilator. He had also tested positive for the Coronavirus, COVID-19. Due to these circumstances, Mr. Smith cannot have any visitors," the receptionist said in a robotic, trance-like state.

Avalina was undoubtedly disappointed. She decided to leave the hospital. The young witch didn't want to expose her new body, to a disease that was so contagious and deadly, especially since she still needed the body to carry out her vengeance. Avalina would have to check on him in a few days. *I'm not through with his fat ass yet,* she thought. *If that damn corona shit virus doesn't get him, I will.*

⁎
⁎⁎

A few days later, at the Brighten Police station, Chief Valentine walked into Detective Wiretrak's office. The chief was highly upset. It had been over a week since they found the bodies of Anna Nuñez and John Waters, in the lake.

"After all this time, there still aren't any damn leads. I can't believe this shit!" Chief Valentine loudly stated.

"I don't know what to tell you, boss. We haven't found a shred of evidence to determine who the hell the killer is," the young detective replied.

"What makes it worse, is this damn new super bug that's taking away our fricking resources."

"I know what you mean, chief. We've lost two great officers, Williams and Ryan."

"Not only that, but the rest of our men are out in the field being tied up with this shit. They have to make sure that people don't congregate anywhere, as per the governor's mandate."

"Yeah, I know what you mean, boss," Wiretrak replied.

While the two men were complaining about the current situation, one of the forensics men, Charlie Rhodes, was standing in the doorway. Charlie was a young rookie, but he knew his job and he knew it well. Rhodes was holding a plastic bag containing hair samples. Finally, after a couple of minutes of exchanging complaints, the chief of police noticed him standing there.

"Is there something I can do for you, Rhodes, or do you want to join in, too?" Chief Valentine stated.

"We've found something, chief," Charlie Rhodes replied.

"Found something? What the hell do you mean you found something? Out with it will you? I don't have time for games!"

"Well, for starters, both victims, Anna Nuñez and John Waters, had rocks and pebbles buried into the lining and pockets of their coats. The killer probably did that in order to prevent their bodies from floating up and being spotted by anyone."

"Don't tell me something I already know, son. We've been through all of this shit before, you know."

"Yes, I know that chief, but what you *didn't* know was that we found some hair samples in the pockets of the victims, that didn't belong to either one of them."

"Really, and just how did you know that?" the chief sarcastically asked the young man.

"Because, sir, the hair samples we found were from a red-headed female."

"Are you sure about that, Rhodes? Don't be pulling my chain here!"

"Yes, sir, it's a new test that we just used to determine that, and here's her hair, sir."

Charlie Rhodes handed the plastic bag containing the hair samples to the chief of police. Detective Wiretrak also examined it. The two men were in awe. They couldn't believe that a single woman was able to take on these two victims all by herself, unless of course, she had an accomplice.

"And you're absolutely, unequivocally, one hundred percent positive about this, Charlie?" Wiretrak asked him.

"Well, tests don't lie, my friend, tests don't lie," Charlie responded.

"Well, then, let's go find out who the hell this murdering bitch is and put her and whoever's helping her, in jail, right?" the chief commanded.

"I'm on it, chief," Detective Wiretrak replied.

It was now March, 21st. The news media reported 287,000 cases with 11,921 deaths worldwide. In the United States, there were over 21,000 infected with 267 deaths so far. The United States had now surpassed China with cases of infected people. New York State alone had over 9,000 cases with close to 100 deaths already. The governor of New York State had now reported that starting on Monday, March 23rd; all non-essential businesses would have to close. Employers would now have to adapt to a work from home program for their employees.

David Scholl had come by to call upon his girlfriend, Joan. David was wearing a face mask and gloves like everyone else was. He looked at his watch and noticed that it was five o'clock in the evening, but it was still nice outside. David rang the doorbell.

"Who is it?!" Avalina shouted through the door.

"It's me, David!" he replied.

Avalina opened up the front door. She was wearing a sexy, pink translucent evening gown. David stared at her, practically drooling over her. David's eyes became fixated upon her nipples that were protruding right through her gown.

"Wow, don't *we* look sexy?" David said while still gazing at her chest.

"And you, what's with the getup? I'm not infected," Avalina said with a chuckle.

The young witch was happy to see him, but also because she had just found out from her boss that starting Monday, the day that she was due to return to the office, she would begin working from home as a result of the pandemic. Her boss also said it would only be a half of day's work that day. She had just decided to go and check in on Benny Smith's condition in the hospital, but Avalina always made time for her lover. David pulled down his respirator mask and was getting ready to kiss her.

"Wait a minute there, big boy! How do I know that *you're* not infected?" she coyly asked him.

"Ha-ha, touché. Well, I can assure you, my dear, sweet love, that I am *not* infected," David replied.

"Oh, I don't know about that, baby. The man on the TV said you could have it and not even know it. I believe he called it, being a carrier."

"Oh, stop it already. Come here and kiss me, will ya?"

With that, David grabbed his girl and gave her a very long sensual kiss. Avalina practically melted in his arms. She escorted the young man inside and closed the front door behind him. Avalina proceeded to unbutton his shirt and pull it off, exposing David's muscular, hairy chest. The two of them kissed some more before going off into the bedroom.

It was 6:00 am Monday, March 23rd. David was kissing Avalina, or whom he thought was Joan Sanders, goodbye. David had spent the entire weekend with her. He had to go home and contact his boss to find out how the new working arrangements, would affect him. The young man walked down the driveway and went straight to his old Thunderbird. David started up the engine, warmed it up a little and then he took off. Avalina watched and waited for him to leave, then she got dressed. Avalina was going back down to the city hospital to pay Benny Smith one last visit, knowing that she had to be back home at 12:00 noon to log in to work.

Detective Wiretrak was on his way to City Medical Center. The detective had received a phone call from the hospital. It seemed that one of their patients, Mr. Benny Smith, wanted to see him. Wiretrak didn't know what this was all about, but he remembered Benny from a car accident last year. Benny Smith had come to Brighten on business when he hit a deer on the parkway. Wiretrak was on the scene and was instrumental in bringing him to the local hospital. When Benny got better, he came by to personally thank the detective for saving his life and the two of them, really hit it off.

At 7:00 am, after driving for about forty-five minutes, Detective Wiretrak finally arrived at the medical center. He walked on into the hospital lobby and went straight over towards the information counter. The young female receptionist wearing a face mask, looked up from her computer screen to greet him.

"May I help you, sir?" the receptionist asked him.

"Hello, Miss, I'm Detective Wiretrak from the Brighten Police Department," the detective stated while showing his badge to the young lady at the counter.

"Oh, ok, how may I help you, detective?" the young woman asked him.

"I was told by a supervisor here, a Miss Harriet Rosenberg, that you had a patient here, a Mr. Benny Smith that needed to see me."

"Just a minute, sir; I'll call her."

The woman dialed an extension on her phone. Wiretrak looked around and noticed that everyone there was wearing face masks, everyone but him. After a few minutes on the phone, the woman explained the situation to the detective.

"It seems that we do indeed have a patient here that needs to speak with the police, about an encounter he had before he was brought here. The patient, Benny Smith, did specifically ask for you, sir," the young woman told him.

"Where is he at?" Wiretrak asked her.

"Mr. Benny Smith is in room 222."

"Ok, I'll head on up there."

"Not so fast, officer. The patient had tested positive for the Coronavirus and he's not doing well. You'll need to wear this to protect yourself against the virus," the receptionist stated while handing the detective a face mask.

"Thank you, Miss, you've been most helpful."

Detective Wiretrak took the mask and walked towards the elevators. He used a napkin and pressed the button to call the elevator, then he put on his face mask. Within a minute or two, the elevator arrived. Wiretrak got on and pushed the button for the second floor. The doors closed and he started going up. Wiretrak wondered what the patient wanted from him. He thought about what the female receptionist had told him.

The elevator arrived on the second floor and it opened its doors to let Wiretrak out. He walked down the hall and looked for room 222. The detective found the room near the nurses' station. When Wiretrak walked in, he noticed there was a clear plastic curtain around the man lying there in the hospital bed. A nurse had walked in.

"Excuse me, sir, may I help you?" the middle-aged African-American nurse asked him.

Wiretrak noticed the nurse was also wearing a mask. Then, he noticed the sign that read, "Everyone Within This Facility Must Be Wearing a Protective Face Mask!" *I guess this will be the new standard for a while now,* Wiretrak thought to himself.

"Yes, I'm Detective Wiretrak from the Brighten Police Department. I was told that this patient of yours, Benny Smith, needed to see me," Wiretrak responded while displaying his badge again.

"Oh, yes, detective, I'm Nurse Williams, the head nurse here. We've been expecting you. Mr. Smith has been wanting to talk to you about what had happened to him at home. Now, he's very weak, sir and he can't talk because of the tube down his throat, but we gave him a pad and pencil to write with. The only trouble is, you can't take anything from him, not even a piece of paper, that's because of contamination issues," the heavy-set woman explained to him.

"I understand, nurse. I'll just take a picture of whatever he writes with my smartphone."

"Well, I don't know how well that's gonna come out since you can't get closer than six feet to him, even with that plastic tent around him. In fact, you're a little too close to him now, detective; please step back."

"Ok, ma'am, I guess I'll just have to do it the old-fashioned way then."

"How's that, sir?"

"I'll just have to take notes with my book," he said with a chuckle.

"Ok, detective, good luck," the nurse said with a smile as she stepped outside of the room.

Detective Wiretrak turned and faced the patient. He knew this wasn't going to be easy, but the man had to try. After all, the patient *did* ask for him specifically.

"Mr. Smith, Mr. Benny Smith, I'm Detective Wiretrak from the Brighten Police Department. I understand you wanted to see me," Wiretrak said to Benny while displaying his badge to the sick man lying in bed.

Benny slowly turned towards the detective. He reached for his pad and pencil and began writing. Wiretrak was curious to know what the man wanted of him. Benny finally finished writing and held up his pad in front of the detective. The note said, *Avalina Bishop is back and she's trying to kill me!* Wiretrak read the note in disbelief, while copying it down in his book.

"Who is Avalina Bishop, Mr. Smith?" Wiretrak asked him.

Benny started to write again. He knew what had happened to Avalina was a very long time ago. Benny figured that the young detective wasn't familiar with the case; after all, it happened way before he was even born. He finished writing again and showed the new note to the detective that read, *she's a witch that died a long time ago in a house fire. Now, she's back as a red-head. Help me, please!*

At 8:30 am, Avalina Bishop came parading around to the hospital again via Joan's body. She was going to try to eliminate Benny without endangering her body, that's of course *if* he was still alive. The young witch went through the lobby doors towards the information counter and suddenly stopped. Avalina had spotted Detective Wiretrak coming out of one of the elevators. *What the hell is he doing here?* Avalina wondered. She quickly turned around and walked out towards her car. The young witch sat in her vehicle and waited for the detective to exit out of the hospital. Within a few minutes, Detective Wiretrak had walked out of the hospital and went over towards his car, unaware that he was being watched by her. Avalina waited for him to leave before she went back into the medical center. The possessed young woman, strolled casually back to the information counter, and proceeded to hypnotize the young receptionist again.

"I need to know what room Benny Smith is in," Avalina demanded.

"He's in room 222," the receptionist replied in her hypnotic state.

Avalina walked towards the elevators. She pressed the elevator "up" button and waited. When Avalina finally got upstairs, she searched for Benny's room. The young witch cautiously waited until no one was around before walking into his room.

"Hello again, Benny," Avalina coyly said to him.

Benny Smith turned around in horror. He couldn't believe that she was able to get to him in the hospital. He thought he was safe, especially after talking to that detective. However, Detective Wiretrak didn't believe a single word of what he had told him, but unfortunately, Benny didn't know that. The detective thought he was as nutty as a fruit cake. Now, the witch was back.

"I know you can't talk with that thing in your mouth, so hear this, I don't like loose ends, so I've come back to finish the job. It's time to go bye-bye," Avalina said while lifting up her arms in front of him.

"You know, Benny, I'm not going to physically touch you; I don't have to, but I do feel a heart attack is coming your way," she softly said while staring into his eyes.

Avalina waved her arms and exerted all of her powers over Benny. The witch made his heart beat faster. Benny's heartrate continued to climb at a dangerous level. He was clinging on to his life. He reached for the emergency call remote and pressed the red button. Since the nurses' station was nearby, it didn't take very long at all for someone to come to his aid. Within seconds, the nurse came walking into the patient's room.

"Mr. Smith, are you alright? Who are you, Miss?" the nurse turned to ask Avalina.

"I was just leaving," Avalina replied while quickly turning around and walking out the door, disappointed again.

Avalina rushed back to her car and headed back upstate to her home. While she drove, the witch began talking to herself.

"Shit! Shit! Shit! That sonofabitch has got more damn lives than a damn cat! This is ridiculous! I have got to get his ass, one way or another!" Avalina said while clenching the steering wheel with hatred.

Later on that afternoon at the Brighten Police station, Detective Wiretrak was trying to make sense of what Benny Smith had written down on his notepad, back at the hospital. Wiretrak reviewed the message he copied in his book: *Avalina Bishop is back and she's trying to kill me! She's a witch that died a long time ago in a house fire. Now, she's back as a red-head. Help me, please!* The detective wondered if the man had completely lost his marbles. *He seemed genuinely scared though,* Wiretrak thought as he remembered seeing the fear in the man's eyes. The young detective decided to look on the internet and see what he could find out about, Avalina Bishop.

Wednesday afternoon, April 1st, the virus was spreading even faster. There were now 926,095 cases of infected people worldwide. The pandemic had now claimed over 84,000 lives total. New York State had the highest amount of victims with over 23,000 dead already, with the highest concentration being in New York City alone.

After searching for days through the internet and previous case files, Detective Wiretrak had completed his research on Avalina Bishop. He still couldn't make any kind of connection; after all, this was a teenager who was the victim of arson fifty-one years ago in Merryville, New York. There wasn't any real evidence that the girl was involved in the occult. *Benny Smith must be off his rocker,* Wiretrak thought. However, there was one thing that clicked in the detective's mind. Benny had written, *now she's back as a red-head.* Wiretrak also remembered what Charlie Rhodes, from forensics, had said, *the hair samples we found were from a red-headed female.* The young detective tried to put two and two together. *Could it be the same damn woman and if so, who the hell is she?* Wiretrak wondered.

Detective Wiretrak had decided to pay Benny Smith another visit. After he arrived back at the medical center, Wiretrak took the elevator to the upper level. The detective took note of how full the hospital had become since his last visit. The facility was inundated with COVID-19 virus patients. The halls were loaded with stretchers of possible infected patients. Wiretrak made sure he had his mask and gloves on. When the detective arrived at the nurses' station, he was informed that Benny Smith was in a coma and that he had been in that state, since the detective's last visit with him. The head nurse told him that he almost died from a heart attack on that very same day, before slipping into a coma. Wiretrak left the hospital feeling very frustrated. He knew now that he would probably never get any more answers from Mr. Smith. The detective was also well aware of the fact that there was a vicious killer out there, that needed to be caught before any more people could fall prey to her. There still were those haunting questions: who was she and what was her motive?

It was now Wednesday morning, April 8th. The governor of New York State announced on his daily telecast, that the virus had finally hit the apex. The number of affected cases was now leveling off, at least in New York State. New Jersey and Connecticut had not reached their peak as of yet. It had now become mandatory that anyone going into any store, public facility, or medical institution, should be wearing a face mask and gloves. Ads were constantly being shown on television about the importance of washing your hands, practicing good hygiene routines and of individuals maintaining a distance of at least, six feet apart from each other in all public places. Fines of up to one thousand dollars were now being issued to anyone, that didn't comply with the social distancing act. There were limitations of one per customer on toilet paper, paper towels, water, bleach, and other cleaning supplies in all of the supermarkets and grocery stores. Hand sanitizers were nowhere to be found since they were in such high demand. The economy had taken a severe nosedive, ever since the Coronavirus had pulled its horrible reins in on the world. It seemed that this was going to be the new normal for a long time, at least until the medical scientists, developed a vaccine for the new virus and that was going to take at least a year to develop…if not longer.

13

THE BOYFRIEND

Hector Rodriguez waltzed right into the Brighten Police Department on Monday morning in the middle of April. The young Latino was looking for Detective Michael Wiretrak. He had asked the young female officer at the information counter for the detective, then he waited there as she paged him. After about ten minutes, Detective Wiretrak greeted Hector at the counter.

"Mr. Rodriguez, I'm Detective Wiretrak, I understand you wanted to see me?" the detective asked him.

"Yes, I wanted to know if you ever found my girlfriend, Anna Nuñez," Hector replied.

"Yes, we did, Mr. Rodriguez, but I'm afraid it's bad news…she's dead."

"Oh, my God! No, it can't be! Are you sure?"

"I'm afraid so, Mr. Rodriguez. I'm sorry."

"When did you find her?" Hector asked him with tears in his eyes.

"A local fisherman found her body in the lake about a month after you reported her missing, sir," the detective explained to him.

"Why didn't you call me?"

"Well, it was kind of hard, sir, since the number you gave us was not in service; plus, you didn't give us your address or any other kind of contact information," the detective said suspiciously.

"I'm sorry, I got laid off from my job and I had to get rid of a few bills, my cellphone was one of them. Can I see her, officer, please?" Hector pleaded.

"I'm sorry, Mr. Rodriguez, but that won't be possible."

"Why not?"

"The town morgue can only hold a body for up to thirty days, and since nobody claimed it, the town took the liberty of burying her out on the island. I'm sorry."

"Oh, shit, I can't even see her or say goodbye to her?"

"I'm sorry, but we tried to contact her relatives. None of them were even alive anymore, including her teenage daughter."

"Anna had divorced her husband because he cheated on her. She was raising her teenage daughter all by herself, until a cop in New Jersey shot and killed her, right there in the police station. Shit, she didn't deserve that, her only child. Susan was a good girl."

"I know all about that story, Mr. Rodriguez. Her daughter, Susan Nuñez, burned a famous author to death right in her own home. She tied the poor woman up to a chair in the kitchen and then torched her house, but this *good girl*, as you call her, wasn't through yet. After Susan Nuñez got picked up by the police officers and was brought into the station house, she got a hold of an officer's gun, shot, *and killed* the chief of police, of all people. *That's* the way it happened, Mr. Rodriguez."

"I still can't believe that."

"Well, believe it, because that's what *really* happened. Oh, and by the way, we did try to locate her ex-husband, but apparently, he left the country."

"Are you sure the body you recovered was my girlfriend, Anna Nuñez?"

"Yes, according to her dental records, it was her, but whether or not she was your girlfriend, is debatable. Do you have a recent picture of her on you?"

"Yes, I do, on my smartphone."

Hector pulled his smartphone out of his right front pocket and turned it on. He searched through all of the pictures on his phone, until he found the most recent picture of Anna and himself. Hector stared at the picture of Anna and him in her kitchen. The photograph had been taken by her own daughter, Susan. It brought back happier times to him. He showed the photo to the detective.

"This is her, detective," Hector said while getting all choked up.

"Yup, that looks like the woman we pulled out of the lake alright; of course, she didn't look quite like that when we retrieved her body from the lake," Wiretrak stated.

"You're absolutely sure, detective?"

"Come to my office and I'll show you a picture of the body, that's if you can take it."

"Yes, I just need to know for sure."

Detective Wiretrak brought the young man back to his office and told him to have a seat. Wiretrak searched through his computer to find pictures of the two bodies, that were pulled out of Pond Lake last month. He selected the best looking picture of Anna Nuñez and told Hector, to bring his chair closer towards the computer screen.

"Oh, my God! What have they done to my girl? She didn't deserve that sh…"

Hector began to sob in front of the computer monitor.

"I'm sorry again, Mr. Rodriguez," Wiretrak sympathetically said to the man.

"D-do you…have any…s-suspects yet?"

"We have hair samples of a possible killer, but no concrete suspects as of yet."

"Where was she found, detective?"

"Not far from here at all, a place called Pond Lake."

"I know where that is. Everybody has picnics over there. Hey, detective, if there's anything I can do, I mean *anything*, to help catch the sonofabitch that did this shit to her, please let me know, alright?"

"Sure, Mr. Rodriguez, you can start off by giving me your correct contact information, like the number on your smartphone," the detective stated.

"Like I said before, sir, my cell service is turned off until I can afford to pay the bill, but I'll give you my address."

Hector gave Detective Wiretrak his home address and the detective escorted him out the door. Then, Wiretrak returned back to his office and sat down at his desk. Before he got a chance to start thinking about the case, his phone started ringing and he picked it up on the second ring.

"Hello, Detective Wiretrak here," he answered.

"Hello, detective, this is Nurse Williams; I'm the head nurse over here at City Medical Center in New York City. You were here visiting a patient a couple of weeks ago, a Mr. Benny Smith," the nurse reported.

"Oh, yes, yes. I was planning on coming back to see how he was doing."

"Well, that's what I'm calling about. Mr. Smith just expired. I'm sorry."

"Oh, no, did he ever come out of his coma?"

"I'm afraid not, sir."

"I guess I'll never find out what he was trying to convey to me."

"We have been trying unsuccessfully to locate his family. Would you happen to have any kind of contact information on any of his family members?"

"As far as I know from the few times I met the man, he had no remaining family members. Benny was never married and his parents passed away a long time ago."

"Well, I guess that presents a problem then, except for one little thing…"

"And what might that be, Miss Williams?"

"Well, aside from you visiting him, he had another visitor; it was a woman that came by right after you left on that very same day."

"I'm sorry, but is that supposed to mean something to me? I mean, I should hope he had more friends than just me visiting him in the hospital."

"Friend? I don't know about that detective. You see, when I walked into his room, Mr. Smith was experiencing cardiac arrest. This woman, that you think was his friend, didn't think anything of it. In fact, she copped an attitude with me when I asked her who she was. She said she was just leaving. Now, nothing for nothing, detective, but that don't sound like a friend to me. A friend would have been genuinely concerned about him, you know what I mean, detective?"

"Yeah, I suppose you're right, Miss Williams."

"I know I'm right. It just seemed to me that poor ole Mr. Benny Smith was afraid of her. Of course, we'll never know since he went into a coma right after that."

"You said this woman never identified herself at all?"

"That's correct, detective. She said she was just leaving."

"Can you describe this woman, Miss Williams?"

"Damn straight I can. She was young, pretty, probably in her twenties with penetrating blue eyes, and she was tall. Oh, yeah, one other thing, she had this straight, bright red hair. It was long, I mean, it was down to her butt."

"I'm sorry, did you say she had red hair?" Wiretrak said with enthusiasm.

"That's right, sir, bright red hair, long and straight," Nurse Williams reiterated.

"Thank you very much, Miss Williams. I'll let you know if I need any more information from you. Have a good day."

The detective hung up the phone and remained seated at his desk while thinking. He wondered if the woman that visited Benny was his killer. *But why would she travel all the way down to New York City to see Benny?* Wiretrak thought to himself. It just didn't make any kind of sense to him at all. The young detective was going to discuss this matter with the chief. He thought it might be a good idea to bring a police artist down to the hospital to visit Nurse Williams.

A few miles away, in a rented basement apartment, Hector Rodriguez was just coming home from the police station. It was nice outside. The sun was shining with a warm breeze. The young man thought about hanging out with his friends. Maybe they could cheer him up, but Hector really just wanted to be left alone. The twenty-nine-year-old Latino was feeling really depressed. He picked up his mail from the mailbox and wondered, how the hell he was going to pay his bills; they were already piling up. The man needed income badly; he needed a new job. The little money that Hector had in his savings account had already been depleted. *That stupid virus! Shit, I can't even work as a damn waiter in a restaurant,* Hector thought. But what really upset him was the fact that the love of his life, Anna Nuñez, was gone. *Shit, I didn't even get to say goodbye to her,* Hector sadly thought.

The young man had proposed to her just a month before her disappearance, but Anna was still trying to get over her ex-husband. Although Anna was eleven years older than Hector, the age difference did not matter to him. Hector adored her with all of his heart. *She was beautiful inside and out,* he thought. Hector liked the fact that Anna had a lot more experience in bed than he did. *Boy, she really knew how to please a man. Why the hell would any man want to cheat on her? Her ex-husband was an asshole and a scumbag,* he contemplated.

Hector liked her daughter, too; he would sometimes help her with her homework. Hector still couldn't believe that she was responsible for viciously killing two people. The man felt really bad when Anna's daughter, Susan, was shot and killed. He had tried to console Anna, but she just wanted to be left alone, which was totally understandable to him at the time.

Hector looked around in his small, two-room basement apartment, wondering how he was ever going to be able to pay the rent. It was already past due over a week now. *If I don't get some money soon, I'm gonna get kicked out,* he wallowed in thought. Hector sat down on his bed. He pulled out his smartphone from the right pocket of his blue jeans. Hector looked at some of the pictures he had of Anna. One of his favorite pictures was of her laying naked on her bed, twirling her hair and looking extremely sexy. He made sure not to show that picture to the detective. Anna let him take that picture and she told him to look at it and think of her whenever he was lonely.

Man she was so damn hot. What a fine body. What beautiful long black hair, and those bedroom eyes. I'll never ever forget her, Hector thought to himself. He started to get aroused while staring at her picture on his smartphone. Hector grabbed the big bulge protruding between his legs and started to squeeze it, enjoying the good feeling. He thought about masturbating to his late girlfriend's picture, remembering how good she felt to him when they made love together. Hector started to unzip his pants and then he stopped. *No, it wouldn't be right,* Hector thought. *Why should I be able to feel pleasure when she can't anymore? My girl's dead and nothing could ever bring her back to me again.* He started to cry uncontrollably on his bed. Hector's friends always thought that he was tough, but deep down inside, the young man was really very sensitive. However, he would never let them see that part of him; they would think he was weak-minded.

After sobbing for a good fifteen minutes, Hector got up from his bed and went over to the dresser. The man looked through his drawers until he found what he'd been searching for. The young Latino had acquired a .38 caliber revolver from a junkie down in the city, about two years ago. Hector had showed it to Anna while they were dating, but Anna made it quite clear to him that she didn't want anything to do with guns, so he had put it away...until now. Hector stood in front of the dresser mirror looking at his reflection. He stared at the cold metal weapon in his right hand for a few minutes, thinking about Anna and thinking about what a failure in life he had been. Hector did the only thing that he felt he could do. He raised the gun to the right side of his head and squeezed the trigger. The bullet entered his brain and ended his sad life. Hector collapsed onto the light brown carpet of his apartment, in a pool of his own blood, that was spewing from his head. Maybe, now, Hector would be together with Anna again.

14

TIME TO KILL AGAIN

Joan Sanders was just about ready to leave. She had planned to go back down to the hospital early in the morning before working, until the phone rang. Joan's boss wanted her to come down to the office for a meeting between the two of them. She didn't know what he wanted from her, but it sure did sound serious. Joan had been telecommuting using her home computer; everyone was doing that now because of the Coronavirus pandemic. She did have to go down to the office about three times a week, to retrieve the mail for the firm, usually on Mondays, Wednesdays, and Fridays, but it was only Tuesday and Joan was just there yesterday. *What could he possibly want from me now?* She thought.

Joan finally arrived at her place of work, she parked her car on the street and walked into her boss's office. Joan looked at him as he was sitting down at his desk drinking coffee. Richard Johnson, the head attorney over at The Johnson Law Firm, was a middle-aged man with an average build. His salt and pepper hair, and expensive suit gave him a distinguished look that most businessmen had at his age. Richard asked Joan to have a seat near his desk, so that he could analyze the young woman, while he questioned her.

"Miss Sanders, I have a question for you," her boss stated.

"Yes, sir, what is it?" Avalina answered him through Joan's body.

"Are you happy here, I mean *really happy*?"

"Well, of course, sir. I need my job."

"Need is not the same thing as like, or even, love. I need to know, are you really and truly happy here?"

"Sure, *I love my job,* Mr. Johnson!"

"I hope so, because it's just that…well…you seem different lately, maybe even distant."

"Different? Distant? I'm afraid I don't understand what you mean by that, sir?"

"Yes, different, even before all of this working from home business started. I'd say you've changed considerably in the past few months."

"I do my job and I try really hard to get things done in a timely manner, Mr. Johnson."

"Yes, I know, don't get me wrong. You do get your work done; however, it does seem to take you a little longer to complete certain assignments. I was just wondering if there was anything bothering you lately."

"No, nothing that I can think of except, I guess I was just worrying about this virus that's been going around and, how it's going to affect my job here; that's all, sir."

"Yes, I see; everyone seems to be affected by it one way or another. Well, we're chugging along here and as long as we are, I need to know that I can still depend upon you one hundred percent. Right, Miss Sanders?"

"Yes, sir, Mr. Johnson!"

"Good, one other question Joan…may I call you 'Joan?'"

"Sure, sir."

"How are you making out with the technology, Joan?"

"The technology, sir?"

"Yes, how is it working from home? Are you having any

issues telecommuting?"

"Well, sometimes I have to wait for my machine to pull up the clients' files."

"Oh, that's the internet. Since everyone is working from home these days, it's going to be slow. What kind of internet service do you have at home? Is it ISDN, DSL, Dial-Up, cable, or satellite?"

Avalina didn't know what the hell he was talking about, but she didn't want to look stupid in front of the boss. Avalina thought about the bills she just recently paid with Joan's checkbook; one of them was the cable television bill. She distinctly remembered the cable TV bill saying something about internet service charges.

"I think it's cable, sir," she replied.

"You *think*? You mean, you're not sure what kind of internet service you have?" Mr. Johnson asked her.

"Excuse me, sir, I mean it is cable, sir. Sorry."

"Ok, now, Miss Sanders, you can return home and take care of our clients through your computer. Don't forget to come in tomorrow to get the snail mail."

"Alright, thank you, sir. Would you like me to get you another cup of coffee before I leave?"

"No thanks. By the way, make sure you wear your mask the next time you come on down here."

"Yes, sir."

"That'll be all, Miss Sanders," Richard replied.

The possessed young woman walked out of the office and went back outside to her car. Avalina sat down in the driver's seat of the car and had a serious discussion with her host.

"Listen up, bitch, what the hell are you trying to do, get us both fired?" Avalina angrily asked her host.

"Wouldn't that just be peachy, you little parasite?!" Joan retorted laughingly.

"You had better cooperate and help me learn how to do your job properly...or else!"

"Or else what, you witch bitch?"

"If you let *anyone* get suspicious of me and ruin my plans, so help me, I'll kill your mother and *all* of your damn friends, you know I have the power to do it!"

Joan did not reply to Avalina's ultimatum; instead, she just got quiet...for now. Avalina knew that she couldn't destroy her host's spirit, not yet anyway. She still needed her in order to survive in this strange, new world and Avalina needed to be completely familiar with all of the goings on in Joan's world. However, she was going to have to exert more of her powers to suppress Joan, but it wasn't going to be easy. Avalina had noticed that her powers seemed to be growing weaker. *I think my powers were stronger in the other body I had,* she thought to herself.

A man had just walked by on the sidewalk near Joan's car, and since her car windows were partially open, he heard the woman. It had appeared to him that Joan was yelling at herself. The man wondered if she was either on the phone or mentally unstable. He decided to just keep on walking before she noticed him staring at her.

Once Avalina Bishop regained full control over her host, she decided to do what she originally intended to do, before being interrupted by her superior in the morning. The possessed young woman, was going to take a quick trip down to the city to visit Benny

Smith back at the hospital. *I know I'm supposed to get back to work, but I need to take care of this sonofabitch first,* Avalina thought. She had no idea that Benny had already passed on. Avalina drove her host's old car using Joan as a puppet.

Avalina would have to learn everything there was to know about this new, hi-tech world she was now a part of. The young witch wanted to be well prepared to survive here. Avalina had originally planned to only avenge her death and leave Joan's body, but something happened to her, something that just wasn't planned. Avalina fell in love with David Scholl and she wanted very much to be a part of his life. If it meant completely destroying Joan's spirit in the future and assuming her entire life, then so be it; that's what Avalina's new plans were. She drove the old car down the parkway, while thinking about David and how he last made love to her. The young man just wanted to please her in every way possible and of course, the feeling was very much mutual. There wasn't anything that Avalina wouldn't do for her lover.

The possessed young woman finally arrived at the medical center in the city. She parked her car and turned it off. Before leaving, Avalina decided to disguise herself this time, just in case. She rolled up her long red hair and tucked it under a large tan-colored floppy hat. Avalina reached into Joan's white bag, took out a pair of dark sunglasses and put them on. She remembered to bring the face mask this time, that she had in the glove compartment of the car, since it had become mandatory to wear one in public places now.

The disguised witch casually walked from the parking lot into the hospital lobby. Avalina walked right passed the information counter. She headed straight towards the stainless-steel elevators and took one of them up to the second floor. The witch remembered Benny's room number; it was room 222. She eased on by the nurses'

station and headed straight for his room. When Avalina got there, she noticed that the plastic curtain was gone. The room looked like it was in the process of being cleaned up. Nurse Williams had just walked in the room.

"May I help you, Miss?" the head nurse asked her.

Avalina slowly turned around and looked at the nurse. The young witch instantly remembered her from the last time she was there. *Shit, that's that same woman that caught my ass here last time,* she thought to herself. Avalina hoped the nurse wouldn't recognize her.

"Yes, I'm looking for Mr. Benny Smith. Was he moved?" Avalina asked the nurse.

"I'm sorry, he expired," Nurse Williams coldly replied.

"What do you mean he *expired?* We're not talking about a gallon of milk here."

"I mean he's dead, died yesterday morning."

The young witch felt cheated. She wanted to be the one to end his sorry ass life. Avalina wanted Benny to suffer like she did.

"You look very familiar," the nurse said while trying to recognize her.

"And *you* must be mistaken; I'll just be leaving now."

The possessed woman tried to walk out of the patient room, but the nurse blocked the doorway and held her ground. Avalina wasn't looking for a confrontation with this woman, but it looked like it was unavoidable. She removed her dark sunglasses and her mask. Then, the witch stared coolly into the nurse's eyes.

"I knew it was you and I know you had something to do with Mr. Smith's death. You're in a lot of trouble, Miss; I done told the detective all about your ass," Nurse Williams hissed.

"Excuse me, tubby, but I think you better get the *hell* out of my way."

"Who the *hell* you callin' 'tubby', you scrawny ass looking bitch?!" Nurse Williams said while putting her hands on her hips.

"Like I said before, move the hell out of my way!"

The young enchantress waved her arms up and used her powers to send the nurse flying out of her way, without even touching her. The nurse hit the hall wall and fell down on her butt. There were no other nurses around at the station at that time because the hospital was shorthanded. No one was there to see the vicious confrontation happening between the two. The other two nurses were on a break, leaving Miss Williams all by herself. Nurse Williams slowly got up from the floor and charged at her, but Avalina quickly got out of her way. The nurse smacked into the room wall and fell down on the floor. This time, the nurse fell flat on her face. Nurse Williams was no match for Avalina's agility.

"Hey, what's going on in there?!" a patient in an adjoining room yelled out.

"You want some more of this, bitch?!" Avalina roared.

"I'm-a get your skinny ass if it's the last thing I do," the nurse said while trying to get up on her feet.

The witch strolled on over to where the nurse was lying and kicked her hard in the head. The nurse became unconscious as she fell on her back. Avalina looked down in disgust at the heavy-set African-American nurse laying there on the floor.

"Well, will you look at that? It looks like the nurse, needs a nurse, or maybe even a doctor. Wouldn't you say that, bitch?!"

Avalina noticed that the head nurse was slowly regaining consciousness. The young witch knew that she was going to have to eliminate her. Avalina figured that the woman could easily identify her and pose a threat to all of her plans. The witch knew it was time to kill again, even if the woman wasn't her intended target.

"You know what, *bitch*? I'm damn well tired of playing this fricking game with you," she said while the nurse was trying to get up on her feet again.

Avalina kicked Nurse Williams until she was on her back again. She then plunged her right hand deep down into the left side of the woman's chest cavity like a cutting knife. Nurse Williams screamed in agonizing pain, as Avalina reached in for her beating heart and ripped it right out of her chest. The bloody heart was still pumping as she held it in her hand. The young witch squished the organ in her bare hand until it exploded, sending blood and tissue fragments all over her and the room she was in. Nurse Williams let out her final gasp as she perished in a pool of her own blood, while she laid there on the cold, white, vinyl tiled floor. Avalina stared at the woman's eyes that were now fixed open in a horrifying gaze.

"I really didn't want to kill you, but you wouldn't let me leave. You left me no other choice," she said softly to the now lifeless body that was once Nurse Williams.

The sorceress heard someone coming, so she quickly wiped her hands on the bed spread and turned her coat inside out, to hide the blood that was on it. The possessed young woman put on her dark sunglasses and mask, then she casually walked out down the hall, as some people were approaching. Avalina had to get back home to rest. The confrontation had left her weak. She knew there was a limitation to her powers and it had been reached.

Back in Brighten at the police station, Detective Wiretrak had convinced the chief to allow a police artist to work with Nurse Williams.

"I'm glad you finally agree with me on this, chief. If my

hunch is correct, we may be able to catch our killer," the detective told the chief.

"Alright, then, call the hospital first and make sure the nurse is available for questioning, before you and Greg head on down there," the chief stated.

"You got it, chief."

"Oh, and one other thing…"

"What's that, chief?"

"You remember the young Latino fellow you spoke to here yesterday?"

"You mean Hector Rodriguez?"

"Yeah, that's him."

"What about him, chief?"

"It seems that the Midland police force found him dead in his apartment yesterday."

"What?! How did it happen?!"

"It appears he died from a self-inflicted gunshot wound to his head. The landlord heard the gunshot, went down to check on him, found him dead in his apartment and called it in."

"Shit, well that definitely rules him out as a suspect, doesn't it?"

"I suppose it does."

"Alright, chief, let me go call the hospital and find out when that nurse is available."

"Get on it, Wiretrak."

Detective Wiretrak went back to his desk, looked up the number, and called the hospital. When the detective finally got through to the nurses' station on the second floor of the city hospital, he was totally shocked to find out that the head nurse had been slaughtered. The supervisor had informed Wiretrak that Nurse Williams had been murdered in a cruelest and horrifying way, by having her heart extracted from her chest while she was still alive. The supervisor also informed him that the local police were on the scene investigating it right now. Wiretrak was starting to feel sick. He hung up the phone, knowing he would never get to interview her with the police artist. The young detective got up from his desk to inform the chief.

Avalina had just gotten home at five in the evening. She didn't expect to get back home so late. Obviously, it was way too late to work, plus the girl was tired anyway. *I'll just blame it on the computer; I'll say it was down,* Avalina thought. She removed all of her blood-soaked clothes, went to the bathroom, and took a nice hot shower. The young witch was feeling the effects of exhaustion. Avalina used up so much of her energy during the fatal confrontation with the head nurse. She grabbed the special golden pentagram locket around her neck and prayed for strength. Avalina felt the warmth of the power emanating from it while it laid between her breasts. The locket was glowing. The powerful ornament made her feel a little stronger, but she still needed rest to rejuvenate herself.

After her shower, Avalina had put on her white bathrobe and decided to watch a little television before going to sleep. She walked into the living room and searched for the remote control, knowing it was the only way to turn the damn thing on, since there were no buttons or knobs on the television set. *It's on one of those end*

tables behind a lamp, the possessed young woman remembered. Avalina found it, aimed it at the set hanging on the wall above the fireplace, and pressed the power button. The TV set sprung to life showing a male news reporter with a red banner below him that read, *Special Report.*

"Police are investigating the gruesome death of a female nurse today at City Medical Center in, New York City. The victim was identified as Laverne Williams. The police stated that the victim's heart had been removed from her chest by her assailant, while she was still alive. Williams had been a registered nurse for the hospital for over twelve years. Williams had been working alone on the floor at the time; since the hospital had quarantined several of its workers that tested positive for the Coronavirus. The hospital's video cameras were not functioning on the floor at the time, due to a glitch in the security system. Laverne Williams leaves behind her two young boys, Charles, and William. Nurse Williams was thirty-five-years-old when she died. If anyone has got any information regarding the identity or the location of the victim's attacker, please call the number on your screen," the reporter stated while showing a recent picture of Nurse Laverne Williams on the screen.

Avalina didn't want to hear about it anymore, so she turned off the TV set. *The nurse simply got in my way. I didn't want to kill her,* she thought.

"Shit, I didn't know she had kids," Avalina said to herself, feeling somewhat remorseful for what happened.

"So, it was you who killed her. Shame on you," the ghostly spirit echoed in the room.

"Mama, is that you again?" Avalina asked.

"You've killed an innocent woman, a nurse that did you no harm, a nurse that saves lives, especially since there's a shortage of them right now. Have you no shame, Avalina?" her mother's spirit retorted.

"I didn't want to, but she just got in my way mama; that's the truth."

"You're a damn liar. I don't believe you."

"It's true, mama, it's true!"

"You must pay for all of your sins! You must be stopped!"

The ghost of Sabrina Bishop was summoning all of her powers to destroy her own daughter. She was tired of all of the unnecessary death and destruction, that was brought on by her daughter's evil spirit. A raging storm had come over the house and brought lightning, thunder, and an onslaught of hail. The lights started flickering. Avalina's fiery, long red hair and robe were flying in the wind that seemed to have come from nowhere. Windows began to shatter. The young witch was getting extremely nervous. It brought back very unpleasant memories of her younger days, when the windows were breaking in of her house, as it burned with her being trapped inside of it.

"Stop it, mother, stop it!" Avalina screamed at the top of her lungs.

The raging spirit continued to display its anger. Suddenly, Avalina felt a tug on her precious pentagram locket. The apparition was desperately trying to remove it from her neck, knowing that Avalina drew all of her powers from it. Joan's spirit was also crying out and frantically trying to regain control over her own body.

"Pull it off! Pull it the hell off of her neck, *please!*" Joan's spirit cried out through her own lips.

"Nooo!" Avalina shrieked.

Avalina's spirit summoned what little strength she had left and subdued Joan. She grabbed the golden pentagram locket, which was now dangling straight out in front of her face. Avalina held the pentagram tight in her hands and prayed.

"Oh, Prince of Darkness and ruler of all evil, save me from being destroyed. Guard and protect my spirit. Save my soul from my enemies that wish to extinguish me. Let me be allowed to live in this strange new world. Let me complete my quest for revenge and I will serve thee," Avalina chanted.

A dark form had appeared in the corner of the room with glowing white eyes. The figure raised its arms up through its cape as lightning emerged from them. The raging storm, that had come over the house, was now quieting down to a whimper. Then, the storm disappeared along with the ghost of Sabrina Bishop and the dark figure. The evil entity, that was in the corner of the room, never uttered a single word, but Avalina knew who it was and why it came. She had begged the spirit to help her and now, Avalina must return the favor…someday. The young witch was standing in the middle of her living room, looking extremely disheveled with her chest heaving up and down, as she clenched her golden pentagram locket.

Avalina was totally exhausted now. She staggered into the bedroom, holding her golden pentagram, and trying to extract any energy from it. The possessed young woman stumbled into the bed. She covered herself up with the blue blanket using only her left hand, never once letting go of the golden pentagram locket that was still in her right hand. Avalina finally fell asleep. While she slept, the young witch was slowly regaining most of her powers. Avalina would be ready to work again by tomorrow.

15

LOOKING FOR CLUES

On a warm and sunny Wednesday morning, Detective Michael Wiretrak was sitting at his desk at the Brighten Police Department. Wiretrak was thinking of how to put the pieces of this mysterious, murderous puzzle together. *So far, there was one victim in the city that was killed by a red-headed woman. The victim was identified as Michael Resnick. The news media had said that the perpetrator deliberately pushed him into an oncoming subway train. A passenger at the station platform said that the killer was a woman with long, bright red hair. Then, there were the two that were murdered up here, Anna Nuñez and John Waters,* the police detective remembered. Wiretrak wondered if they were all killed by the same person. *Obviously, the victims up here were killed in a different manner than the one in the city last month, but the one shred of evidence that ties them all together, is that they were all killed by a woman with long, bright red hair,* the detective thought.

"One thing's for sure, if it's the same woman, it's not just local anymore…this bitch is getting around," he said to himself.

Detective Wiretrak remembered the last conversation he had with Nurse Williams and what she told him over the phone regarding, Benny's final visitor: *she was young, pretty, probably in her twenties with penetrating blue eyes and tall. Oh, yeah, one other thing, she had this straight, bright red hair. It was long, I mean, it was down to her butt.* The detective also wondered if the red-headed female killer, was also responsible for the recent death of Nurse Williams. *It's too bad there wasn't any security footage of the incident; that would have made it a little easier,* he thought.

Detective Wiretrak only knew of two women in the area that were tall and had straight, bright red hair: Carrie Sanders and her daughter, Joan. Neither of the two women he knew appeared to be the murdering type, but then again, that could be their perfect cover.

They could be in it together, the man assumed. The detective figured that the killer had to have help. *Maybe, just maybe it was time to question the both of them,* he thought to himself.

A few miles away, Avalina and her human puppet were waking up to the sunshine that was beaming right through the windows. The young witch felt sweaty, but Avalina was refreshed after all of that energy-draining work she experienced just yesterday. Avalina didn't realize that she slept all night long, holding the gold pentagram locket in her right hand. It had become her security blanket in times of need.

"Wow, that's probably why I feel so damn strong and so revitalized. I feel like I can take on the world," she said to herself.

The young witch decided to take a nice, long, relaxing warm bath to wash the sweat off of her body. Avalina didn't think that her host would object to that, but even if Joan did, she didn't give a shit. *it's my body now,* Avalina thought to herself. She got out of bed and dropped her white bathrobe down onto the floor beside her bed, leaving her completely naked.

"Oh, shit! I better get rid of those blood-stained clothes before I take my bath," the possessed young woman immediately said to herself.

Avalina quickly went to the kitchen to get a large black plastic garbage bag out of the pantry. She brought the bag into the foyer where the clothes were still lying on the floor. Avalina threw all of her blood-stained clothes, including her coat and hat, into the black bag and tied it up. The only thing the young woman kept was her bra, knowing how expensive they were to replace, plus it was still clean. Avalina cautiously went out the back door that was on the rear deck, making sure that there was no one around; after all, she was completely naked and the woman didn't want to give anyone a show. Avalina walked down the stairs, opened up the green garbage can, and carefully placed the bag into the container. Then, she closed the lid, walked back up the steps and went back inside the house. Avalina made sure she remembered to lock the door after that.

"Now, that that's done, I can take my bath," she said to herself.

Avalina trotted off into the bathroom and looked at herself in the mirror over the sink, admiring her large and shapely breasts. Her nipples had become large and hard from the cool air outside. She licked her fingers and started to rub her nipples in between them, which made them even more engorged. *Man that feels so damn good,* the young witch thought. Avalina was getting extremely stimulated. She remembered David Scholl fiercely sucking on them like a hungry baby. Avalina picked up her right breast, brought her nipple to her lips, and licked it. Then, she did the same thing to her left breast. *It's not the same,* the aroused young witch thought. Avalina thought about calling David, but he lived so damn far away in New Jersey and she wanted satisfaction right now. Avalina remembered when she was mortal back in the sixties. She always used to love to take a quiet warm bath and give herself pleasure. *That's just what I'll do now, take care of my new sexy body,* Avalina thought while admiring herself in the mirror. *I've seen the way David looks at my boobs,* she thought.

The young enchantress filled up the bathtub with warm soapy water and stepped inside it. She grabbed a big yellow sponge from the shelf above the tub and soaked it in the water. Avalina gently laid down in the tub with her legs spread open wide. The girl had her head up above the water, with her two feet propped up on the top of the tub up against the wall. She was tall enough to be able to do that and still feel completely comfortable. The warm sudsy water felt good all over her body. Avalina took the sponge and rubbed her breasts with it, paying careful attention to her nipples.

Then, Avalina went for the source of her pleasure. She dropped the sponge, took her right hand, and inserted two fingers inside her vaginal area, while massaging it. Avalina's breathing became more intense and rapid as she reached her first peak, while letting out a low moan with a tremble in her body. She continued to stimulate her genitals with her right hand, while rubbing her left breast nipple with her left hand. Avalina picked up the pace, working her right hand like a thrusting jackhammer, until she achieved a second and much more powerful climax. This time, the young witch let out a loud scream as her body quivered so much, that water had splashed all over the floor. She wanted to go for a third peak, but the phone started ringing and broke her sensual mood.

"Sonofabitch! Who the hell is bothering me now?!" Avalina screamed out, despising the interruption.

The answering machine finally picked up after the fourth ring. Joan's boss, Richard Johnson, was on the line reminding her about the video conference that was scheduled for eleven o'clock, this morning. He announced that it was already ten thirty before hanging up.

"*Shit*, I forgot all about that damn meeting," she said to herself.

Avalina drained the tub and rinsed herself off. She only felt partially satisfied. The girl was still in heat, but it would have to wait until after work. Avalina dried herself off and walked out of the bathtub. The young witch thought about just putting on her white bathrobe, but she decided to change her mind. *They'll be able to see me through the computer's camera. I better go and get dressed,* she thought.

In a New Jersey garden apartment, David Scholl was trying to diagnose a customer's computer server over the phone. David had tried to do a screen share with the customer via the internet, but it appeared that the client's mainframe was completely down. The only alternative for David, was to go and drive out to the client's place of business and service the system. He had told the customer he'd be there in about an hour and hung up the phone.

The young man had originally been thinking of Joan Sanders before the phone call. *I can't get her out of my mind, damn it. I really need to see her,* David thought. He remembered the last time they made love together. *It was so much fun and so invigorating for both of us,* he thought. David hadn't been with too many women before. The young man enjoyed his freedom, but ever since his pet bird, Michael, had died, he felt lonelier. David never really fell in love before, but he knew what he wanted and it was Joan Sanders. The sex was really good with her; nonetheless, David couldn't marry Joan. Marriage was definitely not in his future; it would ruin everything for him. He put on one of his old favorite records from the Temptations, "My Girl." David started singing with the old 45 RPM record while getting dressed. He thought about the words to the song and how well they described Joan Sanders.

After about a half hour later, David Scholl was heading out the front door and down the road. David was going to service the computer server for the client. After that, he was going to call his girl, providing she was home.

Carrie Sanders was just coming out of the bathroom when her doorbell rang. *It's not even eleven o'clock in the morning yet. I wonder who that could be,* she thought to herself. Carrie walked on over to the front door and looked out of the sidelight window to see who it was. She didn't recognize the red-headed young man standing there, wearing a black suit and black mask.

"Who is it?!" Carrie asked through the front door.

"It's Detective Wiretrak! Can you please spare a moment of

your time, Miss Sanders?!" he asked while displaying his badge through the sidelight window.

Carrie wondered what a detective would want from her. *Wiretrak,* Carrie thought the name sounded familiar to her. She unlocked and opened up the front door.

"Sure, detective. How can I help you?" Carrie cautiously asked him.

"I would like to ask you some questions, Miss Sanders, may I come in?" Wiretrak asked her.

"Sure, come on in."

Carrie escorted him through the foyer and in to the kitchen where the table and chairs were. Carrie was nervously wondering what the hell the man wanted.

"Would you like to sit down, detective?" she asked.

"Well, don't mind if I do," he replied while taking out his notebook and pen.

"I have some coffee left in the pot if you'd like some?"

"No, thanks, Miss Sanders, I'm trying to cut down; too much caffeine makes me feel jumpy."

"I see. Weren't you the same detective that questioned my daughter while she was in the hospital, after she had gotten shot about two months ago?"

"Yes, Miss Sanders, that was me. How's your daughter doing?"

"She's fine, thanks for asking. Now, tell me, detective, what brings you here, if you don't mind me being so blunt?"

"Well, Miss Sanders, I'm working on a case and right now.

I'm just looking for some clues, that's all."

"Does this case have anything to do with me?"

"I'd be lying to you if I said 'no,' but right now, I'm just trying to get some information. You see, Miss Sanders, I am very thorough in my investigations. I don't leave any stones unturned."

"I see. So, then, tell me, detective, what do you need from me?"

"Well, for starters, Miss Sanders, if you don't mind me being so blunt, where were you on Monday night, February the tenth?"

"Wow, sounds like I'm a suspect in some crime."

"This is just preliminary questioning, Miss Sanders; I didn't say you were a suspect. Now, can you please just answer the question for me?"

"Ok, detective, I'm sure you're very well aware of my job as a teacher at Brighten High School, if you did your homework on me, that is."

"Yes, Miss Sanders, I'm very well aware of your position in that school."

"Good, then you *should know* that on that night, I was at a parent teacher conference."

"No, Miss Sanders, I had no knowledge of any such meeting. I don't have any children in that school; however, I'll check into that, assuming of course, that your presence there can be verified."

"It certainly can be, detective. I was working closely with Principal Sarah Paddington on that evening."

"And about what time did you leave the meeting, Miss Sanders?"

"When it was over, of course, that was about nine-thirty in the evening. By the way, there were witnesses there that saw me leave at that time, including Principal Paddington and some of the parents of my students, just for your information, detective."

"Ok, Miss Sanders. Next question-"

"Wait a minute, detective, what was so important about that date anyway?"

"Oh, nothing special, Miss Sanders, just that a man was murdered on that night."

"Murdered?!"

"Yes, that's right, murdered, but if you were where you say you were, well, then it couldn't be you now, could it? Now, next question, Miss Sanders, do you know a Miss Anna Nuñez?"

"Sorry, detective, I can't say that I do. The name doesn't ring a bell to me at all."

"What about John Waters? Does that name ring a bell to you?"

"Nope, I never heard of him either."

"Well, sure you have. His wife wrote that book that's on your kitchen counter over there," Detective Wiretrak stated while pointing to the book of the late author.

"Oh, that book? *Hope to Stay Alive* by Melissa Waters, what about it?"

The detective got up from his chair. He walked on over to the kitchen counter and grabbed the book. Wiretrak noticed that the book was autographed by the writer.

"Tragic what happened to her, isn't it?" Wiretrak asked her.

"Yes, it sure was," Carrie sadly replied.

"I understand you were a great big fan of hers. You followed her at practically every book signing, am I right, Miss Sanders?"

"Well, yes, I suppose I did, but I just don't see what-"

"I also understand that you became quite chummy with the late Mrs. Waters *and* her late husband, I might add. You were with her at all of her book signings, is that correct, Miss Sanders?"

"Yes, I suppose so, but I still-"

"So, why then did you just lie to me, stating that you never heard of this man before?" Wiretrak asked her while holding up the book showing a dedicated picture of the late author's late husband, John Waters, to Carrie.

"I just don't see-"

"No more games, Miss Sanders. I told you this was just preliminary questioning and I wanted some straight answers."

Carrie knew he was angry. She knew damn well that the detective was a no-nonsense type of a man, but Carrie didn't want to admit why she had just lied to him. The middle-aged woman felt quite embarrassed.

"Detective, wait, listen, I'm forty-eight-years-old. I just didn't want you to think I was some kind of a groupie; even if it were true, I'm so sorry," Carrie sincerely said.

"Apology accepted, Miss Sanders."

"Is there anything else I can do for you, detective?"

"No, not right now, Miss Sanders, but we'll keep in touch. Have a good day."

Carrie Sanders escorted Detective Wiretrak into the foyer

and out to the front door. She wondered why the detective was questioning her. Carrie remembered the horrible way John Waters had died. She also recalled how the man was found dead at the bottom of Pond Lake, but what did that have to do with her? *Am I a suspect in his murder?* Carrie asked herself. She also remembered the detective asking her about Monday night, February the tenth. Carrie tried hard to remember what was so special about that night: *Oh, nothing special, Miss Sanders, just that a man was murdered on that night,* the detective had said to her.

"I don't remember anything about a murder around here, except for Mr. Waters and that woman he mentioned," she said to herself.

Then, it hit her. *A man was killed around that time. Some crazy woman pushed a man into an oncoming subway train, but that was all the way down in the city; he can't possibly think that I had something to do with it, could he?* Carrie mentally asked herself after recalling the whole ordeal. She remembered thinking that maybe even her daughter might have had something to do with it, after hearing the description of the killer on the television news broadcast. After all, her daughter has been acting rather strange lately.

Detective Wiretrak had reached his next destination. He wasn't satisfied with the previous interview with Carrie Sanders; Wiretrak thought she was holding out on him. He parked the car, walked on over to the front door, and rang the doorbell.

"Who is it?!" the woman asked behind the door.

"It's Detective Wiretrak, I'm here to ask you some questions if you don't mind!" the detective stated while displaying his badge in front of the sidelight window for her to see.

Avalina saw his police badge through the window. She remembered the young detective. *What could he possibly want now?*

Avalina mentally asked herself. She unlocked the front door and opened it.

"Hello, detective, it's so nice to see you again," Avalina joyfully stated through Joan, with a phony smile on her face.

"I'm afraid this isn't a social visit, Miss Sanders, I just need to ask you some questions. May I come in?"

"Sure, detective, come on in."

Avalina led the young detective into the kitchen. She was reading his mind as he sat down at the table. *He suspects me and my host's mother of murdering three people, or maybe even more…*, she thought. The young witch knew she was about to get grilled by the detective. *I'll just have to answer his questions cautiously, that's all,* the young witch was thinking.

"I see you have your new attire on," she said while pointing to his mask.

"That's right, it's mandatory now," the detective replied.

"Yours is unique; it's black."

"It goes with my suit and my mood, but we both know I didn't come here to discuss my mask or the rest of my apparel, Miss Sanders. I just need to ask you some questions and I'll be on my way."

"Well, detective, I don't want to seem like I'm rushing you, but I only have about thirty-five minutes before my lunch break is over. You see, I'm working from home now and we're supposed to have another meeting on that computer at one o'clock."

"I'll try not to take up too much of your time, Miss Sanders, but this is police business."

Wiretrak was trying to analyze the attractive, young red-headed woman. He remembered the description Nurse Williams had given him over the phone: *she was young, pretty, probably in her twenties with penetrating blue eyes and tall. Oh, yeah, one other thing, she had this straight, bright red hair, it was long. I mean it was down to her butt.* This woman definitely fits that description, but it still doesn't mean that she's a murderer. The detective noticed that she seemed overly dressed to be working from home. He thought that even though she was wearing a very conservative looking white business suit, the young woman looked incredibly attractive.

"I see that you've recovered quite well from your gunshot wound," the detective said to her.

"Yes, I have, but I still don't have any information for you as to why I was attacked."

"This isn't about that incident, Miss Sanders, I can assure you. I need to know your whereabouts on Monday night, February the tenth," the detective asked her while taking out his notebook and pen.

"Wow, that's over two months ago. Let me think for a bit," Avalina said while trying to come up with a good story.

"Please, take all the time you need, Miss Sanders," Wiretrak declared.

"Well, then, let me see, back then I was still going to work at the office. Since it was Monday, I probably just went straight home."

"Do you have any way of verifying that, Miss Sanders?"

"No, I'm sorry I don't."

"Now, Miss Sanders, you work as a legal secretary for The Johnson Law Firm; that's about five miles south from here, is that correct?"

"Boy, I guess you really did your research on me, didn't you?"

"It's my job to be thorough, Miss Sanders. So, you do work for the law firm, is that correct, Miss Sanders?"

"Yes, that's correct."

"Ok, now that we've established that, we'll move on to the next question then. Do you know a Miss Anna Nuñez?"

"Who?!"

"Miss Anna Nuñez, do you know her?"

"I can't say that I do, sorry."

"What about John Waters, have you ever heard of him, Miss Sanders?"

By this time, Avalina was getting nervous, but she tried not to show it. Avalina knew that the man was trying to put a case together using her and possibly Carrie, her host's mother. The young witch read his mind some more before carefully answering his question. Avalina wanted to see where she stood with him.

"Isn't he the one they found dead in some lake not too long ago?" Avalina asked the detective.

"Yes, that's correct, but other than that, did you know of him?" Wiretrak asked her.

"Only that he was the husband of some author."

"That's right, Melissa Waters. One other thing and I'll let you get back to work."

"Fair enough, detective, because I only have a few minutes left."

"Have you ever been down to City Medical Center in New York City to visit a Mr. Benny Smith?"

"Why would I go all the way down to the city, to visit someone I've never even heard of?"

"Oh, I don't know, Miss Sanders, suppose you enlighten me."

"Did this man claim I visited him, because if he did, I'll call him a liar right to his face?!"

"Well, that may be a little difficult now, seeing that he's already dead."

"I'm sorry, I didn't know, but I still never heard of him."

"That'll be all for now, Miss Sanders. I'll let you know if I need any more information from you; I can see myself out."

The detective got up from his chair and walked out of the kitchen towards the front door. Avalina closed and locked the door behind him. *He knows too much and he suspects me,* she thought. *I'll have to keep a very close eye on him. He's cute; I'd sure hate to have to kill him.* But Avalina *would kill him*. She would kill anyone that stood in her way.

About a half hour later at the Brighten Police Department, Detective Wiretrak was back at his own office. He was sitting down at his desk, thinking. None of it sat well with him. Wiretrak figured that both Carrie and Joan Sanders were trying to hide something; both of them had now become suspects to him, but maybe not prime suspects as of yet. The detective looked at the dark and grainy picture of the perpetrator, that pushed Michael Resnick to his death in February. *I can't tell anything from this shit; it could fricking be anybody,* he angrily thought to himself. The image was definitely of very poor quality. It looked like it was shot from a very old flip phone. A smartphone would have had a much higher resolution camera in it.

The chief of police walked in and took a look at the detective's computer monitor.

"Can I ask you something, Wiretrak?" Chief Valentine asked him.

"Shoot," he replied.

"Why the hell are you harping on that one case when it's not even in our territory?" Chief Valentine sarcastically asked him.

"I have my reasons, chief."

"Yeah, well, do it on your own damn time not on police department time. We've got other cases around here that need to be solved, like those two bodies that were found in the lake."

"I have reason to believe that they're all tied in together."

"Really, you honestly think that this small-town killer got a taste for the *big city life*?"

"Yes, I do. I think *all* of these crimes were committed by the same killer. I just need time to prove my theory, that's all."

"Alright, Wiretrak, you do that," the chief said to him while leaving his office.

Wiretrak really wanted to find the killer or killers as quickly as possible. The detective had especially made it a personal vendetta to find the one who pushed Michael Resnick, in front of that oncoming subway train in February. Wiretrak had decided to verify Carrie Sanders's excuse. He called up Principal Sarah Paddington from Brighten High School. After going through all of the voice prompts in the electronic office phone system, the detective finally got through to Mrs. Paddington. The principal did verify Carrie Sanders's presence on that night of the PTA meeting, which didn't end until nine-thirty in the evening.

"Well, that rules her out of the equation, at least for that incident. There's no way in *hell* she could have made it down to the city at that time," Wiretrak said to himself while hanging up the phone.

Of course, the detective knew it wouldn't rule her out of the other cases. *She's got bright red hair, but not that long, only shoulder-length, not as long as Nurse Williams had stated. However, Carrie Sanders could have cut her hair,* Wiretrak thought. *Then, there was of course, her daughter, Joan Sanders. Now, she really fit the bill and unlike her mother, Joan couldn't verify her whereabouts on the night in question,* Wiretrak was thinking. *Nurse Williams had also said that the girl was young and pretty. Carrie Sanders is pretty, but her daughter does have a younger face.* The detective had wondered what evidence the city police accumulated from the nurse's murder. *I'd sure like to get my hands on that report,* the young detective thought to himself.

16

WHERE IS DAVID SCHOLL?

Friday evening, the last full week of April, David Scholl and his lover, whom he thought was Joan Sanders, had just finished a very hot and heavy sex session in her bedroom. Avalina always liked to be on top of him; she liked having control. Avalina, using Joan's body, had come to another thunderous climax. She looked like a wild animal in heat, tousling her long red hair all over David.

The young witch had collapsed on David. They were both sweaty and exhausted. David put his arms around her as she laid on top of him. The young man was jealous; he wished that men could have multiple orgasms like women do. David stroked her hair and kissed her cheek. The two of them fell asleep together for a while.

An hour later, Avalina had woken up and rolled off of David because she had to go to the bathroom. The young sorceress looked at her hot young lover lying there on the bed next to her, looking so content. It was getting dark outside and there was very little light coming in through the windows. She thought about putting on a lamp, but the young witch didn't want to wake him up. The witch turned and noticed something in the corner of the room. It was a glow of light that looked like two beams close together. Avalina stared at it and tried to focus on it. Suddenly, a chill came over her body. The possessed woman recognized what it was. The Prince of Darkness had returned with its glowing eyes.

"Why the hell is he here? I didn't call him. I don't need him now," she whispered to herself.

After a moment or two, the dark figure that had once occupied the corner of her bedroom, was gone. *I shouldn't fear him, he saved me when I needed him,* the young witch thought. Then, Avalina remembered her last chant to him: *oh, Prince of Darkness, and ruler of all evil, save me from being destroyed. Guard and protect my spirit. Save my soul from my enemies that wish to extinguish me. Let me be allowed to live in this strange new world. Let me complete my quest for revenge and I will serve thee.*

"Holy shit, is it payback time already?" Avalina softly asked herself.

The possessed young woman was getting nervous. Avalina decided to quickly go to the bathroom and relieve her internal pressure before she had an accident. While the sorceress was in the bathroom, she heard a roaring noise emanating from her bedroom.

"Is The Dark One back again?" Avalina had quietly asked herself.

The young enchantress cautiously walked back towards her bedroom. She looked around for those unmistakable glowing eyes of the dark prince. The sound was now getting louder and more frightening. *It's coming from my own bed,* she thought to herself. Avalina stared at David as the bright full moon shone upon him from the window. His chest was going up and down with every loud sound.

"He snores? I've never heard him snore before. Damn, he sounds like an old man," she quietly said to herself while feeling dumbfounded.

The possessed young woman looked around the room again to make sure they were all alone. She held up the mechanical alarm clock towards the window to see the time. It was nine o'clock. *Well, I guess he's staying over again,* Avalina thought. She didn't mind him sleeping over, but something had to be done about that noise of his. Avalina gently nudged him until he rolled over on his right side. Within seconds, David was quiet again. *There you go, much better. End of discussion,* she thought. Avalina got into bed, pulled the blanket up over them, and snuggled up to his back.

*
**

The next morning, Avalina was kissing David goodbye again. She had just made him pancakes and coffee for breakfast. David didn't usually work on Saturdays, but this was an emergency with a very important client.

"It's only ten o'clock in the morning, baby; do you really have to go?" Avalina asked him.

"I do if I want to keep my job, babe. I'll call you later. I promise, alright?" David said while kissing his disappointed woman goodbye.

"I love you, do you know that?"

"Wow, no one's ever told me *that* before. I love you, too," David replied, not really sure if he meant it.

David gave Joan one more kiss; this time, it was a very long and sensual kiss that kept her wanting more. She looked at him with puppy-dog eyes as he turned and walked away. The possessed young woman slowly closed and locked the door behind him. She watched him through the window as he walked towards his car. *He's got a cute butt*, she thought to herself.

Avalina went back upstairs to take care of business. She waltzed into the computer room and turned it on. There was the simple matter of completing her revenge, so that she could move on with David. It was time to find the *real David Scholl*; the one that killed her mortal body years ago with the others. David Scholl was the only one left to kill. This time, the witch was going to use one of those paid people finder sites. She was a firm believer that you get what you pay for. The young witch wanted *real results*. Avalina had Joan's credit card out on the desk and was ready to use it.

"Now, let's see, where the hell is David Scholl?" Avalina asked the machine as she typed.

She found a website that had guaranteed results, but it came with a monthly membership fee of $29.99 a month. Avalina decided to go for it, figuring that she would cancel the membership after finding David Scholl. The young witch looked at the card and entered in the account number and expiration date. Within seconds, the computer responded with a "Declined" message.

"Shit! I thought I paid all of her bills!" Avalina cursed at the machine and her host.

The young witch went through all of the bills on her host's desk. She finally found one that was unopened; it was a VISA credit card bill. Avalina opened the bill and saw that it had an overdue balance of $10,000 on it. She pulled out the checkbook and was ready to write a check, until the possessed young woman noticed that there was only $242.20 left in the account. Avalina looked at the credit card bill again and searched the statement for the minimum payment amount. It was $295.00.

"Shit! Shit! Shit! I'm broke!"

Avalina now realized why her host had taken in a roommate, but that wouldn't work out for her, unless it was her boyfriend. She looked through her host's black purse, looking to see if there was another credit card hidden somewhere. After careful searching, the young witch found a MasterCard. Avalina tried out the new card, carefully entering the information from it into the computer. This time, the computer responded with an approval and a welcome message.

"Woo-hoo!" she shouted.

Avalina had finished entering all of her host's personal information, email address, phone number, et cetera, et cetera, et cetera. Then, she started searching for David Scholl again. After a couple of minutes, the computer came back with two David Scholl's that had fit her criteria.

"I'll just have to kill them both," she said to herself.

One David Scholl was residing in the state of Connecticut and was sixty-six-years-old. The other prospective individual was in Poughkeepsie, New York and he was sixty-five-years-old.

"Poughkeepsie? Where the hell is Poughkeepsie?" Avalina asked the machine.

The young witch went to one of those map sites and looked up the whereabouts of both areas. She had the computer calculate the shortest distance of both locations, then Avalina turned on the black and white laser printer and printed out both maps. The possessed young woman got dressed and left for the closest location: Poughkeepsie, New York.

*
**

Carrie Sanders was driving and thinking about her daughter. She was also recalling all of the questions Detective Wiretrak had asked her. Carrie had tried to call Joan to give her a heads up, but Joan never answered the phone. Carrie would always get stuck with the telephone answering machine instead of Joan whenever she'd call. *Maybe, she's screening her calls and doesn't want to talk to me,* she sadly thought.

After a few minutes of driving, Carrie had arrived at her destination: her daughter's rented home. She got out of her white Ford sedan, walked on over to the front door, and rang the bell.

"Joan, it's me, your mother! Open up! It's important!" Carrie shouted out to the locked door.

Carrie tried to look in through the windows to see if she was home. The middle-aged woman knocked on the door and rang the doorbell several more times, but to no avail. Carrie finally realized that her daughter wasn't home.

"Where the hell could she be?" Carrie asked herself.

Carrie tried to call her daughter's cellphone number, but her call went straight to voicemail. She got back in her car, feeling very disappointed. The woman decided to head on back home. *I sure hope she's not in trouble with the police,* Carrie thought while she was driving.

Avalina had finally reached her destination after driving about forty minutes to Poughkeepsie. The town was further north from her. *I've got plenty of time; it's only one o'clock in the afternoon,* she thought after looking at the clock on the dashboard. The young witch verified the house number with what she had on the computer printout: 315 Fresno Lane.

"Yup, that's it," she said to herself.

Avalina turned off the car engine, put on her face mask and got out of her vehicle. It was an old unkempt ranch house. She looked at the house thinking: wow, *I thought my place was small. You could probably fit this house inside of mine.* The witch was thinking of a plan to get Mr. Scholl to open up his door for her. *Shit, I'm a woman, a very attractive young woman, if I do say so myself. I'll think of something,* she thought while standing there. The witch started walking up the short driveway to the path and towards the front door. Then, she rang David's doorbell.

"Who is it?!" a middle-aged man asked through the door.

"Hello, I was wondering if-!" Avalina said before being cut off by the man opening the door.

"Well, hello there, beautiful! My, you're a sight for sore eyes. I don't know what you're selling, but whatever it is, I'm buying. Come on in," the man stated while ushering her inside his home.

Avalina walked into the man's house while he closed and locked the door behind her. Suddenly, she didn't feel comfortable being alone with this man. He looked at her with hungry eyes, practically undressing her right there. Although, the young witch was perfectly capable of defending herself, Avalina got the impression that the man was a pervert. She looked at him while they stood in what appeared to be the man's living room. The man was about her height, with a muscular build and salt and pepper hair. Mr. Scholl didn't look anything like the David Scholl she had remembered back in high school.

"So, what are you selling, beautiful?" Mr. Scholl had asked her while checking out her breasts.

Avalina was happy that she wasn't wearing anything low-cut that would expose her cleavage. However, she knew that her large breasts were hard to hide, even in the dark pink sweater top she was wearing. The man looked at her as though he were a hungry wolf, ready to pounce on his next feast. Avalina decided to choose her words very carefully before answering the man.

"I'm not selling anything, Mr. Scholl. You are David Scholl, am I right?" Avalina asked him.

"The one and only," he replied.

"Good, I'm taking up a petition. It seems that the town here is looking to build a playground for the children."

"Really? that's news to me...and just where were they considering building this playground, Miss?"

"At that big parking lot about two blocks away from here."

"Really? They sent a beautiful, young woman, like you, on a Saturday afternoon to get names for a petition?"

"That's correct, sir."

"Well, then, where's your clipboard?"

"Oh, yeah, that's right. I left it in my car; I'll go get it."

The young sorceress turned around and changed her mind about killing the man, especially since he didn't look anything like her intended target. She walked over to the front door. All of a sudden, the witch felt a pinch in her right shoulder and she felt very drowsy and weak. Avalina looked at the man and tried to steady herself, until the young woman finally collapsed on the floor right next to the man.

Back in Brighten, New York, Carrie Sanders was finally getting back home. She had stopped by her favorite restaurant to pick up some food before going straight home. Carrie remembered all the good times she had bringing her daughter there to that restaurant. Carrie and her daughter would always have the same thing together: a cheeseburger deluxe with a sweetened ice tea. They would always sit at a booth and talk while eating their burgers. The two of them mostly talked about dad.

Carrie loved Tom Sanders with all of her heart and so did his daughter, Joan. Tom died fairly young from a stroke; he was only thirty-five-years-old. After his death, the two of them lost their faith in religion. Carrie and Joan never went back to church ever again, but they still had a great mother-and-daughter relationship. *Those were the good ole days,* she thought.

Carrie Sanders wondered what the hell had happened to her daughter. She wondered what changed her. Carrie thought it may have had something to do with her being shot. *I really hope she didn't have anything to do with the death of those people, especially the one in the city subway,* Carrie thought to herself. She'd never known her daughter to be the violent type, but Carrie couldn't forget the strange way she had been acting lately, especially when Joan said to her: *Where am I?! What the hell are you doing here?!* It was as if her own daughter didn't know who she was. Carrie walked into her home and went straight towards her bar in the living room. She decided to pour herself a good stiff drink. *Maybe it will calm my nerves. Maybe it will ease the pain,* the woman thought while sitting down on the sofa with a drink in her hand.

Back in Poughkeepsie, New York, Avalina was beginning to wake up. The young witch realized that she was completely naked, lying there on a bed in a small dark and dingy bedroom. Avalina had her arms and legs tied up spread eagle to all four of the bed posts. She didn't know what had happened to her. The young witch didn't even know where she was or what time it was. She only knew that it must have been late in the evening, judging by what little light was coming through the window. Then, the possessed young woman started to remember everything. Avalina noticed something else, too. There was, what appeared to be, dried semen all over her breasts and she was sore in her vaginal area. The girl realized that she had been defiled. *He raped me. The sonofabitch raped me,* the witch thought to herself, feeling angry, sad, and disgusted all at the same time. Avalina just heard a toilet flush followed by impending footsteps. Mr. Scholl approached her completely naked except for his old brown slippers.

"Well, well, well. I see that my luscious sleeping beauty has finally woken up," Mr. Scholl said to her.

"What the hell did you do to me, you sonofabitch?" Avalina weakly asked him.

"Oh, aren't *we* getting feisty, baby? Now, let me tell you something, sweetheart. You were a hell of a lot of fun, even though you were knocked out. This was the first time I got laid since my wife passed away over two years ago. Oh and don't worry about getting knocked up, sweetie. I shot my whole load all over those succulent, big tits of yours."

Avalina felt so revolted. She was going to spare this man's life, but now things had changed. Avalina was raped. She had been taken advantage of. The young witch had lost control and *that*, she did not like, not one bit. *He must pay dearly for what the hell he did to me,*

Avalina thought.

"I just want to know one thing," Avalina said to the man.

"Sure, baby…anything…anything at all," he said while licking his own lips in front of her.

"How the *hell* did you overpower me?"

"Easy, baby, my wife was a registered nurse in the town hospital down the road. She was able to bring me sedatives to help me get to sleep since I've got insomnia. I just injected you with a healthy dose. When you were out, I just stripped your sweet ass, tied you up and had fun with you," the man said with a devilish grin on his face.

"And what do you propose to do with me now?"

"Oh, I don't know. I can't very well just let you go since you could identify my ass. Maybe, I'll just keep you here as my little love doll. As a matter of fact, I can go another round. Can't you see? I'm getting horny all over again just looking at you."

Avalina noticed the man's penis was growing big and stiff. Mr. Scholl grabbed his big member with his right hand and started stroking it while he approached her. It appeared that Avalina was having a change of heart. The young witch seemed to be getting turned on by the man with his muscular build, hairy chest, and large penis. She gave him a sexy smile and started slowly licking her lips.

"Well, it looks like you really want it, don't you, baby?" Mr. Scholl said to her in a sexy voice.

"It's just that, I've never seen anything that big before in my life," Avalina replied in a sultry voice.

"I knew you'd come around and see it my way, baby. You see, I believe we *all* have a sensual basic instinct inside of us. We just need the right person to bring it the fuck out."

"And that person is you, sweetie?"

"That's right, honey. I may be sixty-five, but I'm in great shape. Can't ya tell?"

"I sure can. Why don't you just come on over here and stick it in my mouth?" Avalina said with a sexy look on her face.

"Really, do you think you can handle this shit, baby?"

"Sure I can. Come over here, honey. I want to taste you. I want to eat you all up," she said while breathing hard.

The middle-aged man got up on the bed and was on his knees, straddling her stomach. He looked into her bright blue eyes, getting hornier by the minute. David was dying to get a blowjob from her sweet lips. By now, the man had become so excited that he was dripping pre-ejaculate on her breasts.

"Come here, baby, I can't reach you from there. Come and put it in my mouth," she said while looking extremely aroused, licking her hungry lips.

David moved closer to her head and inserted his shaft into her mouth. Avalina began sucking on him, then she started humming. The young witch felt the man's member growing even bigger and harder right there in her mouth.

"Oh, shit, yeah…that really feels so damn good. Keep it up…keep it up, baby…I'm almost there," David said.

Avalina used her strength to break free from the rope ties, that restrained her hands to the bed posts. She grabbed David's ass, pulling him even closer to her head. Then, the hungry young witch sucked his penis deeper into her mouth, suppressing her gag reflex. The man was so turned on by this that he didn't even realize she was free.

"Oh, shit! Oh, shit! I'm gonna cum!" David screamed out.

Avalina pulled him in as far as she could, then the possessed young woman did the unthinkable. The witch chomped down hard on his manhood and bit it right off.

"Owww, bitch! What the…" David screamed out in pain while grabbing her hair.

Avalina pushed the man off of her and spat out his bloody penis. David Scholl was going into shock. The man was bleeding profusely all over her and his bed. His hands were holding what was left of his manhood in between his thighs. The young witch used her strength to yank her feet out of the restraints. She rolled off of the bed while blood was shooting out all over the place, from David's new wound.

"I guess we'll just have to call you 'stubby,' won't we? Look at it this way, baby, you died satisfied…well…almost anyway," Avalina said to the dying man.

David Scholl's heart finally stopped beating after running out of enough blood to pump. Avalina grabbed the man's penis that was left on the bed, took it into the bathroom and flushed it down the toilet, just like the piece of shit that he was. The young woman got into the tub and took a shower. She wanted to get all of David's blood and semen off of her body. After that, Avalina dried herself off and looked for her clothes. Avalina found all of her belongings on the green living room sofa. She got dressed and went back to the small bedroom where it all happened. The young witch gave the dead man on the bed a disgusted look.

"That'll be the last time you take advantage of a woman. Goodbye, asshole," she said to the corpse.

Avalina walked out the door and closed it using only the sleeve of her sweater. She went to her car, started it back up and drove off. Avalina noticed the time on the dashboard clock; it was already nine-thirty at night. *This didn't go the way I planned it, but at least there's one less scumbag left in the world,* Avalina thought as she drove back home. *He...he raped me...I've never been raped before in my life.* The girl kept driving and noticed that it was starting to rain. She pulled her car off the road and on to the shoulder. Avalina realized that it wasn't rain, after all. She had been crying because of what happened to her. Avalina blamed herself for letting it happen. She punched the dashboard of the car several times. The young witch sat there for a good ten minutes crying her heart out. Avalina was distraught, but most of all, the girl was disappointed and mad at herself. The young witch thought she could handle just about anything, but Avalina was wrong...dead wrong. She would never turn her back on anyone ever again.

The next morning, Avalina woke up to David Scholl's voice. Her boyfriend was calling and leaving another message on her telephone answering machine. Avalina knew he had left several messages on the home phone machine. David had also left several messages on her cellphone.

"I'd love to talk to you, baby, but there's the little matter of another David Scholl that I've got to get today," she said to the answering machine, knowing that David couldn't hear her.

The possessed young woman got home late the previous night and was very tired. All she wanted to do was go straight off to bed. Avalina leaned over in her bed to look at the clock; it was already going on ten-thirty. She got up out of bed, had breakfast and headed for Connecticut. Avalina was looking for the other David Scholl. This time, she was armed with a clipboard, paper, and a pen.

It was now one o'clock in the afternoon. Avalina had been driving for about an hour and a half. The young witch was tired; she wasn't used to driving so long. Avalina parked the car in front of the house number that was on her printout. She verified it again before getting out of the vehicle.

"Yeah, this is it alright, 615 Sycamore Road," the girl said to herself.

It was cool and overcast outside, which reflected Avalina's mood. She looked at the large brick faced ranch house and figured that *this* David Scholl, must have some money. The young witch hoped that this was the right guy and that he was home. After all, it was Sunday and people usually went out to church on Sunday. Then, it hit her: *there aren't any church services anymore, thanks to the Coronavirus pandemic,* she recalled. The possessed young woman grabbed her mask, the clipboard, and her pen. Avalina closed her car door and walked towards the front door of the house. She rang the doorbell and waited. Within seconds, the young witch heard a large dog barking.

"Shit, now I've got to be on the lookout for a fricking dog," she said to herself.

"Who is it?!" a man yelled out from behind the door.

"Hello, I'm looking for a Mr. David Scholl?!"

"Hold on a minute, let me lock up ma dog."

Avalina waited by the door with her clipboard. She noticed a playground a few blocks away that was in dire need of repair. The witch was going to use that as her excuse for the phony petition. After a couple of minutes of waiting, the man had returned and opened up the front door.

"Oh, hello, you must be one of them Census folks, come on in. My, you sure are a pretty one, aren't you?" the middle-aged man said as he led her into the kitchen.

"Why, thank you, Mr. Scholl…you are Mr. Scholl, right?" Avalina asked him.

"Yup, that's me. Come on in and sit fer a spell, won't you?" Mr. Scholl said while pulling the chair out for her to sit down.

Avalina noticed that the man was very trusting and friendly. She remembered something about a Census form that came in the mail, but Avalina threw it out. *If he thinks I'm here for that, then fine,* she thought while sitting down at the kitchen table with the man. Mr. Scholl didn't look anything at all like the David Scholl she had remembered back in high school. The man was shorter than her and stocky. He had a cowboy hat on, but the possessed young woman suspected the man was bald.

"So, tell me something, Mr. Scholl, have you ever been in New York, especially as a kid?" Avalina asked him.

"I don't recall I have. As far as I can remember, I was born and raised right here in Connecticut," Mr. Scholl replied.

"Then, you've never heard of a town called, 'Merryville' in New York?"

"No ma'am. Me and ma wife have been living here for over forty years now. She's visiting her sister right now, but she'll be back tonight."

"So, it's just you and your wife living here, right?"

"Yeah, that's about right, Miss. Ma wife is barren; we never could have any kids, so we just keep a dog. It helps..." David solemnly said.

"Ok, Mr. Scholl, thank you for your time."

Mr. Scholl offered her some coffee and cookies, but Avalina refused. She followed the man out to the front door, never once turning her back on him, especially after the previous ordeal she had with the other David Scholl yesterday. Avalina was disappointed again, but at least the girl wasn't attacked this time. *This guy was a true gentleman; he even pulled out the chair for me to sit down in,* she thought. The witch thought the guy had reminded her of the actor, Dan Blocker, the one who played Hoss Cartwright on that western television show, *Bonanza*.

Avalina got back in her car and drove back home. *Another damn wasted trip and a waste of money. I spent $29.99 on that stupid ass computer for nothing,* she thought to herself. The young witch wondered if she would ever find the *real* David Scholl, the one that had tried to burn her alive with his hoodlum friends, fifty-one years ago. Avalina didn't want to kill any innocent people unless they got into her way.

17

THE INTRUDER

Avalina was sleeping soundly in her bed, until she heard a noise in the middle of the night. The possessed woman noticed that the moon was very bright and full, as it shone through her windows. Avalina turned to look at the alarm clock, but she still had to strain a bit to read the dial on the clock. It was three-thirty. Avalina thought that she was hearing things, so the young witch rolled back over in her bed. A few seconds later, the noise came back again. Avalina was startled; she knew it wasn't her imagination this time. *Mother? It can't be you again, could it?* the possessed young woman wondered. Avalina was sure that the Prince of Darkness took care of her mother for her, and yet, there was that noise again. It sounded like it was coming from downstairs, but the witch was so darn tired. She was warm and cozy under the blanket. *Maybe it'll go away,* the young witch thought. She tried to go back to sleep, but then there was a much louder noise this time. It sounded like a crash, as though someone had knocked something down and broken it.

"Someone's in the house. Man, I don't need this shit," Avalina softly said to herself.

She wondered where the flashlight was. Avalina knew there were no weapons in the house, except for the kitchen knives, which were all the way downstairs. She could see herself now going downstairs to the intruder and asking, *excuse me, sir, can I please get a knife from the drawer to defend myself?* No, that wouldn't work at all. The sorceress would have to resort to what little witchcraft she had. Avalina had learned that her powers were useless when she was taken by surprise and that, it only worked on one person at a time. Also, the girl had noticed that she had to be calm or angry for it to work, not scared as she was right now. The possessed young woman remembered one other thing, too; she would be absolutely powerless when injected with any kind of drugs. The noise started back up again. It sounded like there was someone downstairs looking for something.

"I think it's a burglar," she quietly said to herself.

The young witch stayed in bed debating on what to do. There was no phone in the bedroom and her cellphone was in her bag downstairs. *I wish David was here*, the nervous sorceress thought. The footsteps sounded as if they were getting closer. Whoever was downstairs was slowly approaching the staircase. Avalina looked at the open doorway in the bedroom; she could see what appeared to be the flickering of a flashlight in the hallway. The footsteps were getting louder and closer. Then, it sounded like the intruder was starting to climb up the steps. Avalina was shaking in the bed with fear. The sorceress covered herself completely up with the blanket, wishing she had closed and locked her bedroom door. The young witch hoped that the prowler would turn around and leave.

The intruder slowly climbed up the steps and walked over towards Avalina's bedroom. Suddenly, the footsteps stopped right outside of her doorway. Avalina's vessel had a strong urge to urinate, but she held it in with all of her might. The footsteps started up again; this time, the intruder walked down the hall. Avalina heard a toilet flush. *Shit, he's using my bathroom...of all the nerve!* she angrily thought to herself. After a moment of silence, the footsteps started back up again. The prowler decided to go back down the stairs again. The witch was relieved. *I hope he's leaving*, she thought. After a few more footsteps, Avalina heard the best sound ever: the sound of the front door opening back up and closing shut again.

"Yay, he's gone," she quietly said to herself with great relief.

The young witch decided to go relieve herself in the bathroom, but she didn't want to use the one upstairs, not after that stranger just used it. Avalina put on her white nightgown and slippers; then, she went down the stairs. The girl locked the front door, then she went to the downstairs bathroom to relieve her bladder. *I must have forgotten to lock the front door when I came home yesterday,* she thought while sitting on the toilet bowl. The young witch flushed the toilet and washed her hands. Avalina was relieved that the burglar had left. She didn't put on any lights, because it would have made it harder for her to fall back to sleep. The young woman carefully walked around the mess that the invader left. She felt her way around towards the staircase, until someone suddenly grabbed her from behind and put her in a choke-hold.

"Don't move, bitch, I've got a gun pointin' right in yo back," the intruder stated in a low, gruff voice.

"I won't…I promise," Avalina barely said while struggling to breath.

Avalina felt something sticking her in the back. *Oh, shit, he really does have a gun at my back,* the nervous young witch thought. She realized of course that the man never left the house; it was a trick, and now, the young enchantress had locked herself inside with this criminal.

"What do you want from me?" Avalina asked.

"Let's go in the kitchen, bitch. I've got plans for you," the intruder replied.

"I don't have much money, but you're welcome to anything here. Please, don't hurt me!" Avalina begged him.

"I'm glad you feel that way, bitch, but I didn't come here for any money."

"Wha-well, what did you come here for?" Avalina nervously asked him.

"I came here for *you, bitch*! Now, keep it moving, sister."

The man ushered the woman right into the kitchen, using the moonlight that was coming in through the windows as guidance. He didn't want to put on any lights, either. The home invader never released his grip on the young woman while they walked into the room. The prowler kicked out one of the kitchen chairs from under the table.

"Now, sit yo ass down, bitch," he said in a nasty tone while pushing her down into the chair.

Avalina looked up at the man, trying to get a good look at him with the moonlight that was coming in from the windows. The intruder towered over her. He was a big, burly man. The prowler was wearing a black full face mask, a black cap, black leather jacket, black jeans, and black leather gloves. The young witch had no idea who the hell he was. More importantly, Avalina didn't know what the man wanted from her. She was still breathing heavily while sitting in her chair. In fact, the young witch noticed that the man was watching her breasts move up and down with every breath she took in.

"Are you going to rape me?" Avalina asked him, hoping he would say 'no.'

"Shit, now what the hell would I want with a skinny ass white bitch like you? I've got to have me a woman with some meat on her bones," the intruder replied.

"Well, if you don't want my money and you don't want me, then, what *do* you want?" she nervously asked him.

"Oh, I want yo ass alright, but not in the way *you* think I do," he said while waving the gun in her face.

"You're gonna kill me…aren't you?"

"Bingo, you just won the double jeopardy question of the day."

"Wh-why? What did I ever do to you? I just offered you

everything I could think off."

"Do the name Laverne Williams mean anything to you?"

"No, I'm sorry, it doesn't."

"Alright, then. Let's be clear, *bitch*, Nurse Laverne Williams, the nurse who worked in the City Medical Center as a head nurse up on the second floor! Do it ring a bell now?"

"Yes, it does."

"I bet it do. What the *fuck* did you do to her?"

"I-I didn't do anything to-"

"The hell you didn't, bitch! I was there! You tore her ass up!"

"I don't know what you're talking-"

"Excuse me, did I just hear you say you didn't know what I was talking about? Now, let me tell *you* something, bitch. I walked right past your ass in the hospital hallway. I saw you when you came out the room she was in. Now, I know why you had your damn coat turned inside out. You must have had her blood all over yo ass, *didn't you?*"

"I-I don't know-"

"I was just going there to take ma woman out to lunch. I was going there to try and win her ass back. I loved her, but I messed up by cheatin' on her. When I saw what she looked like, I turned around and followed your ass. I followed you out to the parking lot. You lucky I didn't have ma ride with me. I saw you get in your car and I got your plate number. I could have told the police, but I wanted to handle this shit myself. She was the mother of my two kids, the love of ma life. Now, you've taken all that shit away from me. You took ma two little boys' mama away from them. So tell me somethin'. Give me one good reason why I should spare your scrawny ass right now? Tell me, bitch!" the man screamed with a cry in his voice.

Avalina didn't know what to say. Clearly, the man had the goods on her. There was nothing she could do or say that would persuade him in her favor. The young witch felt really bad. Avalina didn't intend to kill the nurse; she just got in her way.

"I-I'm so-so sorry, Mister...I didn't mean it," Avalina breathlessly said.

The young sorceress held her head down in shame while crying. She knew she'd broken up a family. Avalina took the two young boys' mother away from them and now, she was going to have to pay the ultimate price. Avalina wasn't going to fight it either. The young witch didn't want to die all over again, especially now that she had David Scholl to look forward to, but Avalina knew she was wrong...dead wrong. Avalina just wanted revenge for all the ones that did her wrong; she really didn't want to kill any innocent people.

"I won't fight you, you're absolutely right, I screwed up. I'm so sorry about your wife. I really didn't mean to kill her," she said sobbing.

"I can't believe I'm hearin' this shit. You actually feel sorry fo killin' ma woman? Why, then? What the *hell* did she do to yo ass?" the man asked her in disbelief.

"She-she wouldn't let me leave. I came there for someone else, but she wouldn't let me go. I was defending myself, that's all," the witch said in despair.

"Defendin' yourself? Is *that* what you called that? You a monster, there ain't no gettin' 'round that. You just a damn ass monster, and now, *my ass* is all alone. Ma sons got grandma since I can't take care of them. I got to work, but I-I ain't got no one. Ya see, we was never married, but after bein' with her on and off for over five years, I finally realized she the one fo' me. I wanted to marry her, but after what happened…" the man trailed off and he, too, started crying.

She knew this man was going to kill her; it was just a matter of time. The young witch extended a comforting hand to the man standing right in front of her, holding a gun.

"Don't you touch me, bitch!" he exclaimed while recoiling from her.

"I'm sorry, I just don't want to see anyone cry," she timidly replied.

"You think you could just talk yo ass outta this shit?!"

"No…no…I just wanted to-"

"Comfort me? You know what? I had enough of this shit! It's time to kill yo ass!" the man said as he cocked his gun and pointed it at her face again.

"Wait! I have one last request before you shoot me," she said to him.

"I suppose I could do that…dependin' on what it is. What do you want…a last cigarette or some shit?"

"No, it's nothing like that."

"Then, what already? I'm-a runnin' outta patience wit yo ass already!"

"It's just…well…I'd like to see your face."

"Ma face? What the hell you need to see ma face fo?"

"I want to see the face of the man that's going to kill me."

"Yeah, alright."

The intruder took off his face mask and hat. Avalina stared up at the man and looked into his eyes. The young witch knew that there was no way in hell, that she could change the mind of this, angry and heartbroken African-American man.

"You have such kind eyes; I can see the hurt inside of them. I wish I could just take away your pain and sorrow. I wish I could take back what I've done to you and your family. I'm really very, truly sorry. I didn't mean it…I swear," Avalina sincerely said to him.

The man looked at her and knew that she was really sincere. He knew that killing this young woman could never ever bring back his beloved Laverne Williams, nothing could. Laverne was gone. He stared at the girl sitting there in the chair, looking so helpless. It was hard for him to believe that this seemingly innocent young woman, could be capable of such a horrific act of violence. Then, the man thought about his own life and how he cheated on the one woman, that loved him with all of her heart, the mother of his two sons. His life would never be the same again.

He was going to ask her for her forgiveness, and then propose to her after all this time. Dwayne Worley pulled out the engagement ring from his right jacket pocket and looked at it. He bought the ring for Laverne with his credit card. Dwayne had planned on asking for Laverne's hand in marriage the day she was killed by Avalina. Dwayne marveled at how the diamond sparkled in the moonlight, then the tears started flowing from his eyes. Dwayne Worley quickly pointed the gun to his right temple and pulled the trigger. He collapsed and died right in front of Avalina while she screamed uncontrollably. The young witch was hysterical. She got up out of the chair still screaming and heaving. Avalina went over to the toilet bowl, crouched down, and vomited.

A little while later, after she had calmed down, Avalina started to call the police on the kitchen phone, then she quickly hung the phone back up on the wall.

"What the hell am I doing?" she asked herself.

Avalina knew there was no way to explain this scenario to the police. *How could I explain to them the reason why this man came here to kill me, and that he decided to kill himself, instead,* she thought while thinking of a solution. Avalina looked at the dead body on the floor. Blood had been pouring out of the gunshot wound in his head and onto the white tiled kitchen floor.

"I'm really sorry for your loss and thank you for letting me live," she said to the body.

Avalina wondered what she was going to do with him.

"How did you get here?" Avalina asked the dead man, as if he could answer her.

He must have a car outside, she thought. The young witch went over to the family room and turned on the outside light. She looked out the window facing the driveway and noticed that a big black SUV was parked there. *It must be his favorite color,* she thought; then, it hit her.

"Shit! I don't just have to get rid of him; I've got to get rid of his truck, too," Avalina voiced to herself.

The young witch knew the best place to take him; it was where she had taken Anna Nuñez and John Waters after she killed them: Pond Lake. Avalina tied up her long hair into a bun and put on the blue rubber gloves, that were on the kitchen counter near the sink. She took the gun from the hand of the dead man and cleaned it off. *This could come in handy around here. A girl needs some protection, you know,* she thought. The young witch placed the gun in the back of a silverware drawer. Avalina grabbed a big black garbage bag from the box, placed it over the deceased man's head and tied it around his neck. She wanted to prevent any more blood from leaking out all over the place.

Avalina put on a dark blue jacket, a blue baseball cap and some comfortable sneakers. She dragged the body out through the back sliding door to the patio. Avalina slowly, but steadily, dragged him down the stairs, struggling with each and every step, until she reached the driveway. The witch opened the passenger door of the man's SUV and propped the body up against the seat. She went around towards the driver's seat and got in. Then, the possessed young woman grabbed his underarms. She summoned up all of her strength and power. Avalina pulled the man up into the passenger seat of his own vehicle. The young witch took the keys from his jacket pocket, inserted it into the ignition and started up the engine. She got back out to close the passenger door. The girl looked around to make sure no one was watching her. Avalina got back into the SUV and slowly drove off with no lights on, until she got away from her neighborhood. The young witch was driving very cautiously since she wasn't familiar with the vehicle, especially one that large. The sorceress noticed that it was starting to get light outside; she would have to hurry. Avalina took a turn a little too fast, then the corpse fell over onto her lap.

"Oh, shit! Get the hell off of me!" she yelled in horror.

Avalina finally arrived at Pond Lake at about five-twenty in the morning. She turned off the vehicle and put it in neutral. The young witch used all of her strength and whatever power she had, to push the vehicle down into the lake. Avalina stayed there and watched it sink, then she started walking back home. Pond Lake was over four miles away from her home. The witch knew it was going to be a long hike back to the house, especially since most of it was uphill.

*
**

It wasn't until seven o'clock in the morning when Avalina finally got back home. She was cold and tired. Her feet were killing her, even though she had on comfortable sneakers. The young witch just wanted to go back to sleep, but there was work to be done...cleanup work. She took off all of her clothes and put them in the laundry basket. Avalina kept her blue rubber gloves on and went over to the kitchen cabinet. She took out the bleach, then Avalina opened up the kitchen window all the way to vent the fumes. The possessed young woman got down on her hands and knees and scrubbed the floors, cleaning up all of the spilled blood from the intruder. She picked up the man's hat and mask from the floor and threw it into the garbage bag, along with her blue rubber gloves. Avalina found the small diamond engagement ring the invader was holding in his hand. She remembered that there was a pawn shop in the town. *I could get some money for this rock,* the girl thought to herself. Avalina decided to put it into one of the kitchen drawers for now.

The young witch took the garbage bag out towards the back door again. She looked outside to make sure that no one was around, then the young witch opened up the green garbage can, tossed the trash bag in and closed the lid. She went back upstairs to the bathroom and looked at herself in the mirror. *Man, I look like a mess,* she thought to herself. Avalina got in the bathtub and took a nice hot shower, reliving everything that had just happened to her. It was almost nine o'clock when she got out of the bathroom. The young woman knew it was almost time to work, but she was tired and needed some sleep. *I'll start work later,* she thought. The young witch went straight off to her bed and under the covers. Avalina instantly fell back asleep.

18

ONE LAST TRY

On Wednesday morning, April 29th, Detective Wiretrak had just received a call about another missing person. A woman claimed that she hadn't seen her son in over two days. The woman also mentioned that she had been taking care of his children, since their mother had just been murdered. Wiretrak had just hung up the phone when Chief Valentine walked right in.

"Hey, Mike, I need for you to go down to the coffee shop, pick me up a regular coffee and a buttered bagel. Here's ten bucks; that should cover it," the chief said.

"Well, wait a minute chief; you didn't even say 'good morning' to me. You just barged in here and asked me to get you coffee, while I had something very important to tell you," Wiretrak replied.

"Yeah, you're right, what is it Mike?"

"Well, it seems we got another one, chief," the detective stated.

"Another what?" the chief asked.

"Another missing person, that's what."

"You're kidding, right?"

"No, I'm not, chief. Some woman just called me up and said that she hadn't seen her son in over two days."

"Did you get a description?"

"Yes, I did."

"Well…out with it already!"

"Eh, you still didn't say 'good morning.' I mean you could at least offer to buy *me* coffee-"

"Mike!"

"Yes of course chief, the description."

"Please!"

"Ok, chief, we have a thirty-year-old African-American male that goes by the name of 'Dwayne Worley.' His height is six-feet-five inches and weighs in at about two hundred and fifty-five pounds."

"Wow, he's a big guy, alright. He should be able to defend himself."

"His mother didn't think so at all. She said he's been so distraught and unstable ever since his girlfriend was murdered...and get this, chief..."

"What, Mike?"

"You'll never guess who his girlfriend was."

"I'm afraid to ask."

"Well, I gonna tell you anyway: Nurse Laverne Williams. Remember her?"

"How could I forget? You were supposed to interview her with the police artist, until we found out that she was brutally murdered."

"Eh, I have a theory about this, chief."

"What is it, Mike?"

"Well, just suppose that Mr. Dwayne Worley is at the bottom of Pond Lake, too."

"That would be too easy, but you know what? It's possible. I want every man out at Pond Lake searching for him, pronto."

"You got it, chief. By the way, chief…"

"Yes Mike, what is it now?"

"What about a coffee and a bagel for me too?"

"Mike!"

"Yes chief, I'm on it."

Detective Wiretrak went and notified several police officers to go out and search Pond Lake, for Dwayne Worley's body. The detective had a hunch that Dwayne Worley was dead and that he was probably murdered, by the red-headed female killer. After that, Wiretrak went out to get the chief his coffee and bagel, knowing he would have to pay for his own breakfast.

A few miles away, Avalina and David had just finished a very steamy sexual encounter in her bedroom. The hot young witch wore him out so much, that he immediately fell asleep after his climax. David had struggled to keep up with her, thinking that she was like a tiger on steroids, but he enjoyed every minute of pleasing her.

Avalina gently got up out of bed without disturbing David. She needed to relieve herself in the bathroom. Suddenly, the young witch saw a very familiar figure again standing there in the corner of the room, with glowing eyes. The Prince of Darkness had been watching her all along. This made Avalina furious.

"Where the *hell* were you when I needed you? I almost got shot!" she yelled at the black figure.

The evil spirit raised its arms in anger, sending Avalina flying back into her bed with a crack of lightning. She looked back up and found that the creature had disappeared from the room. David Scholl was startled out of his sleep with all the noise.

"Ha-honey, what just happened?" David groggily asked her.

"Nothing, dear, absolutely nothing," she replied.

"But I thought I just saw something and there was this-"

"You were probably just having a bad dream, that's all. Why don't you just go back to sleep, honey?"

Avalina gave him a quick kiss; then, she went off to the bathroom. The young witch was thinking while she was on the bowl. *Was this some sort of a warning or a test?* Avalina wondered what the prince wanted from her. This was the second time he had appeared to her, other than the time she had summoned him for help. *It's always in my bedroom after having sex with David. What could he possibly want from me?* Avalina wondered. She flushed the toilet, washed her hands, and went back to sleep with her lover.

*
**

Over at Pond Lake, search crews, led by Detective Wiretrak, were out looking for the body of Dwayne Worley. The detective had a hunch that Worley's body was down at the bottom of that lake. Officer Radcliff made a discovery.

"Hey, Wiretrak, I just found something," Officer Radcliff stated.

"Yeah, what did you find?" Detective Wiretrak asked him.

"We've got some tire tracks over here leading right into the lake, sir."

"Tire tracks?"

"Yes, sir, come here and check it out!'"

The detective followed the officer over towards the edge of the lake. Wiretrak noticed that the officer was correct; there was a set of tire tracks that led directly into the lake. Wiretrak also noticed that there was a set of footsteps near the tire tracks. The detective took out his smartphone and started taking pictures, then he let forensics do the rest. After careful examination from the forensics crew, one of them discovered a small patch of oil floating on top of the water.

"Hey, Wiretrak! There's some oil over here!" Hans Wilfred from forensics shouted.

Detective Michael Wiretrak looked at the oil patch and knew deep down in his gut what it was. He got on his radio and called the dispatcher. Wiretrak wanted a tow truck with a winch sent over, pronto.

An hour later, after divers had gone down to hook up the submerged vehicle, the tow truck was hoisting up Dwayne Worley's black SUV under the direction of Detective Wiretrak. Officer James, the youngest cop there, was the first to see the vehicle and Worley's remains rise up.

"Wiretrak, here it comes!" Officer James shouted.

"I've got a bad feeling about this," Wiretrak stated.

"I take it you don't think it was an accident or a suicide, do you?"

"We'll know soon enough, won't we, James?"

The detective went over towards the vehicle with the officer. One of the men opened up the driver's side door on the vehicle. As more water poured out of the SUV, Wiretrak and Officer

James saw a body slumped across the two front seats of the vehicle.

"You still think it was an accident or a suicide?" Detective Wiretrak asked while taking pictures of the victim.

"I guess not," Officer James replied.

"Why would someone put a bag over his head, then push him and his vehicle into the lake? It seems like overkill to me. Go ahead; take that bag off of his head!"

The officer carefully cut the black plastic garbage bag off of the victim's head. Wiretrak took some more pictures. Hans Wilfred from forensics looked at the body and shook his head in sorrow.

"Is that our man, detective?" Hans asked.

"He certainly fits the description," Wiretrak replied.

Detective Wiretrak called Chief Charles Valentine on his smartphone. The detective told the chief what they found. Wiretrak also mentioned the footprints that he found near the tire tracks. *The lake is becoming a dumping ground for murderers,* Valentine stated over the phone.

The next morning, the possessed young woman woke up alone. David had gone back home yesterday afternoon to take care of his clients. Avalina decided to take a personal day off from work today. She had decided to try, for the umpteenth time, to fulfill her quest in her search for the *real* David Scholl. Avalina had planned to give it one last try. The girl was quite upset. She had spent almost thirty dollars, money that Avalina couldn't really spare, for that computerized people-finder website, which had given her poor results. The possessed young woman had made up her mind. If she couldn't find her David Scholl after today, Avalina was definitely going to call it quits.

The young witch got out of her bed and went on over to the computer room. She turned on the machine and let it warm up. Avalina went downstairs, turned on the coffee pot and started to pour herself some cereal into a bowl. She wondered where that crazy machine upstairs was going to send her to next.

Avalina finished her breakfast and was getting dressed. She decided to wear a loose-fitting pink blouse and a pair of blue jeans. The young witch didn't want to wear anything sexy, or too revealing, especially after what had happened to her last time. She put on a light brown jacket and was back on the road again. The computer had kicked out two more David Scholl's: one in Long Island and one in Brooklyn, New York.

"At least, they're both in the same state this time," the young witch said to herself in a consoling tone.

Avalina was going to the closest one first: The David Scholl in Brooklyn.

After about an hour of driving, Avalina had arrived in Brooklyn, New York. She was happy that the weather had held up; it was a nice, cool sunny day. *Gee, it sure is a nice change from all of the rain that we've had lately,* the possessed young woman thought. Avalina looked for the old apartment house that was on her printout.

"That's it, 615 Herriot Street," she said to herself.

Avalina parked her car across the street from the tenement. She walked towards the building while putting on her mask. Avalina didn't care for the seedy neighborhood. *Ghetto, that's for sure,* the possessed young woman thought. Avalina was lucky the lobby door was open. She pressed the button for the elevator and waited. When it arrived, the young witch got on and pressed the button for the sixth floor.

Upon arriving at the top floor, Avalina noticed that the apartment number on her printout was listed as 6I. She walked down the hallway searching for the right apartment. The witch was hoping that this would be the end of her quest.

"This is it, apartment 6I," she said while ringing the doorbell button.

"Who is it?!" the man behind the apartment door shouted.

"Hello, I'm looking for David Scholl?!" Avalina asked.

The man inside looked at her through the peephole. After about a minute, the man in the apartment started unlocking the door. Avalina was nervous, especially after what happened with the other David Scholl. The young witch had no idea what this man looked like, since there wasn't a picture available for him online. Finally, David Scholl had opened up his door to her.

"Mmm-mmm and who might you be, Miss Fine?" David had asked her.

"You-you can't be David Scholl," Avalina timidly stated.

"Oh, but I is. Come on in, sugar; you just what the doctor ordered, a red hot red-head."

The young witch just stared at the middle-aged African-American male and knew in an instant, that she had the wrong David Scholl. Avalina felt the man's eyes slowly undressing her, making her feel very uncomfortable. She knew it was time to leave.

"I'm sorry, I obviously got the wrong apartment," she shyly said.

"No, you don't, mama. Come on in here," David said while grabbing her left arm.

"Let go of me! You're hurting me!" Avalina cried out.

This time, Avalina took control of the situation. She was *not* scared. The young witch was fuming. Avalina, using the very same arm that David was grabbing on to, flung the man all the way back into his apartment so hard, that he smacked right into the opposite wall about ten feet away. David Scholl was unconscious as he slid down the wall to the floor. Avalina pulled his apartment door closed, recomposed herself and took the elevator back down to the street level.

*
**

Avalina walked out on the street watching some kids playing on the street corner. The young witch found it really strange that they weren't practicing social distancing, given the fact that the COVID-19 pandemic was still going on. Avalina began frantically looking everywhere for her car.

"I know I parked it across the street from this building. Where the hell is it?" Avalina asked herself.

The young witch walked down the block and around the corner. After a while, she realized that her car was gone.

"Shit, it's gone! My car is gone! I can't believe it!" she angrily yelled out on the street.

Avalina was devastated; she wondered how she was going to get home. *I know it was an old car, but it was all I had. How am I going to get back home?* Avalina mentally asked herself. She thought about calling the police, but Avalina didn't want to draw any more police attention, since they already suspected her of murder. *I know what I'll do...I'll call David...my David,* she happily thought to herself.

Avalina looked in her bag for her cellphone, an old flip

231

phone. She remembered David making fun of her about it. *You really need to get a smartphone, baby, it's the new millennium. Those things are outdated,* he had told her. Avalina didn't even know what a smartphone was until she saw his. The young witch was still amazed at having a pocket-sized wireless phone. Avalina finally found the phone at the bottom of her bag. She called David up and got his voicemail. Avalina began to cry while leaving a message for her boyfriend.

The possessed young woman decided to take another walk around the block, when she heard a car crash. Avalina tried to follow where the sound came from. After walking for about two blocks, she came across her car, which was smashed into another car at an intersection. Avalina hurried over towards the vehicle. Both her car and the other car were destroyed. The man in the other car was hurt and unconscious. A young African-American woman came over to her.

"Did you see that shit? Those two young kids was driving all over the street like they was high. They cut his ass off at the light. I saw the whole damn thing," the woman told Avalina.

Avalina looked in her car and saw one African-American kid at the wheel. The youth was either dead or unconscious; she didn't know or care. All Avalina knew was that she was inconvenienced.

"My car! It's ruined!" Avalina said.

"Oh, shit! That was your car, Miss? They stole your ride?" the woman asked her.

"Yes, it was. Now I got no way to get back home. Shit! I thought you said there were two kids."

"There was, one of them got away."

Avalina looked at the wreck as smoke was billowing out

from under the crumpled-up hood. She heard the sound of a siren; the police were coming. The young witch thought about running away, but she knew they would find her with the license plate numbers on the car. Avalina also knew that it would seem suspicious to them if she ran away. The woman next to her was a witness and she was thankful for that. The blue and white patrol car had pulled over towards the two wrecked vehicles. A young African-American police officer got out of his vehicle to investigate the situation. The officer checked out the middle-aged man in the red four-door sedan, since he was finally conscious and calling for help. After getting information from the other vehicle's driver, the officer came over to check on Avalina's car. Officer Jerome White checked on the youth that was behind the wheel of the old black Ford, the four-door sedan that was registered to Joan Sanders. Officer White shook his head and looked at Avalina.

"Did you see what happened here, Miss?" Officer White asked her.

"No, but this lady did…" Avalina said while pointing to where the woman was just standing.

"What lady?"

"She was here just a moment ago, a young black woman."

"Sure, she was."

"Well, she was. Anyway, that boy stole my car, officer, you should arrest him."

"That's your car, Miss?"

"Yes, arrest him!"

"That *boy*, as you called him, won't be giving you any more trouble. He appears to be dead."

"Oh, I'm sorry. I didn't know."

"License and registration, Miss."

Avalina went into her purse and searched for her host's credentials. She gave the officer Joan's insurance card, her driver's license, and the registration for the vehicle. Officer White called for an ambulance on his radio for the two victims, plus two tow trucks for the damaged vehicles.

"Here you go, Miss. Here's the number for the police station. Call them in three days and they'll have an accident report for you. My name is on there, too," Officer White stated as he gave Avalina the paper.

"But how will I get home?" Avalina asked with a cry in her voice.

"Would you like for me to call you a cab, Miss?"

"I live all the way upstate; I don't have enough money for that."

"I can't help you there, lady. Take the train."

Officer White waited for the ambulance to arrive and then he left. Avalina started to cry, wondering how she was going to get back home. Suddenly, her cellphone started ringing. David was returning her call. Avalina was overjoyed to hear her lover's voice over the phone. The young witch begged David for a ride back home. Avalina told her boyfriend that she would explain everything when he got there. David couldn't understand why Avalina went all the way down to the city in the first place, but he said that he should be there in about an hour or so. *I'll program my GPS for the shortest route,* David told her. Avalina felt somewhat relieved.

It was about four o'clock in the afternoon. Avalina had been waiting close to two hours for David Scholl to arrive from New Jersey. She was just about ready to give up hope until the young witch saw David's car pull up around the corner.

"Joan, come on!" David yelled out of the car window.

"I'm comin', baby!" Avalina yelled as she ran to his car.

"Honey, what the hell are you doing in such a sleazy ass neighborhood as this?"

Avalina jumped in his car and hugged him as tight as she could. David was still waiting for an answer. The young witch started to think up a good lie, one that wouldn't be so far-fetched.

"Believe it or not, my boss has a client here that I had to go check on," Avalina replied.

"A client? Here in this poor ass neighborhood?" David asked her.

"Yes, he knows that the man can't really afford him, so he's doing him a favor and representing him."

"Well, what did the guy do?"

"Um…it was a hit-and-run car accident. That's all I can tell you. Can we please leave now?"

"Sure, honey, let's go."

David drove them down the streets and took the ramp onto the highway. They were both heading northbound towards upstate to Joan's home in Brighten, New York. The possessed young woman explained to her boyfriend that her car may be totaled, leaving her with no transportation. Avalina also told David that she didn't have any money to buy a new car, but she needed one to get around. *We'll cross that bridge when we come to it*, David told her.

The next morning, Detective Wiretrak was back in his office

going over his notes. The case was driving him crazy. Wiretrak was happy it was Friday. *A new day in a new month; maybe, things will be better in May,* he thought. The young detective was convinced that all of the murders were tied in together to the same killer: a woman or women with long red hair and blue eyes.

A few miles away, Avalina had woken up next to her young lover. David Scholl had stayed the night again. Avalina got up to relieve herself in the bathroom. The young witch realized that aside from David, she was not alone. In a dark corner of her room, the Prince of Darkness was once again watching her and David. Avalina noticed The Dark One, but she didn't say anything. Avalina didn't want to wake up David, but she knew there was something peculiar about this spirit. *There must be a reason why it's always here when David comes over,* she thought while going to the bathroom.

Later, in the early afternoon, Avalina got a call from "Joey's Garage" in Brooklyn. The mechanic on the phone said that her auto insurance company was going to total the car. Due to the age and mileage of the vehicle, it wasn't worth repairing. Avalina, posing as her host, Joan Sanders, called the insurance company and found out that the book value on her old car was only going to be five hundred dollars.

"I'm ruined! Where am I going to find a car for a measly five hundred dollars?" Avalina asked herself.

"Did you say something, hon?" David asked her while he was coming out of the shower.

"The insurance company is totaling my car and they're only giving me five hundred measly dollars for it. I know that car was worth more than that. Where am I going to get a car for only five hundred dollars?" Avalina said with tears in her eyes.

"Oh, baby, don't worry. I've got a good friend that owns a used car dealership out in New Jersey. I'll just give him a call; I'm sure he can hook you up with a good car if I ask him to."

Avalina looked at David with loving eyes. She gave him a hug while he stood there naked in front of the bathroom doorway. The young witch felt his member growing right through her white night gown as they hugged. Avalina knew she was going to have to do something about that.

The next day, as promised, David had taken Joan over to his friend's auto dealership in New Jersey. The possessed young woman settled on an eight-year-old white, Chevrolet four-door sedan. The car had 95,000 miles on it, but it was in good shape. The only problem was that it cost her nine hundred dollars, which was four hundred dollars over her budget.

"I can lend you some money, babe. Pay me whenever," David told her.

"Oh, you're a doll. I don't know what I would do without you," Avalina told him with loving eyes.

The two of them walked into the salesman's office so that Avalina could sign the papers. Avalina almost made the mistake of putting her own name down on the forms, instead of her host, Joan Sanders. David gave her a check for five hundred dollars. Avalina tried to put the rest on her credit card, but it was declined. David wrote another check out, essentially paying for the whole car. The two of them drove back to her place in separate cars; the young witch had followed David in her new used car.

After they arrived at Joan's home, the possessed young woman unlocked the front door and the two of them walked inside her home. Avalina went into the kitchen with David and turned on the radio to an oldies station.

"Oh, shit! That's my jam, man! The Temptations, 'My Girl!'" David exclaimed.

"You know that song?" Avalina asked with a curious look on her face.

"Hell yeah! It's my favorite song," he said while singing along with the song.

"That came out *way before* you were even born, boy," Avalina said with a shocked look on her face.

"Come on, let's dance, Joan."

David grabbed his girl and started dancing with her in the kitchen. Avalina smiled and put her arms around him. The two of them were happy twirling around the floor to the song. They really made a cute couple. Avalina listened to David sing every word of the song in her ear as they danced.

Avalina woke up Sunday morning with a mission on her mind. She was going to go to Long Island to look for the last David Scholl on the computer printout. Avalina would have taken care of it yesterday, but she had to wait for her boyfriend to leave. It was nice out, a real nice day for a drive, too nice for a kill, but it had to get done. Avalina put on her loose-fitting pink blouse again and a pair of blue jeans. She got into her new old car, armed with the printout and the directions. The young witch headed south on the Long Island Expressway.

After driving for nearly an hour, Avalina finally arrived at her destination: Bethel, Long Island. She drove off the exit ramp and went on to Beach Way Road. The girl cautiously drove to the house that was on the computer printout: number 41. Avalina parked her car across the street from the house. She put on her face mask, straightened her hair a bit and walked out of the car, while turning around every few feet to make sure that her car was in a safe spot. She wasn't taking any chances with her car this time. There was one real neat feature about this car that the other one didn't have: an alarm system. Avalina made sure she set the alarm before leaving the vehicle. The possessed young woman walked across the street towards the target house. This time, she brought a gun with her, the one she obtained from the recent intruder in her home. The young woman stood in front of the old ranch house and rang the bell.

"Who is it?!" a male voice from inside yelled out.

"Hello, I'm looking for David Scholl!" Avalina replied, hoping she had found the right man this time.

The man from inside the house was staring at the raving beauty from the sidelight window. David wondered what this beautiful woman wanted from him. *Man, she's drop-dead gorgeous; I've got to let her in,* he thought. David opened up his front door and stared at her some more.

"I'm David Scholl, what can I do for you?" he said with a smile.

"Hello, my name is Joan Sanders. I'm putting together a high school reunion and I wondered if you would be interested in participating," Avalina replied.

"Sure, be glad to!"

"I just wanted to make sure I have the right 'David.' Which high school did you attend in 1969?"

"That's easy, Merryville High School."

Avalina was ecstatic. She couldn't believe that after all this time and all of this work searching for David Scholl, she finally found him. The computer finally kicked out a winner, even though the middle-aged man, didn't look anything like the David Scholl she remembered from high school. Avalina shrugged it off, thinking that everyone changes as they age. This David was completely bald with a grey beard, grey mustache, and a pot-belly. The man was about her height, wearing a torn, white t-shirt and an old worn-out pair of blue denim jeans. The young witch smiled from ear to ear, then she took out her clipboard from her bag. What David didn't know was that the clipboard was just a prop. He didn't know that this was just a ploy for her to get into his house and kill him. David was blinded by her good looks and he wasn't about to turn her away.

"We have *so* much to talk about, David. May I come in?" Avalina asked with a devilish smile on her face.

"You sure can, come on in, honey," David replied.

David let the young woman inside his house and closed the door behind her. When the man turned back around towards her, he was shocked. Avalina was pointing a gun right at him. This was *not* going to turn out the way he thought.

"Hey, what's this all about, Miss?" David asked her.

"Do you remember what you and your friends did to Avalina Bishop in 1969?" she asked him.

"I thought you said your name was Joan Sanders?"

"Just answer the question, asshole. I ain't got time for games."

"I can't, because I don't even know who the hell she is."

"You said you went to Merryville High. If you did, you should know damn well who Avalina Bishop was."

"Wait a minute now, I think I remember something about

who she was."

"I thought you would, asshole."

"Wasn't she the chick that burned up in a house fire back then?"

"Yeah, that's right. You and your homies started the fire, do you remember that, too?"

"No way, ma'am; I had nothing to do with it…honest."

"Bullshit, you're lying! Any last words before you die, sucker?"

"I didn't do it…I swear."

"Stop lying! No more bullshit! I'm tired of all this shit! It's time to say 'goodbye,' asshole."

David tried to lunge at her. He tried to get the gun from her hand, but it was too late. Avalina had already squeezed the trigger. The bullet entered his skull, right between his eyes. David Scholl collapsed on his back, up against his front door, blocking it as blood poured out from his head wound. Avalina put her gun back into her purse. The possessed young woman bent down and pushed David out of her way as he bled to death. Avalina composed herself. Then, she walked out the front door and closed it right behind her. The young witch got back into her car and started driving, feeling completely satisfied. *I finally got him. I finally got his damn ass,* Avalina thought to herself as she drove off. *I got them ALL! Now, I can completely focus on my new life with my new love, David Scholl.* Avalina was beaming gloriously while she drove her new old car back to her home. Her mission had finally been accomplished.

19

GRUESOME DISCOVERIES

On a lovely Monday morning, May 4th, a UPS delivery man was pulling his big brown truck into the driveway of David Scholl's home. Jerome, the young UPS carrier, was checking the address on the small package he pulled from his truck. The man wanted to be sure he had the right address.

"315 Fresno Lane, Poughkeepsie, New York. Yup, that's it," he said to himself.

Jerome had noticed that a signature was required for the package. He was hoping to just drop it off on the customer's doorstep, but that wasn't the case for this particular package.

"It must be something expensive," Jerome said to himself.

Jerome grabbed his electronic tablet from the truck with the package and headed straight for the front door. He rang the doorbell two times before deciding to leave a note on the door. Jerome pressed the self-adhesive notice on the door and watched it open up. Apparently, it wasn't closed all the way.

"Mister Scholl?! It's UPS! I have a package for you that needs a signature!" Jerome yelled as he entered the house.

The carrier suddenly became overcome by the stench of death, even with his mask on. The pungent odor was making him sick to his stomach. *I didn't sign up for this,* he thought to himself.

"Mr. Scholl, are you alright?" he asked.

The UPS carrier cautiously followed the revolting odor into the bedroom. Jerome was shocked! David Scholl had been lying dead on his bed with dried blood all over him and the mattress. The deceased was still holding what was left of his male genitalia between his thighs. Flies, maggots and other bugs had been swarming all over his remains.

"Oh, my god!" Jerome screamed out in horror as he tried to choke back his oncoming regurgitation.

The young UPS carrier ran right out of the house with the package and his tablet, while vomit was dripping from his mouth. Jerome ran back to his truck and called the police on his smartphone. The man started his truck back up and left as fast as he could.

A few hours later, Detective Michael Wiretrak was in the break room of the police station all by himself, watching the news on television.

"ACB breaking news, a UPS carrier in Poughkeepsie, New York found a gruesome discovery this morning. Jerome Robinson, of UPS, was delivering a package over at 315 Fresno Lane in Poughkeepsie, New York, when he noticed that the front door was open. The carrier walked in and detected a rancid odor emanating from inside the home. Jerome called out to Mr. David Scholl, the owner of the house, but there was no answer. The carrier then found the body of Mr. Scholl dead and covered in blood on his own bed. Police later found out that the victim died from a massive blood loss, due to having his penis severed," the reporter stated, while showing a picture of the victim and some footage of his home on the screen.

"Jesus H. Christ, what a way to go," Detective Wiretrak said to himself.

"Police did find some clues on the scene; mainly, there were long strands of red hair clenched into the victim's right hand, as if he tried to defend himself from his attacker. Police are having it analyzed," the reporter added.

The detective jumped out of his seat when he heard that

comment.

"Red hair? Sonofabitch! She gets around, doesn't she?" Wiretrak said to himself in shock.

Detective Wiretrak decided to stop in to the chief's office, before heading back to his own office. Wiretrak figured it had to be the same killer that's been striking around here, New York City, and now further north in Poughkeepsie. The young detective was going to try to connect all of the murders and all of the victims to that one, or two, female serial killers.

In the town of Brighten, NY, Avalina had been watching the same news broadcast that Detective Wiretrak had just seen.

"Well, well, well...they finally found that scumbag," Avalina stated to the television set that was hanging up on the wall above the fireplace.

Avalina had decided to have her breakfast in the living room while watching television, but she didn't expect to see *that* story. All of a sudden, her front doorbell rang. The young witch was not expecting company either, but Avalina had a feeling she knew who it was. The possessed young woman got up to answer the door; sure enough, she was right. It was David Scholl.

"Hey, babe, I thought I'd come over and pay you a little visit," David said.

"What a nice surprise, honey," Avalina replied while giving him a great big hug and a kiss.

Avalina escorted David into the living room and sat down on the sofa with him. The front doorbell rang again before they got comfortable.

"Wow, it's getting to be like Grand Central Terminal around

here," Avalina sarcastically stated while getting up again to answer the door.

David grabbed the TV remote and started channel surfing. A minute or two later, Avalina came back into the room with a perplexed look on her face.

"Honey, there's a woman at the door that wishes to talk with you," she stated.

"She wants to talk with *me*? Did she say who she was?" David asked her.

"No, but she says it's important."

"Well, what did she look like, babe?"

"Middle-aged, heavy-set with black and grey hair…more grey than black, though."

"Ok, let me go see who it is."

David walked towards the front door where the woman was standing. Avalina was right behind him. She sensed that David was unnerved by the news.

"What are you doing here?" David asked the middle-aged woman.

"I need to ask you something…in private," the woman told him while looking at Avalina.

"What the hell did you do, follow me here? You had no right!"

David was really uncomfortable about this woman that was visiting him; his face showed it by turning really pale. Avalina noticed the change in him, but she still expected an explanation.

"Joan, this is my mother, Laurie," David told her with an

annoyed look on his face.

"Mother? Is that what you've told her? How rude," the woman replied.

"Nothing for nothing, and no insult to you, Miss, but she looks a little too old to be your mother, David," Avalina said while looking questionably at David.

"She...she had me when she was very young, didn't you, mother?"

"If you say so, *son*; now, I really need to talk with you in private."

"Sure. Joan, honey, can you please excuse us while we step outside for a bit?"

"Of course, dear, go right ahead," Avalina responded.

Avalina watched her boyfriend and his so-called mother go outside to chat. The young witch was watching the two of them talk out in the driveway. She tried to hear what they were saying to each other, but they were talking too softly and they were too far away to be heard. Avalina didn't believe David; she didn't buy it at all. *Why would he lie to me after all we've been through?* Avalina asked herself. She watched David hand the woman something out of his pocket; it looked like some money. David said a few more words to the woman, then, they parted. He was coming back inside while the mysterious woman walked into her pink car and drove off. Avalina opened up the front door to let him in.

"Come on now, David, who was she really?" Avalina asked him.

"I-I told you, baby, she's my mother. Don't you believe me?" David asked her with pleading eyes.

"Yeah…I do, come on back in."

Avalina wanted to believe him. She couldn't resist his loving eyes, but something deep down inside of her said that it just seemed suspicious. Everything about the whole ordeal just didn't sit right with her. She'd leave it alone for now…until next time.

Two days later in Bethel, Long Island, New York, Maryanne Scholl was ringing her father's doorbell. *Gee, it's only nine o'clock in the morning, where could he be?* Maryanne thought questionably to herself. The twenty-nine-year-old girl rang the bell a few more times. It was a wonderful morning. The sun was shining with a cool breeze in the air, but Maryanne was deeply concerned.

"Daddy, it's me, open up!" she called out loud.

The young woman became nervous; her father should have been home. Maryanne opened up her handbag and searched for the extra set of keys her father had given her. When she found the keys, the girl inserted them into the locks. She turned the doorknob and opened the door. Maryanne walked into the house and tripped over her father's body lying there on the floor. The girl nearly collapsed in horror while she stared at his remains.

"Daddy!" Maryanne screamed in terror.

The young woman noticed the gunshot wound in his head. She knelt down at his side, trying to get a pulse, but Mr. Scholl had no pulse. He was stone-cold dead. The heartbroken woman grabbed her smartphone from her purse and called the police.

"9-1-1, what's your emergency?" the operator asked her.

"My…my father's been…shot," Maryanne hysterically cried out.

"Ok, ma'am, what's your location?"

"I'm at 41 Beach Way Road in Bethel."

"Ok, ma'am, I need for you to stay with me now and focus. What's your name?"

"My name is Maryanne Scholl."

"Ok, now, Maryanne, is he breathing?"

"No, and he's ice-cold."

"Where was he shot, ma'am?"

"He has a bullet hole in his head…I don't know who would want to kill him," she cried to the 9-1-1 operator.

"Alright now, Maryanne; help is on the way. I need for you to stay with him."

Maryanne dropped the phone and helplessly hugged her father's ice-cold body. She cried hysterically all over David Scholl's lifeless body, knowing he'd been dead for quite some time now. Within a few minutes, the police and ambulance showed up at the residence.

*
**

On Friday morning, Detective Michael Wiretrak was at Joan Sanders's front door ringing her bell. This time, the detective brought along a fellow police officer with him. The two of them waited patiently for Miss Sanders to open up her front door. Joan finally came to the door wearing a light pink house dress, expecting her lover, David Scholl to be there.

"Good morning, detective, what can I do for you this time?" Avalina sarcastically said with a smirk on her face.

Detective Wiretrak and Officer Rosa had no way of knowing, that the woman standing right in front of them was being inhabited by a vengeful spirit. Wiretrak noticed that something was different about the way she looked; it was her hair. *She's got a new hairdo,* he thought to himself.

"Miss Sanders, I need for you to come down to the station house to answer some questions," the detective stated in a monotone voice.

"The police station? Am I under arrest, sir?" Avalina asked them.

"No, ma'am, I just need for you to come downtown with me to answer some questions, that's all."

"Now? I was ready to go to work."

"It won't take long, Miss Sanders."

"Alright, then…give me a few minutes to get dressed and I'll be right out."

Avalina closed the door on them and let them wait outside. She then went back upstairs to get dressed. The young witch knew that the detective was on to her. Avalina was going to have to come up with a good plan of action. *He's not going to spoil my plans. I won't let him,* she thought.

Later on that morning, David Scholl was in front of Joan Sanders's home ringing her doorbell. *Gee, I wonder where she could be. It's Friday morning; I thought Joan would be working from home,* David thought as he rang her bell once more. He decided to call her cellphone, but the call went straight to her voicemail. Finally, David gave up on her and went back to his car.

Joan Sanders was at Detective Wiretrak's office answering

his questions in a matter-of-fact tone of voice. The possessed woman tried to read his mind to get a jump on the questions, so that it would allow her more time to come up with a better lie.

"Were you ever at 315 Fresno Lane in Poughkeepsie, New York, the home of David Scholl?" Detective Wiretrak asked her.

"No. Never," the possessed girl replied.

"Did you kill David Scholl?"

"No, I did not."

"Miss Sanders, I must tell you, I'm growing very tired of your lies."

"I am not lying!"

"Your hair was found at the scene of the crime."

"Was it *really*? Why don't you just cut a sample of my hair and send it to a DNA lab? You'll see it's not me."

"You would agree to that?"

"Yes, I would. Go on, get the scissors. I'll cut it off myself if it makes you happy."

The detective didn't know what to make of it. Wiretrak ordered the young officer next to him to get a pair of shears. When the officer returned with the scissors, Wiretrak cut a lock of Joan Sanders's hair from behind her head. The detective had the hair sample sent to the DNA laboratories. Then, he temporarily released Joan Sanders and told her not to disappear.

"You *are* going to bring me back home, aren't you?" Avalina asked him through Joan's body.

"Yes, I am give me a minute, please," Wiretrak replied to her.

On the other side of town, David Scholl was driving back home from Joan's home. David kept wondering where Joan was. *I guess I should have called before I came over; it would have saved me a wasted trip and wasted gas,* he thought to himself. All of a sudden, something very familiar caught David's eyes.

"Shit, a pink Cadillac!" David said to himself.

David noticed the old car had just passed by him going in the opposite direction. He knew there was only one classic pink Cadillac in the area and he knew who the owner was. The young man made a "U" turn at the next intersection and proceeded to follow the car. After a few miles, he finally caught up with the driver. David tailgated the car all the way back to the home of Joan Sanders. He stopped the car, got out and started to approach the driver. The middle-aged woman was already leaving her car.

"Hey! What the hell are you doing here?!" David angrily asked her.

"I think your girlfriend should know the truth about you," Laurie Reynolds replied in a serious tone.

David grabbed the woman by the arm and prevented her from getting any closer towards his girlfriend's home. The woman was startled, but she still remained firm to him. Laurie looked deep into David's eyes, seeing only hatred for her.

"Stop it! You're hurting me! Do you really hate me all that much, David?" Laurie asked him.

"No, I don't, but I don't want you to ruin my plans either," David replied as he eased up his grip on her.

"Do you love her?"

"I don't know for sure yet…maybe."

"Then, you must be truly honest with her. You must tell her the truth. Tell her who and what you really are."

"I can't do that...not now."

"You must, you must, you must!"

"It would ruin everything! Can't you understand?"

"David, surely you don't intend to marry her, do you?"

"No, I know I could never do that. I know I can't get married."

"Well, then, you must break it off with this woman!"

"I cannot. Please understand, it's the least you could do for me, especially after all I've done for you."

"You did what you were *supposed to do*!"

"I didn't have to buy you that expensive classic car. I didn't have to get you that nice ass apartment that you live in rent-free every month. I sure didn't have to see to *all* of your needs. No, I've done *far more* than I had to do for you. Now, I'm asking you nicely, just turn your ass around and go back home," David said while loosening his grip a little more on her arm.

They stared at each other face-to-face for a moment. Laurie knew that he was right. David *had* done everything for her and she was deeply indebted to him. Laurie thought about it some more, but then the woman realized that she couldn't let him get away with this shit again.

"Look, David, you know I love you very dearly. I will always feel obligated to you, even if you don't feel the same way about me, but this is wrong. I must stop you," she said with a cry in her voice.

"I'm sorry you feel that way, dearie," he sadly replied.

David hugged her really tight. Laurie had no idea what to expect next. She didn't feel the knife until it quickly penetrated her heart from behind her back. Laurie was slowly collapsing in his arms in pain, growing weaker and weaker as her dying heart struggled to pump life giving blood to her organs.

"How could you? How could you do this to your own..."

Laurie tried to finish her sentence, but it was too late. Her heart had finally stopped. Laurie Reynolds was gone. David cried over her; he really didn't want to kill her, but she had left him no choice. Laurie would have ruined everything for him. David carried her limp body back to her car, struggling with her weight. He removed his knife from her back and cleaned it off on her black leather jacket. Then, David sat her up in the driver's seat of the classic car that he purchased for her, a few years ago. The young man was thinking of what to do with her body, until he heard an automobile approaching. David left her right there in her car; he quickly got back in his own vehicle and fled the scene of the crime.

Detective Wiretrak was bringing his suspect back to her home. Wiretrak knew that it was just a matter of time, before all the evidence would close in on Miss Joan Sanders. The young detective kept glancing at her through his rearview mirror, as she sat in the back of his car, until he finally spoke to her.

"It's a real gorgeous day out today; don't you think so, Miss Sanders?" Wiretrak asked her.

"I didn't notice," the possessed woman replied.

"Yes, it is. It's a great day to do some yard work...take in the fresh air."

"I don't care to."

"Well, frankly my dear, I don't care what you do; just please *don't* get into any more trouble. Remember, I'll be watching you," Wiretrak said in a threating manner as he arrived towards her home.

The detective pulled up behind the pink Cadillac that was parked near the driveway. Wiretrak turned around and faced his suspect. He then gave her a very suspicious look.

"Are you expecting any company, Miss Sanders?" Wiretrak asked.

"No, but I did see that car before," Avalina replied via Joan's body.

"Well then, let's just go see who it is, shall we?"

The two of them got out of the detective's blue four-door sedan and walked over towards the Cadillac. Wiretrak knew that something wasn't quite right. He had a gut feeling about it; his cop instinct was kicking in. The woman was slumped over in her driver's seat, then he noticed some blood behind her.

"Miss, are you alright?" Wiretrak asked as he placed his hand on her shoulder through the open car window.

The woman fell completely forward towards the steering wheel, exposing the knife wound in her back. Wiretrak noticed that the body was still warm. He checked her pulse, then the detective shook his head 'no.' Avalina screamed in horror as she witnessed what the detective just experienced.

"She's dead! She's dead! Oh my god! She's dead!" Avalina screamed.

"Pipe down, Miss Sanders! Please, get a hold of yourself!" Detective Wiretrak shouted while grabbing her by the shoulders.

Avalina started crying in front of him. Wiretrak wondered if she knew who the woman was. One thing was for sure though; the woman and her classic car were not there a few hours ago, when he and the officer had arrived to pick up Miss Joan Sanders.

"Miss Sanders, please get a hold of yourself. Do you know this woman?" Wiretrak asked her.

"Ye-yes…I-I've seen her before," she said through her tears.

"Who is she?"

"She's…she's my boyfriend's mother."

"Your boyfriend?"

"Yes, when he last visited me a few days ago, that woman came by to my house looking for him. David said it was his mother."

"David, is that your boyfriend?"

"Yes, his name is David Scholl."

Detective Wiretrak thought that name sounded familiar. *I've heard that name before…I know I have…just recently,* he thought to himself.

"I assume you know where he lives?"

"He lives in New Jersey, but I can call him."

"You do that while I call for an ambulance and the chief."

Detective Wiretrak took out his cellphone and called for an ambulance, then he called Chief Valentine and explained the whole situation to him. Wiretrak knew that this was going to get complicated; the woman's car had New Jersey license plates on it. The detective searched her bag for identification. *Laurie Reynolds of 15 Maiden Lane in Holton, New Jersey,* he read on the dead woman's driver's license. Wiretrak also noted that the woman was born in 1966. *Shit, she looked a hell of a lot older than that,* he thought to himself. The detective figured that the woman either had a hard life or she was a drinker.

Joan Sanders was staring at the handsome young detective, while the parasitic spirit, that inhabited her body, was being preoccupied by thoughts about her lover. Joan thought that Detective Wiretrak was cute, so did Avalina; however, Avalina only had eyes for David Scholl. The vengeful spirit was worried that she may have gotten David in trouble with the law. *I shouldn't have mentioned David's name to the detective,* Avalina had thought, but it was too late. Wiretrak wanted to question David Scholl, that was a given. Avalina *still* didn't believe that the dead woman sitting in the pink car was David's mother. *She just looks way too old to be my darling's mother,* the young witch thought to herself while the detective was making his calls. The other thing that bothered Avalina was the fact that, the woman had a different last name than David. Avalina overheard the detective say that her name was Laurie Reynolds, not Laurie Scholl. *Of course, that could be her maiden name,* Avalina thought. Avalina never got David Scholl on the phone; she had to leave a message on his voicemail.

20

THE DARK ONE

David Scholl was down in Detective Wiretrak's office in New York being interviewed. David was putting on one of his best sorrowful acting performances, but Wiretrak wasn't buying it. The detective had felt that Mr. Scholl's grief and misery just didn't seem genuine.

"So, tell me again, Mr. Scholl, who do you think would want to murder your mother?" Wiretrak asked him again.

"I-I, just don't know, officer," David tearfully replied while blowing his nose.

"If Miss Laurie Reynolds truly is your mother, then why do you two have different last names?"

"Like I told you before, officer, 'Reynolds' was my mother's maiden name."

"It's detective not officer, Mr. Scholl."

"Sorry, detective."

"Where were you today, Mr. Scholl?"

"Am I a suspect, detective?"

"Please just answer the question, Mr. Scholl, where were you?"

"I was working from my home in New Jersey."

"And you can prove this?"

"You could come over to my house and check my computer logs."

Manuel Rose

"Computer data can be completely altered. You don't have any verifiable witnesses to prove your whereabouts, do you?"

"No, I don't."

"This just doesn't sit right with me, Mr. Scholl. Tell me, why do you think Miss Reynolds would come all the way from Holton, New Jersey, just to stop over by your girlfriend's house in Brighten, New York?"

"She probably thought I was there and just wanted to visit me, that's all."

"Wouldn't it have been easier and closer to visit you in your Campton, New Jersey apartment, instead of driving all the way to New York? I mean you and your mother are only two towns away from each other, it just-"

"I don't know what the reason was detective; maybe, she had something important to tell me and it just couldn't wait."

"Alright, Mr. Scholl, I have all of your information here. We'll keep in touch."

Detective Wiretrak escorted David Scholl back into the waiting area, where Joan Sanders was patiently waiting for his return. He had called her back after receiving her voicemail message. David gave Joan a reassuring hug before they walked out of the police station, hand in hand. The young witch escorted him into her car and drove him to her home, as the sun went down.

Avalina got up from her bed at three o'clock in the morning to relieve herself. She looked at her lover with the light of the moon shining through the window. David was still lying there in her bed, snoring. Avalina's lover had taken *really* good care of her last night. The young witch lost count of how many times David had brought her to a climax, but the girl knew it was more than she could count on one hand. *Oh, man, he's so damn sexy, but I have GOT to do something about that damn snoring of his,* she thought to herself. Avalina carefully walked towards the bathroom, making sure she didn't wake him up.

"Y-o-u, o-w-e, m-e-e-e," a ghostly voice hissed out.

Avalina was so startled that she almost tripped on the pile of clothes on the floor. The witch turned around and was shocked to see that The Dark One had been right behind her. *Holy shit! It's back and it speaks,* she surprisingly thought to herself.

"That's right, I c-a-n s-p-e-a-k," the eerie spirit uttered.

"You can read minds, too?" Avalina asked.

"Y-e-s, I c-a-n, A-v-a-l-i-n-a."

"You know who I really am, how?"

"I kn-ow e-v-e-r-y-t-h-i-n-g...everything about y-o-u. You've picked a r-e-a-l nice b-o-d-y."

"Wh-what do you want from me now?" Avalina whispered to it.

"Y-o-u, o-w-e, m-e-e-e," it slowly repeated to her.

"I understand, but how do I repay you?"

"H-i-m...you must kill him for meee."

"No! Please, anyone but him," she softly pleaded with the mysterious evil spirit.

"You are w-e-a-k."

"Please, oh, Dark One. I will do whatever you wish, but spare this one for me."

"You deserve better than this piece of s-h-i-t. He is u-s-e-l-e-s-s to meee."

"But not to me, oh, Great One. Please, spare him his life so that I may serve you better," Avalina begged.

"Why do you want him so?"

"Because…I love him."

"Love? He does not know the meaning of l-o-v-e."

"Yes, oh, Magnificent One, he does. David loves me, too."

"This one only loves h-i-m-s-e-l-f."

"No, I don't believe that at all."

"He m-u-s-t be d-e-s-t-r-o-y-e-d, but I cannot dooo i-t. You m-u-s-t!"

"No, I can't and I won't."

"If only you knew the t-r-u-t-h about him, y-o-u w-o-u-l-d."

"I know all there is to know about David Scholl."

"Nooo…you don't."

"Honey, who are you talking to?" David asked while waking up to the conversation going on in the room.

"N-no one, dear, I'm just thinking out loud. I'm sorry if I disturbed you," Avalina replied, noticing that the spirit had already disappeared.

"Why don't you just come back to bed, babe?"

"I will, honey, but first I have to go pee."

David was getting aroused, while he was looking at her naked body in the moonlight. He stared at her with hungry eyes as she walked by him. The young man waited patiently in heat, for his young lover to return from the bathroom. David wanted another round of fun with her. Avalina sat on the toilet bowl thinking about what The Dark One had told her. *Why does he want David dead? What did he mean by saying, if I only knew the truth about him, I would destroy him? Why can't HE kill him himself if he really wanted David dead?* All of those distressing questions were swarming around in Avalina's pretty little head, taunting her. The young witch wondered what David could have done to make the great evil one want him dead. It certainly had peaked her curiosity, but one thing was for sure though, she wasn't going to ask David about it. Avalina would have to find another way to learn the truth about David Scholl, if she really wanted to know. The girl was blinded by love.

Avalina had yet another problem; she had missed her period for quite some time now. In fact, it had been well over a month since she last had it. The young witch decided to check herself with the home pregnancy test she recently purchased at the supermarket. Avalina looked at the results on the device's display. She tested positive. *I'm pregnant! How am I going to tell him that?* Avalina asked herself. She went back to the bedroom, turned on the lamp that was on the nightstand and sat down on the bed, next to his face.

"Hey, what's up?!" David bellowed.

"Honey, I have to tell you something very important. Please, don't get mad at me..." Avalina begged him.

"*Girl*, you just killed the damn mood; it had better be important."

"It is important. I'm pregnant. I thought you said you couldn't make me pregnant."

"No, it can't be."

"But it is! *See?* Look at my test results."

David sat up in the bed while he was still partially under the covers. He looked at the device in her hand. David was bewildered, but at the same time, the young man was highly upset.

"I don't care what the *hell* that thing says, Joan! It ain't mine."

"Oh, yes it is. I haven't slept with anyone else but you."

"It's impossible! I haven't been able to get any girl pregnant, since…"

"Since what, David?"

"Never mind. I'm sorry this had to happen, especially to you, my dear."

"What do you mean you're sorry? I love you and I wanna keep this baby. I want us to be together. Don't you love me, David? Don't you want to marry me and help raise our child?" Avalina cried.

"Marry? Yes, yes of course I do. Come here, dear."

David grabbed Joan and tenderly started kissing her. The young witch got back into the bed with him under the covers, feeling very excited. David rolled over on top of her and peeled himself back from her. The possessed young woman anxiously waited for him to insert his growing manhood inside of her.

"Oh, yes, honey, stick it in. I'm all ready for you…just stick it in and feel our new baby growing inside of me," Avalina said in a sexy, husky voice.

"I'm so very sorry, darling," David said as he reached for something under his pillow.

"Stick it in, p-l-e-a-s-e," she moaned.

"Oh, I will," he said.

"Stick it, huh-" Avalina yelped.

David buried his eight-inch stainless-steel hunting knife deep down into her stomach. It was the same one he just used to kill Laurie Reynolds. David pinned her down with his knees and his free hand. He began twisting the long blade back and forth and moving it around, as if he was carving out a large hole. Blood began pouring out of Joan's abdomen while she looked at him so shocked and heartbroken. The possessed woman was in an enormous amount of pain, struggling to breathe and struggling to stay alive. How could he do this to his lover, now the mother of his unborn child, a child that would never ever see the light of day?

"Wh-why? I thought...you...loved me?" Avalina said as her mortal life began slipping away with her human host.

Avalina and Joan were both in agonizing pain. The young witch was growing weaker by the minute. Her heart was struggling to pump blood. It all just kept on pouring out of the large open wound in her abdomen.

"Sorry, dear, but I can't ever have children. That wasn't part of the arrangement," David stated in a matter-of-fact tone of voice.

"You...you killed...your own...mother. Didn't you?" she quietly uttered.

"For the record, she wasn't my mother, but yes, I killed her. I had to do it. She was going to ruin everything for me...and now you. I'm really truly sorry about this shit; I really liked you. I liked you a lot...the sex was *really* good. I don't know how the hell I managed to get you knocked up, but it must be terminated, along with you, my dear. I have to right my wrong in order to survive here."

David took his knife out of the nearly helpless body of Joan Sanders. Joan was dying and she was taking Avalina's spirit with her, so that she may die again. Avalina was taken by surprise, but she still had one card left up her bloody sleeve. The failing witch used what little power she had left, to leave her dying human vessel and return back to the inanimate object from where she came from: the golden pentagram locket that was still around her neck. David plunged his knife back into her belly, stabbing it several more times like a human jackhammer, until the woman, whom he thought he loved, breathed no more.

David got off of her body and got out of the bloody bed, still naked with a fierce hard-on, wearing Joan's blood all over him and his knife. He went into the bathroom and washed his knife in the sink, then David jumped into the bathtub. He took a shower and washed all of his dead lover's blood off of his own body. The young man was still sexually aroused. It seemed that killing Joan had made him even more excited. David masturbated, until he climaxed, screaming with delight. The man was completely relieved. He rinsed and dried himself off, paying extra special attention to his pleasure member. David walked back into the bedroom to collect his clothes and get dressed. He took one last look at Joan's lifeless body. The woman, whom David thought he loved, was lying there on the bed with blood all over her, the sheets, and the light blue blanket. Then, he noticed something. The dark spirit was looking down at her from the ceiling above the bed.

"You! I might have known you had something to do with this shit," David hissed at the spirit hovering way above him and Joan's body.

"You'll p-a-y for t-h-i-s," The Dark One hissed back at him.

"Sorry it didn't work out for you. No child. Oh well…sucks for you."

David quickly got dressed and went down the stairs. The young man turned around when he got to the bottom of the steps, checking to see if the dark spirit was behind him, then he walked out the front door, closing it behind him. The Dark One was still looking down at the woman's lifeless body in her bedroom. He was disappointed. He had been betrayed. David did not stick to the original plan, even though The Dark One had kept his end of the bargain…to a degree, that is. David had been right about one thing; the spirit *did* help Avalina get pregnant, but only because he wanted to end the agreement he had made with David Scholl years before. The Dark One realized that David was never going to get a girl pregnant. This infuriated The Dark One and he quickly realized that David was totally useless to him and that he must be destroyed. He was not through with David yet. The dark spirit was going to devise a new plan to get even with David Scholl.

Later on that morning, Detective Michael Wiretrak was ringing Joan Sanders's doorbell. Wiretrak wanted some more information from her about her boyfriend, David Scholl. He looked at his wristwatch; it was only eight o'clock. *Where could she be?* Wiretrak asked himself, knowing perfectly well that Miss Sanders was working from home. He rang the front doorbell some more.

"Miss Sanders, it's Detective Wiretrak! Open up, please! I need to ask you some more questions!" he shouted.

Still, there was no answer. Then, as if by magic, the front door opened up all by itself. What Wiretrak didn't know was that The Dark One was on the other side, opening up the door for him.

"Miss Sanders, is that you?" Wiretrak asked.

The detective cautiously entered the premises as the spirit disappeared. He looked behind the front door, expecting to find Joan Sanders standing there.

"Miss Sanders, its Detective Wiretrak. I'm inside your home, are you decent?" he asked, wondering if she was in the shower, or getting dressed.

Wiretrak walked into the kitchen, then the living room. Still, there was no sign of Joan Sanders. Wiretrak called out to her again.

"Miss Sanders where are you?!" he shouted.

All of a sudden, the telephone began to ring. After the fourth ring, the answering machine picked up with Joan's recorded greeting.

"Hello, thanks for calling, but I'm not available to take your call right now. If this is a telemarketer, *buzz off.* Anyone else can leave a message and I'll get back to you soon. Wait for the beep," Joan's recorded voice said.

"Hello, Joan, this is your boss, Richard Johnson, remember me? Why aren't you online for our video conference? Don't you value your job?" Richard asked before hanging up the phone on the machine.

Something's wrong; she's supposed to be home working on the computer, Detective Wiretrak thought to himself. Wiretrak's cop gut instinct kicked into high gear. He pulled out his service revolver and started walking up the stairs to the second level. The detective cautiously started going from room to room. He checked the small guest bedroom, the computer room where Joan worked from, then Wiretrak went into the master bedroom.

"Holy shit, Miss Sanders!" Wiretrak exclaimed.

The detective walked closer to the once beautiful girl lying there on the bed, covered in her own blood that was emanating from the big gash in her abdomen. He looked closer at the body. There were cut up sections of the young woman's intestines protruding from her stomach wound. Wiretrak was feeling disgusted. *Who would do this to this beautiful young creature?* Wiretrak asked himself.

Detective Wiretrak didn't want to admit it to himself, but he *was* very attracted to Joan Sanders. He loved her beautiful smile, her fiery, long red hair, penetrating deep blue eyes and, her figure. The young detective had hoped she was innocent and had nothing to do with the murders. If she was innocent, he was probably going to ask her out. Now, it was way too late. Joan was gone, murdered in her own home, slaughtered like an animal in her own bed…but by whom and why? That's what the good detective was going to have to find out. Wiretrak felt the body. *She's still warm; the murderer couldn't have gotten very far,* he thought. Wiretrak took out his smartphone and called Chief Charles P. Valentine. The detective explained what he discovered at the residence of one of his murder suspects, Joan Sanders. Chief Valentine told him that obviously, she's no longer a suspect.

"Her mother's going to have to get notified about her," the chief told him over the phone.

"I know…I'll do it. Also, send forensics over." Wiretrak replied.

"There's something else I have to tell you, Wiretrak."

"What is it, boss?"

"The DNA results got back from the lab…the hair samples don't match. It looks like Miss Sanders may have been innocent."

Wiretrak felt remorseful; he thought he may have been wrong about Joan, after all. Of course, Detective Wiretrak didn't know that Joan was wearing a good quality wig, made of human hair. It was *that* wig the woman had worn on the day she gave her hair sample. Avalina had thought of everything, even destroying the wig by burning it in the fireplace the very same evening.

"What a shame, what a waste. She was absolutely gorgeous. Who would do such a terrible thing to such a beautiful woman like that? I'm gonna find that sonofabitch that did this to you, if it's the last thing I do," Wiretrak pledged to Joan's body.

"D-a-v-i-d S-c-h-o-l-l," The Dark One whispered into the detective's ear.

"What? Who said that?" Wiretrak asked.

The detective turned around and looked everywhere, but there was no one there. Wiretrak figured that he was just thinking out loud. The girl's boyfriend would definitely become a prime suspect. He knew that everything wasn't always peaches and flowers with any relationship. *The couple could have had a serious fight. Who the hell knows?* Wiretrak thought.

Detective Wiretrak took some pictures on his smartphone of the crime scene. Wiretrak looked suspiciously at the deceased's hair. *Her hair looks a little brighter and a lot longer since the last time I saw her. She could have dyed her hair, but there's no way in hell it could have grown that much in such a short period of time,* he thought.

"Hey, there's something funny going on around here…and I don't like it," the detective suspiciously said to himself.

He took out his pocketknife and cut a piece of Joan's hair off. Wiretrak put the hair sample in his pocket with the full intent, of having it analyzed for its DNA content. The young detective stuck around until the ambulance and police had arrived.

Carrie Sanders was sitting down at the kitchen table eating a peanut butter and jelly sandwich. She wanted to watch the afternoon news, but the cable was out. The cable TV company was upgrading to fiber optics, so the service was going to be out all day.

"Shit, I pay all this damn money, over a hundred and sixty dollars a month and I can't even watch television," she angrily said to herself.

Carrie decided to call her daughter and see how she was doing. She went over to the phone on the wall, then the doorbell rang.

"Jesus, it's always like that. Every time I go to call someone, there's someone else at the door. I'm coming!" she yelled.

Carrie went to the front door. She pulled the curtain back on the sidelight window to see who it was. *Oh, shit! It's that fricking detective again. What the hell does he want now?* she mentally asked herself. Carrie opened up the front door and put a fake smile on her face.

"Oh, detective, what a nice surprise. What can I do for you?" Carrie sarcastically asked him.

"Miss Sanders, may I please talk to you? It's about your daughter…" Wiretrak sadly said while looking down.

"What did she do now?"

"Please, may I come in? It's important."

"You're scaring me…sure, let's go in the kitchen."

Carrie Sanders ushered the detective inside and closed the door behind him. The woman led him into the kitchen where she was just eating and asked him to sit down.

"Would you like some coffee? I can put a fresh pot on for us," Carrie asked him.

"No, ma'am, but I think you should sit down, too," he told her.

Carrie sat down next to him at the table. She began to feel nervous, knowing the good detective must have some bad news about her daughter.

"Miss Sanders, your daughter's been murdered. I'm so sorry to have to tell you this," Wiretrak somberly said.

"No…it can't be…not my baby! No, no, no!" she buried

her face into her hands and cried helplessly.

"I'm so sorry."

"Who killed her? Why?"

"We don't know yet, but we're checking all available leads."

"Wh-where was she?"

"I went over to her home this morning to ask her some questions, after ringing and ringing her front doorbell, the door just opened up by itself. I thought she was behind the door, but she wasn't. I later found her lying in her own bed, covered in blood. Your daughter had a severe abdominal wound, probably made from a large sharp object, like a knife. I'm really very sorry to have to tell you this. Miss Sanders, did your daughter have any enemies of which you might know of? We already have one suspect in mind: her boyfriend, David Scholl."

"Who? I never even knew she had another boyfriend. Oh, God, my only living baby. She hasn't had any luck with boys. The last one was a nut; he wound up killing himself. Where is she now, detective?"

"She was brought over to Brighten Medical Center."

"That shithole? Of all the damn places, why the *hell* did they have to bring my baby over there?"

"It was the closest one, ma'am."

"Yeah, right."

"Miss Sanders, is there anyone else you could think of that might have wanted your daughter dead?"

"No. I'm sorry, detective, but could you please leave me now? I just want to be alone right now."

"I completely understand, Miss Sanders. I'll call you when we get any more information."

The young detective saw himself out of the woman's home. He closed the door and shook his head. Wiretrak got back into his car, wishing there was something else he could do. The sun was shining and it felt nice outside, but Detective Wiretrak felt anything but nice. The young detective decided to head on back to the police station. He wanted time to make out his report; plus, the man wanted to send Joan's hair sample down to the laboratory. Wiretrak felt really bad about what had happened to Joan Sanders, but he was also aware of the fact that his prime suspect in almost all of the murders, was now gone. Wiretrak was going to have to start from square one all over again. *Shit on me*, he thought, *shit on me*.

21

MARCELLA O'SULLIVAN

The ambulance, that was now carrying the body of Joan Sanders, was only a few miles away from Brighten Medical Center. A young female emergency medical technician was looking at the gold necklace that was around Joan Sanders's neck. She appeared to be fascinated by it.

"Glory be, that sure is a lovely hunk of gold around her neck. You won't be needing it any longer," the EMT said to herself in her Irish brogue.

"Did you say something O'Sullivan?" her partner, the male paramedic, asked her as he drove the ambulance.

"No, no, laddie. I'm just talking to me self, that's all," she replied.

Marcella O'Sullivan had recently come over to the United States from Belfast, Ireland. Marcella was a medic in Ireland, but there were severe cutbacks in her home country and she was one of the many, to be let go. Working in America had its challenges for her. Marcella had to get used to driving on the opposite side of the road, even though the girl couldn't afford her own car as of yet in the states, but there were times when she rented one. Next, the young woman had to get the job for which she was originally trained. Then, Marcella had to find an affordable apartment to live in.

The twenty-eight-year-old woman knew that the money was good in the United States, especially in New York. Marcella was very pretty. She had long, straight, light brown hair with a nice shine to it. The girl was also very thin. Her partner, James Strange, fell in love with her soft blue eyes and Irish brogue. Marcella wasn't really interested in her partner or any man just yet; she was only interested in excelling in her career. Also, the young woman loved helping people out, especially if they were ill or down and out.

This was almost the end of her first full week on the job, but it was the first time Marcella had ever seen anyone look so cut open in her life, especially a woman. Marcella looked at the once beautiful young woman lying there on the stretcher. *My god, so much blood. Did he really have to stab her so many times to kill her?* she asked herself, assuming that the victim was slaughtered by a man. The EMT felt bad that she couldn't help her, but at the same time, Marcella felt extremely compelled to take the young victim's necklace. *I know stealin' is a sin, but something is tellin' me to take it. Oh, Lord, I must have it,* she thought while removing Joan's, or, really, Avalina's gold pentagram locket and chain off of her neck. Marcella looked at the shiny necklace in her hand and she was mesmerized by it for a moment. Then, she placed the jewelry in her pocket.

"We're almost there, Miss O'Sullivan. Get ready to leave the bus soon," Paramedic Strange told her.

"Sure, laddie, and stop looking at me ass," Marcella replied.

"I just love your accent."

"It's called a brogue, an Irish brogue, darlin'."

Paramedic Strange pulled the ambulance into the driveway of the Brighten Medical Center, towards the emergency entrance. They both knew that any doctor on call in the ER would pronounce the victim dead on arrival, then she would be placed in the hospital morgue, while the hospital tried to notify her family. The paramedic stopped the ambulance and the two of them got out. Paramedic Strange helped EMT O'Sullivan bring the body into the hospital. Marcella would never admit it, but this time, she was the one that was checking out her partner's ass, especially since James was leading her.

*
**

David Scholl was finally getting ready to relax and eat his frozen pizza when the front doorbell rang. David had a feeling he knew who it was. He went over towards the door and shouted.

"Who is it?!" David asked.

"It's Detective Wiretrak!" the young detective replied.

David knew it would be him again. He unlocked the front door and opened it.

"Well, well, well, aren't you a little out of your jurisdiction, detective? After all, this is the state of New Jersey, not New York, you know."

"I'm very well aware of that, Mr. Scholl, but I came by here to ask you a few questions. May I come in?"

"Sure, detective, come on in."

David knew that if he refused to talk to the detective, it would make him look suspicious. He showed the detective into the living room. David sat down on the sofa and Wiretrak sat down on the chair adjacent to him, as he pulled out his book and pen.

"Well then, what can I do for you, detective?" David asked him.

"Where were you early this morning prior to eight am?" Wiretrak bluntly asked him.

"I was right here in my bed. I woke up at eight-thirty to get ready for work. Since, I'm mostly working from home these days, I don't see much reason to get up any earlier."

"Really? I was under the distinct impression that you went

home with Miss Joan Sanders after our interview yesterday. Am I correct?"

"Yes, I did, but I didn't stay over. After a while, I kissed her goodbye and then I went home."

"So, you're saying that you didn't stay over this time?"

"I hardly ever do."

"Is that so? Well, that's not the understanding that I got from Miss Sanders. She once told me that when you come over, you usually stay over, and that's quite often. Miss Sanders also told me that you two were very close. She considered you her boyfriend."

"Are you checking up on me, detective?"

"Maybe. Maybe, I just want to get the facts straight. Now, let me ask you again: did you, or did you not stay over at Miss Sanders's home last night after you left the police station?"

"No, I didn't. If you don't believe me, then why don't you just ask her yourself?"

"That's going to be quite difficult to do, Mr. Scholl."

"And why is that detective?"

"Because Miss Joan Sanders is dead. She was murdered early this morning, Mr. Scholl."

"What?! No!" David said with a fake cry in his voice.

"That's right. I was over at her house at eight o'clock this morning. She was stabbed multiple times in her abdomen. The poor girl was all covered in her own blood, lying there in her own bed. Who would do such a thing to her, Mr. Scholl? Do you know?"

"No...no...no, I haven't the slightest idea."

"There's something else, Mr. Scholl."

"What is it?"

"Her body was still warm when I got there."

"You, you think I had something to do with her death? I-I loved her."

"Did you really?"

"Yes, yes I did."

"Can you prove you were here last night? Did anyone see you?"

"No, I can't. No one saw me, but I swear to you, I was here all night."

"What time did you leave Miss Sanders's home last night?"

"It was early...like about...oh, I don't really remember exactly...probably around seven in the evening."

"Do you have any toll receipts or an EZ Pass to verify that you went over the bridge?"

"No and besides, you should know that you only pay for going in one direction, on the bridge and the tunnels over here. It's when you go to New York from New Jersey."

"Ok, Mr. Scholl, that'll be all for now. We'll keep in touch if we need more information. Oh, and for what it's worth, sorry about your loss."

Detective Wiretrak left Mr. Scholl's home and headed out to his car. Wiretrak knew all about the bridge toll setup; he was just toying around with him. *Shit, it's nighttime...I hate driving at night,* Wiretrak thought to himself. The detective believed that David Scholl had something to do with the death of Joan Sanders. David didn't look genuinely upset or surprised about her death. Now, the only thing that the young detective had to do, was to find some way to prove it.

On Monday morning, June 1st, the birds were out enjoying what was left of the beautiful spring weather, before the impending thunderstorm approached. Marcella O'Sullivan woke up to her alarm clock in the bedroom of her three-room apartment, in Merryville, New York. Marcella lived on the top floor of the old apartment house, that was slightly run down. The young woman hated it there, but it was all she could afford on her salary. What Marcella really hated about the old building, was the fact that it was a five-story walk up, which made it rather difficult for her to carry groceries upstairs when she was tired. Marcella still felt a little tired, but the young woman knew it was time to get up and get ready for work. She slowly got out of her bed. Marcella had a very strong compulsion to go over to the laundry basket, that was on the floor, sitting in the corner of the room. Marcella went through her dirty clothes until she got to her uniform pants.

"Something is callin' me here," she said to herself.

Marcella went through her pants pockets until, she pulled out the golden pentagram locket. *I had completely forgotten about this little trinket; it almost went into the wash,* she thought. The young lady took the necklace over towards her oak dresser and stood in front of the mirror.

"P-u-t, i-t, o-n," a ghostly voice ushered her on.

Marcella placed the golden locket and chain around her neck. Suddenly, she felt very strange. Her reflection in the mirror was replaced by a strange new face. It was the face of a young woman with long, raven-colored hair. It was a girl she had never seen before in her life. Avalina Bishop was checking out the new body she was about to inhabit.

"Who are ya, lassie?" Marcella asked the strange young lady in her mirror.

"I'm gonna be your worst nightmare, honey. I need you to go back to sleep so I can take over your body," Avalina replied.

"No! I won't let ya, dearie. Besides, I've already slept. I'm not tired anymore."

Avalina tightened up the necklace around the girl's neck into a choke-hold. Marcella began to struggle for air.

"Stop it…I-I can't breathe," Marcella begged her.

"That's the idea. Now, don't argue with me, Miss, and I'll make this as quickly and as painless as possible for you," Avalina commanded.

"Ok, ok," Marcella begged her.

Avalina waved her hands in the mirror, forcing Marcella flat on her back on the bed again. Avalina tightened the necklace some more until Marcella was unconscious. Then, she loosened her grip on her so that the girl could breathe again. Avalina's spirit slowly consumed her new human host, possessing Marcella as she slept. Avalina had crept into the young woman's mind and stole all of her knowledge and memories; until she knew all there was to know in order to become Marcella O'Sullivan's puppeteer.

Later on in the afternoon, Avalina was waking up in her new body. It was the sound of the ringing telephone right next to her on the nightstand, that woke her out of a deep, restful sleep. She leaned over on the bed to answer it.

"Hello?" the possessed young woman said over the phone.

"O'Sullivan, this is your supervisor, Lieutenant Palin. Why

aren't you here at work? I had to send your partner out with someone else!" the angry man barked over the phone.

"I-I'm sorry, sir, I'm feeling a little bit under the weather today," Avalina replied through Marcella's body.

"So, you're sick, eh? You should have called in earlier. I'm lucky I had someone to cover for you on such a short notice."

"I'm sorry, sir, it won't happen again."

"How long are you staying out for?"

"Just for today, I hope. I should be back in by tomorrow, sir."

"What's ailing you, O'Sullivan?"

"It's my head, sir. I have a splitting headache that just won't go away," she replied, trying to sound sick over the phone.

"Well, alright then; go take some aspirin and make sure you're in here tomorrow, alright?"

"Yes, sir, I'll see you tomorrow," Avalina said as she hung up the phone.

The young witch got out of bed and walked over to the large mirror above her dresser. The possessed woman took off all of her clothing. She began to check out her new body in the mirror's reflection.

"Not bad...not bad at all, but I kind of preferred the last one better. Joan Sanders was more voluptuous; her boobs were much larger and I kind of got used to that, fiery red hair that she had. *This* bitch is on the scrawny side, almost flat-chested, with not much of an ass. Shit, but I guess she'll have to do," Avalina said to her reflection.

"Well, I'm sorry ya don't approve of me, darlin'. Just

remember, dearie, I didn't ask for this shit either!" Marcella's partially subdued spirit retorted.

"Now, you listen to me, you little shit! You be quiet and stay away and *maybe, just maybe,* I'll let you live when this is all over. You hear me, bitch?!" Avalina snapped at her host's spirit.

"Yes, I hear ya, you wicked, wicked witch," Marcella somberly replied.

The possessed woman sat down on the wooden bedroom chair and started thinking of how she was betrayed, by David Scholl. Avalina had loved him with all of her spiritual heart. The physical body she possessed at the time was even carrying his baby. *He murdered me and he murdered his own unborn child...OUR child! How could he do such a terrible thing? Did he ever love me at all?* Avalina mentally asked herself all of those questions, but mostly, she was bitter...very bitter. The young witch only thought about one important thing: revenge. *David used me like I was his own whore, his love slave. He led me on,* she thought with sorrow and despair. Avalina really wanted to kill him like he had killed her, but the young witch wondered if she could ever really carry it through.

"I loved him. I loved him dearly. How could he do this shit to me, after all we've been through? How? What the hell did I ever do to deserve that?" she asked herself with a cry in her voice.

The young witch buried her new mortal head into her hands and cried. She thought about the last thing that had upset him.

"All I did was tell him I was pregnant with his own child," Avalina said with a cry.

The witch remembered what the dark spirit told her before David had killed her. He said, *if I only knew the truth about him, I would destroy him.* She wondered what the dark spirit meant by that. What was the truth? Avalina remembered how David had killed that strange woman before her, the one that was parked outside of her house, the one whom he claimed was his mother at the time. She had wondered who the hell the woman really was to him. More importantly, Avalina wondered how many more women there were before her that met the same fate as her.

"David Scholl is nothing but a conniving murderer. He must be dealt with, accordingly! He must be stopped," she said while crying to herself.

Avalina finally pulled herself together and looked around her new surroundings. It was nothing special. The whole apartment had been painted in white-wash, which looked more like a dirty dark tan with age. Parquet wood floors dominated the whole place. There was a small portable TV on a stand in the living room and a cream-colored sofa. The kitchen was very small. There was a little round wooden table and four chairs under it. The kitchen floor was covered with an off-white linoleum floor covering. That was it.

"This place looks like a shit house," she emphatically said to herself.

The witch knew that it was a far cry from the nice home her other host lived in. She wished that it was all just a dream. Avalina wanted nothing more than to go back home with her mother and father. She wished that she was a teenager again back in 1969. The witch wished that none of this ever happened to her, but she knew that this was now her new reality. She knew that both of her parents were dead and there was no turning back now.

In Campton, New Jersey that afternoon, David Scholl had just finished helping a female customer over the phone. The woman had issues getting the office server to boot up. *Damn, her voice, she sounded just like Joan Sanders,* he thought to himself. David couldn't get her out of his mind. He really regretted killing his hot young lover.

"Why the *hell* did she have to get knocked up? I thought I was safe. I miss her ass. She was so fine and beautiful...*shit!*" David said to himself.

David was both sad and angry that it had to end that way. It took him a very long time to find another girlfriend ever since his first love, Janet, met up in an untimely death. David really thought that Janet Michaels was the one for him, until Janet had found out the truth about him. David just couldn't let her get away with that shit. The bitch knew way too much.

Janet threatened to expose him to the authorities. David had pleaded with her; he told her to relax and think about what she was doing. *They'll never believe you,* David had told her. After talking back and forth without getting anywhere with David, Janet got in her car and drove off to the nearest police station. Janet started picking up speed going down a road with sharp curves. She tried to apply the brakes, but the car would not slow down. Janet's car flew past a turn; then, it went over the guard rail, became airborne and finally landed in the river. Janet and her vehicle were never found. David didn't really mean to rig her car so that she would lose control; it was just something that had to be done...just like with Joan Sanders. Now, David would have to find another girl to please him. David got lucky with Joan. *She* came to *him. The odds of me knocking up a girl are really slim. I know that fricking dark ass spirit did that shit. He helped me get her pregnant. I know it,* David angrily thought to himself.

Later on in the evening, Avalina decided that she wanted to go back to her old home, the home of Joan Sanders. Avalina remembered she had put David Scholl's address in her little black phone book. *I'm pretty sure I put it in my top dresser drawer,* she thought. The young witch wasn't exactly sure how to get to David's home, without the driving directions he had given her. She had written the instructions in her book, along with his address. Avalina frantically searched Marcella O'Sullivan's brain to find her car keys.

"Holy shit! This bitch doesn't even have a damn car? It's bad enough I have to be stuck in this small ass run-down apartment, but now I'm trapped in here like a stinking rat! *shit!*

"How the *hell* am I supposed to get there?" Avalina angrily said out loud.

The angry spirit used her new host to go through her own purse. Avalina found $89.52 in the bag, plus a VISA credit card. She looked around for a cellphone, but the girl didn't have one in her purse. The young witch figured that her host either didn't have one, or it was hidden somewhere else. The possessed young woman was through wasting her time. She looked through the phonebook for a taxicab service. After picking the one with the biggest ad, Avalina gave them a call using the phone on the nightstand. One way or another, she was going back for David's address. The young witch wanted to pay him a very special visit.

An hour later, Avalina arrived at her old place of residence, the house where her lover, David Scholl, had just murdered her in bed. It was after six o'clock in the evening, but the hot sun was still burning brightly outside. Avalina tipped the cabdriver and walked towards the old house. *Maybe I should have asked the cabbie to stick around; I'm not going to be here long,* she thought. The young witch realized that she didn't have any keys for the house anymore. *I could try to unlock the door with witchcraft; if not, I'll just break a window,* Avalina thought. As she approached the front door, Avalina noticed a sign with yellow tape around it that read: "POLICE LINE DO NOT PASS."

"Shit!" she said aloud.

"Freeze!" a young police officer shouted from the side of

the house.

Avalina didn't notice the police squad car that was parked near the house. The young officer was assigned to keep a watch on the home, until some more developments came up for the case. Avalina was so startled that she nearly dropped her purse.

"I'm afraid I don't understand. What did I do?" Avalina timidly asked.

"Put your hands up, Miss. Who are you and what are you doing here?" the officer asked her while having his service revolver trained on her.

"I'm-I'm here to-to visit my friend," Avalina stammered.

"Your friend? What's her full name?" the officer asked her.

"Ava...excuse me...J-Joan. I wanted to see how she was doing...that's all."

"Joan, what? What did she look like?"

Avalina was so nervous that she couldn't even remember anything else about her previous host, especially with that handgun pointing right at her. The young witch tried her best to remember, but it was no use.

"Alright, you're taking *way* too long, Miss. Keep your hands up; we're going down to the police station."

Officer George Landing was new on the force. He had always wanted to be a police officer just like his dad. At only twenty-two-years-old, George's dream finally came true when he passed the interview, physical and required training for the Brighten Police Department. Unlike his father, though, George was overzealous. The young rookie cop was trying really hard to take every promotion he could get his hands on. George was always neat in his attire; he kept his brown hair short in a crew-cut fashion and he was always clean-shaven. The young cop was also a regular member at the gym; he worked really hard to stay fit and trim.

Officer Landing turned Marcella around and handcuffed her while reading the young woman her rights. Avalina started crying through Marcella's body, pleading to the officer that she did nothing wrong. Officer Landing put the young woman into the back of the police cruiser and drove off.

About a half hour later, Officer Landing had arrived at the Brighten Police Department with his new prisoner. Landing got out of the squad car and removed Marcella from the back seat. Landing then escorted the young lady into the police station, like a proud son trying to impress his father, after shooting a game animal during a hunting session.

"Hey, George, what you are doing with that EMT chick?" an older fellow officer called out.

"I'm bringing her in," Landing replied.

"On what charge?" Detective Wiretrak asked as he came towards the front desk.

"She was at the scene of that recent murder victim, Joan Sanders," Landing answered him.

"Now, I don't think this pretty young woman, who saves lives, had anything to do with it, don't you, Miss...?"

"O'Sullivan, EMT Marcella O'Sullivan; and no, I didn't do anything, sir," Avalina replied.

"You see, Officer Landing? It's got to be some sort of a misunderstanding. I've seen her and her partner at a recent homicide. Bring her into my office."

"But, sir, shouldn't she be brought into the chief's office?" Landing asked.

"The chief took the evening off; he said he had stomach cramps. He also left *me* in charge," Wiretrak replied.

Avalina recognized the detective. *He's the one who practically accused me of murder. He even took some of my hair for a DNA test,* she remembered bitterly.

The three of them walked into Detective Wiretrak's office. Wiretrak told Officer Landing to remove Marcella's handcuffs and, to leave his office while he interviewed her. The detective sat down at his desk and asked the woman to have a seat. Wiretrak began questioning her.

"So, Miss O'Sullivan, what *were* you doing at the home of our recent victim, Miss Joan Sanders?" Wiretrak asked her.

"I went to visit a friend; that's all there is to it," Avalina replied.

"You knew Miss Sanders, well?"

"Yes, we were close."

"How close?"

"You could just say that we were one of the same."

"Oh, like you two shared each other's thoughts?"

"Oh, yeah…we've shared our minds, bodies and spirits."

"Well, Miss O'Sullivan, I'm not asking you to tell me all about your sexual preferences here. I just want to know what you were doing at the victim's home this evening."

"Like I said before, detective, I went there to visit a friend; and I'm *not* gay, if that's what you're implying. By the way, did my hair sample prove my innocence?"

"Excuse me, what did you just say?"

"My hair sample. Of course, it was a different color back then, but what did the DNA results show?"

Avalina caught herself before she pressed him any further, knowing it would be next to impossible to make the detective believe, that she was a reincarnation of Joan Sanders. The possessed young woman tried really hard to read his mind, just to see if she could find out what he was thinking about her, but it was no use. Her powers were weak, very weak. In fact, Avalina was beginning to wonder if she had any powers left after her latest transition.

"Miss O'Sullivan, I don't exactly know what kind of game you're playing here, but I don't like it. I've seen you only once at a recent crime scene. What would I want with your hair sample, unless of course, there's something you're not telling me?" Wiretrak asked her.

"No, no, I'm sorry, sir. I'm just feeling a bit under the weather lately; you know, a little stressed from work and well, I guess I'm a little tired. I just wanted to visit my friend; I haven't heard from her lately. I didn't know she was dead...I'm sorry," Avalina said with a phony cry in her voice.

"And that's the *real reason*, Miss O'Sullivan?"

"Yes, yes, it is."

"Ok, then, I see no real reason to keep you here for now. Come on, I'll take you back to the front desk."

"Is there a phone there that I could use to call for a cab?"

"You don't have a cellphone, in this day and age?"

"I've seemed to misplace it."

"You misplaced your cellphone? Really? Wow, I thought everyone slept with their phones nowadays."

"Well, I don't, and I *did* misplace it."

"Alright, then; come on, I'll show you where the house phone is."

Detective Wiretrak brought Marcella O'Sullivan back to the front desk and let her use the desk phone. Wiretrak watched her intently as she made the call for the car service. *What the devil did she mean by that remark about a hair sample? The only hair sample I took recently was that of the deceased, Joan Sanders,* he thought. Wiretrak started to become very suspicious of her. *I think I'll just keep a close eye on Miss Marcella O'Sullivan for a while,* he thought to himself. The detective wanted to watch her until she left, but he had gotten a call and had to leave.

22

TIRED OF LIVING

Carrie Sanders was lying in her bed having a bad dream involving her daughter, Joan. In her dream, Joan was trying to tell her something. She was talking about the evil spirit that had been possessing her. Joan was also telling her mother about the pain in her stomach. Joan had mentioned to her that she was dying, and so was her baby.

"No! No! Don't die, Honey! No!" Carrie screamed out loud.

Carrie jumped up into a sitting position in her bed, bathed in a cold sweat. She was still barley covered by the blue quilt on her queen-sized bed, still heaving from the very vivid frightening scene that played in her head. The middle-aged woman realized that she had been having a nightmare. Carrie looked at her alarm clock on the nightstand; it was only three-thirty in the morning. *God, it's way too early in the morning to bother my daughter, but I've got to know if she's alright,* Carrie thought. She picked up the black phone that was sitting on the nightstand and dialed her daughter's number. Then, after Carrie heard a few tones, a recording played saying that the number she dialed had been disconnected.

Joan hadn't paid any of her utility bills in over two months; so one by one, the services were being turned off: including the cable TV, her phone, and the electricity. Suddenly, Carrie started to remember everything. She remembered the detective coming to her house the other day. Detective Wiretrak had come over to bring her the grim news that her daughter, Joan, was dead. Joan Sanders had been brutally murdered in her own home, in her own bed, just five days away from her twenty-second birthday.

"No...it can't be...it must all be just a horrible dream...or maybe an extremely cruel joke brought on in tremendously poor taste by some asshole. My Joan can't be gone...not my last surviving child. It isn't fair…it just isn't…" Carrie tried to finish saying.

Carrie Sanders began helplessly crying to herself on the bed, knowing very well, that it wasn't a dream at all. It wasn't a cruel joke. Her daughter was gone and she was never coming back. Joan had been taken away from her by a selfish, monstrous killer: her own beloved boyfriend, David Scholl. Of course, Carrie didn't really know who had killed her own daughter, but she speculated, just like Detective Wiretrak did after what he told her about David. The two of them firmly believed that David definitely played a big hand in it. Carrie cried so much that her eyes were getting red and puffy. The woman's formerly beautiful, long; straight red hair was becoming matted.

Carrie kept thinking about the idea of having to bury yet another child, her last surviving offspring. Joan had been the last of her three born children. Her first baby and her only son died during childbirth. The baby was a breech birth that had experienced head entrapment and died, due to a lack of oxygen. Carrie was devastated; she had named him Dalton. All Carrie kept saying to everyone was, *I carried him for nine months, just to give birth to a corpse.* Since baby Dalton had never seen the light of day, Carrie told her husband that she was done with making babies. *Either YOU have a vasectomy, or I get my damn tubes tied,* she firmly said to him. Carrie didn't want to go through the pain of losing another child, but a year later, Carrie got pregnant again. Carrie's husband lied to her; he never did have the vasectomy, and baby Sarah was born.

Once again, the Sanders became a happy family. Carrie stayed out of work for almost a year just to be with her little newborn child. Carrie and Tom both spoiled their daughter. The couple enjoyed shopping for clothes and toys for their little girl. Carrie loved to dress up her new baby. When Sarah got a little older, Carrie braided her long red hair into pigtails or into a ponytail. One fateful morning, Carrie was bringing their daughter to her first day in kindergarten. She drove down the road heading towards the school. Carrie made sure that the child was well secure in her car seat, in the back of the family's green four-door sedan. All of a sudden, she heard her daughter crying in the backseat.

"No, mommy, no! I scary'd! No wanna go to school," Sarah had cried out.

Carrie had turned her head around and told her little daughter that it was ok, and that she would love kindergarten, but Carrie didn't see the big black SUV that was swiftly coming towards them. She was too preoccupied consoling her little girl. The sports utility vehicle had taken the light at the intersection. It came barreling along at a high rate of speed. The oncoming SUV plunged right into the left side of Carrie's car, directly hitting the backseat where little Sarah was sitting in her car seat. Her tiny neck snapped just like a dried-out twig during the impact. The poor little child was killed instantly. It all happened so fast that Carrie couldn't comprehend what had happened. Her brain went into overload and she just passed out. Sarah had only turned five-years-old on that very same day.

Carrie Sanders was lucky, although, she didn't see it that way. The woman had survived the accident with only a few cuts and bruises. Her car was a total loss. When Carrie regained consciousness in the hospital emergency room that afternoon, it was her husband, Tom, who had given her the bad news. *Honey, our daughter didn't survive the crash,* he solemnly told her. Once again, Carrie Sanders was distraught. *A parent shouldn't have to bury her own child...twice,* she had cried out to her husband in the hospital.

However, a year after Sarah's death, Carrie got pregnant again with Joan. This time it was Carrie that wanted another child; that was over twenty-one years ago. Now, her last surviving child had been cruelly taken away from her by a horrible killer. Carrie couldn't even lean on her husband, Tom, this time since he had passed away over five years ago from a stroke. Carrie was an only child; she didn't even have any siblings to turn to either. Her mother and father were both killed in a boating accident close to ten years ago; so in essence, she had no one to turn to and nowhere to go. The woman did have one real true friend, Mildred A. Stark, a fellow schoolteacher; but Mildred had been in a comatose state, ever since a loose brick from the school building fell upon her head. Mildred had stopped right outside of the structure to answer a text, while she was leaving to go home. That's when she got hit. It had been almost six months ago since it happened. Mildred's husband was not ready to take her off of life support, even though the doctors claimed that the woman showed no evidence of brain activity; so, she's been in the hospital ever since.

Carrie decided to get out of bed and go through the old photo albums in her dresser drawers. She looked at all of the old photographs of happier times. The woman viewed the snapshots of her second child, Sarah and her husband, Tom, with a half-smile on her face. Carrie looked at the pictures she had of Joan as a baby, as well as those of the ones she had of when she was growing up. There were no pictures of her first baby, Dalton. The woman didn't want any pictures of a dead infant. It would have only reminded her of what could have been.

"Here I go again, burying another one of my children and, I don't even have my dear Tom at my side for support. Shit!" Carrie said to herself.

Carrie spent over two hours reminiscing about the past with her photo albums. All in all, the grief-stricken woman went through five books of pictures. Carrie finally closed up the big white books and tearfully, placed them back in the drawer of her dresser. She noticed that the sun was coming out. Carrie looked at her alarm clock; it was a little after six o'clock in the morning.

On the other side of town, Detective Wiretrak was in the shower thinking about the workday that was ahead of him. Wiretrak was concerned about several things. One thing that had alarmed him was the fact that after a downturn in the COVID-19 cases, there seemed to be an upswing all over again. People were not practicing social distancing like they should have been. Some were throwing house parties and others were holding rallies, without wearing any face masks, especially the young people.

"Young people seem to think that they're impervious to anything harmful. They think they're superhuman; that's just being plain irresponsible and stupid," he said to himself.

Wiretrak knew that once the warm summer weather came in, everything would probably ease up and return back to normal, but there was no normal, not as of yet anyway. There wouldn't be any normalcy until a vaccine was available for the Coronavirus and that, probably won't happen until next year.

The other thing that bothered Detective Wiretrak was what Marcella O'Sullivan had told him at the police station, the day she got arrested for trespassing at the crime scene of Joan Sanders. *By the way, detective, did my hair sample prove my innocence? Of course, it was a different color back then, but what did the DNA results show?* Wiretrak kept playing her words over and over again in his head, like a worn-out recording. He became obsessed with what Marcella had said to him that day. *She knows something; I don't know how or what, but that woman definitely knows something,* he was thinking to himself while rinsing off in the bathtub. Wiretrak wondered what the *real* reason was for Marcella's presence at the murder scene. *Did she really know the deceased? Maybe, she's closer to Joan Sanders than I thought she was, or was it something else?* he asked himself. The young detective dried himself off and stepped out of the bathtub. Then, he went back into his bedroom and proceeded to get dressed for his day at work.

"I still think David Scholl had something to do with the murder of Joan Sanders, but I need proof. I need to know what motive he had. There I go talking to myself again," the detective said to himself.

Wiretrak knew that the prime suspect in most murders was usually the spouse. The detective also knew that nine times out of ten, the motive had to do with money and/or sex, wanting to be with someone else. Since Joan Sanders was not wealthy, it had to be about sex. Wiretrak was also well aware of the fact that Joan Sanders and David Scholl were not married, but they were together. *Maybe, she was closer to him than he really wanted her to be. Maybe, he was just using her for sex; of course, that still didn't give him a reason to kill her, especially like that. They were both single. David could have easily just left her,* he thought. Wiretrak had finished getting himself dressed and he was just about ready to leave, until his cellphone rang.

"Detective Wiretrak here," he answered.

"Wiretrak, it's me, Chief Valentine," the chief replied.

"Hey, chief, I was just about ready to leave. Why is your number showing up as unknown?"

"It must be a network problem; anyway, I got some news for you from the medical examiner. It's about Joan Sanders."

"Well, spill it, chief. Don't keep me in suspense."

"It seems our victim, Joan, was not alone."

"What do you mean by that, boss?"

"Miss Joan Sanders was in the early stages of pregnancy."

"Well, well, well and I can only make an educated guess at who the hell the father is."

"David Scholl?"

"Glad to see we're on the same track. Thanks, chief, I'll be right down."

Detective Wiretrak was happy; the pieces of his puzzle were finally coming together. Now, there was a motive for David Scholl to murder his girlfriend. It became obviously clear that David wasn't quite ready to become a father yet. The detective knew he had to give this information to Joan's mother; he just didn't feel like depressing her anymore, not now anyway. Wiretrak hated giving people bad news, especially to inform them that their child or spouse had been killed. He left his apartment and went to his car. The young detective started up his vehicle and thought for a bit while the engine warmed up. *We're going to need a DNA sample from David Scholl,* he thought.

Back at the home of Carrie Sanders, Carrie really needed someone to talk to; the woman needed to vent. On a whim, she decided to call the hospital that her friend, Mildred, was in. Carrie wanted to see if she had finally come out of her coma. Carrie dialed the number of the hospital and waited for someone to answer the phone.

"Good morning, Brighten Medical Center, may I help you?" the receptionist asked.

"Hello, can you please transfer me to room 305, Mildred Stark's room?" Carrie asked.

"I'm sorry. Mrs. Stark expired two days ago."

"Oh my God, no!"

"I'm sorry. Is there anything else I can do for you, Miss?"

"No, thank you."

Carrie dropped the receiver back on the phone's hook and wept some more. She knew for sure that there was no one else to turn to. Then, the teary-eyed woman started to remember her recent dream.

"My daughter's spirit was trying to communicate to me through my dream," she said to herself.

The woman tried to recall the dream as vividly as possible. In her dream, Joan was talking about the spirit that had possessed her.

"What spirit? Was that why she was acting so weird lately?" Carrie asked herself.

Joan was also telling her mother about the pain in her stomach. Joan had said that she was dying.

"The detective said that she was stabbed in the stomach, multiple times," she reiterated.

Then, Carrie recalled the last thing her daughter had actually said to her in the dream. *I'm dying momma, and so is my baby.*

"Baby, what baby? She never mentioned anything about a baby to me. Was I going to be a grandma? Maybe, that's why she was stabbed in the stomach. That sonofabitch! He made sure he not only killed her, but the bastard had also killed her baby! Shit! it isn't fair!" she screamed out loud.

Carrie now firmly believed that Joan was killed by her own boyfriend, David Scholl. She figured that David wasn't ready to become a father yet. *He probably wasn't the fatherly type,* she thought. Carrie presumed the sonofabitch wanted to escape child support by killing off his girlfriend and their unborn child.

"I-I could have been a grandma…now, I don't have anything…nothing at all…except a funeral for my dead daughter. I have nothing to live for…not a goddamn thing. You sonofabitch, you killed my daughter and my grandchild! I hope you fucking rot in hell, you scumbag!" Carrie cried out as if her daughter's assassin was right there in the room with her.

Carrie Sanders tried to pull herself together; she was

supposed to go online via the school's website today to teach her class. Carrie's students would be waiting for her, but Carrie was in no shape to teach her children today. The woman looked disheveled and she was emotionally distraught.

"I've had three children and none of them even met each other. My first born didn't even see the fricking light of day," she miserably stated.

The depressed middle-aged woman finally got out of her bedroom after wallowing in her self-pity. Carrie walked on over to the kitchen and brewed herself a fresh pot of coffee. She poured a bowl of cold cereal, filled it with milk and waited for the coffee to finish brewing. When her coffee was ready, Carrie filled her cup up halfway, then added milk and sugar. She took her breakfast into the living room and turned on the TV to watch the news.

"Police are on the lookout for any information leading up to the arrest of the killer who slaughtered twenty-one-year-old, Joan Sanders. Miss Sanders was found brutally stabbed to death in her own home," the male reporter said with a split screen showing an old picture of Joan smiling.

Carrie dropped both her cereal bowl and her cup of coffee, upon seeing the breaking news story about her daughter. The tears started to well up in her eyes all over again.

"She looked so happy in that picture," the woman sadly said to the television set.

Again, she began to break down and sob. Carrie Sanders was literally consumed with grief. There was nowhere for her to go and no one for her to turn to.

Carrie went downstairs to the basement and went through her late husband's workbench. Carrie was looking for some heavy rope.

"This, I'll do...this, I'll do, nicely," she said to herself after finding it.

Carrie cut a few feet of the rope and fashioned herself a noose out of it. She brought the noose upstairs to the dining room. The saddened woman moved all of the chairs, except one, out of the room and into the hallway. Then, she moved the table out, too. Carrie then stood up on the remaining chair and took the loose end of the rope in her hand. The woman was meticulous in terms of taking into account for her height, the height of the ceiling and the height of the chair, while she was measuring the length of the noose. Carrie was a perfectionist.

"Everything just had to be right...or you wouldn't do it at all," she said to herself.

Carrie snuggly attached the cord to the top of the chain closest to the ceiling, that held the small chandelier. She made sure to triple the knot around the chain of the light fixture, for added strength and support. She gave the noose a firm tug with both of her hands to check for its strength. Carrie placed the noose around her neck, making sure that all of her red hair went over it, not under it. Carrie kicked the chair out from under her feet, until she was dangling from the ceiling light fixture. The dying woman kicked up a hell of a dance. Carrie looked just like a marionette while her homemade noose choked the life out of her. After a few moments of struggling and gasping for air, it was all over for her. Carrie Sanders was dead at the age of only forty-eight. She simply just got tired of living and tired of being disappointed in life. Maybe, now, she could be with all of her children and her late husband. Maybe, now, Carrie Sanders could rest in peace.

23

THE TRUTH

Avalina was waking up in the body of Marcella O'Sullivan and getting ready to go back to her former host's home. She was going to try it again. *This time there'll be no slipups. If the police are still there, I'll just use my powers to put them to sleep,* the witch thought to herself. She fixed herself a bowl of cereal and some hot tea with milk and sugar. After Avalina finished her breakfast, she washed up and got dressed. The possessed young woman went through the phone book and called the same car service back up again.

Later on that morning, the taxicab arrived back at the home of Joan Sanders, with Avalina Bishop inside of Marcella O'Sullivan, her human puppet. Avalina tipped the driver and cautiously got out of the car. She noticed how dark and cloudy it was. The young witch looked at her watch. It was nine o'clock in the morning, but it could have easily passed for being nine o'clock at night. Avalina carefully looked around the perimeter of the home that still had, the yellow crime scene tape wrapped around it.

"So far, so good; I don't see any cops around," she said to herself.

The possessed woman slowly approached the driveway. She noticed tire tracks leading from the end of the driveway towards the back yard. The girl went into stealth mode by slowly peaking behind the house. Sure enough, there was a police squad car parked hiding behind the house. No one would have noticed it unless they walked towards the backyard and looked around the house.

"Shit," she quietly said to herself.

Avalina observed the police officer that was sitting in his

vehicle, playing with his phone. She focused and concentrated her powers onto the officer.

"Now, you will go to sleep. You will go into a very deep sleep. Your eyelids are getting very heavy. Resist the temptation to stay awake. You cannot fight my command. You must go to sleep. Sleep just like you were a newborn baby. Ease your mind and sleep, until I give you the command to awaken," Avalina slowly chanted.

She repeated the chant again, but nothing happened. The officer was still wide awake and playing with his phone. Avalina realized she was powerless.

"What the hell happened to my powers?" Avalina quietly asked herself.

The young witch wondered what she was going to do now. There was no plan "B." The witch leaned on the side of the house and thought for a bit. *How the hell am I going to get rid of him and get into that house?* Avalina had wondered. All of a sudden, the officer picked up the microphone that was attached to his two-way radio and began talking into it. After a moment, the police officer hung up his microphone and started up his vehicle. Avalina had gotten the lucky break that she had wanted; the cop had gotten a call and had to go. She waited for him to leave. Avalina was very careful not to be seen. The officer slowly drove his car back onto the driveway pavement and then he took off.

Avalina went straight to the front door and tried the lock. It wouldn't budge. She tried using her powers to unlock it, but that had failed her, too.

"I'm powerless! What the shit happened to me?" Avalina asked herself again.

The young witch felt like she was becoming mortal. Avalina

went around the back and climbed the deck steps. She checked the sliding glass patio door to see if it was unlocked, but unfortunately for her, it was locked. Avalina didn't have any keys. She didn't even have the remote keyless entry for the garage door. Everything was locked up in the house.

"The car! What about Joan's car?" Avalina cried out.

She remembered just recently acquiring the eight-year-old white, Chevrolet four-door sedan with David Scholl, in a used car dealership in New Jersey. *That was such a happy day. David was so sweet. He completely paid for the car without ever asking me for his money back,* Avalina happily recalled. The young witch figured that the car must still be locked up in the garage.

"A lot of good that's gonna do me now," she bitterly said to herself.

Avalina was growing both frustrated and furious.

"I've got to get inside that damn house and get David's address and directions," she said through clenched teeth.

Avalina looked around the backyard for a rock. She didn't come all this way, twice, for nothing. The possessed young woman kept scrounging around the yard for a rock to throw. Finally, Avalina had found what she was looking for: a small grey rock. The young witch looked around to make sure that none of the three neighbors, were out and about. She walked back up the stairs leading towards the rear deck of the house. Avalina thought about smashing the sliding glass door, but she didn't want to create such an obvious mess, nor did the woman want to make that much noise. Instead, Avalina decided she would smash the kitchen window that was right next to the door. Avalina broke only enough glass so that she could reach her hand in and unlock the window. The young witch lifted the unlocked window up, being careful not to cut herself in the process. Avalina climbed in through the window and stepped onto the kitchen countertop. She then cautiously climbed down to the floor while stepping on some broken glass.

"I made it! Damn, I'm great," the witch said to herself.

Avalina went upstairs towards the master bedroom. When the young witch walked into the room, she was taken aback. It was still just the way it had been the last time Avalina had seen it…before she died. The queen-sized bed, with its white sheet, two white pillows, and a light blue blanket on top of it, were all still covered in blood…her blood; but in reality, it was the blood of Joan Sanders. Avalina became somber. She still had trouble accepting the reality that the love of her life, David Scholl, had done this to her.

"This is where it all happened. This is where David stabbed me to death. He had destroyed my precious body…my favorite host…just because I got pregnant with his child," she sadly said to the empty room.

The young witch tried to compose herself; she remembered the real purpose of her visit there. Avalina went through her old dresser drawers and finally found what she was looking for: her old black address book with David Scholl's address and directions in it.

"Bingo, this is just what I came here for," she said to the book.

Avalina saw something else in the drawer that was hidden under her old garments, something she wasn't really looking for, but the girl was happy to have found it. It was her gun, the gun she took from the home invader the night he committed suicide, right in front of her eyes.

"Oh, yes, this will certainly come in handy, especially since I don't have my powers anymore. Hopefully, they'll come back soon," she said to herself.

"Noooo, they won't," a voice said from inside the room.

Avalina recognized that voice. She looked around, but she did not see him.

"Where are you?" Avalina asked.

"I am here; looook up," the voice called out to her.

The young witch looked up at the ceiling. The Dark One had materialized and was floating above the bed, looking down at her. He was in the same exact spot that Avalina had last saw him, while she was dying in the body of Joan Sanders.

"Where the hell were you when I needed you? You saw me getting stabbed to death by that, that heartless monster, and you did nothing…nothing at all," she bitterly stated.

"Did you sayyy mon-ster? I thought you loveddd him?" The Dark One slowly replied.

"He murdered me and our unborn child. I was going to have his baby."

"Pre-cise-ly why I tolddd you to des-troy him in the fir-st pla-ce. He's no gooood."

"Yeah…well…I guess I should have listened to you. I screwed up."

"So, now, do we have a mu-tu-al un-der-stan-ding of what must be done?"

"Yes, we do. I want his ass bad. I want him to pay for what the hell he did to me and my baby."

"Goooood."

"Just one thing: what the hell happened to my powers?"

"You've relin-quished them in your last trans-form-ation."

"How?"

"Ev-ery time you possessss a mere mortal body, you looose some of your po-wer. Not coun-ting your original body, this is your third body. If you die againnn, you may ne-ver return againnn."

"You mean; this might be my last body?"

"Cor-rect. Make sure you accomplishhh your mis-sion. You may ne-ver get ano-ther chance againnn."

"Please, you must help me!"

"I cannot."

"Why? Why can't you help a poor little powerless witch like me?" Avalina pleaded with a helpless look on her face.

"Be-cause I made a dealll with Da-vid Sch-oll years ago."

"What kind of deal?"

"Have you taken your fulll re-venge against your ori-gi-nal assassinsss?"

"What do you mean by that?"

"The ones that burneddd you alive when you were young?"

"Yes, I finally killed them all, including David Scholl; except of course, the David that I dated."

"You have not killeddd them alll. You have not killed Da-vid Sch-oll."

"I killed the old David Scholl, not the young one, not the one that slaughtered me there on that bed."

"You have killed an inn-o-cent man...not the one you were loo-king for."

"No, that's not true. The last one I killed was in Long Island and he admitted to me that he went to my high school; that's why I killed him. I knew I had finally got the right one."

"Noooooo, there were two David Scholl's in your schoool at that time. You have killeddd the wrong one."

Avalina started to remember. The young witch recalled that the middle-aged man, the one she had killed in Long Island, didn't look anything like the David she remembered back in high school.

"You're telling me I killed an innocent man?" Avalina asked the spirit.

"Precisely," The Dark One replied.

"I failed. I searched and searched for him and still I can't find him."

"Oh, but you have."

"No, I give up."

"Noooo, do not be weak! Do not be a quitter! Don't be a fooool."

"The only other David Scholl I have found was the one I loved, the young David that had killed me right here on that bed," she said while pointing to the bed that was all covered in the blood of her former host.

"It is ti-me for you to know the re-al tr-uth."

"What truth?"

"They are both one and the sa-me," The Dark One slowly hissed out.

"WHAT? No! It can't be. He is much younger."

"Nooo, he is not. He is old. He is the David Sch-oll that tried to burnnn you alive in 1969, with his friends."

"But he can't be. He doesn't look anything like the David Scholl I knew back then."

"He has had his faceee chan-g-ed."

Avalina was shocked. In fact, she was so stunned, that the possessed young woman dropped the book and gun she was holding on the carpeted floor, right in front of her feet. The young witch tried extremely hard to digest what this evil spirit, dressed in a black cloak and black hat, had just told her.

"I don't believe it…it just isn't possible," Avalina softly said while trying to figure it out.

"Oh, but it is po-ssi-ble. I made it possible for him. I have en-chan-ted him," The Dark One confirmed.

Avalina still couldn't believe it. Part of her didn't want to believe it was true. Then, the young witch began to remember certain things. Avalina remembered how every time she would search for the name "David Scholl" on the computer, her boyfriend would be the first one to come up. *His apartment was decorated like it came out of the sixties,* she recalled. At times, David acted very old-fashioned around her. David had even talked like he came out of the past. *That old song, "My Girl" by The Temptations, he said that was his favorite song,* she remembered David saying. Suddenly, it was all coming together for her.

"If this is true, it gives me even more of a reason to despise him. It gives me more reason to really want to destroy him. But I need to know how and why you did it?" Avalina asked the spirit.

"Da-vid saw his fa-ther die young of a very rare ill-nesss. It was an ill-nesss that made him pre-ma-turely age at a very rapid rate.

306

David was nine-teen yearsss old when his fa-ther died. It made such an im-pression on him, that he sum-moned me. David beg-ged meee for ever-las-ting youth, thinking that he, too, would suffer from the same fate as his fa-ther did. That was before David had rea-ched his twentieth birth-day," The Dark One explained to her.

"So, you granted his wish?" Avalina asked him."

"I had made a de-al with him. Da-vid would remain looking nine-teen yearsss old for-ever, or, until he impreg-nated a woman with his seed. How-ever, David failed to men-tion the fact that heee had a very low sperm count. He neglected to men-tion that very im-portant det-ail to meee. Da-vid had essen-tially lied to meee; so, I helped him im-preg-nate you so that I could col-lect. It was timeee to col-lect...," the spirit slowly said.

"Collect what? What did David have to do for you in order to stay young?"

"He must re-lin-quish his soul to meee once he plants his seeeed...then, his time would be up."

"Is he immortal?"

"Nooo. You can kill him, but I cannot, as per our con-tract. Once David's mate gives birth to his child, he will inst-antly age to his cor-rect age, and if he, tooo, has the disease, David will con-tin-ue to age until he dies. That is when I can col-lect what is right-fully mine."

"That's why he killed me...because I got pregnant. I got in his way and he wanted to survive. Shit! That selfish, self-centered sonofabitch!"

"Correct. So, do we have a mu-tual agree-ment?" The Dark One asked her.

Avalina thought long and hard. Clearly, the young witch still had some strong feelings for David Scholl, but she couldn't dismiss what he had done to her…twice. Avalina had to set aside her love for David. She knew he had murdered her and her unborn child right here in this room, but Avalina did not know that he was the same one that helped murder her, when she was only a teenager, about fifty-one years ago. The possessed young woman had already made her decision.

"Yes, we do. I must destroy him for what he has done to me," Avalina said as she turned and faced The Dark One.

"Very goooood," he hissed.

"So, tell me, if I need your help in a hurry, I mean, since I'm powerless right now, what may I call you?"

"You may call me Na-tas."

"Ok, Natas, that's easy to remember."

Natas had disappeared right in front of Avalina's eyes. She stared at the empty bed that was covered in blood for a moment. The young witch was both hurt and extremely angry. Avalina bent down to pick up the gun and the address book. The witch was also worried because her powers were all gone. Avalina was going to have to be very careful, since this may be the only body she has left. Avalina left the bedroom all teary-eyed. The young sorceress walked down the stairs and went out the same exact way that she came in: through the kitchen window. Avalina knew in that moment that she would never return to this house again.

Later on that evening, Detective Wiretrak was getting ready to pay Marcella O'Sullivan a visit. Wiretrak was getting a little suspicious of the young female EMT. He started to walk out of his office until Chief Valentine summoned him into his office, over the intercom. *Shit! What does he want now?* the young detective mentally asked himself. Wiretrak strolled over to the chief's office and knocked on his door.

"Who is it?!" Valentine barked behind his door.

"It's me, Wiretrak. You wanted to see me, chief?" he asked through the door.

"Come on in."

"What can I do for you, chief?" Wiretrak asked him as he stepped into the chief's office.

"We're going to have to get a court order for David Scholl. The sonofabitch refuses to give us a DNA sample," Valentine angrily replied.

"I figured he'd play hardball."

"Where were you going off to?"

"How did you know that I was going out, chief?"

"You look like it. You got your jacket on and it's summer."

"Well, I thought I'd go pay Marcella O'Sullivan a visit."

"Oh, Jesus H. Christ. Will you leave the damn girl alone and let her do her own job for Christ's sakes? What, do you have a thing for her, like Joan Sanders? You think I didn't know about that, huh?"

"No, boss, I just want to question her, that's all."

"Did you tell Carrie Sanders that her late daughter was pregnant?"

"No, chief, I'll get right on it."

"Don't bother. She's dead."

"What? How? When?"

"She was found hanging from her dining room chandelier this afternoon."

"Shit! Who found her, chief?"

"The cable TV repairman. It seems that there was a crew of technicians doing some work in her area. They were still upgrading the service area with fiber optics. One of the men rang her doorbell; he wanted to inform Miss Sanders that there would be some service interruptions again, while they replaced the lines. The service tech figured she was home, since he could see her dining room light on through the window. When Miss Sanders didn't answer the door, the man decided to go and knock on her window to get her attention. That's when he noticed she was hanging right there from the ceiling light fixture. The next thing I know, we got a fricking call to go check it out. Horrible, isn't it?"

"Yeah, it really sucks, but you know what, chief? It doesn't surprise me, not one bit. You should have seen the look on her face when I told her that her daughter was murdered."

"I can imagine. The woman didn't have any other family members; they're all gone now. Joan Sanders was her last living youngster. Yep, you really wanna know what the hell killed Miss Carrie Sanders? I'll tell you what killed her...depression; that's what did it. Once depression gets a hold of you, it locks you up tight in its ugly grip, until you pay up...usually, with your damn life. That's what the hell happened here, Wiretrak."

Detective Wiretrak solemnly left the chief's office. He felt really bad about what happened to Carrie Sanders. Wiretrak also knew that his prime suspects in the string of recent murders, were both gone. There were no more women in the area that featured bright red hair; at least, none that he knew of. *I guess it's back to the damn drawing board for me,* he miserably thought to himself. Wiretrak left the police station, hopped into his car, and drove off.

✳
✳✳

A few miles away, Avalina Bishop was returning back to Marcella O'Sullivan's apartment. Avalina wasn't crazy about her new host's body or the shabby ass apartment that she lived in. *Well, I guess it'll have to do,* the possessed young woman thought as she left the cab. Avalina walked on into the lobby of the old tenement and proceeded to climb up the stairs. When she got up to the top floor, Avalina caught her breath enough to complain.

"Shit, I lose a nice, big ground floor house, only to get stuck in an old five-story walk up," she angrily said to herself.

*
**

The young witch walked down the corridor towards her flat. She unlocked the door and went inside her three-room apartment. Avalina walked into the living room and sat down on the cream-colored sofa. The possessed young woman began thinking about everything that Natas had told her today. *He is old. He is the David Scholl that tried to burn you alive in 1969, with his friends,* The Dark One had said to her disbelief. She was just about ready to cry until the doorbell rang. The possessed woman got up and walked towards the front door.

"Who is it?!" Avalina yelled out.

"It's Detective Wiretrak, you got a minute?!" he shouted back through the door.

"What the hell does he want now?" Avalina quietly asked herself.

The young witch unlocked the door and begrudgingly let the detective inside. Wiretrak followed her to the living room and sat down on the sofa.

"Nice place you got here," he said to her.

"You must be joking, right? This place is a dump," she replied.

"But it's your place, your home."

"Don't remind me; anyway, I'm sure you didn't travel all the way across town just to talk about my home."

"No, I didn't. What do you *really* know about Miss Joan Sanders?"

"She was my friend."

"We've established that already. Is there anything else you'd like to tell me about her?"

"Yeah, she was murdered."

"Come on now, we all know that, too."

"I also know who her killer was."

"Really? The truth now. No bullshit, who was it?"

"It was David, David Scholl, her boyfriend," she said with a tear in her eye.

"Forgive me for feeling skeptical, but how do you know this? I mean, do you have any proof, Miss O'Sullivan?"

Avalina had thought long and hard before answering his question. She tried again to read his mind, but it was no use. Natas was right; her powers were all gone.

"No, I don't, but I know he did it," she sadly said.

"You had asked me something in the police station when you were there. Do you remember what you asked me?" Wiretrak asked her.

"No, not really."

"You asked me about your hair sample. You wanted to

know what the DNA results were. Now, do you remember?"

"I, I wasn't really myself that day, detective."

"Oh, come on, now, Miss O'Sullivan! what the hell kind of a game are you playing here with me?! You knew I never took your hair sample!"

"I'm not playing any game! I think you ought to leave now. There's nothing more I have to say to you, detective. Please just go," Avalina angrily said to him.

"Fine, thanks for your help. I can see myself out," Wiretrak sarcastically said as he got up and let himself out through the door.

Avalina got up and locked the door behind him. She was worried. The last thing the girl wanted was to be arrested all over again. *I should have never asked him about my hair sample. That was a very stupid thing to say to him. Now, he suspects me…again. shit!* she bitterly thought to herself. Avalina walked into her kitchen to make herself a peanut butter and jelly sandwich. She noticed that the phone on the wall had a flashing red light. Avalina realized that the phone must have a built-in answering machine. *Modern technology,* she thought. Avalina pressed the flashing red button and the machine began playing her messages.

"Hello, is this Anna? Anna, if it's you, please pick up the phone. Anna? I guess I have the wrong number," the woman said before hanging up on the machine.

"I guess you do," Avalina said to the telephone on the wall.

The machine beeped and gave the date and time; then, it moved on to the very next message. Avalina stood there and listened to the next recording.

"EMT O'Sullivan, this is your supervisor, Lieutenant Palin. Why the hell didn't you show up for work again today? This is the second time. I'm putting you out on AWOL with no pay. You can see the chief tomorrow morning at nine. He'll figure out what he's going to do with you," the angry supervisor said on the recording.

Avalina didn't give two shits about him *or* the damn job. All she really wanted was to get even with David Scholl. The young witch had a serious score to settle with him. The machine beeped again and said, "end of messages," in a robotic voice.

Avalina was tired. She took a warm shower and went to the bedroom. The young witch was happy about one thing, though. She noticed a window mounted air conditioner in the bedroom window. It reminded her of the one her parents had in her old home. Avalina turned on the unit. *Well, at least I can sleep cool tonight,* she thought while hopping into the big queen-sized bed.

24

PAYBACK TIME

On a hazy, hot and humid Monday morning in early July, Marcella O'Sullivan had been officially notified of her termination from her place of employment as an emergency medical technician. This was due to failure of her attendance on the job and failure to attend any counseling for it. It didn't seem to faze Avalina Bishop at all as she read the letter to herself.

"So what? Who the hell cares? I didn't give a shit about that job anyway. Besides, I only wanna be here long enough to kill that sonofabitch, David Scholl. After that, I care less what happens to me *or* this mortal," Avalina angrily said through Marcella's body.

The young witch had become completely disheartened and bitter. She no longer wanted to stay here on Earth possessing a mortal body. Avalina was only interested in seeking her revenge against David Scholl. After that, she would be ready to leave this world and return back to the darkness, back to where she came from. Avalina used to have high hopes of marrying her lover, David Scholl and raising a family together, but now, that was just a distant and wishful memory for her.

"There *Is* no happy ending for me now…I guess there never really was a chance for me. There are only happy endings on TV shows and movies. That kind of shit doesn't really happen in real life. It's just bullshit and stupid ass fairy tales," Avalina solemnly said to herself in Marcella's apartment.

The depressed young witch thought of the only thing that would make her happy: getting even with David. She went to the bedroom dresser and got her gun and address book from the drawer. Avalina packed the items into her host's black purse. The scorned witch then went to the kitchen phone and called up the car service company.

*
**

A few miles away, Detective Michael Wiretrak was in his office receiving a package from a young police officer. He opened up the large Manila envelope and pulled out the papers. Wiretrak started reading the report with disappointment in his heart.

"I was right. I was right all along," the detective sadly said to himself.

The detective wasn't eager to share the news with anyone, but he knew it was his legal responsibility to inform the Chief of Police. Wiretrak took the whole report and brought it over to the chief's office.

"Hey, chief, I solved the cases of at least two of our murdered victims," Wiretrak told his superior.

"Really? Which two, Mike?" Chief Valentine asked him.

"The first two victims we found in Pond Lake, Anna Nuñez and John Waters."

"That's great news, Wiretrak! who's the culprit?!" Valentine excitedly asked.

"Well, you're not going to believe this, chief."

"Oh, come on now, Wiretrak. I wanna hurry up and lock this sonofabitch up already."

"Well, that's going to be a *big* problem, boss. Actually, it's going to be impossible."

"Just what the hell do you mean *impossible*?! Nothing's impossible, Mike!" Valentine barked.

"Take it easy, Charlie, remember your blood pressure," Wiretrak said in a calming way.

"The hell with my goddamned blood pressure already!"

"I'm sorry, boss, but it's going to be really impossible to incarcerate this killer."

"And just *why* is it impossible to lock this killer up? What is it? You don't know his whereabouts? Did he leave the country or something?"

"No, boss, the perpetrator is already deceased."

"No shit, he took the easy way out?"

"Not exactly, and for the record, it was a female not a male."

"Sonofabitch, you mean Charlie Rhodes was right about that new test?"

"That's right, chief. It also confirmed *my* suspicions of it being a woman all along."

"Really? Alright, enough with the damn games already. Who the hell was it and how the hell did you find out?"

"It was our latest victim, boss: Joan Sanders."

"You're putting me on, right?"

"I wish I was, chief, but the DNA tests don't lie."

"But we did a DNA test on her! It came back negative remember?"

"Yeah, I remember, but she must have had a wig on that day, probably made of human hair. When I saw her last at the crime scene, her hair was a slightly different color, *and* it was a whole lot longer than when she was here on that day. There's *no way in hell* her hair could have grown that much in such a short time."

"I still can't believe it. She didn't look all that strong, you know."

"Believe this: it's the DNA test results from the hair sample that I took from her body at the crime scene."

Wiretrak handed the chief the DNA report. Valentine read it in disbelief while shaking his head from left to right.

"I still think she had help. I just can't believe that one girl had the strength to overpower all of those people. What about the others? The nurse and that black guy in his SUV, Dwayne Worley?" Valentine asked the detective.

"I'm not sure about them, boss, but I've got a gut feeling, that she was responsible for pushing Michael Resnick in front of that oncoming subway train in February," Wiretrak firmly stated.

"Really? You know I think forensics found some strands of red hair on Mr. Worley's body. Two guesses at who it belongs to, Mike," the chief said while shuffling through a bunch of papers that were piled up on his desk.

"It's possible, chief, but Worley was a big beefy guy. I just couldn't see Joan Sanders going toe to toe with him," Wiretrak said while scratching his head.

"If there's one thing I've learned after being here all these years, it's that anything is possible. She could have seduced him, for whatever reason, then shot him in his head, bagged him and drove him to the lake in his own SUV. After that, Miss Sanders could have gotten out of his vehicle, put the damn thing in neutral and pushed it into the lake with him in it."

"But why, chief? What the hell was her motive?"

"That's what the hell we have to find out."

Later on that afternoon, Avalina had finally arrived at David Scholl's garden apartment house in Campton, New Jersey. The young witch paid the cab driver and walked out of the car. *Shit! That was a hell of a lot of money*, she thought. *Well, he had to drive me from New York to New Jersey; plus, I had to pay for his return toll going over the George Washington Bridge, and his damn gas.* Avalina thought and looked at the directions David had written for her.

"Apartment 1A. Ok, let's go find it," she said to herself.

Avalina walked around the complex looking for David's apartment number. She remembered that he lived all by himself on the first floor of the two-story building.

"Here it is; this is his apartment," Avalina softly said to herself.

The young witch put her address book back into her purse and rang the doorbell, wondering what exactly she was going to say to him to let her in. After a moment, David came towards the front door. He looked through the peephole in the door and was pleasantly surprised. *Wow, what luck, another pretty girl coming to visit me!* David thought.

"Who is it?!" David asked.

"Hello, I'm here from the census bureau! Are you David Scholl?!" Avalina shouted through Marcella's body.

"Yes! Just a minute, miss!"

David unlocked the front door. He stared at the pretty young woman for a moment as she stood there, wearing a light green blouse and a pair of blue jeans.

"Did anyone ever tell you that you have the most beautiful, soft blue eyes?" David asked her.

"Yes, I've been told that before. May I please come in, Mr.

Scholl? You are Mr. Scholl, correct?" Avalina asked, already knowing it was him all along.

"The one and only. Come on in," he happily replied.

David led the young woman in and closed the door behind her. He took the girl into his living room, getting ready to pounce on her. *She may not be as fine as Joan Sanders was, but she is a pretty young thing,* David thought while leading her to his sofa. Avalina had remembered his apartment so well, including the banjo clock that was hanging up on the wall. She recalled the bright green shag rug that was on the living room floor. Avalina also remembered the purple lava lamp that sat on the old-fashioned desk, sitting in the corner of the room. Avalina recalled the old glass-top coffee table that was in the middle of the room. She even recollected the large picture of her favorite band, The Beatles, that hung prominently on the wall in the foyer. The young witch reminisced about the first time she had come here and, all the sensual fun they had here together. *Shit! Why did it all have to end? It pains me to see him all over again,* Avalina wretchedly thought to herself. The two of them sat down on David's green sofa sitting next to each other.

"You know, nothing for nothing, but I could have sworn I sent in that census questionnaire; unless of course, you guys didn't get it yet," David told her.

"I really didn't come here for that, David," she sternly said.

"I was gonna say, where's your clipboard?""

"Right here," Avalina said while standing up away from him and pulling out her gun on him."

"What the hell? Who the hell are you and what do you want?"

"You killed me twice, you, sonofabitch! Now, it's *payback*

time!"

"M-Miss...you must be m-mistaken...I ain't never seen you before in my life," David nervously stammered.

"Get your damn hands up!"

"But, Miss, I-"

"Get 'em up now!"

David sat there helpless, not knowing what to do or say to the young woman. Clearly, things weren't going the way he had thought they would. The woman had the gun trained directly at his cranium, as he sat there on his sofa.

"Before you kill me, Miss, can you *please* just tell me what the hell this is all about? I couldn't have killed you. You're standing right there holding a gun at-"

"Shut up! Just shut the hell up already. I came here to kill you. I came here to see you fuckin' die, you, piece of shit. You screwed up my life...twice," she said while choking back the tears.

"I still don't know how."

"Does the name, 'Avalina Bishop' mean anything to you?"

"I-I haven't heard that name in years, but y-yes, it does."

"Do you remember what *you* and your hoodlum friends did to her back in 1969?"

"No, I don't. I wasn't even born then."

"Well, let me refresh your memory. I remember back then hearing you say in the cafeteria to your friends and I quote: 'Man, later for her ass. If she really was a witch, she got what the hell she deserved, unquote.'"

"How did you know that?"

"Because I *heard* you say that shit to your friends in the school cafeteria that day."

"It was a stupid thing that we all did together back then. We were kids and it wasn't even my idea."

"Oh, so you *do* admit that you were around back then. You all murdered me in my own damn house that day."

"What? You, you weren't even there, lady."

"Oh yes I was, you, asshole. I remember hearing all five of you chanting outside: 'burn, witch, burn! All of you repeated it over and over again. It's been ingrained inside my brain ever since, you, sonofabitch.'"

"How the hell can you possibly know that, Miss?"

"Like I just said before, asshole, I was there. I remember everything, including *you* trying to get fresh with me, until I squeezed your balls. Remember that, David?"

David was wondering how this young woman knew about all of those details from over fifty years ago. *It can't be her. She's been dead for years and this girl, doesn't look anything like Avalina Bishop,* he nervously thought while staring up at her and her gun. Then, David noticed something else about her. She was wearing a very unusual gold necklace with a pentagram hanging from it. David remembered seeing it before on someone else, but he couldn't remember who or when.

"How do you know all of this shit? I've got to know before you kill me." David said to her.

"I keep telling you…I *am* Avalina Bishop…reincarnated," she responded.

"You expect me to believe that shit?"

"I don't give a rat's ass what the hell you believe, but it's true. I came back just to get *all of you*, and I have, including that bitch, Melissa Conley, or whatever she changed her damned ass name to."

"You've killed them all?"

"That's right, asshole, and I've saved the best one for last...*you*!"

"T-then, you really are a witch, aren't you?"

"That's what I've been trying to tell you, asshole. To think I actually fell in love with your ass, shit!"

"When did *you* fall in love with me? You despised my ass in school."

"Just recently, dickhead. All I did was tell you that I was carrying your fricking baby, then you stabbed the shit out of my stomach, until you killed me *and* our unborn baby in my own damn bed. It was a nice sexy body, too. Remember all the fun we had together?"

"How...how the hell did you know all that shit?"

"Because it was me, too."

"Nah, no way, man, I don't believe that shit."

"Well, stupid, explain how the hell I knew all that then."

"The murder...it was all over the internet... that's how you knew that shit."

"Really, and did the internet say that I was pregnant, and that's why *you* killed me? Did the police lock your ass up yet?"

"No, and I can't explain that; unless of course, you were

friends with Joan."

"Oh, so while you were killing Joan Sanders, she got on the phone and called me? Did you see that shit happening because I sure as hell didn't. You left my ass for dead. I never got the chance to call anyone. I never got the chance to call for help," Avalina said with tears in her eyes.

"I still can't believe it. It's just way too far-fetched."

"While I was dying, I asked you something. I asked you if you killed your own mother and you admitted it, but then you said that for the record, she wasn't your mother. Now, how the hell would I know that?"

"I don't know."

"Who the hell was she, David?"

"Her name was Laurie Reynolds; she was my daughter."

"Your *daughter*? That old lady? She looked like she was your grandmother!"

"When I was young, I had sex with an older woman. I was thirteen years old at the time. She told me she was pregnant with my child. The woman was crazy, she wanted to marry me, but shit, I was too young and she was too old for me. After her baby was born, the woman got depressed and killed herself. Hell, I don't even remember her name. My folks felt so bad, that they took care of her baby, until they died, then I took care of her. Laurie Reynolds had also inherited the disease of premature aging, just like my father."

"Wow, really?"

"Yeah, really. She was going to spill the beans on me to the police so…"

"You killed her."

"I had to…didn't want to…but I had to."

"You know; I can still remember the first time I came here in Joan's body. I had come by here to kill you, but when I found out that you were David Scholl, well, I nearly fainted. You were so depressed because your pet bird had just passed away. You invited me into this very same room, being a perfect gentleman, and then you brought me a cool glass of water, remember?"

"What happened next?" David anxiously asked her.

"You knew I was upset. You gave me my water. We talked for a little bit after that, then you gave me a kiss on the cheek. I had kissed you back on the lips. You got so damn horny; your dick was growing right in your pants. I played with it for a little while and then I gave you a blowjob right here on this sofa. After that, we went into your bedroom and screwed all night. I remember it very well," Avalina said with a half-smile on her face while reminiscing.

David was getting aroused all over again listening to her sexy memories. *It has to be her, only Joan could tell that story so vividly,* he thought. David wished he could have screwed her right there and then, but since she had her gun pointed on him and he still had his hands up, that wasn't happening.

"That girl…the red-head…Joan Sanders… that really was you. wasn't it?!" David asked her.

"It was, until you killed me. That was my favorite body. Heck, I liked it better than my own real body, even though Joan was a little bit older than me. I especially loved her long, flowing bright red hair," she replied to him.

"And her big breasts," David added.

"Yes, those, too. Like I said before, you killed me twice and now I know why. I know all about you, Mr. David Scholl! You're nothing but an old fart, a dirty old man and a murderer."

"I wouldn't talk if I were you, you know. If you're *really* Avalina Bishop, then you're just as old as I am."

"Ah-ah, I've got myself a young body. *You*, on the other hand, well, that's just a disguise given to you from our friend, The Dark One."

"You know about him, too?"

"Who do you think helped me? Natas claims he helped you to impregnate me, and he's pissed off at you, asshole. He's pissed that you destroyed my host *and* your baby. Natas says it's time for you to pay up, and I'm going to help him collect; but before I kill you, David, I just wanna know one thing."

"W-what?"

"Did you ever really love me, or were you just using me for sex?"

"I-I don't know, babe. I really did have strong feelings for you; well, at least when you were Joan Sanders, but I don't know for sure if it was really love. It's been so long since I've been in love, that I've forgotten what it felt like, but I sure came close to remembering how it all felt with you. Killing you was very hard for me. I wish I didn't have to do it. I'm sorry, babe."

"I'm sorry, too, but I just can't let this shit go," Avalina said while wiping her tears with her right hand, the hand that was holding the gun she had pointed on David.

David saw a golden opportunity and took it. He smacked the gun right out from her hand and knocked Marcella off balance, until she fell flat on the floor behind his green sofa. David frantically searched the floor for the gun. All of a sudden, a shot rang out and hit his purple lava lamp, spewing broken glass, water, and melted wax all over his desk. Avalina had found the gun first lying under the sofa.

"Ok, ok I give up!" David yelled out.

"Stand up with your hands up! I don't want to kill you lying down on the ground," Avalina said in firm voice.

David slowly got up with his hands high above his head. He knew now it was the end of the road for him. Avalina had completely run out of patience with him.

"Will you please grant me just one final request?" David sincerely asked her.

"I know you don't smoke...what is it?" Avalina asked him.

"May I have just one last kiss from your sweet lips before I die?" he asked her with an adoring look on his face.

Avalina looked at him with trusting eyes. She couldn't resist his seemingly loving expression. Avalina let her guard down, but she still held on to her gun.

"Come here, baby, for old time's sake," she softly told him.

David slowly and cautiously walked over to Avalina. He put his arms around her and tenderly kissed her on the lips. Avalina had her hands around him, too, while still holding on to her gun. David grabbed her ass, while he rubbed his growing manhood against her thighs, trying to get her horny. Avalina was getting very excited, until she felt the blade of David's knife pierce right through her back. David had reached for it in his pocket. It was the same knife that he had used to kill her once before, when Avalina was in the body of Joan Sanders. The young witch was in agony, as David started to turn the sharp stainless-steel blade within her, but Avalina was *not* going to die from his hand again. The injured sorceress kneed him hard in his balls until he released her. Then, he collapsed back down onto the floor while grabbing his crotch. Avalina stood over him and shot him in the chest. The bullet had entered David's heart. David Scholl was now flat on his back, screaming from the excruciating pain, knowing that his life was finally coming to an abrupt end. Avalina dropped the gun and went over to him. The young witch cradled his head in her lap, while she sat on the green shag carpet with him.

"I'm so sorry, but I had to do it. You left me no choice, David," Avalina sadly said to him.

"He's come…to watch…me…die," David barely said while trying to point at the ceiling above him.

Avalina looked up to see what David was pointing to. Natas, The Dark One, was hovering right above them at the ceiling level. Avalina started to cry.

"You were my only true love in life. I just wanted you to know that," she told him while the tears streamed down from her face.

David Scholl was changing as he died. Avalina watched, first, in awe, as David Scholl's face changed, to the David she remembered back in high school in 1969. After that, David started aging at a very accelerated rate. Now, Avalina was watching in horror, as the man she once loved, was rapidly deteriorating right before her very eyes. David's hair was turning snow white and began falling out of his skull, leaving him bald. His skin was getting dried up and wrinkled like an old prune. David Scholl's heart had finally ceased beating, but Natas wasn't through with him yet. He made sure that David had contracted the same disease of premature aging that his father had. David was aging even more to the point that his remaining skin and organs began dissolving.

"Stop it! Stop it! Haven't you done enough already?!" Avalina screamed at Natas.

"Why dooo you care so muchhh a-bout him?" Natas slowly hissed at her.

"I don't know why. Even after all he has done to me…I-I still loved him."

"You are no-thinggg but a foooool."

The previously handsome young David Scholl was now nothing more than an unrecognizable skeleton, with its skull still lying in Avalina's lap. Avalina slowly pulled herself away from what was left of David Scholl. She tried to stand back up, but the pain was too unbearable from the knife that was still embedded into her back. Natas waved his arms, ejecting the knife from her back. Avalina's bleeding had stopped and her wound was completely healed. The young witch was now able to stand up and look at Natas, who was still floating above her.

"Thank you," Avalina told the spirit.

"Con-sider it pay-ment for what you have acco-mplished," Natas slowly replied.

"What more do you need from me?" Avalina asked him.

"No-thinggg more my dear chi-ld. You have performed admirably well. You may go now," Natas slowly hissed to her.

But Avalina didn't believe him. She knew that he would call upon her services again. Avalina picked up her gun and put it back into her purse. She took one last look at the crumbling old skeleton that was lying there on the floor, the remains of what was once her handsome young lover, David Scholl. Then, the saddened witch walked over towards the kitchen phone. Avalina picked up the receiver of the wall phone and called for a cab to take her back home. While she waited for the car service to come, the young witch contemplated everything that had just transpired between her, David, and The Dark One. *I guess I had to kill him, or he would have killed me again. He sure tried to. Well, it's all over now. I guess I don't need to stick around here anymore. This is nothing but fond memories for me now,* the young witch sadly thought to herself.

After a while, the private car service came by to pick Avalina up. She walked out the door, got into the car and left. It was getting dark outside. Evening was coming, but it was still bright enough for Detective Wiretrak, to have just seen the woman leave David's apartment, in the car that was marked, "Jim's Car Service."

"How many damn women does this man really have?" Wiretrak asked himself.

The young detective had come by with a court order to get a DNA sample from David Scholl. Wiretrak approached David Scholl's apartment. He wondered why the front door had been left open. Wiretrak walked into David Scholl's apartment and began to look around while calling his name.

25

THERE'S NOTHING LEFT FOR ME

Detective Michael Wiretrak was back in the chief's office the following Tuesday morning with his findings. The central air conditioning system had just broken down in the building. Chief Charles Valentine was already having a field day with it, demanding it to be serviced.

"The hottest fricking day in July and that *shit* breaks down. Where the hell is that damn service tech already?! I want that system fixed now! Where is he?!" Valentine hollered.

"I don't know, boss, but I didn't come in here for that," Wiretrak said to him.

"Well then, what the hell *did you* come here for?"

"I came in here to tell you about David Scholl."

"Oh, so you finally got a DNA sample from his ass, Mike? We got the court order now. I gave it to you and I don't wanna hear any bullshit!"

"Well, not exactly, chief. I didn't get-"

"Ah, come on, now. What the hell did I just tell you? No bullshit!"

"He wasn't there, boss. He just wasn't there!"

"What?! He wasn't there? Well, where the devil is he? Find him, that's what you're getting paid for!"

"Look, chief, please calm down and let me just tell you exactly what the hell happened. I went over to Scholl's apartment in Campton, New Jersey yesterday. I brought the court order with me to get a DNA sample from him. When I got near his apartment, I saw a woman just leaving his place. She got into a cab and left in a hurry. David's apartment door was left wide open, so I walked in and announced my entrance to Mr. Scholl as I looked around. He never once answered, by the way. I searched high and low for the man in the whole damn apartment, but there was no trace of him anywhere."

"Maybe, he left with that woman. He might have already been in the cab when you got there."

"That's possible, chief, but Mr. Scholl doesn't really strike me as the type of person that would just leave, without first closing and locking his front door. I mean, the man's got three damn locks on his door. He looks like Mr. Security to me, boss, if you know what I mean."

"So, what the hell are you trying to tell me here, Wiretrak? Are you saying that Mr. David Scholl, our suspect in a homicide, has been kidnapped?"

"I don't really know, chief; but here's the thing, I *did* find something very strange in his apartment. It was on the floor of his living room."

"Well, what the hell did you find already? Out with it, will you?! You know I hate suspense!"

"Well, you see, boss, David has this bright green shag rug right down on his living room floor. There was some strange white residue, like a white powder on the rug."

"Maybe, he's doing coke. Did you bring back a sample of it?"

"I sure did, chief; the boys in the lab are analyzing it right now as we speak."

"Good, if anything, we could just bring him in on drug

charges."

"There's just one more thing that bothers me, chief."

"What's that, Mike?"

"That white powder that was on his rug…it was in the image of a skeletal body."

"Shit, that's kind of creepy. What about the woman? Did you get a good look at her? Do you even know who the hell she is?"

"No, I didn't and no, I don't know who she is either. However, I did get the name of the car service that she took last night."

"Good, why don't you give them a call and find out who the hell they picked up yesterday at that address? It may be the only damn lead we have on Mr. Scholl."

"I'm on it, boss. Oh, and nothing for nothing, chief, but you'd better get yourself a small fan in here while you're waiting for them to fix the A/C. You're sweating bullets."

"Get out of here already!" Chief Valentine barked while fanning himself with the papers that were on his desk.

*
**

Detective Wiretrak went back to his office, making sure that *his* fan was on the desk and working. He remembered writing down the name of the car service, the one that the woman had used yesterday when she had left David Scholl's apartment. Wiretrak searched his little black book until he found it.

"Ah, here it is: Jim's Car Service," Wiretrak said to himself as he read from his book.

The detective looked them up on his office computer. After searching for a few minutes, Wiretrak found their telephone number and gave them a call.

*
**

A few miles away, Avalina Bishop was waking up again in Marcella O'Sullivan's body. She had a bad night. The young witch kept playing yesterday's scenario over and over again inside her head. It was like a DVD player that was stuck and playing the same movie repeatedly.

"There's nothing left for me to do here. I killed them all, including my handsome young lover, David Scholl," Avalina sadly said to herself.

Then, she remembered how David Scholl had last looked. *He wasn't so young and handsome anymore. He wasn't young at all, was he? David Scholl was old, old, and ugly,* the young witch thought to herself. Avalina wondered if she should even stay here on Earth. *I don't really belong here anymore,* she thought. Avalina had a purpose here before. She wanted to take revenge on the five miserable souls, that set her childhood house on fire and watched it burn down, with her inside of it. Avalina had accomplished her mission. She got her revenge against them all. The witch wanted to get even with David Scholl, her ex-lover, for the way he ended her life again by brutally stabbing her and her baby, while it was growing inside of her womb. She had accomplished that, too. David was dead now…by her own hand.

"What else is there for me to do?" she questioned herself.

Avalina thought about starting a whole new life for herself all over again, but the young witch didn't know what she would do for a living. Avalina certainly did not want to be an EMT again, riding around in an ambulance and saving lives all day; she knew that was Marcella O'Sullivan's dream, not hers.

"I liked being a legal secretary for that law firm when I was

Joan Sanders. I should apply for the job, being that there's an opening for it now. Maybe, just maybe I can even find myself another hot young lover and start a new life," she told herself.

Avalina looked at herself in the mirror, wondering what her host would look like as a redhead. *Yeah, I guess I'll stick around for a while. No more revenge and no more killing. I'll be a good girl now. I've got myself another chance and I'm not going to blow it*, Avalina happily thought.

About an hour or so later, someone was ringing Marcella O'Sullivan's doorbell. Avalina had just gotten out of the bathtub with a red towel around her. She wondered who it was.

"Who is it?!" the possessed young woman asked from behind the entrance door.

"It's Detective Wiretrak!" the detective firmly shouted out loud.

"Shit, what the hell does he want now?" she softly asked herself.

"I need to ask you some more questions, Miss O'Sullivan! It's imperative!"

"Alright, alright give me a minute!"

Avalina went over to her host's bedroom closet. She picked out a rose-colored house dress and put it on. Avalina walked back over towards the entrance door to let the detective in.

"So, what is it now, Mr. Detective?" Avalina asked him in an annoyed tone.

"I need to ask you some more questions, Miss O'Sullivan, may I come in?" Wiretrak asked her.

"Sure, let's go back in the living room again."

The young witch led the investigator into the living room and the two of them sat down on the cream-colored sofa. Avalina wanted to crush this man in his blue suit, like the unwanted pest that he was. Wiretrak took out his notebook and began questioning her.

"Now, Miss O'Sullivan, just where were you yesterday afternoon?" Wiretrak asked her with his pen in hand.

"I was here all day," she responded.

"Really? That's rather strange; you know why?"

"No, detective, why?"

"Because I have sources stating that you were elsewhere yesterday, like in Campton, New Jersey."

"Your sources are wrong. I was here all day yesterday."

"Have you got anything to prove your whereabouts from yesterday?"

Avalina tried really hard to read his mind, but she couldn't. *The Dark One really was right, I'm completely mortal and powerless*, she angrily thought. Knowing that the good detective was on to her, Avalina decided to come clean with him, at least to some extent.

"You're right, detective, I was in New Jersey yesterday visiting a friend," she somberly replied.

"Good, now we're getting somewhere; and did that friend happen to be a Mr. David Scholl?" Wiretrak asked while looking at her eyes.

"David Scholl? I don't even know who the hell he is."

"Oh, I think you know *damn well* who he is. For starters, you claimed that you were Joan Sanders's best friend. Surely, she must have mentioned her boyfriend to you, or am I going to catch you in another lie, Miss O'Sullivan?"

"Oh, *that* David Scholl."

"Yeah, *that* David Scholl. Secondly, I spotted you leaving his apartment early evening yesterday. Now, to be truthful, I didn't really get a good look at you, but the car service you took yesterday verified picking you up. So, are we on the same page, now, Miss O'Sullivan?"

"Yes, detective, we are."

"Good, I'm glad we're heading in the right direction. So, you *do* know David Scholl, correct?"

"David and I are just friends, that's all. I went over there to reminisce about Joan with him, you know."

"Yes, I see. Tell me, Miss O'Sullivan, where is Mr. Scholl now?"

"I assume he's back home."

"Well, he isn't. You see, Miss O'Sullivan, after you left him yesterday, I took the liberty of going inside his apartment. It was easy since you left his front door wide open when you left him. I found it rather strange that Mr. Scholl, himself, never even closed his front door after you left him…and now I know why. He was never there. You claim that you've seen him yesterday, but yet, he wasn't home. Now, just how do you explain that, Miss O'Sullivan?"

"I-I went over to visit him, but he had to leave in a hurry. I wasn't feeling good. I had a bad headache, so David gave me some aspirin and told me to stay until my headache went away. David asked me to close the front door when I left. I guess I just forgot."

"And that's the story you're sticking with now?" Wiretrak asked her while watching the nervous expression on her face.

"Yes, sir, that's the whole truth," Avalina replied with a conspicuous tremble in her voice.

Detective Wiretrak did not believe her far-fetched story. In fact, he expected something a little better than that from her. Avalina sensed that the good detective didn't believe her excuse, but she couldn't think of anything else to say on such short notice; after all, the man had her on the spot and he was on a roll.

"There's still one more thing that really bothers me, Miss O'Sullivan," Wiretrak indicated.

"Mr. Detective, I've told you everything there is to tell, sir," the witch stated.

"No, not quite, not quite at all. You see, Miss O'Sullivan, there was this strange residue on Mr. Scholl's green shag carpet in his living room, a white powder, if you will. It was a white powder in the shape of a human skeleton. Now, I took a sample of that powder, brought it down to the lab, had it analyzed, and you know what? It turned out to be tiny human bone fragments. Now, isn't that strange, Miss O'Sullivan? What do you think about that?" Wiretrak asked her in a suspicious tone.

"I-I don't know."

"You don't know? You know what I think, Miss O'Sullivan? I think you went over to Mr. Scholl's home to get even with him. I think you suspected him of killing your best friend, Joan Sanders, and you didn't like that. You didn't like that at all. You were going there to kill him, Miss O'Sullivan, weren't you?"

"No...no I wasn't...that's not true...that's not true at all!"

"Isn't it? Come on, now, tell me the truth, Miss O'Sullivan!"

"Stop! Stop it! He was a monster and he deserved to get what he got! I tried to love him, but it wasn't enough!"

Avalina was getting hysterical. The detective was making her crack; he knew she must have had some feelings for David Scholl. It was beginning to look like a love triangle to him, but the detective wasn't quite through with her yet. Wiretrak wanted a confession.

"Do you confess to the murder of David Scholl, Miss O'Sullivan?" Wiretrak asked her.

"M-my name is not Miss O'Sullivan," she said in between her tears.

"It isn't? Then, what *is* your name."

"It's, Avalina, Avalina Bishop."

"That's the second time I've heard that name mentioned."

Wiretrak looked in his notebook to see what he had on an 'Avalina Bishop.' He read his notes and looked up at Marcella.

"Now, let me get this straight. Avalina Bishop was a teenager, a teenager that was the victim of arson over fifty years ago in the town of Merryville, New York, right?" Wiretrak asked her.

"That's correct, sir," the possessed young woman replied.

"And *you* expect *me* to believe that that's you, a teenager from the sixties."

"It's true, detective, I am Avalina Bishop. I was Joan Sanders, too."

"You know what? You're making me frustrated with all of this bullshit, Miss O'Sullivan."

"I tell you, I'm *not* Miss O'Sullivan. I'm Avalina Bishop and I *was* Joan Sanders. This body you see is just a shell. I'm possessing Miss O'Sullivan and I can prove it."

"Really? Well, I sure as hell would like to see that," he said while laughing.

"Do you remember what I asked you in the police station that day when I was arrested?"

The detective stopped laughing. He looked at her intently.

"You asked me if your hair sample proved your innocence. Ok, you've got my attention now," Wiretrak told her.

"Good, I asked you about my hair sample because you took it from Joan Sanders, which was really me at that time. You came by quite often accusing me of murdering all of those people. I knew all along that that's what you were doing, and do you know what? You were absolutely right."

"How's that?"

"I *did* kill all of those people. I did it for revenge. All of them were involved in burning down my house with me inside of it."

"Even the nurse from the city hospital, Laverne Williams?"

"No…she just got in my way…so did Anna Nuñez."

"And what about Dwayne Worley? He was found at the bottom of Pond Lake in his SUV with a black garbage bag over his head."

"The black guy? He was an intruder. He came by to kill me because I murdered his girlfriend, the nurse; but instead, he wound up killing himself with his own gun. I *had* to get rid of him. But the others, Melissa Conley or Waters, her married name, Gilbert Johnson, Benny Smith and Michael Resnick all had to go."

"What the hell did Michael Resnick ever do to you?!"

"Oh, do I detect a note of sensitivity here? Well, for the record, Michael, like the others, *did* kill me back in 1969. I found him in a bar down in New York City. The dirty old man that he was, tried to pick me up and take me home to his apartment. We got as far as the subway, then he started to get fresh with me, so I pushed him down the tracks in front of the oncoming train."

"That's a lie! Michael would never do that! he was a perfect gentleman!" Wiretrak said while getting emotional.

"And just how the hell could you be so sure of that, Mr. Detective?" Avalina said sarcastically.

"Because Michael Resnick was my father."

"But you two have different last names."

"You ever heard of name changing? People do it all the time, you know. Miss O'Sullivan, I thought I was going to get a confession from you about what happened to David Scholl. I think I've sat here long enough listening to all of your bullshit. Now, I'll admit you almost had me going there for a while, but you know what I honestly think, Miss O'Sullivan?"

"What, detective? What *do* you think?"

"I think you need help…psychiatric help."

"I'm not crazy, if that's what you think!"

"Now, look who's getting sensitive here," Wiretrak said.

"You know what? I give up on you, detective. I have tried to tell you the truth, but you obviously don't believe me, but that's alright. You know something? You're kind of cute when you're angry…and…well…I haven't had sex ever since I was in the other body…"

Avalina got up from the sofa and stood up in front of him. She pulled off her rose-colored house dress and threw it across the room, exposing her fully naked body. Wiretrak tried to turn away, but she grabbed his chin and turned it towards her.

"You *will* look at me, boy. I'm hot for you, detective. I'm hot and I want you right now," Avalina said in a sexy voice to him.

Wiretrak stared at her inviting young breasts. Although, they were small, Miss O'Sullivan's breasts were crowned with large, fully erect nipples that would beg for *any* man's lips. Wiretrak knew that the young girl had a very nice shapely body, but there was nothing he could do about it. Avalina sat back down next to him and put her hand on his thigh, trying to feel his penis.

"Stop it, Miss O'Sullivan!" Wiretrak shouted as he grabbed her hand and pulled it off of him.

"Don't you find me attractive enough, detective?" Avalina said in a disappointed pout.

"Yes, I do, but you won't find anything down there, Miss O'Sullivan."

"What do you mean by that?"

"I had an operation many years ago, a sex change operation. You see, Miss O'Sullivan, I was the one who had my name changed, and my sex for that matter. My name used to be Michelle Resnick," he said softly.

"Oh…I'm sorry…I didn't know," Avalina said while pulling herself away from him and feeling weird.

Wiretrak didn't want to tell her, but it just slipped out. He saw how she reacted. It was the same reaction every other woman had when he told them the truth. *She thinks I'm a freak. I really liked looking at her nice little body. Now, she's going to get dressed again…shit!* Wiretrak thought, while watching the young woman stand back up and reach for her house dress on the floor. Wiretrak loved women, but he was trapped in a half-ass female body. The operation wasn't a complete success. The young detective had no feeling in between his thighs. He didn't have anything there that could actually satisfy a woman. The detective had thought about suing the doctor, but he wanted to avoid any embarrassment, especially on the job. Wiretrak just looked at Marcella O'Sullivan, wishing he could make love to her, even if she *was* crazy. *It would be my word against hers and who the hell would believe her anyway after they heard her talk?* Wiretrak thought, but realizing it wasn't going to happen and understanding that, making love to her was just completely out of the question, he had decided to talk to her some more.

"Please, don't be sorry. You couldn't possibly have known. Nobody knows except my boss, Chief Valentine; and at this point, I couldn't care less who knew. I am what I am and I do my job well. Tell me something, Miss O'Sullivan, where did you get that unique pendant from?" Wiretrak asked while pointing at the gold pentagram locket that was hanging around her neck.

Avalina was putting her rose-colored house dress back on, knowing that she couldn't do anything with the young detective; at least, not sexually anyway. She sat back down on the sofa, but further away from him this time, as if he had a contagious disease. Then, she pulled the locket out from under her dress.

"You *do* remember this, don't you?" Avalina asked while holding the locket in her hand.

"Yes, now I remember where I've seen that before. Miss Sanders had one similar to it around her neck," Wiretrak replied.

"No, it wasn't similar, it was the same exact one. Here, look at the inscription," she said as she moved back closer to him on the sofa so that he could read it.

"Avalina: Goddess Of Eternal Life," Wiretrak read.

"You see, detective, I have been telling you the truth all along," Avalina responded.

"Oh, come on, now. You could have had that thing made somewhere."

"It's an original. It was given to me by my grandmother when I was young. She was a witch too in Salem, Massachusetts."

"Sure, she was. So, I guess I'm not getting a real straight confession from you regarding David Scholl, aye?"

"Screw him! He murdered me and his unborn child."

"How did you know that Miss Sanders was pregnant? Did David tell you?"

"I told you already! I *was* Joan Sanders, too! That baby I was carrying in her body was his and mine together. He killed me because I got pregnant with his child. *Now*, do you understand?"

The detective started thinking and wondering how this girl knew so much. No one knew that Miss Sanders was pregnant, except for maybe David Scholl. Something, in what this young woman was telling him, did make some kind of sense, though. If it were true, it certainly did prove his theory about why David Scholl had killed Joan Sanders. It would have been David's motive to murder her and avoid child support. Detective Wiretrak had decided to arrest her after all.

"Miss O'Sullivan, I'm afraid I'm going to have to bring you in," Wiretrak said in a matter-of-fact tone of voice as he stood up.

"You're arresting me?" Avalina asked him in a surprised voice.

"I'm afraid so, Miss O'Sullivan."

"On what charge?"

"For the suspicion of murdering David Scholl."

"Oh, so you believe my story then?"

"No, not really, Miss O'Sullivan. What I *do believe* is that *you* murdered David Scholl because he murdered your best friend. You told me at the police station that you and Miss Sanders were extremely close. I believe that now, in more ways than one. In fact, you, Mr. Scholl and Miss Sanders may have had some kind of a love triangle for all I know. Obviously, Miss Sanders trusted you enough to tell you about her pregnancy. Then, of course, there's my other theory that you could have wanted David Scholl all along to yourself, but when he rejected you, you killed him."

"You've got a sick and twisted mind, detective," Avalina angrily said while standing up to face him.

"Look, I'll let you put on something that's a little more presentable, but please hurry it up," Wiretrak said while now pointing his service gun at her.

"Is that really necessary?" Avalina asked while looking down at the barrel of his gun.

"I'm afraid so, Miss O'Sullivan. Please, hurry up; you're wasting my time."

Avalina strolled into her bedroom with Wiretrak following close behind her. He sat at the edge of the bed in front of her dresser, waiting for her to pull off her house dress again, so that he could get another look at her inviting young body. Avalina stood in front of her dresser, pulled off her rose-colored house dress again and flung it behind her. The dress had landed right in the detective's face, temporarily blinding him while she searched for her own gun in the drawer.

"Hey, what gives?" Wiretrak asked while trying to remove the dress from his face.

"I'm sorry, detective, but there's been a change of plans," Avalina said.

The witch shot the detective in his chest, barely missing his heart. Michael Wiretrak collapsed down on the floor in front of her feet, bleeding profusely from his wound.

"You'll…never…get away…with this," the detective said to her while he was in agonizing pain.

"Oh, but I will. I know I will. Say goodbye, detect-"

Suddenly, a bullet came out of Detective Wiretrak's gun as he squeezed the trigger. The bullet entered Avalina's heart and prevented the woman from ever finishing her sentence. She grabbed her bloody left breast and collapsed to the floor.

"No…not again…can't die…again," she struggled to say while lying down next to the detective and looking at him.

Wiretrak didn't want to kill her, but she left him no choice by shooting him first. Avalina grabbed her golden pentagram locket and tried to get any kind of strength and power from it. She knew her host's body was failing fast. Avalina was struggling. She kept trying to put her spirit back into her pentagram locket. After a couple of grueling minutes of trying to pump precious blood to its vital organs, Marcella O'Sullivan's heart had finally stopped beating from the bullet wound and massive blood loss. Detective Wiretrak rolled over onto her. He put his bloodied arms around her and cried.

A few weeks later in early August, Detective Michael Wiretrak was back at work in his old office again. He had solved most of the murder cases, simply blaming them on Joan Sanders and Marcella O'Sullivan. The only one snag was finding David Scholl's body; that was of course, until the DNA sample from the bone fragments in his apartment had turned out to be his. No one exactly knew how David Scholl's body had been reduced to bone fragments, no one knew who or what did it. Wiretrak still thought about the two women: Joan Sanders and Marcella O'Sullivan, especially

Marcella. He kept remembering the way she came on to him and how sexy she acted. The young detective opened up his desk drawer and grabbed something to help bring him close to her; it was the golden pentagram locket that she wore around her neck. Wiretrak just couldn't let that get buried into the ground with her…could he?

I hope you enjoyed this story; if you did, check out:

Death on the Railway, Second Edition

Manuel (Manny) Rose

ABOUT THE AUTHOR

Manuel "Manny" Rose was born in Brooklyn, New York. He is the exclusive owner and CEO of MMRproductions.com. Manuel is an author of both children's books as well as adult thrillers. Manny started his own business in 2000, which has evolved and had branched out into multiple avenues, including some of his how-to educational products. As an avid professional audio/video producer, writer, singer, and voice actor, he provided the screenwriting and narration for the instructional films that he produced, as well as character voice-overs for his line of children's audio books, including his project: "My Child Storytime VOL. 1," which is a CD that features all original stories and songs. Manny is also a proud member of ASCAP.

Please Visit His Websites at:

https://manuelrose.com/

http://mmrproductions.com/

https://twitter.com/ManuelRose

https://www.facebook.com/Manuel-Rose-Writer-101580988342731/

https://www.youtube.com/user/MMRPRODUCTIONS

https://www.amazon.com/Manuel-Rose/e/B078J5QKVX

https://soundcloud.com/user-112846907/a-murderers-music-box-demo

https://www.goodreads.com/ManuelRose

Thanks so much for reading!

If you enjoyed this book, please take a minute to leave a review on Amazon.com, BarnesandNoble.com and Goodreads.com. Reviews make a huge difference to an author's sales and rankings—the more reviews, the more books I'll be able to write.

My readers mean the world to me, and I'd love to stay in touch. You can keep up with me on Goodreads.com https://www.goodreads.com/author/show/17650713.Manuel Rose
and Amazon.com https://www.amazon.com/Manuel-Rose/e/B078J5QKVX/ref=dp_byline_cont_pop_ebooks_1

Also from Manuel Rose

Death on the Railway, Second Edition

A Murderer's Music Box

On the evening of an impending winter storm, in the quaint suburban town of Merryville, New York in February 1969, fifteen-year-old Avalina Bishop becomes the victim of a cruel and heinous crime committed by her best friend and four other classmates, as they attempt to burn her alive in her own home for being a witch. What they do not know is that Avalina was given a special gift from her grandmother, who is a true witch from Salem, Massachusetts. This gift is a golden pentagram locket which harbors the power to preserve Avalina's spirit and enable her to walk the Earth once more. Over fifty years later, Avalina's soul is reawakened, but it is now darkened by pure rage and her own insatiable desire to smite all those who have wronged her. She embarks on a quest for revenge and begins possessing the bodies of young mortal women in an effort to carry out her own evil deeds. However, Avalina's plans frequently get derailed as she initially struggles to navigate a strange, new, digital-driven world amidst a deadly pandemic. After her spirit inhabits the body of twenty-one-year-old, Joan Sanders, Avalina also begins to regain some measure of humanity when she falls in love for the very first time, and she believes that she has been given another chance to have a happy life. However, Avalina discovers that the man she falls in love with has a ghastly secret of his own that could very well lead to her own demise once again, for their destinies are intertwined in far more ways than either of them could have ever imagined. Find out what happens in this new, mystical thriller by Manuel Rose.

$15.99
ISBN 978-0-578-35395-1
51599>

9 780578 353951

CPSIA information can be obtained
at www.ICGtesting.com
Printed in the USA
BVHW030720090123
655867BV00005B/117